Prince

HOUSE OF MISFITS

CAMBRIA HEBERT

A baby is born in privilege, blooming under the warmth of his parents' love. Jealousy sprouts and brings with it malevolent intentions. A king and queen cursed with an empty kingdom. A child abandoned in revenge.
A misfit, the boy should turn hard and cold among the thorns he grows in. Despite lifelong attempts to destroy him, this child does not wither. Underneath his insecurity, he maintains a heart with the tenderest center.
A heart that plays the most beautiful music.

Not far from this misfit but in a whole different world, a dashing prince lives with a crown of expectations adorning his golden head.
A prince raised with honor and duty. A prince expected to marry.
Alas, during a simple walk in the forest, he is enchanted by a different song.
And so a fairy tale is woven, two worlds colliding, secrets revealed, love everlasting
And a realization that not all fairy tales require a princess.

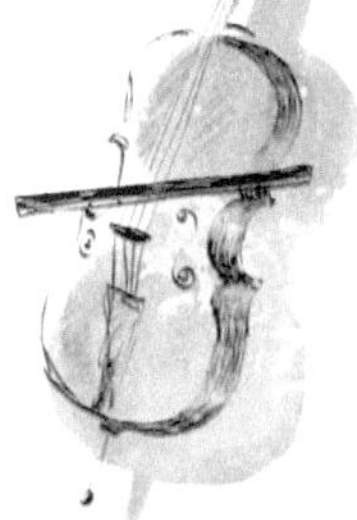

For Amber B,

BL wouldn't be the same without you

and neither would this book.

Prince

HOUSE OF MISFITS

CAMBRIA HEBERT

*Once upon a
Time . . .*

A woman with stars in her eyes is scorned and hate blooms in her heart. Her victims reach far and wide, but the most tragic of all… a baby.

Prologue

Many years ago…

Villain

Hell hath no fury like a woman scorned.

And this night, fury was not contained in hell but crept among the privileged down a long hallway padded with an expensive rug, the folds of a long cloak rustling silently in the shadows.

They thought their money would keep the evil at bay. Their arrogance overcame all common sense, giving way to opportunity in the form of revenge.

Misery loves company, and I wouldn't be the only one to suffer. He would forever rue the day he made a mockery out of me.

Cursed are the hearts who dare to love, what once beat soft and steady, glowing pink and infused with the passion of red. More than an organ filled with youth and life, but the encasing of a soul, a soul who shriveled under rejection and plight, turning so cold and small the casing also began to decay. Veins of black spread like snakes, circling, squeezing until there was no more pink and no more passionate red.

Armor-like vines took over. Wicked thick thorns with piercing points locked away what once loved, and a cold, howling wind echoed through the heart, beating only for a sole reason.

Retribution.

Though the word went unspoken, it whispered through the passages of the vast home, echoing through the quiet to stop at the door like a hunting dog who found its prey.

Reaching out from the concealment of my cloak with a steady hand, thickly veined fingers wrapped around the doorknob ornately designed with pewter. The monied, well-installed design only aided in the silent way I slipped into the room.

The room was dark except for the glow of a nightlight casting stars across the ceiling, which was painted blue and adorned with hand-painted white clouds.

The rug underfoot was plush, muffling my footsteps, and the gently swaying mobile over an ornately carved crib made jealousy swell my chest until I was fisting my hands.

This house.

This room.

The softly playing violin echoing through the air.

Gritting my teeth until I heard them grind, I moved forward, keeping my head down, not looking. Not yet.

With careful, unhurried movements, I lowered the hood, allowing the fabric to fold and settle against my nape. Dark strands of hair clung to the back of my neck, curling around my throat like the same vines that choked my heart.

A curl fell across my forehead, and I brushed it away. As I lifted my chin, taking in a deep breath, finally, my eyes gazed down upon the small wrapped bundle sleeping without a care in the world.

This baby.

It all was supposed to be mine.

Instead, I was tossed aside as if I hadn't mattered at all,

replaced easily enough with someone more fitting to the role I was already cast in.

The faintest of sound, a barely there sigh, snapped my attention to the slumbering babe. A tiny fist broke free of the blue he was swaddled in, waving wildly before finding its way into his mouth.

As he suckled, his eyes locked on mine. The color of honey… just like the one who'd betrayed me.

Somewhere in the house, a dull sound echoed, and I remembered why I was here.

Reaching into the crib, I lifted the child, settling him against my bosom. I expected him to cry and wail, to be pierced by the barbs caging my soul.

Lifting my hand, I readied to shove it against his face to muffle any sounds he was sure to release… but he didn't cry.

The baby smiled.

That shriveled, lifeless speck of my soul lying listlessly inside me jerked, and when it did, the rest of me did too.

Anger so hot and swift burned my skin, making the cape stick to my body and my clothes dampen with sweat.

How dare this child! How dare he try to manipulate me?

Just. Like. His. Father.

And just like that, our fates were sealed. I disappeared into the dark of night with the child who should have been mine, cursing us all to a miserable fate.

A child denied its right by birth by a woman denied her right by love.

And them?

A king and a queen left behind, cursed forever with an empty kingdom.

ETHAN

THE DOUBLE DOORS LEADING INTO MY OFFICE BURST OPEN, distracting me from the mountain of paperwork piled on my desk. Shoulder blades coming together with instant annoyance, I glanced up, ready to scold whoever the hell dared to just barge right in.

The reprimand died on my lips as the glossy, light-stained wood parted, revealing a figure I was very familiar with. Moving past him, my gaze landed on Bree, who hovered nervously at the threshold, apology plain on her face.

I couldn't be mad at her. Even my assistant was no match for him.

Delivering her a small smile and a nod, I motioned that all was okay, and she nearly deflated in relief, scurrying forward to pull the doors closed behind him.

She wasn't relieved I wasn't angry. No, she was relieved she wasn't the one having to deal with Adrian Abbott.

That was my job. A job assigned to me at birth.

"Father," I greeted, leaning back in my chair as he went to the minibar across the room to help himself.

"We need to talk."

"In the middle of a business day?" I asked, surprised he

would interrupt me because, frankly, he was a giant workaholic and thought everyone else should be as well.

"This is about business." He confirmed, turning with a crystal glass in his broad hand and about a finger length of dark liquid in the bottom.

"You heard back on the UK deal?" I questioned as he came to sit on the other side of my desk, his red tie the only color to his basic attire of a black suit and white dress shirt.

"It's time you got married."

A strangled sound twisted in my throat, and I was pretty sure I choked on the spit I usually swallowed without thought.

"Married?" I asked, the word coming out hoarse.

"You had to know this was coming." He spoke as if I wasn't about to asphyxiate.

Clearing my throat, I gave a very neutral response. "I'm not dating anyone at the moment."

"And whose fault is that?" The blame was punctuated by the sharp snap of his glass on the top of my desk. "You're the one who let Ivory run off with some… *street rat.*"

"Dad," I practically groaned.

"Do you know how embarrassing that was for your mother and me? Our own son, the most eligible bachelor in all of New York, bested by a no one."

Even though it irked me, I didn't bother to explain Neo was not a no one. My father was so old-school money and so deep with the Upper East Side elite he wouldn't hear anything I said regardless. And on top of that… if I wanted Ivory, I would have had her. No one "bested" me unless I allowed it.

"I wasn't in love with Ivory. I never was. And she didn't love me either."

"What's love got to do with it?" he exclaimed. "This was a perfect business opportunity we had been working on since you both were born. And what did you do? Tossed it all aside."

"I'm not getting married for business," I retorted.

"Well, the rate you're going, you aren't going to get married for love either. Might as well make some money."

A dull ache started at the base of my skull, shooting pain behind my eyes. "Can we argue about this another day?"

"I found someone."

Lowering my thumb and index finger from the bridge of my nose, I gazed up. "Pardon?"

"I found you a wife."

If I'd been drinking something, it would have been all over the surface of my desk and his serious face right now. Was he for real? "Did you and Mom go shopping at the wife boutique?"

"They have those?" he asked. "How distasteful."

I made a sound in the back of my throat. "Much more distasteful than arranging a marriage for your son when he was just a child."

"You and Ivory were well-matched. Upper East Side royalty," he said, shaking his head sadly. "You liked her. And your mother is very worried, thinks you have a broken heart."

I sighed heavily. This was my own fault. Ivory and I were the ones who went along with the betrothal, never speaking out against it and just sort of allowing everyone to assume our fate.

If I'd said no from the time we were old enough to really refuse, this wouldn't be an issue right now.

But I hadn't said no. For reasons I didn't care to explain.

"I don't have a broken heart, Father. I'm happy for Ivory. I like Neo."

He gave me a blank look.

"The street rat." I clarified.

He blanched. "How could you possibly like him?"

"Because he saved Ivory's life more than once. Because he treats her well." *Because he's man enough to step into this world and be who he is with no apologies.*

"He's from the Grimms, Ethan."

"He's also got an upcoming art exhibit in the prestigious gallery just up the street to showcase his work."

"A showcase he wouldn't have if not for Ivory's name." My father was very good at arguing, probably the reason Abbott Group was one of the top real estate and hotel conglomerates on the East Coast.

"Ah, yes. I forgot money also buys talent," I rebuked coolly. I was good at arguing too. I was his son after all.

"Pope Enterprises," he said, completely disregarding the conversation we were having. I went with the change because it was a conversation I didn't want to have either.

"The real estate investment firm out on the West Coast?" I said, running the name through my mind to recall everything I knew about them. Admittedly, it wasn't much.

"I talked to Stefan Pope on the phone this morning. I think a partnership between the biggest firms on the East and West Coasts would be very profitable."

Pursing my lips, I thought aloud. "And who's to say a partnership like that would even work in our favor?" We were always the biggest company in any deals we made. It was the reason we were so successful. *He who holds the most power reaps the most reward.*

"Which is exactly why I think a little assurance is necessary."

Clearly, he already had something in mind. If he didn't, he wouldn't be sitting here in the middle of the day. I said nothing. Instead, I waited for him to spit out whatever it was his conniving mind had worked up.

"I've invited his daughter, Sienna, to visit and be a special guest at our upcoming events. She's always wanted to visit New York City, and I have assured Stefan that you would be a most accommodating tour guide."

"You didn't," I deadpanned, an uncomfortable knot tying itself in my intestines.

"I did, and you will." He spoke like we were in a board meeting and he was laying down the law to his employees. "She's single, beautiful, and worthy of someone like you. A marriage between our families would make our businesses the most powerful in the entire country and, when this UK deal goes through, in all of Europe." Getting up from his seat, he finished the liquor in his glass and turned to go.

"No."

He turned back, lifting one eyebrow. "No?"

"I'm not interested in her."

"You haven't even met."

"And yet you're already planning the wedding." A metallic taste filled my mouth, and the throbbing behind my eyes intensified. *Great.* I really didn't have time for this.

"So you're interested in someone else?" Father asked, looking at me expectantly.

He knew damn well I wasn't, and I couldn't lie and say I was because I'd already said earlier that I wasn't seeing anyone. Bastard.

He nodded once, as if my silence somehow proved his point. "She'll be here in less than two weeks. She's staying with your mother and me. I expect you to be very accommodating."

A protest opened my lips.

He held up his hand. "At least meet her. You might like her. She could be your one true love."

He let himself out of my office just as easily as he'd let himself in.

Slumping back into my chair, I let out a harrowing sigh.

Moments later, Bree bustled in with a gleaming silver tray, presenting it before me. Glancing over, I saw the single glass filled with water and, beside it, an ornate napkin with our company logo and two pills in the center.

"You know me well," I said, tossing back the pills and downing the water.

"I pushed back your next meeting. You have two hours until your next conference call."

A pushed-back meeting meant I'd be working later, but I didn't care. Two hours of freedom seemed like a gift at the moment.

I stood up, grabbing my suit jacket from a nearby hanger, and turned. "Why don't you order yourself something special from the private Gucci sale going on? Just give my name when you call."

Her eyes went wide. "Mr. Abbott?"

"Consider it an apology for having to deal with my father and also a thank-you for taking care of me."

"That's not necessary—" She began, and I made a noise, cutting her off.

"I saw you browsing the private listings this morning when I came in. You want that bag."

Her cheeks turned pink, and she glanced away. "Well, you weren't in yet, and I just received your invitation—"

"Go buy it. Seriously. And thank you." Pausing at the door, I called back, "I'll be back in two hours."

"One hour and fifty minutes!" she yelled back.

Laughing under my breath, I kept going, reaching into my jacket pocket for a pair of black sunglasses.

"Thank you!" Her voice echoed down the hall as I stepped into the elevator.

Finally alone, I leaned against the wall and let out a breathy sigh. "She might be your one true love." I mocked my father's words.

A humorless laugh escaped me.

I wondered what he would say if I told him she most definitely was not. That she could be the most beautiful, angelic woman in the entire world and she still wouldn't be my type.

No woman was.

Two

The tall, mirrored building stretched to the sky. So high my head tipped back as far as possible and my eyes squinted up, still unable to see the top.

The mirrored windows making up the side glinted with sunlight, reflecting the city behind me. Cabs zoomed by, horns honking and mixing with the usual sounds of the city. Even with all the noise, it was a little quieter here. A little... nicer.

I wasn't quite used to the difference between the Upper East Side and the Grimms, but maybe someday I would be.

Pulling my chin down, resolving to try again next time to see the very top of Ivory's building, I caught sight of my reflection.

It became blindingly obvious why I wasn't used to this elite part of the city. I didn't fit here. I looked sorely out of place.

Baggy, scuffed-up jeans. Hand-me-down sneakers from Beau. A loose T-shirt that was technically Neo's, but I wore it more than he did. All of this topped with a mane of floppy hair that swished when a large truck rumbled past at a speed he probably shouldn't be traveling.

A man wearing a tailored dark suit passed between me

and my reflection, a pristine leather briefcase gripped in his palm.

Looking down, I saw my own "briefcase," faux leather, beaten and ripped, decorated with stickers I picked up almost everywhere I went.

Smiling, I patted the case fondly. "You're so much better than some stuffy old case filled with paperwork," I told her lovingly.

Nearly tripping on the hem of the too-long jeans, I went inside the building, ignoring the obvious stares I garnered. People always stared at me here. I was used to it.

Sort of.

Feeling a light flush creep up the back of my neck, I went toward security, a genuine smile filling my face when I saw who was manning the check-in.

"Fletch, my man!" Dennis called, white teeth bright against his ebony skin. "It's been a hot minute. How you been?"

Despite being dressed in a fancy fitted black suit, shiny black loafers, and adorned with a black earpiece at his ear, the guard was more like me than anyone else in this building.

I held up my fist, and we bumped it out. "Hey, Dennis!" I called, my voice enthusiastic. "I'm great. Been super busy. How're you?"

"It's all good here. Just standing around in my penguin suit. You catch the game last night?"

When I nodded enthusiastically, my hair fell into my eyes, and I swiped it away while answering, "Of course! Can you believe that last-minute shot?"

Dennis whistled. "Damn near spilled my beer!"

The woman at the reception desk across the way cleared her throat loudly.

Dennis straightened and gave me a bored look. "Who are you visiting today, sir?"

Fishing my visitor pass out of my back pocket, I held it up for him to scan. "Just came by to see my sister."

Dennis nodded, the scanner beeping over the barcode on my ID. "Thank you, sir. You may go in now."

"Thanks!" I said, moving through the little gate. "See you next time," I said, waving over my shoulder.

He winked.

"Hi, Bethany!" I called to the woman at the reception desk.

Her head snapped up because I was being loud again and dragging her into it. She acted like this lobby was a museum.

"You look pretty today." I went on.

The sour look melted from her face, and she smiled. "Thank you, Fletcher. I'll call up and let Ms. White know you're on your way up."

Behind me, Dennis laughed under his breath, and I stepped into a waiting elevator, settling in for a long ride to the top.

The doors barely opened onto Ivory's floor when a voice floated into the elevator car. "Mr. Fletcher, welcome."

"Agh!" I exclaimed, jolting back against the far wall, gripping my violin case like it was a shield.

Charles (Ivory's right-hand man) also jolted. "Sir?"

"Why do you have to be so creepy, Charles?" I wheezed out, straightening with a hand over my chest. "Mr. Fletcher, welcome," I mocked, my voice morose and weird.

"I didn't realize my greeting was creepy," he said, not even the tiniest bit impressed with my dead-on impression.

I was actually pretty bad at a lot of stuff. But I was good at useless stuff, impressions being one of those things.

"You should try out for a horror movie," I suggested. "You'd make a great creepy butler who's actually the killer but no one thinks is actually the killer because you're so boring."

His eyes flickered with a little amusement, but it didn't

hang around long. "I'm afraid my schedule with Ms. White keeps me busy enough."

The elevator doors started to close, and I was still inside. Diving forward, I made it out before they could ding. In my rush, I tripped over the hem of my jeans and toppled into Charles.

He actually wasn't much bigger than me, so we both fell to the ground.

"Sir!" Charles exclaimed.

"Sorry!" I untangled my legs from his and jumped up, offering a hand to the man. He glared at it and then stood on his own.

Clearing his throat and adjusting his jacket, he motioned. "Please, right this way. Ms. White is waiting."

I felt my eyes go wide. "Is that why you were there? You knew I was coming?" Rushing to catch up, I said, "Are you telepathic?"

He glanced at me out of the corner of his eyes, his voice dry. "Bethany called from the lobby."

"Oh yeah." I remembered.

He stopped at Ivory's door and knocked twice.

I didn't wait for her to call out. Instead, I went past him to push open the door.

"Sir!"

"Family doesn't knock," I said.

"Fletch!" Ivory called the second I opened the door.

"Thanks for the escort," I told Charles, and he smiled politely before pulling the door closed between us.

"He's kinda weird," I whispered loudly as I moved across the huge office.

Ivory laughed, standing up behind her massive sleek glass desk and coming around with a big smile on her face.

She was the most beautiful woman I'd ever seen. Glossy black hair, big blue eyes, and skin as white as snow. She was small and austere looking, wearing a body-hugging, light-colored dress and a pair of heels. I didn't know how she walked in them. I could barely walk in sneakers.

I probably would have been intimidated by her if I'd met her like this first. But she'd wandered into my world, her fancy aura ruffled and overcome by the unknown. She was kind to me and my brothers, even if she did screech a lot at first. She even overlooked that time I got her arrested.

Neo fell in love with her, and now she was my sister.

Setting my case on the couch nearby, I met her halfway, hugging her tight and breathing in her light scent. "I missed you," I told her.

She pulled back but kept hold of my arms. "If you missed me, why didn't you come see me sooner?"

Oh yeah. She had tried to get me over here a couple times.

"I was busy."

Her rose-colored lips pursed. "What did I say about lying?"

"I was!" I insisted. I was busy not doing much. A person could be busy doing anything.

"Where's the coat I bought you?" she demanded, looking at my T-shirt and then at the couch where I'd tossed my stuff.

"I forgot it," I mumbled.

"It's getting cold out. It's not summer anymore." She scolded.

"I know."

Releasing me, Ivory picked up the phone on her desk and hit a button. "Charles, can you put in an order for some hot chocolate—" Her words were interrupted. Then she smiled. "That's why I can't live without you," she added a moment later, then hung up the phone.

The door swung in seconds later, and Charles appeared, pushing a small cart with a white cloth draped over the top. In the center was a plate of pastries and two paper cups.

My eyes widened when I saw the familiar logo on the side, and my tongue darted across my lower lip, already salivating for the rich chocolate flavor. "Kismet!" I exclaimed, bouncing on the couch.

Ivory laughed lightly. "It's your favorite. Even Charles knows by now. He'd already ordered ahead."

"Sorry I called you creepy earlier, Charles." I apologized, reaching for the paper cup with no lid because it was piled high with whipped cream and chocolate drizzle. The second my fingers closed around the cup, the drizzle dripped farther down the side and over my digit.

"Yes, well," Charles said, clearing his throat as I licked away the sweetness.

Ivory arched a dark brow. "Charles, creepy?"

"He stalks the elevator. It's weird." I elaborated.

"You're very diligent in your profession, Charles. A trait I well admire. Thank you very much for this. You can go back to your office now."

When he was gone, Ivory put her fist on her hip. "You shouldn't give him such a hard time."

"Me?" I asked, lowering the cup from my lips.

Ivory laughed. "You have whipped cream on your nose."

I wiped it away and then took another sip. The hot chocolate from Kismet was literally the best I'd ever had in my entire life. I never knew hot chocolate could taste so good. It was thick and rich, creamy and chocolatey. Sometimes they put mint in it. Sometimes caramel or peanut butter. You could even get it frozen!

It was also way overpriced and in the fancy district, so I never would have had it if we hadn't met Ivory. Sighing appreciatively, I let the warmth of the treat seep into me.

"Eat," she said, sliding the plate of pastries closer while picking up her own cup to check the label on the side to make sure it was the correct way she took her coffee.

I was halfway through a cherry danish when she grabbed a folder off her desk, coming back to the couch.

The sound of my swallow was audible, and my fingers tightened around the cup. I knew where this was going. This was why I'd been avoiding coming here.

I couldn't avoid it forever. I missed Ivory. She was relatively new to our family, but it didn't matter. I tended to get easily attached to people, something Earth always warned me against. I even knew it was a bad idea… but my heart didn't seem to want to listen to my head.

Somehow I felt like I was searching… always searching for family. Even after I found the misfits, there was still this echo of loneliness inside me. I didn't understand it, so I often ignored it, but sometimes it snuck up when I least expected.

Placing her knees slightly to the side, her ankles crossed delicately near the floor, Ivory slipped the folder onto the coffee table between us.

"I can't keep putting off all these offers, Fletcher."

Abandoning the almost devoured bread and glancing longingly at the hot chocolate, I turned toward her. "You don't have to. I already told you no."

A delicate startled sound echoed in her throat. "You can't possibly mean that."

"I do," I rebuked, not a hint of doubt in my tone.

"I don't understand." Her brow furrowed, and she opened up the folder to a stack of neat papers.

Offers. All of them were offers.

Offers I rejected when she asked me the first *and* second times.

"You love to play the violin, Fletch. You are so good at it. Ever since you played at my streetwear couture show, people have been clamoring to hire you."

Glancing down at the fisted hands in my lap, I answered, "I'm not a professional violin player."

"You could be."

My stomach twisted. A dark feeling curled up from the bottom of my feet. "I don't want to be."

"Then why did you play at my show?"

"Because you asked me to," I said quietly. "Because Neo was also there."

Because I wanted to know what it was like just once to play on a stage.

It was amazing. Incredible. Like a world all my own.

Her voice was patient and even reassuring. "We'll be at each of these events that are wanting to hire you."

"I don't even understand why your fancy friends want to hire me. It's not like I'm like them," I muttered, anger building in my chest.

"They aren't my friends. Not really. Just work acquaintances, people from my social circle."

I gave her a pointed look as though she'd just proved what I was saying.

She sighed. "You're talented. You're a new attraction. You're like an undiscovered genius. People like that. They want to show off that they... have access to things other people don't."

"I'm not a zoo attraction."

"I've seen you eat," she deadpanned.

I laughed. Ivory always said none of us had manners. Humor died quickly, though, because it was overshadowed by all the other undercurrents I felt. "No."

"Fletcher. These are lucrative deals. Thousands of dollars in income. You won't have to play in the subway anymore. You won't have to steal."

"I like playing in the subway," I argued. It was true. I did. It was my place. A... safe place.

She pushed more. "This is an opportunity for a better life. A job you're good at."

"I like my life the way it is," I insisted.

"You deserve better."

"I said no!" I yelled, shooting up from the sofa. The drinks on the table rattled with the force in which I moved, my voice taking on a deeper, more forceful tone than usual. "I don't want to do it. I know you all think I'm some little kid who doesn't have his own thoughts and is… easily swayed, but I will make decisions about my own life. I said no. I meant it."

Ivory sat motionless, her eyes wide. I'd never raised my voice at her before. I never really pushed back. Just because I never did didn't mean I couldn't.

I wasn't as dopey as everyone thought I was. *I was tired of saying no.*

Her red lips parted, then pressed together only to part again. "I understand. I'll let everyone know."

I nodded once, not even satisfied I'd won. Heat crept up the back of my neck along with a pinch of guilt because of the way I yelled at her.

"I'm sorry—" I started, but she jumped up, cutting off the apology.

"No, I'm sorry. I shouldn't have pushed. You said no. I should have respected that. I just worry about you. And this is good income."

"Money isn't everything."

"You're right. It's not," she said softly. I knew she wanted to say more, but she bit back the words. "I just want you to be happy."

My heart pinched. "I am."

She looked up, her blue eyes somehow staring deep. "Are you really?"

I felt my Adam's apple bob while an odd feeling wormed around inside me. "Of course."

Nodding, Ivory closed the lid on the folder and carried it away, jamming it under some stuff on her desk.

"I'd better go. I told Earth I'd help with the bar tonight."

"I'll have Charles call a cab for you."

"No. I can get home myself."

She didn't argue, even though I knew she wanted to.

Surging forward, I wrapped my arms around her waist and hugged her tight. "Don't be mad!"

A soft laugh escaped her, and she returned the hug. "I'm not mad."

"Promise?"

"I promise."

Feeling less heavy, I pulled back, planting a kiss on her cheek. "Thank you."

"Take your hot chocolate." She reminded me, pointing to the cup. The whipped cream had melted, so I snapped on the lid sitting nearby.

Before picking up the cup, I shoved the rest of the danish in my mouth. "Rank roo," I called, taking the drink and my violin case.

"Dinner soon!"

I nodded enthusiastically because my hands were full and I couldn't wave. Inside the elevator, I set the case at my feet and sighed.

I didn't really have to help Earth at the bar tonight, but I wanted to escape. Something I'd never really wanted to do before, not with Ivory anyway.

But I didn't want to explain that when it came to me and the violin, there was an oddly fine line between love and hate.

Three

*E*THAN

THE DULL ACHE BEHIND MY EYES AND TIGHT MUSCLES AT THE base of my skull taunted me as I stepped into Central Park, a forest within the city that was currently aglow with autumn. Crisp air swirled around, lazily waltzing among the aged, sturdy trees draping overhead with a kaleidoscope of burnished colors. Golden sunlight filtered through where the trees had surrendered their leaves, sharing their brilliant foliage with the ground underfoot.

I rarely, if ever, ventured into the park in the middle of a workday, but today, my need for fresh air and space led me here and I was content to follow my whim.

A familiar ringtone erupted, and the inside of my jacket began to vibrate. I thought of ignoring the call completely, but the sound was irritating so I plucked the device out of my pocket, intent to shut it off.

Ivory.

She was probably the one call I wouldn't ignore.

"Hey," I answered, Ivory also being one of the only people I could answer so informally.

"Sorry to bother you in the middle of the day," she said, her voice sounding as tired as I felt.

"Is everything okay?" I asked immediately, turning to look in the direction of her office building.

"Yes, of course. Long day."

I made a sound and started walking again. I could understand that. "What's up?"

"I just wanted to tell you that he said no."

I paused, searching my brain. When I couldn't find the answer, I asked, "Who said no?"

"Fletcher. I know you wanted him to play at your upcoming hotel opening."

The mention of Fletcher made my heart skip just a little. And then disappointment made me frown. "He said no? Really?"

Ivory sighed heavily. "I know. I can't believe he would turn down these opportunities. I just don't understand. But he was adamant."

"Opportunities?" I said, picking up on the plural.

"Oh yes, I have an entire pile of offers here for him. I feel like I have a side job as his manager, but he won't even look at any of them."

"He didn't strike me as someone that stubborn."

"I didn't think so either," she said softly. "But I won't push him anymore."

"Okay. Well, thanks for letting me know."

"Is everything okay?" Ivory always was good at reading me.

I made a soft humming noise in the back of my throat. "Everything's fine. Just fighting off a headache."

A small sympathetic sound echoed in my ear. "Okay, well, if you want me to send over my masseuse, just let me know."

The muscles in my neck and shoulders begged me to accept. "You're the best," was all I said, and then we ended the call.

This time, I made sure to power off my phone before

tucking it back into my pocket. An hour of peace wasn't too much to ask for.

Turning into a part of the park that was a little less busy, I walked along in quiet, stewing over the meeting I'd just had with my father.

I'd never much been bothered by him dictating my love life before… but I cared now. The thought of playing knight and shining armor to some West Coast princess over the next few weeks was enough to make the headache I was fighting off turn into a full-on head rager.

Soft music stroked over my frayed emotions, soothing me in a way I'd never experienced before. The air vibrated with a deep timbre, a low melody almost somber in nature. It was melancholic but beautiful all at once, not at all off-putting, instead like a beacon of cautious optimism.

The tune was slow but never-ending, and I walked toward it, drawn inexplicably by the way it made me feel. Leaves overhead seemed to dance to the same song, the forest within the city coming alive in a completely new way.

The noise of cars and urban life faded away, and it was as if I were truly transported into another place where only I and the grass underfoot existed, the golden sun sparkling on everything it touched, the very air enchanted with only the song and faded clip-clopping of the horses and carriages traveling along nearby paths.

Rounding a small bend, I stared, almost transfixed, through the dark sunglasses at the lithe figure up ahead, his body swaying as if the music didn't come from the instrument in his hand but from his body.

Footsteps stalling, I watched the vibrations of each note bubble up from somewhere deep inside him, escaping through the strings he navigated with so much skill it was again like he himself was the instrument and not the wood he held.

Head bowed toward the violin, his hair looked like spun

golden thread as it swayed with every note he played. Familiarity rippled through me, but I didn't think it through. I couldn't think about anything just then. All I could do was feel.

The tune moved me. It felt as if actual pieces inside my chest were being rearranged and adjusted according to this song. As if this boy who played this song knew exactly where pieces of me belonged and he would arrange them so I wouldn't have to.

Emotion so stark and overwhelming punched me. I actually bent a little at the waist. Tears sprang to the corners of my eyes, but I held them at bay.

Absolutely entranced. Absolutely owned.

Absolutely besotted by the sound of this boy.

I didn't even know a person had a sound. A song unique to only them. But now that I'd heard, it seemed to be so obvious because no one else could possibly ever sound like him.

This went far beyond the sound of a voice or even a whisper against your ear.

This was… *This is the sound of someone's heart.*

In my chest, my own heart pounded, thumping heavily and slow but so powerful breath was hard to draw.

I stood there listening, not really breathing. Not really seeing. Totally alive and aware with senses I'd never used before.

When the last note was played, it hovered thick like the air after a heavy rainstorm. It caressed my nerves with small aftershocks, stroking them as if they were trying to build a memory.

As if I could ever forget.

Laughter was what drew me back to the woodland. A sound not quite as musical or delicate as the violin, but a sound as equally engaging.

He was no longer holding the violin. He'd placed it on the

bench behind him, the instrument lying there unaffected by the magic he'd just made it produce. The crisp breeze caught the fabric of his T-shirt, ruffling it, plastering it against a thin frame.

More laughter filled the air as he knelt into the grass, sticking an oversized hand into a white paper bag to draw out a handful of something. I watched him toss whatever he held out away from him, sitting back on his haunches to smile.

He was surrounded by animals. Squirrels, a few birds... even a bunny.

He was feeding them, kneeling right there in the cool grass, tossing out what must have been roasted peanuts to the animals who were impossibly unafraid.

Yes, in this park, the wildlife was accustomed to people, and yes, people sometimes fed them... but this was unlike anything I'd seen before.

The bunny hopped just a little closer. He said something I couldn't hear and tossed a peanut toward it. A squirrel darted close, chattering at him almost like it was jealous for attention.

As I watched, I became jealous for attention too.

A stronger fall breeze cut through the air with my thought, the leaves rustling overhead, playing a song all their own. A song that would never be as enchanting as this boy's.

Hair rustling wildly, he lifted his head, noticing me. I didn't bother to pretend I wasn't staring. I wasn't doing anything wrong.

Even though there was distance between us, I felt our gazes collide.

Familiarity came for me again. This time, the ability to think didn't disappear.

Moving back on his haunches, the boy slowly rose, still clutching the paper sack.

His body rotated toward mine, and I saw.

I saw him with my eyes this time, not with my heart.

Fletcher. A boy I already knew. A boy I'd just spoken to Ivory about.

"Ethan," he called out, waving to me with the bag because his hand was still stuck inside.

Cute.

Lifting a hand in acknowledgment, I started walking in his direction, not willing to turn away even though a whisper foretold this chance meeting in the forest would likely change everything.

Four

Fletcher

My stomach felt weird. The second I looked up and saw him standing there with the sunlight practically spotlighting his broad figure, it started jumping around like I'd eaten too many of these roasted peanuts.

My nose wrinkled. *But I haven't eaten any of them.*

The closer he got, the squirmier my stomach became, making me shuffle from foot to foot, wanting to look away but not able to force my eyes elsewhere.

He really does look like a prince.

Tall, broad-shouldered with chiseled features and stylish blond hair. His eyes, which I knew were blue, were hidden behind a pair of shades, but even the dark lenses couldn't hide the intensity of his stare.

Shifting again, the toe of my sneaker caught on the hem of the jeans, and I pitched sideways, the paper bag rattling because my hand was still stuck inside.

"Agh!" I yelled, yanking my hand free, causing nuts to fly everywhere, landing with gentle but audible thuds all over the grass.

The ground came fast, so fast I knew I wouldn't be able to catch myself. "*Oomph,*" the sound rushed out of me before I even realized what happened, my body still bracing for the hit.

No hit came. In fact, I wasn't even falling anymore.

Huh? Prying open one eye, I peeked up.

My heart stopped.

That sharp jaw was incredibly close. So close I could see the very faint stubble there. He was staring down, brows furrowed over the sunglasses, and his naturally contoured cheekbones looked fiercely sharp.

"We keep meeting like this." He spoke softly because, again, he was so close.

The vivid memory of the day at the hospital when I'd almost fallen flashed behind my eyes. He'd caught me then too.

Releasing the breath I'd been holding, I made no move to get up because I was still marveling at his proximity and how his one arm supported my entire weight without any trouble at all. The muscle didn't even quiver from the effort.

But me?

My stomach wasn't the only thing quivering anymore.

"You okay?" The deep timbre of his voice made a small shiver race up my spine.

I tried to scramble up, completely alarmed, but it only made me fall into him harder.

"Up you go," he said, echoing the same words from that day in the hospital. Then I was on my feet again, blinking, still staring.

"Your jeans are too big," Ethan pointed out, gesturing at the too-long hems.

"I like them," I argued, staring at the way his suit fit him perfectly.

Nearby, a squirrel chattered, and I spun. "You ate it all already?" I admonished. Its tail was twitching impatiently as it stood a bit farther back than before and stared at the bag in my hand.

"You better be careful with these. I think they might be bad!" I whispered loudly as I leaned down to scatter the rest of what I had around the lawn.

"They're bad?" Ethan said, his hand wrapping around my upper arm, somehow dwarfing the appendage. "Did you eat them? Are you sick?" Concern was clear in his tone as he drew me up and around, searching my face for signs of illness.

When he didn't find any, he pulled the bag from my hand to look at it instead.

"Fletcher. Did these make you sick?"

I jolted from his voice. Not because he was loud or harsh but just because, for a moment, everything around us was muted.

"Huh?" I wondered, blinking.

He held up the empty bag, and I remembered the conversation.

"Oh, no. I didn't eat any. I bought them for them." I motioned toward the animals all eating happily.

"Then why did you say they're bad?"

Palm patting my belly, I said, "My stomach feels weird."

He reached out like he, too, was going to pat my belly, and I sucked in a breath. Noting my reaction, he stopped and pulled his hand away.

The tips of my ears grew so warm I wondered if they might be on fire. Slowly, the heat spread from my ears toward my cheeks.

"Sit down." Ethan directed me to the bench.

We both sat, my violin resting between us.

"I heard you playing," he told me, looking down at the instrument.

The heat in my face turned into a full-on blush, and I ducked my head to try and hide it. "Sometimes I just feel like playing."

"Did you write that song?"

"It's not really a song. I was just playing what I felt."

"You mean you made that up right there on the spot?" Why did he sound so awed?

I shrugged. "I mean, I could play it again. It's not really made up." Using a much softer tone, I couldn't help but add, "It's how I feel."

"It was a melancholy tune."

My head whipped up. "Was that an insult?"

His lips, which kinda always seemed puckered, stretched out with his smile. "Melancholy means sad."

"Oh."

"Your cheeks are pink," he mused. "Are you blushing?"

"No!" I complained, ducking my head again. I forgot I was supposed to be hiding it.

"Cute."

My head whipped up again. *Did I hear him right? Did he just call me cute?* "What?"

Sitting back, he cleared his throat. "Is something wrong? Is that why your song sounded so sad?"

"No. I'm fine."

"You know Ivory just called me." Ethan started, and I panicked.

"I lied to her!" I burst out, guilt washing over me. That was probably why my stomach felt so weird. "I didn't mean to!"

Ethan paused, his head tipping slightly sideways. The wind blew, ruffling his blond hair. "You lied to her?"

"She knows, right? Is she mad? Oh man." I started to worry. I didn't want Ivory to be mad. "It was only a little white lie," I told Ethan. "I didn't think it would be that big of a deal."

Pursing his lips, he regarded me seriously. "What did you lie about?"

I blinked. "She didn't tell you?"

"She would never break your confidence."

I nodded. Of course she wouldn't. "I told her I had to help out at the bar tonight, but I don't. I just needed to get out of there."

"Mmm." Ethan made a sound. "And so you came here."

"I don't get to come here much because I live in the Grimms. I like it here, so I thought I'd stop by…"

"I don't think Ivory knows you lied."

"But you just said she told you!"

"I said she called me. I didn't say we talked about you."

"You tricked me!" I said, bolting upright.

The bow to my violin slid forward, and I gasped. Ethan caught it before it could even teeter off the bench. "How about you put this away where it's safe?" he said, handing it to me. "You're very clumsy."

"I am not," I argued but tugged the case into my lap, opening it to put away my violin.

"Ivory didn't seem to know about the lie, but we did talk about you."

I glanced up. "You did?"

Ethan made another sound of agreement. I liked the sounds he made. Kinda rumbly, kinda indulgent. Every time he made one, I wanted to lean closer.

"She said you rejected the offer I made to have you play at an upcoming business function I have."

I felt my eyes widen. "One of those offers was from you?"

Surprise flickered on his face as he leaned back, propping up his elbow on the back of the bench. The fabric of his jacket sort of strained around his bicep. "You didn't look at them?"

Does he work out? How is he so big? He's bigger than all of my brothers.

Leaves rustled overhead with a particularly strong wind, making a few deep-colored leaves break free and lazily fall to the ground. A chill wrapped around me as the sky dimmed a bit, the sun hidden behind a cloud.

"You cold?" Ethan's sharp voice snapped me out of my inner thoughts. I got lost in them a lot.

"Huh?" I asked this a lot too.

"Why aren't you wearing a coat?"

"I forgot it," I told him, not even worried about the coat or the cold air. "You really wanted me to play at your event?"

Ethan sat forward, his knee almost brushing mine as he peeled the suit jacket off his shoulders and down his arms. Beneath, he was wearing a steel-gray dress shirt that looked a little shiny and a gleaming white silk tie.

"Wh—" Before I could even ask what he was doing, the jacket was draped around my shoulders, the warmth from his body seeping through the thin fabric of my T-shirt and causing actual goose bumps to rise along my arms.

"I don't need this," I protested, offended.

But I didn't pull it off.

Ethan ignored my words just like I had, pulling the lapels closer under my chin and then smoothing it out over my shoulders.

"What would Ivory say if I let you get sick?" He spoke softly as though he was telling me a secret.

No one ever really spoke softly to me. Sometimes Ivory, but that was just her voice. My brothers were all loud and gruff. And Snort wasn't named Snort because he was silent.

I laughed at the thought.

"What are you giggling about?" Ethan asked.

My eyes snapped up. "I wasn't giggling!"

A blond brow arched over the glasses.

"We have a dog named Snort." I laughed—*not giggled* —again.

After a moment of pause, Ethan settled back against the bench. "So why'd you turn me down?"

"I didn't turn you down," I hurried to say. The jacket

slipped back on my shoulders with the force of my words, and I grasped it, pulling it tightly around myself once more.

The scent of pine with just a hint of something else, some spice, wafted up around my head, and I breathed in deep.

Without thinking much, I dipped my chin, pressing my nose into the collar of the jacket to breathe in deep. He smelled like Christmas, more specifically like the tree stand I helped out with last year in the Grimms.

"Are you smelling my jacket?"

A new fierce blush exploded across my cheeks, spreading to the back of my neck. "You stink." I lied, feeling bad for it.

I wasn't good at lying.

"Oh?" Ethan leaned forward. "Better give it back, then."

I launched away from him, clasping the lapels from the inside. It was bigger on me, my frame not nearly as wide as his, so I was able to hide inside it completely.

"I turned down all the offers to play," I said, hoping to distract him from taking the coat.

I wasn't ready to give it back.

He dropped his hand. "Why?"

"I'm not a professional."

"It's a shame. You play beautifully. I would have enjoyed listening to you again."

"You would?"

He nodded. "You played for Ivory's show," he pointed out.

"Ivory is my sister."

He made another one of his sounds and gazed out across the park. His profile was just as perfect as the rest of him, almost like he was carved by a sculptor.

Without realizing, I scooted a little closer across the bench. "I'm sorry I turned you down. I didn't know you put in an offer."

His head turned, and despite the sunglasses, I felt the weight of his gaze. "Does that mean if you had known it was me, you would have accepted?"

The sound of my swallow was audible. The hair hanging over my forehead caught in the breeze, and the scent of pine swirled into my nose.

I nodded. It was all I could do. My stomach was back to feeling funny.

"Well, I still haven't found someone." He started, and I realized what I just did.

I jerked upright. "No! I—"

"I waited so long for your answer, and the event is in two weeks. It puts me in a bind, having to find someone else this close."

I blinked, feeling bad for ignoring the offers for so long. "What kind of event is it?"

"A hotel opening."

"You really won't be able to find anyone else?"

"No one like you."

I gave in. "Okay."

"Okay?"

"I'll play at your hotel opening. I feel bad I made you wait so long. And since we're friends…"

"Are we?"

His question stopped me, and I glanced away quickly, totally embarrassed. "W-well, I—" I began, stuttering.

Warm fingers latched gently onto my chin, bringing my face back around as soft laughter filled the air around us. "I was teasing,"

"I didn't think you knew how."

"Me either," he confided.

Falling into silence, I searched the lenses for a glimpse of his stare, wanting to see the look in his eyes, wondering what I would find there.

"You look like a puppy," he murmured, his thumb stroking the underside of my chin.

My face screwed up. "I do not."

"Yes," he refuted simply. "Big, innocent eyes. Clumsy big feet and hands. Floppy hair… A trusting nature."

Pulling out of his grasp, I nearly toppled against the back of the bench. "I should go," I said, scrambling up.

Turning away, I grabbed my violin case, wishing I had more stuff to grab so I could stall for time.

When I turned back, he was standing too. I wouldn't say I was really short, but maybe I was compared to him. He stood so close I had to look up to meet his eyes.

Oddly, I didn't feel intimidated or even like he was trying to assert some kind of power over me. Instead, I felt… at peace.

It was weird.

Just like my stomach.

"Here," he said, extending a card between us.

I took it and looked down. It was his business card.

"Come to my office tomorrow afternoon, and we'll sign the contract and go over the details of your performance."

"Okay. What time?"

"It doesn't matter."

"Aren't you busy?" I asked. If his schedule was anything like Ivory's, then he must be. That made me wonder. "What are you even doing here in the middle of the day?"

"I needed some fresh air," he told me, tipping back his chin to gaze at the sky. "And yes, I'm busy." Glancing down, he leaned in. "But I'll make time for you."

I fumbled back, but he caught my arm, keeping me upright.

"See? Nothing but a puppy."

Is he teasing me again? Do I like it? Shaking off his grasp, I pulled the coat from around me and held it out.

He took it, draping it over his forearm. "I'll see you tomorrow, puppy."

The violin case bumped against my leg as I turned to

leave. Even though I was blushing hard, I was chilled from the lack of his coat.

I had to take the job, I told myself as I made my way out of Central Park. *I left him in a bind. It was the right thing to do.*

It definitely didn't have anything at all to do with the weird feeling still squirming around in my belly.

I LOOKED AT THE CLOCK MORE TIMES THAN I WANTED TO admit. Despite my busy schedule, the morning seemed to drag on.

By late afternoon, I grew restless, tossing down the pen and standing from behind the desk. Tucking my hands into the pockets of my trousers, I turned toward the large window behind me, staring out across the city, eyes straying toward Central Park and the multicolored treetops.

I sighed. *Where is he?*

I told him afternoon, and it was going on dinnertime. The sun already hung low behind the tallest buildings in the city, the sky growing dimmer with each passing minute. Soon, the sun would be gone and the city would be illuminated by thousands of lights.

Could he have agreed to meet just because he didn't know how to say no?

My head shook at the thought. Fletcher might be innocent, nice, and maybe even eager to please, but he didn't strike me as someone who couldn't say no. After all, he did tell Ivory no.

Without even looking at the offers.

A tsking sound escaped from between my lips. *Such bad business.*

A brisk knock on the door brought me around. "Come in," I called.

My heart rate escalated when the door pushed open and then dropped when Bree stepped inside.

"What is it?" I asked, words gruff.

She paused at my tone but didn't acknowledge it further. Gesturing to some files in her hand, she came closer. "Here are the files you were waiting for and the finalized contract. Oh, your last conference call scheduled at five had to reschedule. I've got it down for later this week."

"No one has been here to see me this afternoon?" I questioned.

After placing the papers on my desk, she straightened. "No. Was someone supposed to?"

"So if the call is canceled, then that's all for today?"

"Besides these, yes." She agreed, pointing at the papers. She didn't bother pointing out I didn't answer her question.

"You can go, then."

"Are you sure? I can stay until you've looked over—"

"I can handle it. Just go."

"Should I order in some dinner for you before I go?"

"No. I'm not hungry." I paused. "But thank you."

The assistant seemed to relax with my added offer of thanks. It made me feel slightly guilty for my tone before. I often tried not to take any mood or stress I might be feeling out on my staff, as it only created a harsh working environment and made everyone uncomfortable.

Every time my father stepped into this wing, it served as a clear reminder of that.

"Okay, well, have a nice evening," she said.

"Bree," I called out, turning away from the window, leveling my stare on the light-haired assistant.

"Yes?"

"Thanks for everything. Have a good night."

She smiled. "See you tomorrow."

When she was gone, the silence of the room echoed around me.

Where is he? Why am I so disturbed that he hasn't shown up?

I thought about calling, but he didn't have a phone. How could he just go around without a phone? What if something happened? How would he call for help?

"This is not for you to worry about," I muttered, planting myself back into the seat to look over the newly delivered files.

A short while later, a sound of frustration filled the office, and I pushed the papers away.

I want to see him.

There. I admitted it.

Just allowing myself to think it alleviated some frustration, but not nearly enough. Now I had to wonder why I wanted to see him so much.

One afternoon in the park, not even an hour's time. That shouldn't be enough to make me this way.

A memory of his wide golden eyes staring at me flashed into my mind.

Fuck.

A knock on the door caught my breath. Instead of calling out, all I did was make some odd sound.

The door swung open anyway, and Ivory walked in wearing a white body-hugging pencil skirt with a white military-style jacket adorned with gold buttons. Her heels were white with straps that wrapped around her ankles to the lower part of her slim calves.

The hem of the jacket was slightly frayed, and her onyx hair was sleek around her shoulders.

"Bree wasn't at her desk, so I just let myself in."

"You're welcome anytime," I told her, standing up out of habit and respect.

"Working late again," she observed, walking across my office to where my private bathroom was located. Draped over her arm was a large black garment bag. Beside the bathroom was a built-in closet with a hook jutting out from the front.

When she got there, she looked up and frowned.

Chuckling, I went to help her, taking the bag and hanging it on the hook she obviously couldn't reach.

"What's this?" I asked.

"Your suit for the opening. It was done a little early, so I figured I'd bring it by."

"Ah, thank you."

"I should thank *you*. It's free advertising when you wear my clothes."

"Why wouldn't I wear them? I always look good when I do."

"Charming," she mused, patting me on the chest.

"Do I need to try this on now?" I asked, not even moving to open up the bag.

She made a dismissive gesture with her hand. "You can do it later. Just let me know if there is a problem with the fit."

There wouldn't be a problem. There never was with Ivory's designs, and her design house, Reflections, had made me enough clothes that they probably knew my measurements by heart.

"Have you talked to Fletcher today?" I blurted out.

It was unlike me. I very rarely blurted out anything without thinking first. It just went to prove how unsettled I was by his lack of appearance.

She swung around, the glossy strands of her hair sweeping out like a curtain. With a wrinkled nose, she asked, "Fletcher?"

Nodding, I explained. "I actually saw him in the park yesterday after I spoke with you. I brought up the event I'd wanted him to play at, and he agreed to do it."

Her blue eyes widened. "He did?" she exclaimed, clearly happy. "How'd you get him to agree?"

"I just told him it would be a hardship to find someone this short notice to take his place."

"Maybe if you were anyone other than you," she quipped, giving me a look.

I shrugged. "I thought you wanted him to have a job."

Her red lips pursed. She was indeed a very beautiful woman, and she was also likable. It was a shame I wasn't attracted to her at all.

"You're right." Her nod was brisk. "Thank you."

I wasn't interested in her thanks right now. I wanted to know where Fletcher was.

Ivory might not be your type... but he is.

"He was supposed to be here this afternoon to sign the contract. He never showed." The thoughts echoing through my head made the tension in my voice palpable.

"You're worried." Ivory stated, clearly not asking.

The tie at my neck suddenly felt a bit tight, and I reached for it, loosening it a bit. "Are you saying I don't need to be? Does he no-show often?"

"Actually, no. Fletcher is very reliable, and he's a terrible liar."

"I noticed." I agreed, fondness filling my chest when I thought of his honest eyes and blushing cheeks.

I was used to people who bluffed and put on a front. I'd learned to take everything everyone said with a grain, or two, of salt. Honesty seemed like a commodity the rich couldn't afford, which was ironic because people thought the rich could afford everything.

Clearly, not everything could be bought.

"He could have gotten distracted, though. He often plays in the subway and sometimes forgets the time."

"He spends his time in the subway," I echoed, displeasure curling my lip.

Surprise widened her eyes a bit, and she said, "He likes it down there."

"It's filthy and filled with rats."

"There is that," she allowed. "I could call the apartment and see if he's there," Ivory offered. "I'd call Neo, but he's with Virginia right now. She had an appointment earlier today."

"How is his sister?" I asked, genuinely interested in her well-being. She was a beautiful girl that got dealt a shitty hand in life, but the time I'd met her, she still had a bright spirit.

"She's good, hopeful this surgery will help her walk again."

"If there is anything I can do, anything at all, please let me know."

Stepping close, Ivory put her hand over mine, giving it a squeeze. "Thank you. Truly. It means so much to me that you accepted Neo and his family into my life. Into our lives. Your acceptance of my relationship really helped to smooth things out in our, ah, social circles."

Even my acceptance of heiress Ivory White's relationship with a misfit from the Grimms didn't keep tongues from wagging. In fact, I think they wagged a little more because I just allowed my betrothed to be snatched away. My father basically said as much. However, Ivory was probably the richest woman in this entire state—hell, maybe even this country—so the tongues just wagged a little quieter.

However, my family name and my reputation here was also nothing to sneeze at, so I understood the reason she was thanking me. I could have made things much more difficult.

My father would have preferred it that way.

Me?

I wanted Ivory to be happy.

At least one of us can be.

That thought brought another one chasing right after. *Fletcher.*

"So, ah, about Fle—" I was cut off by the ringing of a cell phone.

Startled, Ivory pulled back, her manicured hand delving into a concealed pocket in her military jacket and coming out with her slim phone. Her brow furrowed when she looked at the screen. "Unknown," she murmured.

"Don't answ—"

"Hello?" she said, cutting off my warning.

I mean really, she didn't listen at all. Neo must have been exhausted.

I couldn't hear the voice on the other end of the line, but the way she straightened made it clear she knew who it was.

"Fletcher?" Was that worry in her voice?

She fell silent, and the loud pounding of my heart made up for her lack of sound.

"He's with Virginia. That's why." Pause. "What's happened?"

I wasn't an anxious person. Actually, far from it. I was usually calm and cool, not easily ruffled. In my line of work, in my family, if I was any other way, my head would have exploded long ago.

So why was I having a hard time controlling my breath right now? My heart rate? Why were my fists clenching with the need to snatch away Ivory's phone and demand to know what he was saying?

Ivory gasped, mouth falling open, eyes jumping to mine.

I froze.

"What?" she cried. "I told you—" She cut herself off, drawing in a deep breath. "*Ugh.* I'll be right there."

Pulling the phone away from her ear, she hit the screen, glancing up. "Well. I found Fletch."

"Where is he?" I demanded.

She sighed. "Jail."

FLETCHER

I woke up this morning, and my stomach still felt funny.

I told Earth, and he told me to drink some Pepto.

So I did.

It didn't help.

I couldn't even eat breakfast, but I did wash down that gross pink stuff with some coffee.

I'm going to see him again today. The thought was almost like a heartbeat that had been echoing inside me since I'd opened my eyes.

After taking a shower and pulling on a pair of jeans and a T-shirt, I grabbed the coat Ivory insisted on buying for me. The coat I had before was fine, even if it was a little thread-bare and old.

But this new one was made of material that blocked the wind and was lined to keep me warm. The pockets were deep enough to fit my entire hands, and there was a hood lined with some kind of fur I could pull up when it was snowing.

The label on the inside read The North Face, but I didn't know anything about that brand.

Beau's head popped up from behind his multiple

computer monitors, his red hair somewhat messy around the headphones jammed over his head. "Where you going?"

Obviously hearing him, Earth popped his head out from the kitchen to stare.

"Subway," I answered, picking up my violin. "Then I'm going to go see Neo and Ivory."

Earth grunted. "That explains the coat."

Beau snickered.

"What do you mean?"

"You only wear that when you're gonna see Ivory 'cause she nags you to death about it," Earth quipped.

I thought about yesterday and how she did in fact nag me about the absence of my coat. It was only because she cared, though, and I was grateful she gave me this, even if it was too nice.

Guess if I wear this, I won't be needing Ethan's jacket today.

"What's that look?" Earth barked, pulling me out of my thoughts.

I blinked. "What look?"

"The look you got on your face."

My brothers stared, both sporting mildly aggressive looks on their faces. It made me wonder what kind of face I'd been making.

"I don't have any look on my face," I said, trying to make it so my expression was blank.

"If you need anything, you know where to find us," Beau said, accepting my reply.

Earth was a lot more suspicious, but he didn't say anything, just stared with that intimidating expression on his face.

"I'll see you guys later!" I waved.

"Stay out of trouble." Earth tossed the warning in my direction.

"Okay," I mumbled, feeling like I was fifteen and not twenty-two.

A snort echoed behind me as I let myself out of the apartment. Could have been Earth. Could have been Snort. I really didn't know.

The air was cold this morning, the chill firmly in place as if it had no intention of being chased away by the sun. The wind blew in a single direction down the street. The howling echoed in my ears as my hair lifted away from my forehead.

I still had quite a while before I was to meet up with Ethan, and my plan was to head down to the subway for some busking (aka playing my violin for money). But when I got there, my feet kept going past the steps leading underground, clearly following a mission I didn't know about.

Not far into my unexpected walk, I passed by an alley I knew quite well. Even though I didn't want to, my head turned and my eyes looked.

I mean, really, who was in control of my body here?

I expected the familiar tightening of my gut, the familiar rush of loneliness and fear I felt whenever I passed by this particular place.

All of that was definitely there today, but it was muted by something else.

Someone was in the alley, a boy. He was younger than me, maybe late teens.

I'd never seen this kid before, but I recognized him.

I recognized the way he crouched against the building, how his bare arms wrapped around pulled-in knees. Fear clung to him like a scent, and his vacant stare was pointed straight ahead.

Instead of continuing on, my footsteps paused, body rotating.

The second he saw me approaching, he straightened, jolting up to his feet. He was thin and dressed a lot like me actually.

"Hey." I started.

"What do you want? I don't have any money!"

I held out my hand. "I don't want anything. I was just wondering if you needed help."

His expression changed instantly, fear morphing into aggression as though I'd somehow offended him. I understood. Pride meant a lot here in the Grimms because for a lot of people, pride was all they had left.

"Why would I need help?" he snarled.

I shrugged. "Haven't seen you around before. I know most everyone here."

"I'm just passing through."

The tough bravado wasn't unfamiliar, but I wasn't about to call him out. "Yeah, okay. Cool."

"I'm out of here." He sniffed, sauntering away from the wall.

"Hey."

He swung around, the slight worry in his eyes replaced with hardness.

"Here," I said, unzipping the coat and holding it out.

"What the fuck, man?"

"You and I both know you're scared as hell and probably not sure where you'll go next." Before he could denounce the truth, I motioned to the coat, extending it a little farther. "You have goose bumps. Wouldn't hurt to be warm while you figure out your next move."

His face was wary as if the call for some protection against the elements was going to outweigh his pride.

I understood that too.

I shrugged. "I don't want it anyway. I stole it last year. It's about time I got an upgrade."

When I let go, the coat fell to the ground between us, and I left it there, turning to leave. As I was walking away, I heard the rustle of the fabric as he bent to pick it up.

"Oh, hey." Even though I didn't turn around, I knew he froze at my words, and the coat fell back on the ground.

"If you go two blocks over to the tiny diner in the alley,

Heather will hook you up with a free meal. Tell her Fletch sent you."

He said nothing, and I continued on my way, not stopping or looking back until I was around the corner and partway down the street. When I did turn back, I saw him fleeing in the opposite direction, the fur on the hood of the coat easy to spot. He was heading in the direction of the diner.

Tucking the hand not carrying my violin case into the pocket of my jeans, I turned and continued along my way. It wasn't much, what I'd done, but at least he would be warm and get a meal. It was more kindness than these streets usually offered.

If it weren't for my brothers, specifically Neo who found me in that very same alley, I might not even be here at all.

The moment I stepped onto a familiar street, the weird feeling I woke up with was replaced with knots of tension, weariness in my limbs and shoulders that slumped under the weight of what was to come.

Why did I do this to myself?

You know why.

Now I knew why my subconscious brought me here. Because if I'd known I was coming, I'd have told Earth and Beau. They would not have been happy and tried to stop me. I didn't want to argue with them. Not about this.

This was something I had to do. Something I couldn't just walk away from even if sometimes I wanted to.

The buildings here were rundown, the townhomes all needing paint and repair. Even the sidewalks had cracks and dips as if the concrete were tired of holding up this street.

Brown weeds reached weakly between those cracks, stretching across the pavement like they had died in the process of trying to escape.

Some pipe must have burst somewhere underground

because massive white puffs of smoke rose from a grate in the street, bringing with it a rotten stench.

Tucking my chin against my chest, I walked past the abandoned apartment whose door wasn't latched so it shook and creaked in the wind. Past broken beer bottles, cigarette butts, and various pieces of trash littering the ground.

For long moments, I was swallowed whole by the steam, everything turning a milky white, eerily closing in like some kind of horror flick.

On the other side, there were two kids playing, one riding a bike that had more rust than paint and the other swinging a stick like it was a sword. Both of them looked up when I passed, and I gave them a little wave. Neither of them had on coats, and I wondered if they were cold.

My destination was at the end of the block. A cracked clay pot filled with plants that had died long ago stood lonely on one of the crooked concrete steps. The railing was only present on one side. The other side probably hadn't been put in at all.

The wooden door was cracked and faded. The metal mailbox fastened to the side of the building creaked as the wind blew.

Reaching toward the door handle, I noted the violin case clutched in my chilled hand.

Panic seized me, tossing my heart into my throat. With a tight chest, I tried to breathe, giving up when my lungs wouldn't cooperate. My fingers trembled as I backtracked down the few steps and around the side of the building.

Glancing around to make sure no one was watching, I bent to an old yet familiar spot. Even though it wasn't obvious to the eye, I knew. My fingers went right to the loose brick, wiggling until it came out. I repeated the action with a few more and then shoved my case into the small opening, the already beat-up exterior earning a few more scrapes in my impatience.

Once it was in, I replaced the bricks, standing back to make sure it wasn't obvious.

Despite the cold air, my palms were sweaty, and I wiped them down my jeans as I made my way back around the house and up the rickety stairs, sparing a glance at the lifeless, brittle plant.

I couldn't help but wonder if that was what my fate would have been if I'd stayed here. I definitely was partway there when I met my brothers.

Pulling a key from my pocket, I let myself in, the door groaning stiffly on its hinges.

Inside was dim but not dark. Just in front of me was a crooked staircase, tilting oddly away from the wall. The third one up was caved in, the wood having given out long ago. To my right was a wide doorway leading into the living room where light filtered in from the dirty front windows, dimly illuminating the tidy but rundown space.

Swallowing, shoving my hands into my pockets, I stepped farther inside.

"I'm here," I called out.

A faint sound from the back of the house made my shoulders stiffen, and then her tall, thin frame materialized like a lurking shadow.

"Who's there?" she called out, stepping into the room and therefore the light. I started to smile and offer a greeting, but she cut me off. "Oh. It's you."

Swallow. "Hi, Mom."

Her eyes swept over me, making me feel cold in a way the wind outside never could. She didn't smile. In fact, my mother smiling was something like a unicorn. Maybe it existed, but I had yet to see it.

"Where the hell have you been?" she asked, regarding me not as a son but as an annoyance.

Well, that's what you are.

"I've been working a lot lately."

She laughed, but it was not a humorous sound. Instead, it smacked of sinister sarcasm, audible doubt, and most of all, bitterness I couldn't understand.

"*You?* Work? You couldn't hold a job if your life depended on it."

"I've been doing okay lately," I refuted weakly.

She made a sound, her nearly midnight eyes fixing on my face like a whip. "Okay," she nagged. "If you're doing okay, then why the hell am I still living in this ghetto?"

She came closer and, with her, a faint smell of alcohol and anger. She was always angry. "You been living it up, out there spending on yourself, forgetting about everything I've given up for you?"

"No," I hurried to say, hating the way my knees slightly trembled. "Of course not. I just meant I've been able to make a little money."

My shoulders ached under the weight of her scrutiny. My heart ached from her indifference.

She laughed again. "I'll believe that when I see it."

"Here," I said, eagerly reaching into my pocket.

It was good I wasn't wearing my coat. If I was, she definitely would have thought I was being selfish.

Pulling out all the money I'd made in the last week busking in the subway—and maybe a little I'd swiped from unsuspecting pockets—I handed it all over.

She took it without hesitation, sitting down on the worn sofa to promptly count it out in front of her on the coffee table. When she was done, she glanced up.

"See? I've been working hard."

A sound vibrated her throat. "This is the least you could do."

Her lukewarm words felt like a compliment, so much so that my aching heart felt just a little better. "I did good?" I asked.

"I wouldn't go that far." She sniffed.

"I'm glad it made you happy, Mom."

Grabbing the money, she folded it up and pushed it into her pocket.

A strong wind blew outside, whistling through the windows, causing a bone-chilling draft to float through the room and tap against the back of my bare neck.

Suppressing a shiver, I moved around to perch on the edge of a wooden seat near the couch. "How have you been?"

"Like you care."

"Of course I care. You're my mom."

"If you really cared, you never would have been born."

Hurt pinged my heart, making me look down at my hands, which were clasped together in my lap. The truth was I didn't want to be here. I didn't like the way she acted or the words she spoke.

"You better not have earned this from doing what I forbade you to do!"

I shook my head adamantly. I might not be a good liar, but I could lie to her. "Never." I swore. "I've been helping out down at the fish market."

"Hmph." Her lips pursed with the sound. "I'm surprised your scrawny arms could even haul half of those fish."

"I'm stronger than I look."

Her eyes shot up at that, piercing me with their dark depths, almost like she was trying to find something she thought was there.

I hated when she looked at me like this. Like she knew I was hiding something or she saw something even I didn't know I contained.

"Are you talking back?"

I shook my head.

"Didn't think so."

"Well," I said, rubbing my palms against my knees before standing. "I should probably get going. I have a lead on another job. I just wanted to stop by and make sure you're okay. Give you that." I gestured toward the money she'd already hidden away. "Do you need anything?"

"I need to not have to look at your face!" She hurled the words, and I felt them like they weighed a thousand pounds.

I nodded. "Okay. I'll come back to check on you."

She said nothing as I shuffled to the door, said nothing when I paused with my hand on the handle, and silence followed me out the front door.

Once it was shut between us, I let out a long, shuddering breath, leaning against the cold, uneven wood.

She didn't ask me why I wasn't wearing a coat. She didn't ask if I was cold or hungry.

She never did.

Ignoring the shaking of my limbs, I went back around the house, making sure no one was watching while I unearthed the case I'd stowed away.

As I walked away, my stomach rumbled loudly, and I regretted my choice to skip breakfast. I could go home and grab something, but the second my brothers looked at me, they would know.

I didn't want to face them right now. To see the pity and underlying anger in their eyes.

They couldn't understand why I still went to see her, the woman who'd kicked me out on the street. They couldn't understand why I would give her money, why I let her get in my head.

They didn't understand.

She was my mother.

The only family I had until I met them.

I didn't let her get in my head because she was already there. Her blood was mine. There was no escape from that.

It was quite true she didn't like me. And honestly, I couldn't blame her.

My stomach rumbled again, threatening to eat itself if I

didn't provide something soon. I always got extra hungry when I was stressed out. And right now, I was stressed.

What the hell possessed me to see her this morning?

As if you don't know. Yeah, okay, I knew.

Guilt.

Guilt for defying her demands and taking a violin job.

The heady, warm scent of baking bread swirled around, bringing up my chin and turning my thoughts outward. My chest expanded with the deep breath I inhaled, practically salivating at the idea of a warm treat.

Staring ahead to the corner of the next block, my eyes fixed on the small bakery, an establishment that had been here in the Grimms since before I was. Outside the door were stands set up with mounds of bright red and green apples, along with a pile of oranges.

My feet sped up without my realizing it as I stared at the fruit, all the while sniffing the bread-scented air.

A small bell rang when a customer stepped out holding the handles of a paper sack. A long golden baguette peeked out from the top, almost as if it were taunting me.

I felt a dark cloud roll over me, my usually unruffled mood suddenly affected with darkness. Anger tainted my brain, and unreasonable frustration consumed me.

I'm hungry and have no money to buy some simple bread.

I can't go home because I don't want them to know.

I am cold, and she didn't even notice.

Scuffling right by the bakery, my quick hand shot out, slipping two apples into the pockets of my jeans. Moving at the same unhurried pace past the door, I didn't look to see if I'd been caught. Eyes ahead, I fixated on the woman hunkered down in her coat as she walked, that damn baguette still teasing.

It looked like a full bag, as though she'd bought lots of fresh bread.

Moving quickly along, I silently, quickly grabbed the end and pulled it from the bag.

I started to shove it inside my coat—*shit! I'm not wearing one anymore!*

"Hey!" the woman yelled, her voice angry and loud.

Jolting, I looked up, realizing too late I'd been caught.

Behind me, the bell on the bakery door jangled angrily, and pounding feet hit the pavement. "Hey! Stop! Thief!"

Momentarily glued in place, I looked at the bread clutched in my hand, then divided my stare between the angry woman and shop owner who were coming at me from both sides.

Willing myself to move, I took off, darting backward, avoiding both my pursuers. As I darted across the street, a cab honked wildly, barely missing me, but I didn't look back because people were still shouting.

Glancing down at my feet, I willed myself to go faster, clutching the bread like it was some hard-won prize.

Slam! My entire body collided full force into something and bounced back, my feet unsuccessfully staying on the ground.

One second, I was running with my riches, and the next, I was staring at my too-big shoes as they came above my head.

Oomph! All the wind was knocked out of my body, leaving me to gasp and groan for more. While I was shaking off the stunned feeling, the sound of more shouts infiltrated my spinning head.

"Stop him! Thief!"

Scrambling up, I prepared to run off again, but a hand clamped around my upper arm, swinging me around and slamming me into a nearby building.

Another painful groan escaped my lips, and I looked up.

"Gotcha," the familiar voice crowed.

Feeling my eyes widen, I tried to take off once more, but

the hand holding my arm moved to my neck where the overzealous cop pinned me, barely allowing room to breathe.

I sagged into the building, dropping the bread onto the cold concrete.

Fig. The Grimms' dumbest, most arrogant cop. He lived for trying to catch me and my brothers in the act of anything he could use against us.

I'd been caught more than anyone else, but I always managed to get out of it.

"He stole my bread!" the woman called breathlessly, huffing and puffing as she came close.

"He stole fruit from my stand," the shop owner added, equally out of breath.

They really should try and work out more.

"Got you red-handed!" Fig preened as if he'd caught me robbing a bank, not just trying to pinch a snack. "There's no getting out of it this time."

I glanced at him, then at the angry people gathered round.

Shit. Today really wasn't a good day.

Seven

Ethan

"Pretty sure this is a no-parking zone," Ivory said when my white Mercedes glided to a stop at the curb near the entrance of the police station.

Could this place even be considered a police station? Great gods, it looked like some rundown, seedy establishment where criminals committed the crimes, not where they were punished for them.

Turning off the engine, still staring at the building, I shrugged. "I'll pay the parking ticket."

Ivory didn't argue. There was no reason to. She was too worried about Fletch and the fact that he was locked up here.

I was worried as well, but seeing this place in person skyrocketed that feeling by like one hundred.

How long has he been sitting in there?

Out of habit, my palm hovered over her lower back as we walked toward the entrance. It was fully dark now, the sidewalk only lit by the awful fluorescent lighting of the station.

"Thank you for coming with me. You didn't have to," Ivory said as I reached around to open the door for us.

"Like I would allow you to come to a place like this alone."

"I've been here before," she replied, so nonchalant I wondered for a moment if aliens had snatched her body.

"Sometimes I really wonder what you see in him," I muttered, partly a tease and partly the truth.

Ivory elbowed my waist, giving me a look. "Neo wasn't the reason I was here."

The second we entered the precinct—no, scratch that. This place just didn't merit that name. Let's just call it the station. The second we entered the station, all thoughts of Ivory and her time here fled my mind.

All that remained was the urge to lay eyes on Fletcher.

The air was tinged with stale coffee, cigarette smoke, and… Oh God, was that *urine*? My loafers squeaked over the cracked tile floors, drawing attention to us as we walked.

The second I felt eyes on us, I straightened to my full height, pursing my lips and glancing around with purpose. The eyes of every single cop, as well as the woman at the front counter, fixed on us.

Feeling her stare, I glanced across the counter. "Good evening, ma'am."

Her lips parted, and a half-vacant look took over her eyes.

She probably wasn't used to people with manners.

Ivory knocked on the counter in front of the woman. "Hello, ma'am. I'm here to get Fletcher—"

"Never thought I'd see you in here again," a new voice said, cutting off her words.

I felt rather than heard Ivory sigh, which automatically made me suspicious of the police officer.

"Hello, Fig," Ivory said, polite but not friendly. "Are you the one who arrested Fletcher?"

My back teeth smacked together.

"I always knew that boy was trouble. Finally caught him in the act."

"Caught him in the act of what, exactly?" Ivory asked.

"Theft of property. Two counts."

"And what is your evidence?" I asked, speaking up for the first time.

Fig's eyes flicked to me, then came back, widening just a bit. "Y-you—"

"Officer Fig, this is my friend, Ethan Abbott. You—"

"I know who he is. I see the news," Fig muttered. "I shoulda known you two would know each other."

I didn't have time for this. "This is hardly an appropriate conversation right now. I'm asking you about the charges you have brought against Fletcher. I want to know what evidence you have to detain him."

Fig straightened a bit, a flash of panic in his eyes before it was replaced with smug righteousness. "My evidence? Those two people right over there." He pointed.

Looking past him, I saw a woman in a dark coat with a paper bag at her feet sitting beside a middle-aged man with gray hair, weary features, and a shirt with the name of a bakery on the left breast.

"Explain," I said, still staring as the two people spoke to an officer.

"That's who he stole from. They're pressing charges right now."

An abrupt, shrill scream cut through the entire building, practically shaking the crappy lights overhead. It echoed, bouncing around until finally dying out.

"Damn drunk," Fig muttered, rubbing one of his ears.

Ivory's face had gone pale. "I want to see Fletcher."

"Not possible," Fig rebuked.

She fidgeted, bringing her hands up to wring them together. "You don't have him in the same cell with that… man, do you?"

"What do you think we are, animals? We got Dan locked up alone. In the cell next to the little criminal."

Another ear-piercing shriek shook the building.

"Hey, shut up, would ya?" one of the officers yelled down the hallway.

"He's back there?" I asked, rotating to go find Fletcher

myself. The thought of him locked in a cell alone for God knew how long beside some insane drunk turned my stomach and created a tight knot at the base of my skull.

"Whoa!" Fig's hand shot out, pushing against my chest. "You can't just go back there. Personnel only."

I glanced down to where his hand was "stopping" me, then back up at him.

Face flushing, he pulled his hand away. "You must work out," he said, his voice a little high.

"Yes. I do. So you either bring him out, or I'm going back there. You can't stop me."

Fig pursed his lips. "You threatening an officer of the law? I could lock you up too."

I leaned down so we were eye level and flashed my teeth. "Try it. I'll have every lawyer in the Upper East Side in this place in twenty minutes."

Fig cleared his throat. "Hatch!" he called. I assumed it was someone's name. "Get the kid. Haul him out here."

"No hauling," I growled.

"No hauling. Just walk him out." Fig corrected.

Straightening, I adjusted the forest-green coat I was wearing.

Ivory tossed me a look of thanks while we waited, and I gave her a slight nod. Thank God I was with her when she got this call. This might be Neo's neighborhood, but I was sure he wouldn't want her coming down here alone.

The distinct rattling of keys, metal bars creaking open, and then another loud shout from the drunkard in the back seemed like background noise as I stared at the hallway, waiting for Fletcher to appear.

Anxiety unlike any I'd never known made my hands clench and my stomach uneasy.

Suddenly, a mop of messy light-brown hair appeared, and honey-brown eyes peeked around the stoic officer leading him. At first, he didn't see us, but when he found Ivory, his entire face lit up. The second he noticed me standing beside her, his eyes went wide and the tips of his ears turned red.

"Fletcher!" Ivory said, hurrying over. "Are you okay?"

He nodded. "I'm okay. I'm sorry you had to come."

"I'll always come," she told him, glancing down to where his hands were cuffed behind his back. Gasping, she pointed, "Is that really necessary?"

"It's policy," Fig declared.

Stepping forward but unable to take my eyes off Fletch, I said, "I give you my word that he won't go anywhere. Uncuff him, please."

The officer standing beside Fletcher started to uncuff him immediately.

"I didn't tell you to do that," Fig complained.

"Give it a rest, Fig." A female officer carrying a donut and coffee walked past. "It ain't like he murdered someone."

"A woman of reason," I declared. "Thank you, ma'am."

She stopped, tipping her chin up to stare at me. "You're even more handsome in person than on the news."

I leaned in and whispered loudly, "The camera adds ten pounds."

She giggled.

"Ow." The small complaint from Fletch had me forgetting all about the woman as I spun to face him.

"Sorry," the officer said, stepping back.

Fletcher's arms fell in front of him as he began instantly rubbing his wrists.

Closing the distance between us, I stalked forward, carefully grabbing his forearm to stare at the red circle ringing his wrist.

"What kind of department is this? Not only is this establishment likely not up to code, behind on protocol, but now your officers are engaging in the mistreatment of the patrons."

"He ain't a patron. He's a thief."

"Innocent until proven guilty," Ivory declared.

Anger made my heart beat hard against my ribs as I turned away, blocking out all the morons surrounding us and sheltering Fletcher from view with my stance.

Lightly, my thumb brushed over the irritated skin. "How badly does it hurt?"

When he didn't answer, I looked up, finding his wide eyes already staring. "Why are you here?"

The emotion in his gaze clogged my throat and made it hard to think. He was looking at me like he was grateful, as if my presence somehow gave him relief.

The urge to protect surged so forcefully my fingers tightened around his wrist.

A small hiss escaped his lips, and I jolted, slackening my hold instantly.

"I'm sorry," I quickly apologized.

"Why?" he asked again, not worried about his wrist.

"You stood me up." It was the simplest answer I could provide, the only one I was willing to admit in the moment.

"I didn't mean to." His voice was forlorn as though he were afraid I was disappointed in him.

"I know."

Wide eyes lifted to me once more, and the innocence in them wrapped around my heart and squeezed. It should have hurt.

"What's the bail?" I asked, spinning back to the rest of the room.

"No bail has been set. We're still filing the charges. He'll have to spend the night."

The drunkard in the back picked that moment to screech again.

"He will not!" Ivory gasped, horrified.

Pinching the bridge of my nose, I sighed.

A small tug on the back of my jacket brought me around.

I turned, muting everyone else once more, focusing on Fletcher.

He leaned in. "I have to pee."

I tried not to smile. The declaration should not have been so cute. "You need to use the restroom," I repeated.

He nodded sagely.

Glancing around, I saw a public bathroom, which frankly, I shuddered thinking about the way it must look. "There," I said, motioning with my chin.

"Can I?"

He was asking me for permission?

Absolutely adorable.

Resisting the urge to smooth his hair, I nodded.

He started off, and one of the officers lunged. "You can't—"

Slam. The palm of my hand in the center of the man's chest stopped him from going any farther.

"There's a toilet in his cell," Fig called.

I recoiled. That was just unconscionable. "He'll be right back," I said, stony.

No one argued.

The door we'd entered through minutes ago banged open, causing everyone to look up. Two men stalked in, anger and purpose radiating off them in waves.

"Earth! Beau!" Ivory gasped.

Focusing on their identities, I realized it was in fact two of the men Fletcher called his brothers. Earth's Asian features were dark and stormy, jaw set, brows furrowed, and black hair mussed like he'd repeatedly run his hands through it. He wore ripped black jeans, black boots, and a black leather jacket.

Beau, on the other hand, appeared less dangerous but somehow still intimidating. A black beanie concealed his red hair, slashing over somber green eyes. His jeans weren't black or ripped, and his shirt was alternating wide stripes of red and blue.

He didn't match at all, but I guess not everyone had style.

"What the hell is this, Fig?" Earth barked, voice deep and intimidating.

Everyone looked at Fig as if no one else wanted to deal with him.

"Just doing my job," Fig offered.

Making a rude sound, Earth and Beau both pivoted toward Ivory. "You should have called," Earth told her, his voice much less harsh than before.

"But he asked me not to," Ivory argued.

"Look, I know Neo and me… have our problems right now, but this isn't the time—"

He thinks it's Neo who got arrested?

"Earth?" Fletcher asked, appearing from behind.

Both Earth and Beau jerked up, swinging toward Fletcher.

"Fletch!" Beau exclaimed. "What are you doing here?"

"I got arrested," he said, then in a smaller voice asked, "Is that not why you're here?"

"You got arrested?" Earth asked.

Fletcher nodded.

"We thought it was Neo," he muttered.

"Neo!" Ivory gasped.

"A couple guys came into the bar and said one of ours got hauled in and that they saw a white Mercedes parked outside the station… We just figured…"

"Neo is with Virginia tonight. Fletcher called, so I came," Ivory explained.

Both men looked at me.

"I came too."

"Come on. Let's go." Earth motioned toward Fletch.

"Whoa, whoa, whoa. That ain't how this works. Now I know everyone on the street shakes in their boots when they see you, Earth, but it ain't like that here. He's in custody. He's staying."

A dark look rolled over Earth's face, creating an equally dark aura around him.

A few men took a step back.

Fletcher began to fret. I could practically hear him worrying about his brother's, ah, reputation and what he might do.

"I'll handle this," I announced, the length of my coat flapping around my calves as I went across the room. "Pardon me." I spoke when the two people pressing charges looked up.

Both their eyes widened, and I smiled.

"Good evening. I came to apologize on behalf of my…" *What is he to me?* "Employee's behavior earlier today. I can assure you that I will deal with it swiftly and effectively so this does not occur again. In exchange, I would like to ask that you not press charges."

It took a few minutes for my words to sink in. Both parties stared so long I was beginning to wonder if they heard me.

"Now wait just a minute." Fig intercepted the exchange. "You can't just ask them to not press charges. That boy stole from them."

"Fletcher." I beckoned. "Come here."

He came, stopping at my side. Glancing at him, I asked, "Fletcher, what did you steal?"

Suddenly, his head bowed like he was embarrassed to say.

"It's okay. Just tell me."

After another silent moment, the woman with the brown bag spoke up. "He took my bread! Right out of my bag!"

"And he stole two apples right off my display!"

Shock rippled through me. "You stole food?"

His head bobbed, though he didn't look up.

Reaching down, I pulled his face up, making him look at me. "Fletcher, you stole some bread and fruit?"

He nodded again.

"Why?"

Even though his face was angled to mine, his eyes slid away. "I was hungry," he mumbled.

My hand let go, arm falling at my side. Ache consumed me, momentarily making me numb.

Hungry.

Was he so bad off that he had to steal just to eat?

Anger rose up, overshadowing the ache his hunger caused, and I spun, pinning Earth and Beau with a heated glare.

Beau seemed just as shocked as me, but Earth's brows were furrowed and his boots stomped forward, intent on Fletcher. "If you were hungry, why didn't you buy something?"

"Don't have any money," Fletch murmured.

"Then why didn't you come home to eat?" Earth demanded again.

"Didn't want to." His voice was small, and it caused the ache to take over my anger once again.

Earth stared at him a second longer and then cursed under his breath. "Milly," he spat almost inaudibly.

Fletcher flinched, stepping back toward me like he was seeking safety.

And if he was, it was me he sought it from.

Angling slightly in front of him, I matched Earth's glare. "That's enough."

"This isn't your place," he snarled.

I didn't recoil or back down. I knew all about his reputation, his secret identity.

I didn't care.

"I'm making it my place."

"Okay," Ivory said, inserting her small frame between us. "This isn't helping."

Fletcher's fingers curled into the back of my coat, and everything else fell away. Shrugging off my coat, I pushed it into his hands while I peeled off the suit jacket beneath it.

Fletcher stared, eyes skimming the dress shirt and gold tie before widening in shock when I draped the jacket around his shoulders.

"You're cold," I said, tucking it close.

"You noticed," he whispered, his voice a little wobbly, as I plucked my coat out of his hands and shrugged it back on.

"Of course I did."

"Where is your coat?" Earth demanded, his voice rough.

"Don't have it," Fletcher replied.

"You had it on when you left this morning." Beau reminded him. "And I also told you to call if you had trouble."

Ivory gasped, glaring at Fig. "Did you take his coat? Give it back right now!"

Earth, Beau, and I went rigid, turning our glares to Fig.

He coughed, then let out a whine. "I didn't take his coat!"

"Then why else would he not have it?" Beau declared.

Fletcher made a small sound. "I gave it to someone."

A heartbeat of silence passed.

"Who?" Ivory asked.

"Someone who needed it more than me."

This boy had to steal food because he was hungry but gave away his coat because there was someone else who needed it more?

The ache inside me intensified until my heart cracked under the strain. I didn't even know people like him existed. How had living this way not made him hard?

Overcome, I turned back to the man and woman, pulling my wallet from the inside of my coat.

Pulling out all the cash I had, I handed it to the bakery owner. "This more than covers the fruit."

"And you," I said, turning toward the woman. "I'll pay for an entire year's supply of bread for your household. You can go every day to his bakery. Buy as much as you want."

Her eyes widened in surprise.

To the owner, I said, "Set up a tab for me." I handed over my business card. "I'll pay it every week for an entire year. Whatever she wants."

The man looked between me and the offered card.

"Surely, you know who I am. You know I can afford it."

His head bobbed.

"Then you also know that I can hire the very best legal team and have this taken care of. I'm offering this now so it doesn't need to go that far. Take the deal."

Both parties agreed, much to Fig's dismay.

"Now just wait a minute! You can't bribe witnesses who were wronged!"

"I'm not bribing anyone. I'm offering restitution and a settlement out of court. It's perfectly legal."

Fig flushed.

Pulling out my cell phone, I lifted it. "Should I call my lawyer to verify?"

"No, no," Fig muttered. "It won't be necessary."

Nodding, I put the phone away. "Good. You can write up the agreement?" I asked the officer who'd been working with the victims.

His head bobbed.

I laid another one of my cards beside him. "Fax the signed paperwork to my office. If it's not there by end of day tomorrow, I'll send my lawyer to get it."

He looked as if he'd swallowed a goldfish when he promised it would be there.

"Thank you for your cooperation, sir and ma'am. I apologize again for the trouble. Please have a nice evening." I turned without waiting for their reply, putting my hand at the base of Fletcher's back. "C'mon, time to go."

His feet stalled, and I glanced down patiently.

"Just like that?"

I nodded. "We all came to an agreement."

Fletcher peeked at Fig who was standing there like he couldn't believe what was happening.

Grasping his chin, I pulled his gaze from the officer. "Don't bother with him. He's not important."

Fig huffed, and I snapped my eyes to him. "I suggest you find a new hobby besides harassing this man. If you don't, you will be dealing with me."

That shut him up.

"Let's go," I said again, this time much firmer.

Fletcher went, allowing me to guide him, possibly pressing back into my palm a little more.

We'd barely made it two feet when he gasped. "My violin! Fig took it! I want it back!"

Following Fletcher's accusing stare, I looked back at the man who really should not have a badge. Did they even check his qualifications before they gave him one?

"Where is it?" Impatience sharpened my tone.

The female officer I'd spoken to briefly walked over carrying the familiar case. Fletcher rushed forward to take it, returning to my side instantly.

"Is that everything?" I asked.

He nodded, and I motioned for Ivory to go ahead of us, Fletch and I following closely behind. Earth and Beau took up the rear as the five of us left the rundown station, stepping out into the cold night air.

"Car's this way," I told him, still keeping my palm flat against his back.

"What the hell was that?" Earth bellowed, his voice carrying with the wind.

Glancing over my shoulder, I gave him an unimpressed look. "That was me getting Fletcher the hell out of there."

"You think you can come in here and throw your money and status around—"

Dropping my hand from Fletcher, I faced Earth. "It worked, didn't it?"

The words knocked him silent for a moment.

Lifting an eyebrow, I took a step closer to the Asian man. "What's the point of working my ass off, having money and status, if I can't use it from time to time?"

"That's not how we do it around here."

The tips of my loafers bumped the toes of his boots. My voice dropped an octave when I met his dark eyes. "Oh, I know perfectly well how *you* do it around here. So I threw some money around. Who cares? It resolved the problem quickly, didn't it? Kept your hands clean, didn't it?"

"You son of a bi—"

"Stop." Fletcher pushed between us. "Hasn't this day been long enough?"

The anger deflated out of me faster than a popped balloon. "C'mon, let's get you some dinner."

"Why didn't you call me?" Earth asked, causing Fletcher to turn back.

"I didn't think the police station was a good place for you to be."

"It doesn't matter. If you need me, I'll be there."

Fletcher went forward and hugged Earth, wrapping his arms right around his waist.

Something unpleasant coated my tongue and I fought the urge to rip him away as I watched Fletch offer easy affection to the grumpy man.

"You could have called me." Beau spoke up, watching them.

Fletch pulled away from Earth and gave Beau the same hug.

I'm the one who got you out of that hellhole. Why aren't you hugging me?

"You would have told Earth," Fletcher said when he pulled back.

Beau chuckled, ruffling his hair.

My lips pressed into a fine line.

"You're okay now?" Beau wanted to make sure.

Fletcher nodded. "I tried to call Neo, but he didn't answer. That's why I called Ivory. I thought Neo might be with her…"

Earth made a sound and looked at me. "So what's your excuse?"

"Pardon?"

"He was with me when Fletch called," Ivory answered.

"All right. Let's go." Earth waved for Fletch and Beau to start up the street.

I made a sound. "Fletcher is coming with me."

Everyone turned to look.

"Why?" Beau asked, more curious than challenging.

"We had a meeting this afternoon, and he missed it."

Beau and Earth turned to look at Fletcher. Even in the dark, I saw his sheepish expression. "It's true. I accepted a job to play violin at one of his events."

"No." Earth's voice was hard. Final.

"But I said I would!" Fletcher rebuked kind of like a spoiled little brother would.

They really did have a family dynamic going.

"I'll just give you some money, okay? You don't need to work with him."

I was about to argue when Fletcher made an angry sound. "What the fuck, Earth?" he shot out.

Everyone froze, staring.

"You're my brother, and I love you. I know you're only trying to look out for me, but I won't keep taking money from you." His eyes swept over Beau. "From all of you. I'm not your responsibility. You should know how important pride is to us."

"You just got arrested for stealing food because you were hungry," Earth muttered darkly.

"Which is exactly why I should take this job. It's good pay."

"What's the point in having good pay if you're just going to hand it off to someone else?" Earth shot out.

Fletcher slumped like all the fight went out of him at once.

Is he giving money to someone? Is that why he doesn't have any?

"Earth, man, enough for tonight," Beau said, glancing at his brother.

Realizing he might have gone too far, Earth backed down. "I didn't mean it. I was just worried about you." His voice was much softer this time.

Fletcher nodded, his one free hand going up to grip the inside of the jacket. "I know. It's okay."

Earth threw me a disgruntled look. "If you want to take the job, go ahead."

Fletch looked up. "Really?"

I couldn't help but be endeared and annoyed that Earth's approval meant so much to him even after he'd basically said he would do what he wanted.

"Of course."

Fletcher looked at Beau.

"I'm down." He agreed easily.

"What about Neo?" Fletcher worried his lower lip, staring at his feet.

"Neo already knows about all your offers," Ivory put in. "He's excited for you."

Fletcher looked up, gaze landing solely on me. I didn't know why, but suddenly, it felt like the sun had come out. "I'll go with you."

"Come here," I said softly, welcoming him.

Every step that brought him closer swelled my heart.

He stopped in front of me, and this time, I didn't resist the urge, reaching up to rub the back of his head. His hair was soft. "Good boy," I whispered.

Backing up, I opened the passenger door, ushering Fletch and his beat-up violin case into the back before adjusting the seat so Ivory could get into the front.

Once both my passengers were enclosed in the vehicle, I went to get in.

"If anything happens to him," Earth warned, menace dripping from his threat, "you know what I'll do."

Glancing over my shoulder, I regarded Earth and Beau standing there with tumultuous expressions.

"I would expect nothing less," I stated, then got in the Mercedes and pulled away from the curb.

Eight

FLETCHER

HE NOTICED I WAS COLD.

I was literally arrested and almost charged, locked up in a cell next to a drunk who did not smell very nice and was very, *very* loud. I was hungry. They made me wait hours for my one phone call, and before all of that, I had to go see *her*.

Out of all of that craziness, the fact that Ethan noticed I was cold was the one thing I couldn't stop thinking about.

The smooth purr of the luxury car's engine lulled me, my body reclining backward, burrowing a little deeper into the jacket he'd placed around me.

Did it really matter if someone bothered to notice I was cold?

It matters to me.

Especially now. Today. Sometimes it felt like people looked through me and not at me, so when someone noticed something as trivial as being cold, it meant something.

Not only did Ethan notice, but he did something about it.

Dipping my chin, I breathed in deeply the scent of rich pine clinging to the warm jacket. *I think it might be my favorite scent.*

Ivory leaned around the front seat, peeking into the back, her blue eyes worried. "Why don't you just come home with me tonight, Fletch? You can talk with Ethan about business tomorrow."

"Will Neo be home?" I asked hopefully. I wanted to see my brother. He always made me feel better about everything.

"Should be soon." She promised with a nod.

"No." Ethan's one-syllable reply interrupted our conversation.

Ivory pulled back to stare at him. "Well, why not?" she argued.

"I waited all day," Ethan said.

"Well, Fletch is probably tired. And hungry. There's tomorrow."

"My schedule is packed tomorrow. It has to be today," he said, no room for argument. But a weird feeling made me look up, and I saw him looking at me through the rearview mirror. His words might have been stern, but his eyes were anything but. "I'll make sure he eats," he said, his tone much softer than before.

"Fletcher?" Ivory glanced back for confirmation.

I nodded. "It's okay."

"Well, you can still stay with us tonight. Ethan can bring you over to the penthouse when you finish your meeting."

I was about to agree, but something had me glancing back at Ethan and the way his big hands clenched around the steering wheel. *Does he not want me to stay with Ivory and Neo tonight?*

My silence stretched on, and Ivory stopped waiting for me to agree, turning back to the front.

A short while later, Ethan pulled up to Ivory's building. "Do you want me to walk you up?" he asked.

"Oh, no, it's not necessary. The doorman is right there," she replied. The doorman was indeed already holding open the big door, watching the car.

"I'll see you in a bit, okay?" Ivory asked, turning to look at me, and I nodded, offering her a small wave.

Putting the running engine in park, Ethan got out of the driver's seat to jog around and open Ivory's door. Reaching in a hand, he helped her out and then escorted her to the sidewalk where she waved good-bye.

I watched him through the windshield as he walked back to the car. The deep-green coat he wore fit his broad figure like it was made just for him and had an oversized, lifted collar that framed his jaw, somehow making him look even more angular. The gold buttons glinted in the headlights, and his strides were powerful as he approached.

He makes me feel safe.

The realization was shocking, so much so that I jolted, causing the jacket to slip off my shoulders. Cold air blew in when the car door opened and Ethan climbed in.

"You want to move up front?" he asked, craning his head around to look at me. I must have looked as shocked as I suddenly felt because his eyes widened and then narrowed. "What's wrong?"

My stomach felt weird again.

"I'll just sit back here," I told him.

"What's wrong?" He pressed, this time reaching out his arm to brace it on the empty passenger seat so he could twist around even more. "Fletcher." He said my name like a warning, but instead of making me afraid, the bottom of my spine tingled in awareness.

What is wrong with me?

"Why did you come tonight?" I blurted out, completely out of sorts.

The concerned expression dropped from his face, everything about him relaxing. "That's what you're worrying about?"

My head bobbed.

"Should I have just left you in jail, then?" Why did it sound like he was teasing me?

"Neo would have come," I argued.

"I was with Ivory when you called. Neo wasn't there, so you got me instead."

I'm glad you came.

"Why were you with Ivory?" I questioned suspiciously, choosing to ignore my inner dialogue.

"She brought me a suit for the event you're playing at."

"I didn't sign anything yet." I reminded him, suddenly wanting to be difficult.

"But you already told me you'd do it, and your word is just as good as your signature. Isn't it, puppy?"

A choked sound ripped from my throat, and I tore my eyes from the window to look at him and glare. "I'm not a puppy."

"Mmm," he grunted and turned back to the front. "You're hungry. What do you want to eat?"

"I thought we were signing a contract?"

"I told Ivory I'd feed you."

"I'm not hungry," I argued.

My stomach chose that moment to grumble so loud that even he heard it in the driver's seat.

Traitor.

"Thai? Chinese? Italian?" Ethan listed, pulling away from the building.

"Can't we just have burgers?" I complained.

I really shouldn't complain after everything he did for me tonight, but I couldn't help it. It was like he brought it out in me.

Ethan's broad frame leaned forward, plucking something up and fitting it in his ear. After tapping on it a time or two, he went quiet for long moments.

"Ah, Jane, have you left for the day?" he asked a few minutes later. "Ah, good. Would you mind ordering in two burgers and some fries...?" He fell silent. A small, deep laugh filled the car. "I'll work it off tomorrow."

Work what off?

"Yes." He agreed again. A pause. A slight glance back at me. "Puppy, you want a milkshake?"

I didn't yell at him for the nickname this time because he was offering me ice cream. Some things were just more important.

"Yes!" I exclaimed. "Chocolate!"

"Did you hear that?" Ethan chuckled. "Not for me. Okay, thank you. Have a wonderful night."

He hit the thing in his ear again, then plucked it out and tossed it back to wherever he got it.

"What kind of phone is that?" I asked, curious.

"It's Bluetooth. It connects to your phone so you can drive while speaking."

"Oh."

"How come you don't have a cell phone?" he asked, glancing back while we were stopped in traffic.

"Don't need one."

"Seems like you could have used one today."

I snorted. "Yeah right, like Fig would have let me use it. He made me wait hours before he let me call Neo! I had to beg to call Ivory when Neo didn't pick up."

"Gross misuse of power," Ethan muttered.

I didn't really know what that meant, so I just stayed quiet.

"Anyway, th-thank you for what you did back there. I'll pay you back." I promised.

"Pay me back for what?"

"The restitution," I said, remembering what he called it.

"It's not necessary. I didn't do it so you would owe me."

"Then why did you?" I asked. This time, the question was more timid than when I'd blurted it out.

"You're my employee," he said easily, as though he didn't even have to think about it. "And a good CEO takes care of his employees."

"I'm just playing the violin at one of your openings," I muttered, not quite sure why his answer didn't satisfy me.

"And until then, you're my responsibility."

I wanted to argue that I was responsible for myself, but the fact that he'd just bailed me out of jail kind of made the argument sound dumb.

A few minutes later, the Mercedes turned into a large ground-level parking garage. Ethan didn't even have to stop at the gate inside because the guard standing there buzzed him through immediately.

Instead of heading to a parking spot like I assumed we would, he pulled around to a wide lit-up entrance that most other places had outside, though this one was fully covered and secure. Leaving the car running, Ethan got out, and a man—a valet—appeared instantly.

"Mr. Abbott, how are you this evening, sir?" The valet's voice floated into the open doorway and the backseat.

"Very well, and you, Jacob?"

"Got an A on my ethics exam!" Jacob exclaimed. His tone was comfortable, as if he'd had a thousand conversations with Ethan like this in the past.

"Well done! I knew you could do it. Hard work pays off. Pretty soon, you'll be coming after my job," Ethan replied happily.

Their easy comradery suddenly made me feel sour, my lip curling with distaste.

"I'll take good care of her for you," Jacob was saying, but Ethan held him off.

Leaning back inside, he lifted the front seat, peering in to where I still sat.

"Don't mind me," I said. "Finish congratulating him."

Ethan looked like he'd swallowed a canary, and then a smile stretched over his features. "Is someone jealous?"

I gasped. "No!"

His warm chuckle called me a liar and also made me want to lean in…

What the hell is wrong with me?

I was going delirious from hunger.

"C'mon, P—"

I glared.

"Fletch." He corrected. "Let's go."

Ignoring the hand he offered, I snatched my violin case and climbed out, moving aside so Ethan could fix the seat.

The valet's eyes went wide. "Oh, I didn't know anyone was with you."

I tugged the suit jacket around me a little tighter. "Hi," I said because I didn't know what else to say.

"Jacob, this is Fletcher. Fletcher, Jacob." Ethan made the introductions like we would be seeing each other more than just this once.

Jacob was a polished-looking young guy with trimmed dark hair, straight white teeth, and a very tidy uniform.

"Nice to meet you," Jacob said, then moved toward the car. "Thanks again for all your encouragement!" he called to Ethan.

"You did all the hard work," he replied, turning away.

Behind us, the Mercedes was driven off, and the men standing at the doors opened them wide for us to step through.

"Good evening, Mr. Abbott."

"Evening, gentlemen," he greeted in reply.

I headed toward the bank of elevators inside the totally swanky lobby, but Ethan made a sound, palming the small of my back and guiding me away.

"This one is mine," he said, leading me to an elevator sitting alone, its gold doors polished and reflecting our images as we approached.

We were completely mismatched, with Ethan being tall

and sophisticated with model-esque looks and style and a presence that commanded attention.

I, on the other hand, was an entire head shorter than him, slim and small beside him, and wearing hand-me-down clothes that didn't fit.

"I think I'll just go to Ivory's," I said, turning away from our reflections to flee.

He caught the back of the jacket, and when he tugged, it went, but I didn't go with it. A low curse behind me made my lips twitch with glee, but then his very wide hand clamped around the back of my neck, stopping the progress I'd made to the door.

"Your dinner will get cold," he said, towing me into the elevator.

I pouted for like two seconds, but really, who had time for that? Curiosity got the better of me, so I asked, "Is this your elevator?"

Ethan made a sound of acknowledgment. "Mm-hmm."

"Like yours and no one else's?"

He glanced at me. "Are you surprised? Ivory has one that goes to her floor too."

Averting my gaze, I just shrugged, glancing down at my shoes as the private car went up and up.

Ivory is different. This feels different.

"Is that why you tried to run off? Are you intimidated?"

Angry, I straightened off the wall, looking him right in the eyes. "You don't intimidate me."

His lips twitched, blue eyes sparkling a bit. *Why did I notice that?* "That's good. I don't want to."

I swallowed.

As he cocked his head to the side, the edge of the large standing collar on his coat grazed his jaw. "So why did you run off?"

"I don't belong here," I muttered, turning my stare back to the floor.

"I think you might." He spoke softly.

Before I could think or do anything, the doors dinged open, revealing the biggest bouquet of flowers I'd literally ever seen in my life perched on a table in the center of the foyer.

"Whoa," I whispered, rushing forward, tripping over the space where the elevator met the floor.

Ethan grabbed my arm to steady me, clucking his tongue. "Who taught you how to walk?"

Tugging my arm free, I frowned. Usually, I wouldn't think twice over a comment like that, but after the day I'd had—after seeing *her*—it kind of stung. "I taught myself."

There was the briefest pause. Then the air around us suddenly shifted as if he read my deepest feelings without any trouble at all. Stepping close, he lifted his hand but held it at bay, silently asking if he could touch me, giving me a choice.

Sucking my lower lip into my mouth, I debated a minute but then nodded once. I had no idea what his intentions were, but this feeling in the air was swirling around and making me drunk.

His hand was so big it engulfed the back of my head, palming me so easily that it made my heart skip a beat. Despite the size and strength his hand possessed, he was gentle when he stroked my hair, the action so soothing my body swayed toward the touch.

"You did well. You taught yourself well." He praised quietly.

Emotions rolled over me like an avalanche in a snowstorm, pummeling and collapsing me, the weight of it all almost too much to bear. My chest turned so tight I found it hard to breathe, so I leaned even more into his touch as if I knew he would fix it all.

Ethan praised me back at the police station, and it pierced my emotions then too.

But this. This is all-consuming.

Fear slammed into me, making me jolt back. His hand was still on the back of my head, cupping it almost protectively in case I jerked too far.

When I was steady, he pulled back, the tingles racing over my scalp in his wake.

Trying to shake off whatever was happening, I turned back to the display. "There must be a thousand flowers in here!" I pretended not to notice how my voice was an octave too high.

Ethan's low laugh made me feel like I'd swallowed a spoonful of honey, coating every part of me as it slid down.

"I didn't count," he said, going along with the conversation with no trouble at all.

"I will." I offered. Maybe counting to a thousand would settle all the nerves racing inside me.

"Later," he said, going to large black double doors with ornate gold hardware. Something beeped after he swiped a card, and the locks made an unlatching sound. "Come on."

Giving one last look to the flowers, I went ahead of him into the apartment.

I knew it would be fancy. I knew it would be big.

Beyond that, I guess I really didn't know what to expect.

But judging from my awed moment of silence, it wasn't this.

The floors were black and white marble tiles laid out in an alternating diamond pattern. A huge ornate dark wood table sat against the wall, a large mirror hanging over it, and various decorations were perched on the glossy wooden top.

Across from that was a staircase that wound in a wide spiral to another level. The stairs were carpeted with thick tan carpet, and the railing was black metal. Sitting in the curvature of the stairs was another table and, on it, another huge arrangement, but this was just greenery without flowers. Beside it was a carved bust, the head of some guy.

"Is that your dad?" I asked.

Ethan's eyes widened, and then he threw back his head and laughed. It was a deep, pure sound that went on a lot longer than it should have.

I was being serious.

But it was okay. I kind of liked the way he sounded.

"It's Julius Caesar," Ethan said, his laugh quieting.

Well, okay. "Do you know him?"

"Julius Caesar was a Roman general who was assassinated a long time ago."

"Oh." *Why does he have some random old dude's head in his apartment?*

"Do you like it?" Ethan asked almost as though he could hear my thoughts.

I shrugged.

"It's okay if you don't." He encouraged.

"It's kinda weird." I admitted, glancing again at the head.

"So if you were to put a statue there, what would you choose?"

"Me?" I asked, surprised.

He nodded.

"I'd get one of Spider-Man."

"Spider-Man," Ethan echoed.

"At least he has cool powers," I said, pretending to shoot webs from my wrists. "All this guy did was get himself killed."

Ethan laughed. "Well, he did a little more than that."

"What's up there?" I asked, pointing to the stairs.

"The bedrooms," Ethan replied, starting past me to go farther into the apartment.

I set my case near the stairs and followed along, eyes going straight ahead to an entire wall of glass that provided a full view of the city. Since it was dark, the buildings were all lit up, twinkling like a million stars.

Passing the thick carpets and cream and black furniture, I

went right to the glass, staring down at the city. "A prince looking down on his kingdom," I whispered.

"What?"

I jumped, not realizing Ethan was standing so close. "Oh, ah, nothing."

"You should shower before you eat."

My eyes went wide. "Shower!"

"Yes, you were just in that filthy jail cell."

"Oh, no, I—"

Grasping my wrist, Ethan tugged me along behind him, tossing the jacket I'd worn the whole way here on a wide, modern sofa. Towing me toward the back of the apartment, he pushed open a door, leading me into a large, pristine bathroom.

The shower was probably four times the size of ours at home, and it was enclosed in glass.

"I really don't—"

"Towels are there." Ethan pointed to a huge stack of fluffy white towels. "Soap and everything else is there." He pointed again.

"But my food will be cold." I tried.

"I'll make sure it stays warm."

"What's the point in showering if I'm going to put on the same dirty clothes?"

"I'll get you something clean of course. Wait there."

Did this guy ever lose an argument?

While I waited, I kicked off my sneakers and leaned against the marble counter. This place was huge, and I'd only seen part of it. Did he live here all by himself?

Does he have a girlfriend?

My back went stiff, and a funny, unpleasant feeling wormed around inside me.

"This stuff will probably be kind of big, but it's the best—" Ethan's words cut off when he looked at me. "What's wrong?"

"Do you have a girlfriend?" I asked, leaning around him to look like she might be standing in the doorway watching us.

"Would you be upset if I did?"

Gasping, I yanked back into position, suddenly wanting to be hidden by his frame. "She won't like someone like me here." I freaked, bending to pick up the shoes, preparing to run.

Ethan sighed, putting a hand on my shoulder. "I don't have a girlfriend."

I deflated in relief. "Oh. That's good."

The disgusting feeling inside me was just starting to go away when he said, "Aren't you going to ask if I have a boyfriend?"

My eyes shot up to his. "You like guys?"

I hadn't realized I'd whispered until he bent at the waist, meeting my eyes, and matched my tone. "Do you have a problem with that?"

"No," I practically yelled. "I don't care."

Pulling back, his eyes scanned my face. "What about you? Do you have a girlfriend?"

I laughed. "Yeah, right."

"A boyfriend, then?"

My eyes widened. "You think I like guys?"

His head cocked to the side. "Do you?"

I thought about the question, *really* thought. I mean, sure, I'd thought about this stuff before, but it seemed like I really wanted to be sure before I answered, like what I said was somehow important.

I must have been silent too long because Ethan placed the stack of clothes on the vanity and turned away. "Come out when you're done. Then we'll eat."

"I like everyone!" I blurted.

Ethan stopped walking but didn't turn around, so I was left standing there staring at the back of his blond head, which was oddly was just as handsome as his face.

"Everyone?" he echoed.

I nodded before realizing he couldn't see. "I-I've never had a relationship before," I told him honestly. "I'm not really datable."

Ethan turned, a scowl on his face. "Who told you that?" he demanded as though whoever it was would pay.

It made me smile. "Ah…" I laughed a little. "No one. I just —that's just what I think."

He crossed his arms, frowning. "That's not true."

Clearing my throat, I glanced off to the side. "I've never really thought about it in terms of boy and girl. To me, it's just love." Saying all this out loud made me so shy, and I felt heat surging to my cheeks.

"Go on." Ethan urged, his voice quiet and almost pleading.

"It's more about meeting someone that makes you feel something. Someone that makes you feel special and that you want to be with all the time. Someone who might… worry about you, who might ask you if you're hungry or cold. Someone who wants to see you even if you can't give them anything."

"*Fletcher.*"

Why did his voice sound like that? So raw and hoarse? Why did it make me want to run to him?

Holding back and more embarrassed than ever, I rushed to finish the words I found I really wanted to say. "To me, it wouldn't matter if it was a girl or a boy if they made me feel that way because love isn't specific and a heart goes by feelings… not by gender."

Suddenly, I was crushed against a wide, warm chest, and his Christmas-y scent engulfed me. I hadn't remembered giving in to the urge to run to him, but I must have because here I was wrapped up in his arms.

Safe.

I wasn't that small, but against him, I was. His wide,

muscular frame nearly devoured mine, but he was gentle, so gentle.

"I'm really glad to hear you say that." The soft words floated over my head. I felt his breath stir my hair.

He held me a moment longer, and my eyes started to flutter closed.

Pulling back, he made a gruff sound. "Get showered. Your food really will get cold."

It wasn't until after he left the bathroom that I realized I was still standing in the exact same place. It wasn't me who had run to Ethan…

Ethan was the one who ran to me.

Nine

Ethan

I'd met him in the hospital. He charmed me.

I'd stumbled upon him in the forest. He enchanted me.

Finding him in jail enraged me.

And now?

Hearing him talk about love captured me.

All my life, I lived by everyone else's rules. I played my role, did my duty.

I hid a part of who I was from everyone... sometimes even from myself. I had things most people would kill for, yet the boy in my guest shower, a boy who literally had to steal to eat, felt something I never did.

Acceptance of who he was.

His viewpoint on love was so pure and innocent, so sweet it made me ache. He had no idea how every word he'd spoken broke me down.

I wanted him.

I wanted the love he spoke of to be mine.

I was well aware that this couldn't be bought. It couldn't be bartered or borrowed.

It had to be earned. It had to be deserved.

Because of that, I wanted it even more.

All my life, my name and money made me worthy. But

with Fletch, those things would work against me. To be worthy of him, I had to be a good man. A good lover and a friend.

I'd never wanted to be worthy of anything as much as I did now.

Feeling shaken, I moved about my walk-in closet, tossing the clothes I'd worn all day in the bin for cleaning. I wanted to shower, but I didn't want to take too long. I wanted to be there when he came out of the bathroom. I didn't want to miss a single second with him.

I smiled at my own thoughts. If Fletcher knew all this was in my head, he'd run so fast I'd probably have skid marks on the floor.

"Spider-Man," I muttered, laughing. "He'd put up a statue of Spider-Man."

So cute.

Opting to just shower later, I pulled on a black pair of Givenchy lounge pants and a flocked logo white T-shirt.

I was leaning against the wall when the bathroom door pulled in just enough for his head to peek out. When he saw me, his eyes bulged, and I wanted to kiss him.

The sudden urge had me straightening from the wall, but I held off, something I really never did. If I wanted something, I grabbed it. I took it. I made it mine.

Not this time. Not with Fletch.

The way I wanted him was far different from any other want I'd known. And so stark desire hung inside me, anticipation nearly crackling in the air.

"What are you hiding in there for?" I asked, utterly charmed by him even as tension coiled beneath my skin.

"These pants are too big."

"Let me see."

"No."

"Come here, puppy," I commanded, my voice just a little sterner than before.

"I said not to call me that." He spoke plaintively even as he pulled the door wide to do as I asked.

A wash of tenderness overcame me, seeing how he shuffled across the floor, swallowed up by the Gucci track pants concealing his oversized feet.

The way he held the waistband as if he were scared they might fall down made my heart feel light somehow.

When he was directly in front of me, I reached for the waistband, but he pulled back with a gasp. "What are you doing?"

"Fixing them so they don't fall off."

"I can do it!" he insisted, hiking them up again.

"If you could do it, why didn't you?" I refuted.

He scowled, and I took the opportunity to grasp the waistband.

"Hey!" He tried to twist away.

I stilled, my hands at his waist. "Are you that shy?"

His ears were already pink, as were his cheekbones.

"I'm not wearing any underwear!" he whispered loudly.

"Well, why not?" I whispered back, ignoring the lick of desire up my spine. "I gave you some."

Fletch widened his eyes, the center of them shining with flecks of gold. "I can't wear your underwear... That's just..." he stuttered.

I leaned closer, unable to resist the urge to tease. "Too intimate?"

The pink on his face flushed red, and he looked away.

Taking mercy, I chuckled and leaned back. "They're brand new. I wouldn't give you a used pair of boxers."

"Oh."

Laughing lightly, I slipped my fingers in the waistband, brushing against his smooth skin. He let out a squeak and stumbled back.

"Hold still," I instructed firmly, ignoring the way my fingertips tingled.

He went motionless, averting his face. I worked quickly, folding over the waistband a couple times and then sinking into a crouch at his feet.

"W-what…?" He started when I grasped the hem pooling on the tile.

"You're going to fall," I explained, cuffing the pants a bit.

His hands went to my shoulders, using them to steady himself for when he lifted each foot, allowing me to roll the extra fabric.

I might have taken a little longer than necessary to complete the simple task because I liked that he was holding on to me.

When I was done, I straightened, giving him back his personal space.

"Are you warm enough?" My voice was soft, my fingers gentle when I tugged the zip-up jacket a little closer around him.

The outfit swallowed him up, making our size difference all the more palpable.

He nodded, about to speak, but his stomach interrupted, giving an angry growl.

"This way," I said, leading him back into the living room, gesturing to the oversized sofa. "Wait here."

Jane, my house manager, had everything already set up on the large white marble island. Two plates were covered with pewter domes, glasses of water already poured. The chocolate milkshake Fletch was so enthusiastic about was in a tall crystal glass, piled high with whipped cream and drizzled with chocolate syrup.

Smiling at her attention to detail, I grabbed a large tray, transferring everything to it, carrying it out to where Fletcher waited.

He was sitting in the center of the couch, nearly gobbled up by the cushions, his legs tucked under him.

The second he saw me, he began to push up to help, but I shook my head. "Just stay there. You look comfortable."

"This is the biggest couch I've ever seen," he said, gazing at it in awe. "My legs don't even touch the ground when I sit all the way back!"

His enthusiasm over everything was something I'd never known a person could possess. Most everyone I knew was bored to tears by life itself. I'd never met anyone who could get excited over a sofa.

The second the tray was in the center of the coffee table, Fletcher slid off the cushions and onto the floor, perching in front of the table. "Is that mine?" he asked, devouring the milkshake with his eyes.

"Well, it's not mine."

Reaching for it, he used two hands because the glass was big and slick with condensation. Before I could offer a straw, his face was practically buried in the whipped cream, his mouth and nose completely out of sight.

I watched because, frankly, I'd never seen anything like it.

When he finally came up for air, he had the white topping all over his nose, clinging to his upper lip and chocolate on his lower lip. "This is almost as good as the frozen hot chocolate I get from Kismet!"

"You know Kismet?" I asked, totally distracted by the tip of his pink tongue darting out to swipe at his lower lip.

"I always get it with Ivory and sometimes Neo."

"Right. Well, they are very famous for their frozen hot chocolate."

"The hot, hot chocolate is good too." He agreed, going back for more of the shake.

Making a sound, I sank down beside him on the floor, picking up a napkin. "You have it all over your face," I scolded, reaching out to swipe at his nose and mouth.

Fletcher glanced up, eyes grabbing and holding mine. The

milkshake he wolfed was suddenly forgotten, the napkin poised between us suddenly unseen.

"Thank you," he said, voice sincere and audible, though not too loud.

"For what?"

He ducked his head, hiding his eyes and whatever else he was going to say.

A few beats passed before I could recover. Clearing my throat, I set aside the napkin and pulled the lids off the plates.

"You should eat."

"When I said burger, I expected something wrapped in paper... not this," he said, staring at the steak burger on a brioche bun with hand-cut steak fries piled high on the side.

"Would you rather have that?" I questioned.

In response, he palmed the giant burger and took a huge bite. As he chewed, he made a bunch of noises around his mouthful, but honestly, I wasn't sure what they meant or even if I should reply.

He took another gigantic bite, set down the burger, and then licked the pad of one finger, making my groin tighten uncomfortably.

"Ah," I said, trying to distract myself, "I wasn't sure if you liked dipping sauce, so we got some of everything," I told him, lifting another lid off a plate filled with cups of different sauces.

His eyes lit up, and he snatched a fry, dipping it in three different sauces before taking a bite and groaning. I watched, completely shook, as he repeated the action but this time with different sauces and shoved the rest of the fry in his mouth.

"Oh," he said, noting the way I stared. "I double dipped. Sorry."

I smiled. "It's okay."

"Aren't you going to eat?" he asked, pointing at my untouched plate.

"Of course," I replied, picking up my burger to take a bite. Truthfully, I'd forgotten I even had food because I was too busy staring at him.

The second the premium beef hit my tongue, bursting with mayo and warm tomato, I groaned.

"See? Super good," Fletch said, turning back to annihilating his plate and using so much dipping sauce I wondered if he even tasted the fries.

"Which one do you like?" he asked, speaking with his mouth full.

My mother would be horrified.

Hell, all of the Upper East Side would be horrified.

I found it endearing as he sat there, lips smacking, chomping away, and pointing at the sauces with his fry like it was some kind of teaching tool.

"Hmm," I said, leaning forward to look at them all. "I've only ever had the homemade house sauce," I said, pointing to one of the cups.

The building I lived in had its own five-star restaurant that delivered to residents upon request.

The offended look that crossed his face made me laugh. "What's that look for?"

"You mean to tell me you have access to all this," he said, waving his hand around, "and you haven't even tried it all?"

"I don't eat burgers and fries very often."

"You can dip lots of things in sauce," he said reasonably.

"I digress." I allowed, trying to keep my entire heart from caving in.

His nose screwed up. "You sound like Ivory, always saying words that no one knows."

"I just mean you're right."

Turning back to the food, he studied the sauces, eating more fries.

"Which one is your favorite?" I asked, taking another bite. *I really should eat these burgers more.* It was damn good.

"Hmm." He considered. "Ranch is a classic. Can't live without ketchup. I don't really know what this one is." He pointed to one. "But it's good. And this one… some kind of barbeque…"

"Which one do you think I would like?" I asked.

"You'd probably pick this fancy no-name one," Fletch said, pointing. "But really, I think secretly you'd like this one." He pointed again.

Leaning up, I looked at the white sauce. "Ranch?"

"Have you ever dipped a fry in ranch?"

"Ah, no."

Completely appalled, Fletcher dipped the half-eaten fry in his hand into the ranch and held it out to me, the white sauce instantly dripping toward his fingers.

Incredulous, I stared for long moments until he flushed and began to retreat. "Sorry, I already bit off this on—"

Cutting off his words and his movement, my fingers circled his wrist, bringing his hand and the fry he'd already sampled to my lips. Without hesitation, I pulled it into my mouth and chewed, still holding on to his wrist.

"Well?" he asked, excitement in his eyes as he waited to see if I would like it.

"I like it," I declared.

His smile was so bright that I momentarily forgot to chew.

I was still holding his wrist when he started to pull back, drawing attention to the ranch on the tip of his finger. Leaning in, I closed my lips around it, using my tongue to swipe off the excess dressing.

His little gasp was quite the reward for my boldness, but though I wanted to, I didn't linger. Sitting back, I stole a glance at the way he was frozen in place, staring at the finger I'd just licked.

Never in my life was I so forward with someone else's person. Grabbing their pants, smoothing their hair, licking their fingers... But I couldn't help it with Fletch. His reactions were too unfiltered, too honest, and utterly engaging.

Watching awareness roll over his entire being every time I invaded his personal space was thrilling.

"You gonna share that ranch with me now?" I asked, snapping him back into the moment.

Snatching the cup, he set it between us, a little closer to me.

"Whoever thought of putting salad dressing on potatoes?" I wondered as I ate another fry.

"You can put ranch on everything," Fletcher said, taking a huge bite of the burger. "*Ah!*" He gasped, making me look up. "I'm sorry!" he exclaimed, scooting back almost like he was putting distance between us.

"Sorry? For what?"

"Is this designer?" he asked, glancing down, "Oh shit, it's designer, isn't it?"

Trying to make sense of his panic, I followed his gaze to where mayo had dripped onto his jacket.

"Fletcher..." I started.

He scrambled back again, jumping to his feet. "I'll have it cleaned. No! I'll buy you a new one."

"Fletcher," I said, rising as well, taking a step forward.

He winced.

I stopped cold, my entire body freezing into place. I felt that wince so deep it echoed in my bones and made my stomach turn.

"I'm sorry," he whispered, shoulders drooping, voice filled with something I didn't quite understand.

Why is he acting like this? Over a stained shirt, no less. It was not a big deal, but he was acting as if it were the worst.

Even though I didn't understand, I didn't want to act as if he were being overly dramatic because I could tell in the set of his shoulders, in the way he almost expected me to erupt, that this was not some kind of act. This was not some game.

"Hey." My voice was gentle, my palms lifting outward. "It's no big deal. Happens all the time."

He glanced up, wariness swimming in his usually innocent stare. "I ruined your shirt."

I shook my head once. "It's not ruined. It will clean. And even if it was ruined, I don't care. It doesn't matter."

"I'm more trouble than I'm worth," he said almost as if he were repeating a mantra, telling the words to himself.

It hurt. It hurt to hear him say that. It hurt that he could think that.

"Fletch, no," I said, forgetting the distance between us and closing it. Taking him by the shoulders, I gave him a gentle shake. "Don't say that." *This is clearly about more than a shirt.* "Don't ever tell that to yourself ever again."

He looked up, deep sadness in his stare. "I'm sorry."

The whispered apology broke me, and the sound I made echoed through the too-big, quiet penthouse.

One tug brought him to me, enclosing him tight. He stood there with his arms at his sides, cheek against my chest as I gently rocked us back and forth, not even realizing what I did.

"You have nothing to be sorry for." I promised, rubbing soothing circles over the small of his back.

I didn't know what else to say or what to do. It was hard to fight a battle you knew nothing about.

My words didn't seem like enough, though. Easing away, I went back to our food, sticking my fingers in one of the red sauces on the table. Making sure he was watching, I wiped my fingers across my chest, smearing the sauce over the white fabric.

"There. Now we match," I said, suddenly thankful I'd saved my shower for later.

A small smile brightened his face, some of the sadness

slipping out of his eyes. I'd ruin a hundred shirts if it made him feel better.

"You wanna finish eating now?" I asked, not wanting to linger on the moment and make him uncomfortable.

Nodding, he came forward, dropping in front of his plate.

I didn't bring it up again but quietly tucked it in the back of my mind to ask about later.

Fletcher

Get a grip, Fletch.

I told myself this as I sat back down in front of the really good food Ethan had delivered. I mean, it was so good that even in the middle of a mental meltdown, I still wanted to eat.

Maybe considering this a mental breakdown was overkill, but I saw the flash of freak in Ethan's gaze when I winced away from him.

I wish I could take it back.

I didn't mean it. I was not afraid of Ethan.

Or are you?

The thought turned the fry in my mouth into chalk, and I dropped the remaining wedge in my fingers back onto the plate.

Staring down without seeing, I got lost in my head for long minutes.

Today was just too much. First, the kid in the alley that brought up a lot of old feelings. Then I saw her, felt her cold stare.

How can my own mother look at me that way? Why do I hope every single time I see her that she will be different?

Being arrested. Sitting in the cold cell while a man I didn't know screamed beside me. I couldn't help but wonder if I would somehow end up like him. Drunk. Alone. Screaming.

And then everything turned one-eighty. I went from the slums to sitting in a penthouse and wigging out because I dripped burger all over a hoodie that probably cost more money than I managed to steal *and* earn in two months.

It was stupid, but I was tired, and the feelings I was usually really good at holding down were fighting back tonight.

But he didn't make fun or press me for answers. Instead, he wiped sauce all over his own shirt to try and put me at ease. No one had ever done anything like that before, except maybe my brothers.

This is different somehow.

"Hey." The gentle voice was like a GPS in my mind, rerouting me, calling me back.

"Huh?" My head popped up, nose nearly colliding with the forgotten fry that was dripping with ranch.

Blinking, I gazed at it and then at Ethan who was holding it out.

"Come on. If you don't eat it, I will." He encouraged, bringing it an inch closer to my lips.

I liked his eyes. They were blue like a summer sky without all the smog from the city. I liked the way he looked at me, like he was studying every single detail about my ordinary face, like maybe it wasn't very ordinary to him.

The weird feeling in my stomach reappeared, and I realized.

I realized it was him.

"Ethan," I whispered without thought, as if it were my heart that spoke and not my tongue.

I didn't even know why I said his name, only feeling in that moment I had to. I had to somehow give weight to this moment before I floated away.

The fry was abandoned, his wide frame leaning in as he carefully reached out to cup my face.

I didn't understand the mood swirling around in this room or how the warmth of his palms made me feel so much calmer.

I didn't understand at all, and my heart was pounding, but I didn't want it to stop.

"You surprised me too." He confessed as if he knew my thoughts.

He feels it too.

The pad of his thumb rubbed slow circles over my cheekbone, lulling me into some sort of haze where the only thing that existed in this world was him.

Slowly, slowly, he drew me in, and the force of my swallow echoed between us.

"Have you ever been kissed?" His voice was husky, and my stare dropped to his lips.

Even though I was shy, I couldn't look away. I shook my head once, my cheek pushing farther into his palm with the action.

"Your first kiss, will you give it to me?"

He could have taken it. I was basically putty in his hands. I was so used to people in this world taking and taking that when he gave me a choice, my pounding heart stuttered.

"You want to kiss me?" I whispered, lifting my eyes to his.

"More than anything."

My ears grew hot, my skin tingled, and I found myself staring at his lips again, wondering what they would feel like against mine.

I nodded once, acquiescing to his request. Gazing up nervously, I expected to find some form of triumph in his gaze, but there was only warmth. Only want.

Thump. Thump. Thump.

My heart beat so hard it almost hurt, and I wondered if he

could hear, but then none of that mattered and a blanket draped over every thought I could have.

The first touch of our mouths made me jolt, and despite the closeness of our faces, my eyes sprang wide.

Pulling back merely a fraction, Ethan smiled softly before tightening his hold and tugging me forward again to settle his mouth completely against mine.

Despite the way his eyes drifted shut, the way I noticed how each of his long dark lashes swept against his smooth skin, I couldn't close mine.

I couldn't do anything but sit and stare. Sit there and marvel at the way his lips moved over mine, giving something I'd never felt. His mouth was soft and warm, moving against mine with gentle yet firm strokes. His breath tickled when it brushed over my moistened lower lip, and excitement raced up my spine when he drew my upper lip firmly between his.

I watched him suck deeply, massaging the sensitive flesh, lavishing attention on something previously ignored.

When he finally released, he didn't lift his head, instead brushing our mouths together once, twice before settling deep again.

I'd never felt anything like this. Not ever in my entire life. I was practically frozen with awe, unable to form a thought, unable to make sense of the emotions rolling over me with every single meeting of our lips.

Easing back, he brought my lower lip with him, tugging it, practically claiming ownership before releasing it back to my custody.

I still stared, eyes wide, sight blurred, and now my lips slick from his.

While he still cradled my face, his breath fanned out with his whisper. "Do you like it?"

Oh, yes.

All I could do was nod.

He smiled, the action making little crinkles at the corners of his eyes.

"Kiss me back, then." He summoned, lowering his head once more.

A surging tide of warmth enveloped me, and this time when he kissed, my lips puckered to meet his, moving against his despite the way they trembled. The feelings arising in me were so heavy my eyes didn't dare stay open, this time closing and giving myself up to everything he offered.

One of his hands slid down to the side of my neck, and I tilted my head a bit when he intensified the kiss. A low moan formed in my throat, filling the air overhead.

I didn't know it could be like this.

My eyes flew wide when his tongue licked across my lower lip, teasing the space where they met.

Instinctively, I parted, and he swept inside, tangling our tongues together, deepening the kiss so much that my hands clung onto his shoulders, seeking an anchor in this dizzy, swaying world.

He continued to kiss, encouraging every response I gave from the slight shiver of my back to the low moans escaping between us. Hands falling away, they slipped around my waist, his palms so wide that when he tugged my body closer, the entire small of my back was possessed by him.

Tongue retreating, I chased after it, probing with mine but coming up lost. I might have felt bereft, but his lips soothed the ache, keeping contact as he suddenly stood, bringing me with him.

My gasp broke our kiss, and for the first time, I noticed how my lungs burned for air.

Entirely focused on me, Ethan sat in the center of the couch, bringing me along so I was straddling his lap.

Still gasping for breath, he smiled, swiping the pad of his

thumb over my lower lip. "You sure you've never kissed anyone before?"

Overcome with bashfulness, I leaned forward, hiding my face in the side of his neck. "Was I very bad?" My small voice was muffled against his skin.

He tried to pull me back, but I resisted, burrowing even deeper against him. How could I look at him knowing how disappointed he probably was?

He'd probably kissed thousands… and he was my only one.

Giving up, he stopped tugging, allowing me to cling. Rubbing his palm up and down my back, his hoarse, deepened voice echoed beside my ear. "Not bad at all, puppy. You were perfect. So much emotion packed into your small body."

Gasping, I sprang back to glare. "I am not small!"

His lips twitched. They were kind of puffy, and I was the reason why.

I want to kiss him again.

I wanted to know if it would feel the same a second time or if it had been like *that* because it was my first.

"You are compared to me."

My face twisted up, and I started to wiggle out of his lap. I wouldn't sit here wanting to kiss him again while he insulted me!

Grasping my hips, his fingers dug in, locking me in place. Look, I might be smaller than him, but I grew up on the streets. I knew how to take care of myself.

Most of the time.

I was about to go all kung-fu ninja on him when he spoke.

"Is that all you just heard? Me saying you were small? Didn't you hear anything else?"

I stilled, meeting his eyes, which I realized were kind of hazy.

You were perfect.

He liked my kissing.

"Kiss me again," I demanded.

Rising off the back of the sofa, his chest collided with mine, fingers sliding into my hair to tug me into a searing kiss.

He wasn't as cajoling as the first time. He didn't ease into it at all, instead attacking at once and dragging me under.

We kissed for an undetermined amount of time, his fingers kneading my scalp, my entire body quaking at the way he consumed me until I had to break free, collapsing against his shoulder to raggedly draw in air.

Oh shit. It wasn't like the first time. *It was better.*

The only thing that kept me from running was the fact that Ethan's chest rose and fell as rapidly as mine, proving I wasn't the only one affected.

Fine. It was that *and* the fact that my legs were shaking.

We stayed like that, with me in his lap, cheek on his shoulder, until our breaths quieted and a coherent thought could be formed in my head. By then, I'd turned languid, my body completely relaxing into his.

With a small sound, I turned into his neck again, tucking closer to inhale his savory scent. Strong arms came around me, and his fingers began to play in the hair at my neck.

My eyelids began to droop, lips parting limply against his skin.

The soft, steady rise and fall of his chest against mine was like a lullaby, and after those kisses, every part of me was lethargic.

Feeling safer than I had in a very long time, my consciousness gave way to sleep.

Eleven

ETHAN

INCREDULOUSLY ENDEARED.

That was how I would describe the emotions literally pummeling me as I sat squished into this couch with Fletcher slumbering in my lap.

I had kissed him, and he fell asleep.

How should one take this?

Should I be offended and worried my kisses were so droll? Or should I feel smug and proud of myself for kissing the consciousness right out of him?

I mean, obviously, we all know which one it was.

I'm far from droll.

Also, I'd like to note that for as small as I said he was, my legs were starting to fall asleep.

Despite the prickling, needly sensation running along my calves and across my feet, I laughed lightly, gathering him even closer, adjusting to make sure he was comfortable.

I didn't believe in love at first sight. I never had. The way I grew up, there was no room in my life for such a notion. It was impractical, silly, and frankly dangerous.

I still didn't believe in love at first sight. I hadn't fallen head over heels for Fletch the day he tripped into my arms in the hospital room. Or when he hid behind a curtain, thinking no one could see him while the sound of his sniffling filled the room.

I wasn't in love with him when I sent an offer over to Ivory for him to play violin or in the park when I heard him play, not even when I fetched him from jail.

I'll admit I was tumbling… sliding into territory where my heart would be claimed.

But then I kissed him.

The awe in his stare and the undeniable euphoria I felt when he finally kissed back—well, I wasn't tumbling anymore.

And now here I sat, utterly lost.

No longer just enchanted.

Completely in love.

So… *love at first kiss?*

Was that a thing? My heart would argue to the death it was.

Seriously, I'm really good at arguing.

I really hadn't meant to kiss him. I mean, I'd told myself, what, an hour before that I would wait. I couldn't resist. I wanted to fill my hands with him desperately, taste him endlessly… quiet whatever it was that tormented him.

We were completely opposite and from two different worlds. The only thing we had in common was our gender, and honestly, that should also work against us.

Impossibly, none of it mattered because here he was, curled up in my lap, his soft breath brushing against my neck and his arm curled around me.

Tenderness rose up, a fragile feeling that oddly gave me strength. I knew this boy sleeping on my chest was actually a man. I knew he'd already lived a life that would harden or break most. Somehow, someway, he'd managed to still hold some innocence, to be pure in his deepest depths.

I wanted to protect that. Protect him.

Shifting, he sighed softly, nuzzling against my skin.

Butterflies took flight in my stomach, making me feel like I'd had far too many espressos and not enough food. Chest tight, heart swollen, I gazed down, pressing a light kiss to his messy, too-long hair.

What am I going to do with you?

I'd barely had the thought before I was so rudely interrupted.

Bang! Bang! Bang!

The loud, thumping knocks echoed through the quiet apartment.

Bang! Bang! Bang!

Tensing, I glanced over the back of the sofa toward the entryway. No one ever just came by unannounced. It was common courtesy to call first.

Bang! Bang! Bang!

And did that person not see the doorbell? Great gods, were they trying to break down the door?

More loud banging, and Fletcher let out a low whine.

Anger turned my eyes to slits, but my movements remained gentle and unhurried when I stood, wincing at the pain as the blood flow returned to my legs.

Leaning down, I laid Fletcher on the cushions, heart constricting when his fingers tightened around me as if he didn't want to let go.

Snagging up a blanket I'd never actually used but only draped around for show, I arranged it over him, tucking it up to his chin.

Bang! Bang! Bang!

I gave him a lingering glance, worried the loud racket would wake him, but he just settled farther into the blanket and kept sleeping.

Stalking through the apartment, I went to the door, which was rattling once more under the assault of my uninvited guest. Irritation coursed through my veins.

The whole frame shuddered when I yanked it open,

scowling menacingly at the man who stood, fist still raised on the other side.

"What took you so long to answer?" Neo scowled, dropping his hand.

"You come to *my* house and beat on the door like a caveman and then scold me?" I retorted, crossing my arms over my chest in challenge.

"Where's Fletch?" he demanded, not even apologizing for this foul and very loud behavior.

He shouldered past me but didn't get very far because of the hand I slapped onto his shoulder, halting his progress.

He glanced at my hand and then at my face. I lifted an eyebrow, daring him.

"Fletch!" he yelled, his voice echoing through the entryway.

"Would you be quiet?" I growled. "You'll wake him!"

"He's asleep?" Neo asked, dark eyes disbelieving, entire face suspicious.

Lifting my hand, I gestured for him to see for himself. His plaid-covered back disappeared around the corner, the black boots he wore echoing on the tile.

When I stepped into the room, he looked up from beside the couch, eyes turning into half-moon shapes. "What did you do to him?" he whisper-yelled.

I had a momentary flashback of the kisses we shared, and awareness tingled my core. Clearing my throat, I answered, "I didn't do anything. He's exhausted. He fell asleep."

"Ivory should have dragged him home with her, but she's too nice for that. I'm here now, and he's coming with me," Neo said, leaning down to pull the blanket away and rouse him.

"Don't even think about touching him," I growled darkly.

Pausing, Neo looked up. "Excuse me?"

Going around the couch, I grabbed him, pulling him away. "He's had a long day."

"That's exactly why I'm taking him home," Neo muttered. "I should have been there."

For the first time since he'd started beating on my door, the anger burning inside me reduced to a small flame. He was worried because he cared. I wanted Fletcher to have people who cared around him.

"I want to talk to you," I said, keeping my voice low and even.

Neo's dark head rose. "About what?"

I hitched my chin at the boy snoozing on the couch. "Him."

"Ivory already told me what happened at the station."

"It's not about that."

Curiosity shone in his eyes, and he nodded once. I motioned for him to follow me into the kitchen, not wanting to disturb Fletcher.

The penthouse was pretty open, so I could still see into the living room from the kitchen, but there was enough distance that hopefully, if we spoke quietly, our voices wouldn't carry.

"Do you want something to drink?" I offered.

Despite the unwelcome greeting we had, I actually liked Neo. I thought he was a pretty decent guy, especially considering he was from the Grimms. He made Ivory very happy, and for that, I was willing to make allowances.

But now there was Fletcher. Fletch considered Neo his brother, and that meant now it was more important than ever we get along.

"Only if you have beer," Neo said, the first hint of weariness in his voice as he dropped onto one of the stools at the island.

Going past him, I pulled open the wide stainless-steel fridge, taking out a beer. Neo raised his brows in surprise when I carried it over, sliding it in front of him.

"Just because I drink wine and scotch at parties doesn't

mean I don't like a good beer," I informed him, grabbing a bottle opener and handing it over.

"Touché," Neo quipped, opening the beer to take a long pull. When he was done, he lowered the longneck to eye the label. "This is pretty good."

"It's from a brewery upstate."

He grunted. "You gonna have one?"

My eyes strayed back into the living room. "Not tonight."

Shrugging, the scruffy-jawed man took another long drink.

"Long day?" I asked, then remembered he was with his sister. "How is Virginia?"

"She's okay," he replied, setting the bottle in front of him. "Just a lot of doctor appointments and shit to see if we can do the surgery."

I nodded. Virginia was a beautiful young woman who was dealt a bad hand in life when an accident left her wheelchair-bound and unable to walk. Before meeting Ivory, Neo spent all of his time caring for her, making sure she had what she needed. Now that he was with Ivory, doors had been opened that were never open before, and there was a chance Virginia could walk again.

"If there is anything you need, anything at all, just say the word," I offered sincerely. Even if I wasn't in love with Fletcher, I would still mean every word.

"Thank you," Neo said, accepting the offer. He was an extremely proud man and didn't accept much for himself, but when it came to Virginia, he would do anything.

A few beats of silence passed, another drink of the beer.

"Why did you bring Fletcher here tonight?" Neo asked, not mincing words.

"I have a contract he needs to sign."

His smile was more like a smirk. "This isn't about a contract."

"You're right. It's not." If he wasn't going to mince words, then why should I?

Neo pinned me with a solid, penetrating stare from across the island. "Are you interested in Fletcher?"

"Yes."

He might have suspected, but my blunt truth caught him off guard. I watched his tongue slide over his teeth and the muscle in his jaw jump. When he looked up, his nearly black eyes were intense. "Fletcher is not a toy. He's not someone you can play with until you're bored or your rich eye finds something shinier."

"It's insulting you would insinuate Fletcher isn't better than that."

"That's exactly why I'm saying it. He *is* better."

"Fletcher isn't a game to me. Far from it."

"Then what is he to you exactly?"

"I think he has the right to hear that first, don't you?"

"So you haven't told him?"

I considered that. I mean, technically, I hadn't said the words, but my tongue did do some talking. "Not exactly." I hedged.

Whatever Neo saw on my face or heard in my short reply ruffled his already ruffled feathers. Pushing up so fast the stool he was on made a screeching sound across the floor, he planted both hands on the island as he leaned in, anger making his jaw look like granite. "So help me God, if you touch him…"

I wasn't about to tell him I already had and would again.

Not because I was afraid but because it was private. Admitting I was interested in Fletch was more than bold enough, at least for me and at least for right now.

"Actually, that's sort of what I wanted to ask about." I deflected.

Making a face, Neo grabbed his stool, dragging it under him once more.

Wincing at the noise he kept making, I shot a look in the direction of the couch. "Would you be quiet? Good Lord, you could wake the dead."

"Obviously not, because Fletch is still asleep," he quipped, tipping the bottle against his lips as though he'd made some kind of epic statement.

"Well, after living with you for so long, he's probably used to sleeping through anything," I muttered.

Neo laughed under his breath and looked up. "I admit I'm curious, so you can ask, but I might not answer."

"Fair enough."

As he crossed his arms over his chest, a look of expectation came over his features.

"Earlier when we were eating," I began, glancing toward the couch to make sure Fletch was still sleeping, "he had some kind of episode."

Dark brows furrowed low, and Neo frowned. "An episode?"

"He spilled some food on his shirt, and his reaction was…" I paused, searching for the right word. "Basically, he panicked, skittered away from me, apologizing. When I moved closer, he flinched."

Neo's upper lip curled. "Did you touch him?"

"Obviously not," I said, holding on to my patience. "He was clearly afraid. I wouldn't do anything to make it worse."

"Then why was he afraid?" he asked suspiciously.

"That's what I'm asking you. Why would spilling something make him panic like that? He didn't even react that way when he got arrested."

Neo went quiet for a moment, obviously turning inward. "He must have gone to see her," he surmised, his voice quiet as if he were speaking to himself.

"Her?" I inquired.

He looked up, suddenly guarded. He wasn't going to answer.

"Earth said a name earlier." I thought back. "Milly. Is that who you are talking about?"

His eyes flared, and even if he denied it, I would know I was right.

"What did Earth say exactly?" Neo questioned.

"Nothing really. He was angry Fletcher didn't have any money and had to steal food. He seemed to think it was her fault."

Nodding, he sighed deeply, rubbing a palm over his face. "Yeah, then that's what it was about."

"Could you explain, please?"

Neo looked up, his expression grim and secretive.

"Please," I implored. *He winced at me, and my heart still aches.*

"Fletcher's had a rough life. He came from a shitty place and endured a lot. When I found him…" Neo's lips smacked together, and his gaze slid away.

"When you found him?" I pressed.

"Look. Bottom line is he knows how to endure, but his endurance has a price. He's gotten a lot better since he moved in with us, but there are still times when everything he's been through causes a reaction. He had a rough day, probably got yelled at repeatedly, and was at his limit."

I digested the words, trying to make sense of it, wanting so much to understand but finding it difficult when I was only given half the picture.

"He's wearing your clothes, right?"

I nodded. "He took a shower. He'd been sitting in a cell all day. And all he had on was a T-shirt."

"He probably thought you were going to blow your lid when he ruined something fancy of yours."

Offended, my shoulder blades came together, and I stood stiffly. "I would never."

Holding up his hand, he waved off my insult. "I know. But he's been on the receiving end one too many times.

Usually, he's good at keeping chill, but as I said, he was at his limit."

Reading between the lines, hearing the words that Neo didn't say, a dark, menacing emotion welled up, turning my voice low and ominous. "Are you telling me that someone has hit him?"

"Look, if you want details, that's for him to say. I'm just letting you know that sometimes he gets… skittish. And I'm also saying that's why you should keep your hands to yourself."

"I wouldn't do anything to hurt him."

"Maybe not intentionally, but Fletcher is… He's not as hard as the rest of us misfits. That's why we're so protective. That's why I'm asking you to back off."

I wondered what Neo would think if he realized that his "warning" just made me more determined to stay close.

I shook my head. "I can't do that."

He stood again, this time quietly, stepping around the island to meet my gaze. "I could make you."

"You could try. But it won't be like with Ivory. I stepped out of the way willingly, but with Fletcher, I'll fight."

Neo snorted, taking another threatening step closer as jealousy boiled his stare. "You think I'm with Ivory because you allowed it?"

I didn't move back, and I didn't break eye contact. "I think Ivory is with you because she loves you. She never loved me, and I never loved her. Not like that anyway."

Grunting, he relaxed his stance a bit, but I knew he was still on guard. "Because you're gay," he stated, tossing it out like he wanted to shock me.

I smiled instead. "If you thought you could shock me, I'm sorry to say you're about a decade too late for that."

Surprise lit up his eyes. "You've known you're gay for that long?"

"Give or take."

"But you date women."

"I dated Ivory." I corrected. "Or rather, everyone thought I did."

"So you're in the closet," he deadpanned.

"Clothes belong in a closet. Not people."

He nodded. "You're hiding who you really are."

I considered his words, then countered with my own. "Not really. I just don't advertise I like men."

"I won't let you make Fletch your dirty little secret."

Since I was taller than Neo, I leaned in, getting right into his face. "I'm getting really tired of you implying Fletcher isn't better than that."

His eyes widened. "That's not—"

"Then stop saying it," I snapped.

"So what? You gonna start showing up at Upper East Side events with him on your arm? You think that's gonna fly here, rich boy?"

"I don't know. How was it for you when you started showing up on Ivory's arm?" I snapped.

Neo's lips pursed. "That's different."

I arched an eyebrow. "Yeah? How?"

"Well, for one thing, Ivory doesn't have a father who would need CPR if he found out the son he wants to marry off to some rich heiress really likes men."

"You son of a bitch," I growled, fists knotting at my sides.

"Tell me I'm wrong," he practically sang. He was such an irritating shit.

But he's also right.

Shoulders drooping, I spun away, stalking toward the other end of the island.

A pregnant silence crowded the kitchen, settling into an awkward hush.

Neo broke it first, sighing deeply. "Look, I know you're a good guy, not the rich douchebag I thought you were when we first met."

"How flattering," I muttered.

"And I'm sorry for giving you such a hard time. If it was anyone else, I wouldn't be like this. But it's Fletcher. He's like my baby brother."

"I don't have it all figured out," I admitted. "And I know it's complicated. But that doesn't change how I feel."

It seemed we were at some sort of impasse, and both of us knew it.

"We should be going," Neo said finally, spinning toward the living room.

"Just leave him," I said, the words ripping out of me almost desperately.

I wasn't used to the unsettled, almost afraid feelings clamoring around inside me. All I knew was that I didn't want him out of my sight.

"Let him sleep. I'll bring him over in the morning."

Neo hadn't turned around, but he was listening. I knew.

"If he's not there first thing tomorrow, I'm coming back." He relented, starting forward again. His footsteps echoed through the foyer, and the quiet opening and closing of the door rang with finality.

I let out a breath I didn't realize I'd been holding, my lungs squeezing with relief. Going back into the living room, I stared down at the sleeping puppy buried beneath a blanket on my sofa.

Reaching up, I rubbed my palm against the soreness in my chest, trying to loosen the ache.

Neo had a right to be concerned, pointing out things I'd yet to consider. I was too blinded by the way he made me feel, too busy falling until it was too late.

There seemed to be a lot stacked against us.

Stuff I didn't even know.

I should have let Neo take him out of here. Maybe it would have been better that way.

Even the thought made the ache in my chest turn into distinct pain, and everything inside me rebelled.

Reaching down, I carefully slid my arms under his curled-up frame, lifting him. The second I cradled him against my chest, he let out a small purr and cuddled his cheek against my shoulder.

The worst of the panic subsided, and my heart swelled with love.

Carrying him up the stairs to bed, I felt his breath against my neck and the rightness at having him in my arms.

Sure, there were a lot of reasons to back off. But none of those reasons came close to how he made me feel, and selfishly, I wanted to know if I made him feel the same. If I didn't, I would let him go.

But if he did?

I would hold on tight.

FLETCHER

My eyes were barely open when memory rippled through me. Gasping, I sat up, the covers falling to my waist as I slapped a hand over my mouth.

He kissed me.

He kissed me like *a lot*.

Still hazy from sleep, I sat there, fingers pressed against my no-longer-virgin lips. The replay of last night held me in that heavy-eyed state.

Pouty lips gliding against mine, warmth coursing through my veins, and being completely surrounded in the best way.

It was as if he cast a spell on me, putting me in some kind of enchanted state.

"*Ah!*" my exclamation echoed around the large room… a room I was not familiar with.

Eyes wide, I stared around the dimly lit space, wondering where the hell I was. I didn't remember going to bed last night, or leaving…

"*Ah!*" Was I still at Ethan's?

Oh my God… was this his bed?

Chest pounding, I stared down at the massive mattress. The bedding was sleek and soft. The navy sheets felt like silk, and the massive comforter was made of the same material, which had a sheen that would probably sparkle in the light.

No way this is his bed.

Thinking fast, I rolled, face planting into one of the many satin-covered, cloudlike pillows to inhale deep.

It smelled like Christmas.

Oh shit!

Bolting upright, grasping the sheet, I held it against my chest as I tried to remember what else happened last night. We just kissed… right?

Right!?

Squeezing my eyes closed and peeling the blankets away from my body, I took a steadying breath and then squinted one eye, glancing, you know… *down below.*

I had on pants. The same pants I'd put on after my shower yesterday.

But my shirt is different!

No. Wait. This was the T-shirt I put on after my shower, but the hoodie I'd been wearing over it was gone.

Breathing out a massive sigh of relief, I fell back, the pillows cushioning my fall. He must have just brought me in here because I fell asleep on him.

I grabbed another pillow and held it over my face to groan. He'd kissed me, and I fell asleep—*in his lap.*

Well, it's his fault for being so comfortable!

Why did the bed smell like him? Was this his room? Did he sleep here too? Surely, a house this big would have more than one bedroom. This was probably just a guest room, and of course the sheets smelled like him. This was his house.

Noise across the room had me freaking, springing back up in a sitting position. I gripped the pillow previously suffocating my face and held it like a shield as the bedroom door swung in.

A little bit of light came in with the open door, but I

couldn't notice that. All I noticed was the man strolling in like he owned the place.

Well, fine, he did own it, but I was in here!

"Ah, you're awake," Ethan said, pausing just inside the room.

My mouth ran dry. I blinked. Blinked again.

"Where were you?" I blurted, finally finding words. But why did they have to be those words?

Surprise rolled across his square-jawed face, and then a small smile curled the corners of his lips. "Why, were you scared without me here?"

Squeezing the pillow tighter into my chest, I rolled my eyes. "I'm not five. Why would I be scared?"

"So you missed me, then." He surmised, chuckling lightly under his breath.

Goose bumps rose along my arms, and awareness tingled my scalp. *Oh, I was never like this until you kissed me.*

The combination of that husky, low chuckle and the fact that he was like half naked and wet… I might be innocent, but I wasn't oblivious, and I definitely was not immune.

"Why do you look like that?" I asked, eyes raking over his incredibly toned arms.

Glancing down at himself, Ethan made a sound. "Oh, this." He gestured to the tank top clinging to his chest because it was so wet. A pair of black shorts covered his lower half, finished with a dark pair of socks and black sneakers.

Palming the end of the white towel slung around his neck, he began patting off some of the sheen from his neck and face. "I was working out."

I gulped. "You mean I was here alone?"

Another one of his small smiles played on his lips as he came closer to the bed. "Of course not. I have a home gym. My trainer comes here in the mornings."

I couldn't even properly process the fact that he had a

home gym and a trainer because I was too busy being incredibly distracted by his wide chest and well-defined shoulders.

The way the damp cotton clung between his pecs, the fascinating rivulet of sweat trailing down the hollow of his throat, down, down to disappear beneath the neckline of the white tank.

It was obvious he was in good shape from the very first time I saw him on television and when my hands clung to him last night when we kissed.

But I didn't know he was this… *godlike.*

I didn't even know people looked like this in real life.

"You look like an Avenger," I whispered, not really meaning to speak out loud.

His teeth flashed bright white, clear amusement on his face. "You think so?"

My head bobbed. "You must work out a lot."

"I get up early and work out every morning before work."

My arms looked like spaghetti noodles compared to his.

"So?" he asked, a little hesitation in his voice. Ethan really wasn't much of a hesitator, so it made me curious as to what he would say. "You like the Avengers?"

I made a sound. "Of course! Who doesn't? They're cool."

"Ah, that explains the Spider-Man statue." Ethan surmised.

"Well, technically, Spider-Man is not an Avenger. He turned them down even though they asked him. Spider-Man likes to work alone."

"I see." Ethan indulged me, smiling down at me once more.

Why does he have to smile like that? Now my stomach feels weird again.

"Here, thought you might need this," he said, holding out a mug I hadn't even noticed.

You try noticing a mug when *all that* is on display.

"What is it?" I asked, leaning up to try and see inside.

Lowering his arm, he showed me the coffee. It was much darker than I usually drank it. I liked extra creamer, the flavored kind. Earth said real men didn't need creamer, but he also said I was the exception.

"Do you drink coffee?"

"You brought me that?" I was surprised.

He nodded. "Of course. I'll have some after I shower."

"But… I can drink it in this bed?" I asked, glancing again at the massive and very expensive bed.

"Of course." He gestured for me to take it, turning the entire cup around, gripping the walls of the mug to offer me the handle. "Be careful." He warned gently when I reached out. "It's hot."

No one had ever brought me coffee in bed before. Well, technically, I didn't even have a bed. I slept on the couch at home. But I didn't mind because it was comfortable.

Well, sometimes I slept on an air mattress with Neo… but I wasn't sure that counted as a bed either.

"Thank you," I said sincerely, pulling the mug close to my chest.

"I added some cream and sugar. I wasn't sure how you liked it, though," Ethan told me, moving across the room. The way his shoulders and back muscles rippled was a total eyecatcher.

Grabbing a small remote nearby, he pressed a button, and the wall of dark curtains started to slowly slide open.

Morning light filtered in, chasing away the dimness and giving definition to everything around me.

The navy sheets definitely had a glossy sheen, and the massive headboard behind me was padded and soft but made with some sort of silver fabric that made it look sleek.

The walls were painted gray, and across the opposite side of the room was a wall of different artwork that made me feel like I was in a gallery.

Neo would like this.

"I'm going to shower. You can watch the view and drink your coffee."

His voice brought me around to the view he'd just revealed. My mouth fell open. *"Whoa,"* I sang in awe. "It's like looking out over a kingdom."

"Coffee okay?" Ethan asked, still dabbing his face with the towel.

I lifted it, swallowing down some of the rich brew. My eye twitched lightly, and I forced myself to not make a face.

Not enough creamer. Not enough creamer.

But I wouldn't say that. Not when he'd made it for me and let me drink it in bed with a kingdom as my view!

"It's good. Thank you," I said after clearing my throat.

"You sure?"

My nod was enthusiastic.

"I'll be out shortly," he said, heading toward the bathroom.

The bathroom that was in this bedroom.

I made a sound. "Is this your room?"

Pausing, Ethan glanced back. "Of course."

"I slept in your bed last night?"

He nodded.

My fingers tightened around the warm mug. "Where did you sleep?"

"Right next to you." His eyes flicked to the wide empty spot that was indeed beside me. The same spot that smelled like Christmas.

"Agh!" I gasped. "You should have left me on the couch!"

Ethan scowled. "A couch is not a bed."

"It's basically the same thing," I kicked back.

"What if you woke up in the middle of the night and felt confused?" he countered.

I made a face.

"Relax. I didn't touch you except to take off the jacket. All we did was sleep."

I let out a relieved sigh, drinking more of the bitter coffee.

"Think about what you want for breakfast, okay? You can tell Jane when we go downstairs."

"Who's Jane?"

"The house manager. She'll make you whatever you want."

"I should be going," I said, suddenly feeling awkward as I sat in his bed, talking about his house lady cooking for me as he stood there looking like… well, like *that*.

Tossing the towel off his shoulders, Ethan's hips rolled smoothly with his long strides as he prowled closer. Gulping, I gripped the coffee and stared as he bore down on me.

"Don't even think about running off while I'm in the shower, puppy." His voice was low and commanding. His arms flexed on either side of me as he leaned in close. "Because if I think you will, I'll have to drag you in the bathroom with me."

My mouth fell open. I closed it, but it fell open again. "I won't."

Chuckling, Ethan pushed back, ruffling my hair with his palm. "After breakfast, I'll drop you off at Ivory's on my way to work."

"Are you sure?" I called after his retreating back.

I can't believe I'm sitting in his bed.

"Positive. Neo's waiting for you."

"Neo? How do you know?"

"He came by last night, but you were already sleeping."

"Neo was here?" I questioned.

He made another noise, which I took as an agreement. I was about to question more, but he stripped off his shirt with one full tug.

His abs were just as defined as the rest of him.

A surge of heat bloomed low in my stomach. I wondered

what it would be like to drag my fingers over that smooth, taut skin covering those hard muscles.

"If you keep staring like that, I'm gonna kiss you again."

I jolted, his words like a bucket of ice water. Ice water that did nothing to cool me down.

Shy and completely incoherent, I turned away, fixing my eyes back on the view while taking another swig of the too-strong coffee.

When I heard the faint echo of his shower, a small prick of disappointment filled me.

I kind of wanted him to kiss me again.

Thirteen

ETHAN

He was no longer in bed when I came out of the bathroom. Panic made my feet stumble as my eyes searched wildly around the big empty bed.

He told me he wouldn't run away... Putting him in bed with me was too much too soon. *How could I put him in a room across the hall when he was curled into my neck like he really wanted to be there?*

Fuck. I really didn't know what to do with myself right now. I was always so much more in control of my emotions. People never got to me like this.

It didn't matter that I knew I was being irrational. I still couldn't get away from the anxiety coiling inside me, ready to strike like a cornered snake.

"I've never seen a view like this. Not even at Ivory's."

My whole body rotated toward his voice, and thrill and relief wared within me.

"Fletch." My voice was breathless.

He seemed oblivious to everything he'd put me through, standing there in the oversized clothes, peering out the window like he was taking in every last detail.

His hair was messier than usual, total bedhead, and his shirt was slightly wrinkled from sleep. One hand was holding the mug I'd given him, and the other was pressed against the glass.

"I've lived here my entire life, and there is still so much to this city that I've never known."

Even though his words held sadness, my heart bloomed with tenderness and love. Before I knew I was moving, I was already at his side, not even glancing at the view because everything I wanted to see was right in front of me.

"You grew up here?"

He nodded, glancing at me out of the corner of his eye before shifting back to the glass. "In the Grimms."

"Have you ever been anywhere else?"

He made a noise. "I haven't even seen all of the city, and you think I've gone outside of it?"

"Just curious," I said, voice tender. "It's okay."

He glanced at me again, this time his head turning with his eyes. I couldn't help but smile and reach out for the wild hair falling across his forehead to push it back.

"You wanna shower?" I asked, moving my eyes over his face, focusing on his lips a little longer than the rest of his features.

He'd been so responsive last night. Even when he had only stared, I felt it.

He shook his head.

"You hungry?"

His bottom lip disappeared under the top row of his teeth, and he nodded.

"C'mon then," I said, smiling softly when I heard him fall into step behind me. *Following along like a little puppy.*

Instead of heading to the bedroom door, I veered left, making his footsteps stutter.

Glancing back, I saw him standing there watching me with suspicion.

"Isn't the kitchen that way?" he asked, pointing to the bedroom door.

"I have a stop to make first," I replied, backtracking to gently wrap my hand around his wrist, tugging him along with me.

He dug his feet into the floor, likely thinking I was tugging him into the bathroom. "I don't want to shower. I just showered last night!" he fussed.

I chuckled and led him into the walk-in closet, which was beside the bathroom.

The second we crossed the threshold, automatic lights came on, an entire track around the ceiling and more in-cabinet lighting in the racks and shelves.

The marble-topped island also glowed.

"Whoa," Fletch murmured, glancing around.

Releasing his wrist, I took the half-finished coffee from his hand, setting it aside. "These are all your clothes?"

"Most of them," I said, going across the large space to a custom cabinet. "I keep some at the office too."

As I passed a floor-to-ceiling shelving unit, it lit up, showing off rows of shoes.

Fletch made a sound and went to them, eyes eating up every pair. "These are sick!" he exclaimed.

Frowning, I went to his side, staring at the black spiked sock neoprene sneakers Christian Louboutin sent me last year. They were brand new. I'd never worn them. The soles were bright red, as was the inside of the shoe.

"Sick? Is there a flaw in the design?" I wondered, picking one up to study it. I didn't find anything that would make them sick.

Fletcher laughed. "Sick means I think they're awesome."

I made a face. "Then why didn't you just say you liked them?"

"You use words I don't know all the time," he countered.

"That's hardly the same thing."

"Why not?" Fletch demanded.

"Because my words actually mean what they're supposed to mean. Sick means being ill, not awesome."

His chin jutted out stubbornly, and a glint came into his stare. "It can mean both."

How could I argue with that face? "Okay." I agreed. "You've taught me something."

Fletcher smiled as though he'd won some kind of prize, and my heart tumbled a little. Clearing my throat, I asked, "So you like these?"

"You don't?" he questioned, obviously shocked.

I laughed lightly. "Yes, they're very nice. But they're too small."

"You couldn't stretch them out?"

One does not simply stretch out a thirteen-hundred-dollar pair of sneakers. But then I thought about the sneakers he had on last night and kicked off so easily in the bathroom. Glancing down at his feet, I said, "What size shoe do you wear?"

Fletcher drew back a little, shuffling as if he were trying to pull his feet away to hide them. "I have shoes. They're…" He made a face. "Hey, where are my shoes?"

"You lost them?" I teased.

He scowled, making me want to tease him more. "A lot of stuff happened yesterday. I—Oh! They're in the bathroom."

"They seemed a little worn out. You were able to kick them off without even untying them."

"Oh, no, that's 'cause they're too big. They're Beau's."

"Why are you wearing Beau's shoes?"

"He has more than one pair. He said he didn't mind."

I sighed. Sometimes talking to him was like talking in circles. "I mean where are *your* shoes."

"Oh, they wore out. I haven't got new ones yet."

"No wonder you trip all over the place. You don't have proper shoes." I scowled.

Fletcher frowned. "My shoes are just fine."

"Put these on," I demanded, shoving the shoe at him.

He took it only because I pressed it into his middle, but he didn't put it on. "Why?"

"Because you need a pair."

"I can get my own shoes."

Stubborn. This puppy was stubborn.

"You don't need to because I'm giving you these."

"I don't want them." He shook his head.

"You just said they were sick."

"Just because I like something doesn't mean I want it."

Something inside me flared to life, possessiveness leaping up unexpectedly at his words as though we weren't talking about shoes anymore but about us. "Are you rejecting me?"

Shock rippled over his features, widening his eyes and slackening his jaw. The hair I'd pushed away from his face minutes ago was clinging to his forehead, almost threatening to shield him from view.

At my hips, my hands clenched. The urge to haul him against me was so great I was also surprised.

"I-I—" Fletcher stuttered.

Blowing out a breath, I forced myself to chill. "I apologize. I didn't bring you in here to argue over shoes."

Turning my back, I went to the cabinet I'd been heading for in the first place.

"Why did you bring me in here?"

Something in my heart lightened, hearing the curiosity in his voice and not any anger as if he wouldn't punish me for my bad behavior. Oddly, that made me feel even worse.

Opening the door, I pulled out a long horizontal rack filled with different-colored fabric. "Actually, I was hoping you would pick out my tie. Then when I wore it today, I would think of you when I looked down at it."

"Really?"

I smiled. "Really."

Fletcher came forward, pushing the hair out of his face

himself. His wide honey-colored eyes focused on all the ties between us. "You have a lot of ties."

"There's more on the bottom row." I pointed.

Fletcher started poking through them. "Lots of different colors," he murmured, still looking.

"A man's gotta make a statement."

Fletcher looked up, doe eyes hopeful. "Do you have one with Spider-Man?"

I actually felt bad I didn't. "'Fraid not."

He made a face and went back to his choices. "This one!" he said, pulling out a hot-pink satin tie.

"All right," I said, taking it and going to put it on in the mirror.

"Really?"

I glanced at him in the reflection. "Didn't think I'd wear it?"

He pursed his lips. "I knew you would. You wear pink a lot."

"How would you know?" I quizzed.

His lips folded in on themselves, and he turned back to the ties, busying himself with pushing the rack away. "I see you on TV sometimes."

I made a noise. "And what do you think of me wearing pink?"

"Not many guys can pull it off. But you do. Just like a prince."

My fingers stalled in the middle of tying. Hands still at my neck, I spun. "What?"

Fletcher's cheeks reddened and his face dipped.

"Fletcher," I called, voice stern.

His eyes popped up. "I said it makes you look like a prince."

I tried to keep my reaction smooth, simply nodding and turning back to finish tying the tie. Inside, my stomach was doing flips, and I was completely charmed.

When I was finished with the tie, I grabbed a different sport jacket than the one I originally planned to wear. Instead of going with all black, I chose a slim-fit grey herringbone, pulling it on over the white dress shirt and black trousers. The pink tie was a nice choice.

"All right, I'm finished. Let's go eat so we can go," I announced a moment later, heading past him for the door.

"Ethan?" His small, hesitant voice stopped me. That tone would forever be my undoing.

"What is it, puppy?" I asked, words gentle.

"These really are too small for you?"

Heartbeat erratic, I rotated, seeing him still holding the one shoe against his middle. Nodding casually, I replied, "Yeah. They were a gift from the designer, but they sent the wrong size. I wasn't about to complain because it was thoughtful of them. So I just bought a pair in the correct size and wore those out to be photographed."

"Really?" Fletcher asked, listening intently.

Smiling, I went back to the shoe rack, reaching up high to pull down an identical shoe to the one he held, just bigger. "See?"

"You did all that for a picture?"

"I get a lot of stuff sent to me by designers because they know that when I go out to events and things, I get photographed, and it's good advertisement for them."

"Oh."

"It's okay." I spoke gently, reaching up to smooth his hair. It was becoming a habit I didn't want to break. "I'm sorry I got mad before. It's just shoes. Don't be upset."

Reaching down, I grasped the shoe still in his arms to tug it free, but his grip tightened. "Fletch?"

"They're my size."

I felt my brows rise. "Are they?"

He nodded.

"How do you know?"

"I looked when you were putting on your tie."

This boy is going to be the death of me.

"Don't feel like you have to accept them. I just thought since I couldn't use them, you might."

"If I wear them… when I look down, I will think of you."

I swallowed thickly, feeling the words he'd echoed back at me.

Is this how he felt when I said that? What the hell will I do if I'm the only one who feels like this?

Trying to breathe normally, trying to keep my composure, I grabbed the matching shoe from the rack and knelt in front of him.

Despite Fletcher's smaller size, his feet and hands were surprisingly large like he was indeed a puppy who had yet to grow into his paws.

"Let's see if they fit," I said, holding out the shoe for his foot.

Reluctantly, he slid it forward, allowing me to slip the sock-style sneaker over his foot. When I was finished, he stepped down, giving a little bounce on one foot.

"I like the red." His voice floated over my head.

Making a sound, I reached up for the one he held, and this time he gave it willingly.

When it was on, I felt for his toes, making sure they really did fit and weren't too big or small.

Despite the black spikes, I was able to determine that these were in fact perfectly sized for his feet.

"What do you think?" I asked, standing up.

He bounced again and took a step. "They have real cushions inside!"

Oh, baby, haven't you ever had new, cushiony shoes before?

"Comfortable, right?" was all I could manage to say.

"We match now." Fletcher beamed, lifting his foot like he needed to show me.

It made me want to toss the Gucci loafers I had on into

the trash and put on the sneakers, not caring at all that they didn't go with my suit.

"You sure it's okay?" Fletcher asked, pulling his foot down.

"I'm sure." I promised, voice husky.

Why did he make me like this? Why did everything about him make me want to spoil and protect him?

"Thank you, Ethan."

"You're welcome," I said, turning to flee. Enough was enough. "C'mon then," I called out. "I think Jane is making pancakes."

"Pancakes!" he yelled. "I haven't had those since Earth made them last Christmas!" he exclaimed, rushing past me and out the bedroom door before I could blink.

I laughed as he raced down the stairs, all the while worried he was going to fall.

What am I going to do with you? The thought from last night reappeared in my brain.

"Is this heaven?" Fletcher's excited exclamation carried from all the way in the kitchen. Jane's tinkling laughter followed directly after.

I smiled to myself, gazing down at the hot-pink tie.

There was only one answer to that question that I could accept.

Keep him.

Fourteen

FLETCHER

THE SWEET FLAVOR OF MAPLE SYRUP AND CINNAMON STILL clung to my lips and the roof of my mouth. The kind of breakfast Jane made for us was the kind I only ever saw on tv before. I think she might be an angel.

They tried to tell me she wasn't.

Maybe they just didn't know.

But I did.

No mere mortal made pancakes that good.

"Thanks for the ride," I said, unbuckling the seat belt and reaching for the handle right after the Mercedes slid to a stop at the curb of Ivory's building.

"That's it?" Ethan said, his words making me pause.

Feeling my ears heat, I turned back to the man sitting in the driver's seat. The gray in his suit jacket made his eyes look a little stormy, and the hard lines of his jaw were only softened by the sunshine hue of his hair.

I liked it when he smiled at me, when he stroked my hair, and the way he fed me a bite of my pancake with his fork.

I liked a lot about Ethan, and honestly, it scared me.

"Oh, uh, thanks for the shoes too. And for bailing me out of jail." Grimacing, I realized something. "I actually owe you a lot."

"I'd like to collect payment in full now."

"What?"

"I'm a businessman, not a bank. I don't do loans."

Reeling, my palms started to sweat, and I rubbed them on the knees of the sweats I was wearing. *His sweats.*

Crap! I owe him for these too!

"I'll wash these clothes and give them right back." I promised, hoping to take a little off the bill.

"Hmm." He nodded, seeming to agree.

"So, ah, how much do I owe you?"

My God, that burger probably cost a fortune. I shouldn't have eaten those dipping sauces—

"Here," Ethan said, tapping his cheek with his index finger.

"Huh?"

"The payment is a kiss." He tapped his cheek again. "Right here."

I gasped. "You want me to *kiss you!*" I screamed.

Ethan winced. He thought I was just going to kiss him in the middle of the street?

I mean, look, I know I said I wanted him to kiss me, but I didn't want to kiss him! How embarrassing.

"If you could refrain from screaming, I would appreciate it," he said, pressing against his ear.

"I'm not kissing you," I declared.

"Why not?"

"Why?" I screeched again. "You can't just kiss people in the street."

"We're in my car."

"Same thing!"

"The windows are tinted."

"I can't," I sputtered. "Just give me a total. I'll pay you back after I get paid from my job." Saying that made me realize. "Hey, I didn't sign the contract!"

He smiled. "Guess that means I'll have to see you later."

Completely flustered, I went to get out of the car. He didn't try and stop me. He didn't get mad or yell. All he said was one word, and it halted my escape.

"Puppy."

God, I hate it when he calls me that.

I turned to tell him just that, but the words died on my tongue. His eyes were soft and twinkling, humor clear in their depths. His lips were slightly puckered, a hint of a smile on his cheeks. He was big inside the small Mercedes, commanding behind the wheel.

Suddenly, I didn't want to run away. Suddenly, I really wanted to stay.

Before I could talk myself out of it, I darted forward, leaning over the center console and pecking his cheek with my lips.

The scent of pine swirled up, mixing with the hint of cinnamon still on my tongue.

He stilled. I heard his sharp intake of breath. My stomach fluttered, and my heart pounded as massive amounts of blood rushed to my head.

When I leaped out of the car onto the street, a taxi honked wildly, swerving out of my path. I barely even noticed because I'd just kissed Ethan.

Slamming the door, I ran around the front, bounding onto the sidewalk, staring down at my new shoes. I really would think of him every time I did that.

Not allowing myself to look back even though the urge to do so was strong, I pushed on, only glancing sideways when a shadow fell at my side.

Startled, I jolted back, gasping at the blond man smiling down.

"Ethan! What are you doing?"

"Walking you to the door."

"I can get to Ivory's penthouse on my own. I've been there lots of times before."

"But I've never dropped you off before."

"What about the car?" I tossed a thumb behind me. "It's in a no-parking zone."

"Watch her for me, will you?" Ethan asked the doorman as we walked right inside. "I will only be a moment. Apologies for the inconvenience."

"It's not a problem at all, Mr. Abbott," the man replied.

"This is ridiculous." I scowled, pressing the button on Ivory's elevator a little too aggressively. "I'm a grown man."

"I know that. But we didn't finish our conversation."

Startled, I glanced up. "What?"

"You ran off before I could say what I wanted to say."

"You mean a kiss wasn't enough?" I exclaimed.

Someone nearby giggled, and I nearly hid in the plant beside me. Thankfully, I didn't have to because the doors dinged open, and I threw myself inside.

Ethan strolled in behind me like he didn't have a care in the world, and I found myself practically snarling at him. Didn't he ever get ruffled by anything?

In the closet when he asked if you were rejecting him.

I shied away from that thought for so many reasons.

"I want to see you again," Ethan said, very direct.

The lurch of the elevator as it went up made me grip the handrail against the wall, but I still continued to grip it even as the ride smoothed out. "Because of the contract, you mean?"

"That's one reason," he allowed.

"I can come by today before I go home to the Grimms," I offered.

"I have meetings until after six."

I frowned. An idea popped into my head, so I went with it. "What about lunch!"

"Lunch?"

"Well, you take a break to eat, don't you? I could stop by, sign it, and then go. I won't take long, so you'll be able to eat."

Varying expressions played over Ethan's face, making me wonder what he was thinking.

"One moment, please," was all he said, pulling out his cell from the inside of his suit jacket. After hitting the screen, he pressed it to his ear, eyes settling on me. "Are you cold?" he asked, suddenly concerned.

How could I be cold? He'd stuffed another one of his designer fleece jackets around me before we left, despite my one hundred protests.

I shook my head, and then his gaze shifted away when whoever he was calling picked up.

"Good morning, Bree," he said, his voice kind and rumbly.

Without thinking, I edged a little closer to him.

Ethan gave a low laugh and then said, "What do I have on my schedule for lunch?"

The elevator stopped, doors opening smoothly. Automatically, Ethan stretched his arm out, making sure the doors stayed open, motioning for me to go first.

As I did, I heard him make a sound behind me. "That's today?"

A pause.

"Yes, of course. Oh. Right."

Another pause.

"No, no. It's perfectly fine. And tomorrow? How late does my day run?"

There was only one guard at Ivory's door this morning, and I gave him a wave. He inclined his head as I knocked on her door.

"Thank you, Bree." Ethan was finishing his call behind me. "I'll be in shortly."

The door swung open before I could ask about his call, Neo standing on the other side.

"Hey, Neo!"

"Fletch," he replied, eyes sweeping over me like he was inspecting for something.

"What's wrong with you?" I asked, glancing down. "Oh! Is it the clothes? I borrowed them from Ethan."

"You okay?" he asked, not mentioning the clothes.

"Why wouldn't I be?"

Behind me, Ethan made a rude sound.

"Fletcher!" Ivory called, coming toward the door.

"Hi!" I replied, leaving them to stand there oddly and going into the penthouse.

Ivory was already dressed for work in a pair of loose light-brown pants that had a big bow at the waist. Her white blouse was tucked in, and she had on some big colorful necklace.

"Did you eat?" she asked right away. "Want some breakfast?"

"I had pancakes."

"I told you I'd bring him. Here he is. Looks fine, doesn't he?" Ethan said to Neo, both men still standing in the entryway.

"What's up with them?" I asked Ivory.

She rolled her eyes. "Just typical men posturing."

I didn't know what that meant.

Suddenly, I gasped.

Ethan's and Neo's attention snapped up.

"What's wrong?" Neo asked.

"My violin! I left it at your apartment!" I said, panicked eyes going to Ethan first.

"It's all right. I'll have Jane bring it over." He promised smoothly.

"But she's busy."

"Nonsense, this is her job." He said it so casually, so surely.

"She'll be careful with it, right?" I asked, chewing my lower lip.

"Aren't you the one who called her an angel this morning?" Ethan teased.

I felt my cheeks heat as my glance slid to Neo who was standing there watching the exchange.

I nodded. "Okay."

"I'll call her in the car."

"Okay," I said again.

"I have to go. Come here."

Neo made a choked sound, then stared incredulously when I listened.

Suddenly self-conscious, I glanced at Neo on my way past him. "He asked nicely," I explained.

Neo choked again.

"I can't do lunch today," Ethan said when I stopped in front of him. "Meetings. But I'll be done tomorrow by five. Can you meet me then?"

"What the hell for?" Neo demanded, totally eavesdropping.

Ethan made a face.

"I have to sign the contract," I explained.

"I thought that's why I left him there last night." Neo accused.

"Neo, for heaven's sake!" Ivory interrupted.

"I can meet you then," I said, ignoring Neo.

"Do you want me to send a car for you?" Ethan asked gently.

My stomach fluttered a little at the softness in his eyes and tone.

I shook my head. "I can manage on my own."

"All right." He relented. "I'll have your violin over within the hour."

I nodded.

"Do you need money? I haven't paid you yet. I—" Ethan reached into his jacket.

"No!" both I and Neo said at the same time.

Ethan glanced up, and Neo kept going. "I'll take care of him. Just go."

"I don't need anyone to take care of me," I announced.

What's it gonna take for everyone to stop acting like I'm a kid?

"If you need anything, call me," Ethan said, gentle voice and eyes just for me.

I forgot I was annoyed and smiled. "I won't need anything."

"Well, if you do, I'll be here." He promised. "See you tomorrow."

"Bye."

"Nice seeing you, Ivory," Ethan called, going to the door. "Neo," he said, but some kind of silent exchange passed between them.

Blue eyes came back to me before he turned and exited the penthouse.

When he was gone, I glanced down at the shoes and smiled.

Fifteen

*E*THAN

I NEVER REALLY MINDED BEING BUSY. IN FACT, I PREFERRED IT to being idle. After all, as the saying goes, an idle mind is the devil's playground.

I didn't want to waste my time or thoughts on what might be, what could be, or even what was. I preferred to focus on the here and now. Set goals and smash them.

I still felt that way, but the last two days, frustration built beneath my skin, making me slightly irritable with the busy schedule I usually didn't mind.

For the first time in forever, I wanted time for myself.

I wanted time to see Fletcher.

I constantly wondered what he was doing. I wondered if he'd eaten, if he was warm. If that nasty rent-a-cop—*What was his name again? Fruit. No... Fig!*—was looking for more ways to drag him into that dreadful station.

I wondered if he was playing his violin. I almost craved the smooth sound of his music. Everything inside me felt unsettled, and this was new to me.

I didn't like it.

Not at all.

It seemed like I'd left him with Neo and Ivory a lifetime ago, not just yesterday morning.

Does he miss me?

Was this what love was? A constant gnawing at your insides, a worry that was never quite quelled? If it was like this, then why did people do it?

It's not like you had a choice. True. It seemed as if I had no choice when it came to Fletcher. My heart chose him, and that was that.

I thought of his golden doe eyes, floppy hair, and the way he snored lightly in his sleep.

The phone near my elbow buzzed, startling me. Snatching it up, I sat forward. "Yes, Bree?"

"I have Preston Willshire on line one."

A tight knot formed in my stomach. "Put him through."

There was barely a delay, and then we were connected. "Preston!" I said with a lot more bravado than I felt.

Odd. I've never had to fake it with him before.

Continuing, I said, "How are you, man? How's everything over in the UK?"

"Ethan," he practically crooned with the Brit accent I always did favor. "It's been too long. How are you?"

"Good, good. Busy as always, which I know you understand. How's business?"

"All's well here on the home front. I was pleased to see the partnership between Abbott Group and The Wills is almost locked down. It seems everything is all in order here." He went on, and I could hear the distinct sound of papers being shuffled.

"Yes, yes. I'm thrilled we could come to an agreement. This will be a very successful venture for everyone involved."

"Well, I won't lie. Took some convincing on my part with the old man, but I finally made him see that an international deal would help grow the company." Preston informed, the rustling papers quieting.

"I do appreciate that, Pres," I said, the nickname slipping out from habit. Suddenly, a lump formed in my throat, but I forced it down and continued the call. "I'll make sure that your word to your father is fulfilled."

His voice lowered, taking on a familiar, more personal note. "You know I'd do anything for you, Ethan."

Those words. That tone. Never before had it made me feel the way I felt now.

Sick.

And no, I didn't mean awesome.

I meant ill.

Clearing my throat, I straightened in my seat because suddenly, I found it hard to sit still.

Maybe he took my silence as encouragement and not the fact that I was trying not to, ah, vomit, because he continued speaking.

"I'm really looking forward to next week. I've already made a reservation at the bistro you like."

Next week?

Shoving some files and contracts to the side, I found my calendar, which frankly, I didn't pay much attention to because I had Bree and she told me everything. Flipping the page, I stared at next week.

ENGLAND DEAL FINALIZATION.

Great gods, I'm to fly to England next week!

I was supposed to leave the morning after the hotel opening where Fletcher was playing.

No. No. I couldn't go. I refused.

"Ethan?" Preston called into my ear.

"I'm here," I said immediately. "Sorry, I, ah, was checking my calendar. Next week really snuck up on me."

"You can't have forgotten." Preston pouted. "It's been two months since I've seen you."

Oddly, it seemed I'd just seen him yesterday, but with Fletch, who I *had* seen yesterday, it felt like months.

"Of course I didn't forget. How could I? This is a major deal." I assured him smoothly.

"Is this trip really all about work to you?" He needled.

Suppressing a sigh, a familiar tightness suddenly clenched the base of my skull, and I bit back a groan. *Not now, please.*

"Are my trips to England ever always about business?" I said, turning my voice velvety.

He laughed lightly into my ear. It was wrong. The sound was all wrong.

Pain radiated up the back of my neck, lancing through my head to pound behind my eyes.

"Listen, I'm sorry I have to cut this short. Bree is sending me the evil eye from the door, and if I don't see what she wants, she'll make my coffee wrong for the rest of the week."

"All right," he purred. "I'll say good-bye. I'll see you soon... *lover.*"

I nearly slammed the phone back onto the receiver, recoiling like the damned thing had the plague.

Groaning, I dropped my head into my hands. *What am I going to do?*

This is why you do not mix business with pleasure.

There was a swift knock on the door that was distinctly Bree, and then she appeared, bustling into the office.

"Can you hit the overheads?" I asked, not looking up.

She did what I asked immediately, turning off the bright lights on the ceiling to switch on an authentic Tiffany lamp near the couch.

"Would you like some medication?" she asked, understanding in her tone.

"Please."

Glancing at the clock, I saw it was getting closer to five.

"Oh!" Bree gasped, startled. On her way out of my office, she nearly collided with my father, who was on his way in. "I apologize, Mr. Abbott, sir."

"It's fine," he said gruffly, stepping aside to let her out first.

She scurried out, and I laughed internally because she

always seemed so intimidated by my father. Though, to be fair, most people were.

"Father," I greeted as he came in, his three-piece suit impeccable as always.

"I came to remind you that your guest will be here soon."

I groaned. Why was everything happening next week?

A lightbulb went on over my head.

"About that." I began. "I was just reminded that I have a flight to the UK next week to finalize the deal there."

"Well, you can't go and just leave Sienna here," he said, indignant.

I knew he'd say that. His plan to get this deal and marry me off really was the most important.

"I've been working on this deal for months, Father. I can't just not go right when it's being finished."

"You've done all the hard work. The rest is just signatures and handshakes." He reasoned.

"Well, I'm not sure that sending someone without the Abbott name is a good idea," I countered.

He frowned, sitting in the chair opposite my desk. "I'll go in your stead."

Surprise made my eyes widen, which caused more pain in my head. Despite the dim lighting, it still seemed too bright.

"You?"

"Well, yes. My last name is Abbott. It was before it was yours."

"But what about your schedule?" I asked, not expecting he would just go. I was hoping perhaps we'd just push the trip or he'd agree to let the man below me go instead.

"I can have it moved around. I'll make it a quick trip. This deal is important too, but you should be here."

With Sienna, my thoughts filled in. I wanted to argue and tell him it would never happen, but honestly, I didn't feel like a fight. And besides, I kind of needed her to show up to get me out of going to England.

I could just tell Preston something came up here and my father would be coming instead. Then once the ink was dry on the deal, I could let him know that our *arrangement* was over.

And Sienna? Well, I could think about that later.

The door to my office was open, and I saw Bree hovering, glass of water in hand. I shook my head slightly, holding her off.

Frowning, she disappeared, returning to her desk.

"Are you sure?" I asked my father.

"Of course. Just focus on the home base."

I would. But my home base was a lot different than the one he imagined.

Commotion brought my attention back toward the door. A voice I'd been waiting to hear floated inside.

"He said to meet him at five."

"You can't just go in there," Bree fussed, and then both of them appeared in the doorframe. "You don't even have an appointment!"

Feeling my and my father's eyes, both people stopped, staring inside as though they'd been caught doing something improper.

"Mr. Abbott!" Bree worried, looking at me, but my eyes went to Fletcher, drinking in the sight of him, finally seeing the person who'd been consuming my thoughts.

Tension drained out of my body, leaving me fatigued. The threatening migraine thumped, reminding me it wasn't just going to let me free.

"Who are you to just waltz right into my son's office?" my father snapped. "Did you just wander in off the streets? What business do you even have here?"

Fletcher's entire body jerked, his lanky frame coiling into a stiff upright position. Nervously, he pushed back his hair like he was trying to smooth it out, and his cheeks bloomed with red. Despite his rigid posture, his chin tilted down, eyes fixing on the floor as though he thought that was where they belonged.

"I-I'm sorry, sir. I h-have an appointment." He began.

"Speak up, boy! What could you possibly have an appointment for?"

All the tension that fled with the sight of him came back tenfold.

No one talked to Fletcher like that. Not even my father.

"Dad!" My voice cracked through the room like a whip.

Everyone turned to me instantly.

Shooting out of my chair, I straightened to my full height, ignoring the pull of my shoulder and neck muscles. It was almost like a rush of adrenaline, the way I suddenly felt incensed to protect. "This is Fletcher. He's the artist playing the violin for the opening next week."

Disbelief filled my father's eyes before he turned back to look at Fletch again. "You can't be serious."

"I am, and I will not tolerate you speaking to him with anything but respect. Am I clear?" I demanded, going around the desk and halfway across the room. "Fletcher, come in here," I called, tone still stiff.

Fletcher hesitated, glancing at my father.

I made a sound, and he snapped out of, coming to stand near me.

"Where on earth did you find—"

Lips thinning, I flicked my eyes to my father, silencing him immediately. Father was a harsh man. He didn't mince words, and he didn't often think about how his words could affect others. He wasn't a mean person, but he didn't often empathize. And he was a total snob.

"Perhaps you remember Fletcher. He created quite a buzz when he played at Ivory's last show. Everyone's been trying to hire him for months."

Recognition lit my father's eyes before they swept over Fletch again.

Feeling his discomfort—*and was that fear?*—I stepped closer, angling just slightly in front of him.

"That was you?" Father asked.

I heard Fletcher swallow, and then he answered, "Yes, sir."

"Why do you look like that, then?"

"Like what?" Fletcher wondered.

"Like you live on the street?"

"Enough!" I snapped. "That's enough. Are we done here? I have business."

"Of course," he said, moving toward the door.

I followed, blocking Fletcher from view.

Father opened his mouth to say something else, and I silenced him with one hard stare. Caught off guard by my fierceness, he stalled a moment, then recovered to say, "I'll have word sent to Willshire about the change in schedule for next week."

"Thank you."

He was clearly a bit surprised at my gruff and suddenly cool behavior, but I didn't care and he didn't question me, leaving my office without looking back.

The second he turned the corner, I let out a deep breath and shoved the door closed, blocking out the rest of the world.

"I'm sorry I embarrassed you." Fletcher's small voice floated behind me.

Half groaning, half choking, I spun, closing the distance between us in seconds flat. I wasn't gentle when I pulled him against me or tender with the way I pushed his cheek against my shoulder. Holding his head against me, my free arm anchored him close as my heart thundered in my chest as if it might explode.

"You could never embarrass me," I swore on a whisper. "It's me who's embarrassed. Me who should apologize." Tucking him even closer, I released a breath. "I'm sorry," I told him. "I'm sorry he was like that to you. He won't ever speak to you like that again."

"It's okay," Fletcher said. "I'm used to it."

My heart broke, pieces of it falling from my chest into my stomach. He deserved so much better than he got.

"I won't let anyone talk to you like that again," I said fiercely.

"You can't stop everyone," Fletcher admonished, but the words were punctuated by the feel of his arms wrapping around my waist.

Up until now, he'd just stood, hands at his sides, accepting my hug but not returning it. Now his arms slipped around, long fingers clutching the back of my coat.

It was as if his words denied me, but his arms called those words a liar.

The time I got to hold him was far too short because Bree's signature knock echoed from the other side of the door. Reluctantly, I pulled back, but not before grasping his face to whisper, "I missed you."

The expression on his face turned a bit to wonder, making me want to stare.

"Come in," I called instead, turning again, putting my body in front of his.

Bree entered swiftly, carrying a silver tray with a glass of water and two pills. "You'd better take these," she said, rushing closer.

I tossed the two capsules into my mouth and picked up the glass, noting how Bree's eyes strayed a little to the side.

Glancing around, I saw Fletcher peering around me, watching us both.

Gulping some water, I swallowed the pills, willing them to work quickly.

Bree and Fletcher were still staring at each other, so I made the introduction. "Bree, this is Fletcher. He's a friend and will also be playing violin at some of our future events."

"Nice to meet you," Bree said, not even batting an eye at his streetwear.

"Hi," Fletcher said, stepping out around me. "Sorry about earlier."

Bree giggled. "If I had known you were coming, I wouldn't have made a fuss," she said, giving me a glare.

I grimaced. "My apologies," I offered sincerely. "You should know he will probably be around here a lot more, so just let him come and go as he pleases. Even if he doesn't have an appointment."

Bree's eyes widened a bit at that, but despite the curiosity clear in her blue gaze, she just nodded.

"You can go for the day,"

"But don't you have a meeting?" she asked, glancing between Fletch and me.

"I can handle it. It's a basic contract. I'll put it on your desk, and you can file it in the morning."

She hesitated. "Are you sure?"

I laughed. "If I didn't know any better, I would say you enjoyed working late."

Bree laughed lightly on her way to the door. "See you tomorrow, then."

"Bye!" Fletcher called after her. When she was gone, he looked at me. "She's pretty."

I scowled. "Why are you noticing that?"

He shrugged. "She kinda looks like a girl version of you. Sunny hair, blue eyes, nice skin."

I blinked. "You think I'm pretty?"

"No. You're handsome. She's pretty."

Reaching up, I rubbed the back of my neck, hand sliding down to loosen the black tie at my neck. I didn't feel like color when I woke up this morning.

"What were those pills?"

I glanced up. "Nothing."

That stubborn glint transformed his face, calling me a liar.

"I have the contract right here," I said, moving toward my desk.

He didn't follow. He stayed planted in the same place, only rotating to watch me. "I want to know."

"Well, I don't want to tell you," I snapped. The second the words came out, I regretted them.

Glancing up, I regretted them even more profoundly.

The stubborn expression was gone, and in its place was a blank one, like he was trying to hide the hurt I knew I'd caused.

"Fletch." Regret hung heavy in my tone. "It's been a long day."

His eyes lifted, shimmering with emotion. "Are you sick?" His lower lip jutted out, wobbling just slightly.

He isn't mad I yelled. He's worried about me.

Groaning, I went forward, but he held his palm out, silently telling me not to come closer. "Are you?"

"No." My voice was rough. "No, I'm not sick. I get migraines. Sometimes they're bad enough that I can't work. If I can catch them early with medication, then I can usually stop them."

Relief seemed to move through him, and just the idea of him being worried about me had me walking closer once more.

His eyes narrowed in clear warning.

"Please, puppy."

He relented, and in seconds, I had him in my arms again.

"I'm sorry I raised my voice," I said, curling around him.

"I don't like it," he said, voice muffled against my chest.

"Okay. I'll work on it. It's been a long day. A long two days…"

"Sit down," he said, pulling out of my embrace. When I

tried to pull him back, he shook his head and pointed to the chair on the wrong side of my desk.

"That's my chair," I said, pointing behind it.

He shook his head and pointed. "That one."

Following his instruction, I sank down, Fletcher instantly moving behind me. "What are you doing?" I asked as he reached for my tie to pull it off.

The action was completely erotic and lit a fire low in my stomach. When his nimble fingers came back and started undoing a few of the top buttons on my shirt, I caught his hand, fingers tight with warning around his wrist. "You're playing a dangerous game," I practically growled.

I felt a light shiver run through him that only served to ignite me more. A bit of doubt filled his expression, but then it was gone, and he tugged his hand from my grasp.

Settling behind me, he pulled my collar open a bit, allowing some air to caress the heated skin on my neck.

The growl of impatience I'd let loose turned into a satisfied groan the instant his fingers kneaded into the muscles of my neck.

Jaw slackening, my chin fell toward my chest, bones practically turning to Jell-O under his ministrations.

Oh, his hands were so strong and so skilled. I knew it was likely because he played that violin, but in that moment, all I cared about was the endless amount of tingles racing over my scalp, down my neck, and into my spine. The tension in my neck muscles fought back, straining against his massage, but even the tight cords of knotted stress were no match for his effort.

Another low moan vibrated the back of my throat. Eyes closed, my head swam with freaking ecstasy. How long had it been since I'd had a massage? One month? Two?

As he worked, pressing and kneading, every other massage I'd had seemed like a waste of money. His hands were magic. And slightly calloused.

As they rubbed down my neck, under my open collar, I could feel the rough texture from playing a stringed instrument scraping over my skin, but it didn't lessen the sensation. If anything, it heightened it.

"You're really tight," he observed, voice low and calm.

I started to reply, but he grabbed a particularly sore area where my neck met my collarbone, sinking his thumb and forefinger into the knot.

Words forgotten, I let out another sound, head rolling to the side, offering even more access. The pain behind my eye started to ebb, and all my thoughts turned fuzzy.

The tense muscle vibrated until it gave way, loosening completely, making Fletcher move to the other side of my neck.

Entire body tingling with pleasure, I couldn't help the swelling beginning in my pants. I hadn't felt this relaxed in a long time, and all it took was his touch. His undivided attention. *Him.*

"Fletcher." My voice slurred.

"Feel good?" he asked, the sound of his voice raising the hair on the back of my neck.

"Come here," I demanded drunkenly.

He laughed lightly, evading by gliding his fingertips up into my hair, massaging into my scalp.

It took effort to stay in the chair and not melt onto the floor. It was a full-on assault, and all I could do was sit there and let it control me.

Fletcher worked the tension out of me that I didn't even know I carried, his calloused, capable hands the perfect combination of everything I needed. He was far better than any pill could ever be.

It went on for a while, me slumped there, pleasure replacing all the blood in my veins until it just wasn't enough. Until I wanted to look at him in this blissed-out state he'd put me in.

Reaching up, I caught his wrist, pulling until his body came around the chair, tugging until he stood between my relaxed knees.

"Feel better?" he asked, eyes hopeful.

Palming his hips, I tugged him closer until he yielded, straddling my hips and settling in my lap.

Fletcher's long legs hung off the sides, feet resting on the floor behind us. Our chests were pressed together so tight I could feel the unsteady beating of his heart.

Still languid, I hunched forward, resting my chin on the top of his shoulder, eyes open but seeing nothing at all.

My arms loosely wrapped around his body, encircling him just enough to keep him close.

"I really like the way you smell," he whispered, palms against my back.

Turning my head into the side of his neck just below his jaw, I nuzzled the skin there as if I could somehow mark him to leave traces of my scent to linger on his body.

Mine.

"That tickles," he said, a light shiver making him quiver.

One more bump of my nose against his neck and I pulled back, finding his stare with my heavy-lidded one.

Everything else in the universe disappeared. All that remained was us, this seat, and the air we shared. Tension coiled around us, almost tethering us together. The space between our already very close bodies was suddenly achingly too far.

Like magnets unable to deny their attraction, the distance closed between us, inch by inch, centimeter by centimeter, until his rapid breathing puffed out against my lips.

"Open for me, puppy," I whispered, not waiting to see if he would obey.

Everything around me tilted the second our lips collided. He parted instantly, and I swept in, staking my claim, diving in to get as close as I possibly could.

Our tongues laved at the other's, caressing, exploring, learning, but never having enough.

Afraid he would pull back before I was ready, I grabbed his face, fixing my thumbs where his jaw hinged, applying just a little bit of pressure to keep him open.

The sound of heavy breathing and lips smacking bounced off the ceiling. The drunken lightheadedness I suffered only grew worse.

His hand curled around the back of my neck, pads of his fingers digging deep into my skin.

I moaned into him, and he responded with a broad lick of his tongue over my bottom lip, making me shudder.

About ready to explode, I pulled back, breathing heavily, our foreheads dropping onto each other's shoulders.

Both of us were rock hard, a fact that was literally impossible to ignore. Part of me was so happy just knowing he was turned on, and the other part of me howled to do something more.

"Ethan?" he asked, hesitation clear in his voice.

My name from his lips caused a tremble in me I'd never felt before. "Yeah?"

"What's going on?"

Pressing close to his neck, I smiled against him. His innocence and inexperience only made me love him more. That and the fact he was willing to ask, clearly not wanting to play any games.

Easing back, I smiled, seeing his dilated pupils, swollen lips, and red cheeks.

"We should talk," I said, never before wanting to define anything like I wanted to define this.

He made a face. "Every time I come to sign a contract, you end up kissing me."

"You kissed back," I pointed out.

His lips rolled in on themselves, and I wondered if he could still taste me. "I like kissing you."

Groaning, I gathered up all my resolve and stood, lifting him off me as we went. My hands stayed on him even when he was on his feet, keeping him close. "How about we do the contract quick and then get some dinner and talk?"

He nodded once, and I wanted to kiss him all over again. Kissing him, it seemed, was going to be something I would never get enough of.

I just hoped he felt the same.

FLETCHER

How could he just sit there like that?

Blandly explaining a contract to me, pointing at words, defining phrases, and basically… *getting on my nerves.*

He'd literally just kissed me until my knees were weak. Seriously, I was standing here beside his chair all wobbly and unbalanced. And now he was talking about these papers like it was nothing.

Was it nothing?

If it was nothing, why did he keep kissing me?

Why did I like it so much? I shouldn't let him kiss me again.

He said we'd talk… I didn't think it would be about this dumb contract.

"Puppy." Ethan's stern voice snapped me out of my inner meanderings.

"Huh?"

"Are you paying attention?"

"This paper says I promise to play at the opening, representing Abbott Group, blah, blah, blah," I said, reaching across his desk for a pen. "Can I just sign it now?"

"You need to understand these things."

"Why?" I complained.

"Didn't you say you were going to take on some other jobs and not just this one?"

I made a face, my stomach feeling slightly queasy.

"Fletch?" Ethan asked, his desk chair gliding closer without any sound, one of his large palms settling on my lower back.

I really wanted to lean into that touch. Like really. But I didn't. My previous thoughts wouldn't allow it. Pulling back, I hunched over the paperwork, flipped to the last page, and signed my name.

Straightening, I dropped the pen on the desk. "There."

He frowned, and my heart tightened a little. The idea that he was displeased with me made me not feel so good. "You should never sign something without reading it first."

"But I trust you," I said, hand curling around the edge of his desk like I needed an anchor. Suddenly doubting myself, I asked, "Should I not?"

His expression changed completely, eyes going soft and luminous, every ounce of disappointment morphing into something else that made my stomach tumble.

I gasped when he tugged me into his lap, anchoring me in place by wrapping his arms around my waist.

"You can trust me, puppy. I won't hurt you." He tugged, trying to get me to lean into him. I resisted at first, but I was weak.

He was big, warm, and comforting. Everything about him made me want to surrender.

When I melted back, his broad chest took my weight with ease, our feet bumping together on the floor.

He sighed in contentment, resting his chin on my shoulder. "Promise you won't sign things that other people give you unless Ivory or I look over them first."

"I promise."

"Good boy," he said, palms rubbing my stomach, making me suddenly self-conscious.

"Stop," I said, pushing at his hands, which did not move.

"Why?" he whispered against my ear, making my scalp tingle.

"Because I'm squishy."

His laugh was like a rumble, like an earthquake shaking around everything inside me. "I like squishy." The words were accentuated by another pat against my stomach.

I turned my head, pouting, but didn't push him away.

Chuckling, he held me tight while leaning up to pull an envelope out of his desk. "Here," he offered, slipping it in front of me.

"What's that?" I asked, picking it up immediately to look inside. "*Agh!*" I gasped, spinning to look at him. "Why are you giving me an envelope of money?"

"That's your pay for the job," he explained patiently. "I usually don't give cash like this, but I wasn't sure if you had a bank account."

I shook my head. "Never needed one."

"We're gonna have to get you one," he murmured, seeming to make a mental note for himself.

"I don't need one."

"That's a couple thousand dollars, puppy. You can't just walk around the Grimms with it in your pocket."

"Who said I would?" I remarked, looking back at the full envelope. I couldn't believe I was getting paid this much just to play my violin for a bunch of rich people eating tiny snacks off silver trays.

It made me feel almost stupid for turning down the jobs before.

Almost. Some money wasn't worth the price.

"Well, if you aren't going to carry it around, where will you put it?" Ethan wanted to know.

"Don't people usually get paid after they do the job?" I replied with a question of my own.

"Usually. But you need the money now. And I trust you."

As I turned slightly in his lap, my stare connected with his. "Really?"

"Of course." I really liked when he talked so softly to me. No one ever talked to me like that before.

"I'll play no matter what." I vowed.

"You didn't answer my question." He reminded me, turning his head a little on my shoulder to stare at me. "Where will you keep the money?"

"Well, I'll give some to Earth for rent, maybe buy some groceries for the house since I haven't been able to for a while and they let me eat." I began.

"What about Milly?"

Her name on his lips nearly shocked me. Body going taut, I almost bolted off his lap and would have if not for the seatbelt he made out of his arms.

"I want up," I said, body vibrating with stress.

He released me immediately, but the fact that his hands hovered close when I leaped away was not lost on me.

"How do you know that name?" I demanded, backing away from the desk.

He watched me carefully, measuring the way I behaved. "I heard Earth mention it at the police station. And…"

"And?" I insisted, wanting to know everything.

"I asked Neo about her."

Suspense and worry made me momentarily dizzy. "What did Neo tell you?"

"He didn't tell me anything. He said I had to ask you."

I relaxed, posture slumping a bit. That was good. *My brothers won't tell him anything.*

Tilting his head to the side, Ethan's eyes played over my features, still drinking in every nuance he could. "Will you tell me about her?"

My lungs expanded so much with my indrawn breath that my chest bowed out, making my back arch. I didn't want to talk about her. Not with him. Not with anyone.

Unable to get the words out, I shook my head.

Frowning, posture straightening in the chair, I knew he was going to ask again.

Knock, knock. The swift rapping sound on the closed office doors brought us both around.

Brows coming together, Ethan glanced at the door. "Come in!"

I really hoped it wasn't his dad. That man was scary.

It wasn't his dad but another man in a suit, the kind without a tie. He was tall, but not as tall as Ethan and not nearly as broad either. His build was thin, and his hair was dark brown. He was probably around the same age as Ethan's dad, but there was something different about him.

Besides the fact that he wasn't scary.

He seemed almost… weary, and it was the kind of weariness something inside me recognized well.

I stared at him, unable to look away, fascinated by the lines around his mouth and the creases in his forehead. His hair was brushed back in some kind of style and his clothes screamed of money, but he was more subdued than most of the other rich people I'd met. Like he was missing that dramatic flair that most of the richies possessed.

(Richies = rich people.)

He smiled, seeing Ethan behind his desk, my eyes following his every move. He was graceful in his movements. Something about him seemed oddly familiar even though I knew I'd never seen him before.

"Ethan," the man greeted warmly, his voice calm. "I thought I might catch you here. Always burning the candle at both ends."

What does that mean?

"Henry." Ethan smiled, standing up to offer his hand over the desk. "I didn't know you were back from your trip."

"Just got back this morning. You know we'd never be away today."

Ethan's face changed. "Ah, yes. That is today."

I made a sound, curiosity getting the better of me.

The man called Henry startled, swinging in my direction. His blue eyes widened when he saw me standing there. "Oh, I apologize. I didn't realize you had a guest."

I waved because he was still staring at me, and I didn't know what else to do. "Ah, I can go—" I began, but Ethan shut that down fast.

"No. Stay. Henry, this is Fletcher. Fletcher is a violinist. He's going to be playing at the opening next week."

"Ah!" Henry smiled, warmth coming into his eyes. "A fellow violinist. That must be why you seem familiar."

I swallowed, taking a tentative step forward. "I seem familiar?"

He chuckled. "Yes. It must be the musician in me recognizing the musician in you."

"You're a musician?" I asked, awed.

Henry chuckled.

Ethan coughed a little. "This is Henry Cossgrove. He's a famous violinist. He often plays on Broadway and headlines his own performances."

"Wow," I echoed, breathless. "You're like a real professional."

He smiled. "Well, I suppose so. What did you say your name was again?"

"Fletcher," I said. "Fletcher Brown."

"Hmm, I thought I knew everyone in the string circle. Where have you played?"

I fell silent, suddenly embarrassed. I spent some time staring at my shoes, not knowing what to say.

"Fletcher played at Ivory's last show. It was his first professional performance."

"Ah, yes. I remember hearing about this young man. People were very impressed. They wanted to hire you for many jobs."

Lifting my head, I smiled. "I'm sure I'm not as good as you."

Henry laughed. "I'm old. When you're old like me, you'll have experience."

"Fletcher is very talented," Ethan put in. "A true natural."

"Well, if Ethan thinks so, then that's saying a lot. Usually, my music puts him to sleep!"

"Not true, not true," Ethan hurried to say, but then he glanced at me and winked.

I tried not to laugh, but a giggle escaped anyway.

Suddenly, everything in the room changed. Henry's eyes bore into me, and this weird look crossed his face.

Suddenly very uncomfortable, I started fidgeting with my shirt and wiggling my toes. I didn't mean to offend him by laughing.

Geez. Why are rich people so prickly?

Thankfully, Ethan picked up on whatever was suddenly swirling around and stepped in front of me.

He made a really good shield.

"Uh, I'm sorry. It's been a long day. Travel, you know," Henry explained.

"Of course." Ethan allowed graciously. "Was there a reason you stopped by?"

"Well, no. Yes. I hadn't seen you since we'd been gone, and I wanted to lay eyes on you, make sure you were well. Samantha also sends her love. She's at home resting before this evening." He paused. "Which is also why I wanted to drop by. Just reminding you about tonight."

"I appreciate you coming by. If I'd have known you were back this morning, I would have come over to greet you. Apologies you had to come all the way here. I'll be sure to get a bouquet delivered for Samantha."

"She'd like that." Henry agreed.

"And don't worry. I'll remember, just like every year."

Another wave of some weird emotion went through the

room, and Henry cleared his throat. "Yes. Well, I do appreciate that. You know that Samantha and I… Well, we're fond of you. It means a lot that you're with us on this evening every year."

"Always," Ethan said, the sincerity in his voice making me sway toward him. "And my parents, have you spoken to them?"

"Oh, yes. They'll be with us this evening," he said.

Judging from the way Ethan shifted just slightly, I knew Henry tried to glance at me. "I hope you won't take offense, but I don't think I'll be able to be there in person tonight. I will still absolutely look up, and I will remember and be there in spirit."

"Of course. I know you are very busy. Just having your thoughts is more than enough."

Ethan made a soft sound, and I couldn't help but wonder what this was about.

"Well, I've taken up enough of your time." Henry began. "I'll let you get back to business. Be sure to take care of yourself. Don't work too much or you'll end up like your father!" He cackled, and Ethan let out a laugh.

Peeking around my large shield, I watched the man move to the door. When he turned back, our eyes connected. I looked away first.

"Give Samantha my love," Ethan said smoothly.

"I will do that." Henry agreed, his eyes finding me again. "I'll look forward to hearing your performance."

Nerves coiled in the base of my spine, making my fingers shake. All I could do was nod.

The second Henry was gone, I dragged in air I hadn't realized I was lacking.

"Who was that?" I asked.

"You really never heard of him?" Ethan asked, a little disbelieving.

"All the musicians I know play in the subway, and something tells me that guy has never set foot in one of those before."

"You have a point." Ethan agreed.

"So?" I pressed, so curious. "How do you know him, and what was he inviting you to tonight? Why did you tell him you couldn't go?"

Ethan seemed offended. "I have plans with you."

"But I'm just… me."

While he strolled closer to me, Ethan's eyes stayed intent on my face, making my ears feel hot and the urge to duck my head intense. I didn't, though. I watched him advance until he stopped just inches away.

"Exactly. And *you* are exactly who I want to be with tonight."

A hint of a smile played on my lips. I couldn't lie. His words made me happy. "But what was all that about?"

"Ah, it seems we both have some questions."

My face fell. He wasn't going to let Milly go. "Never mind," I muttered, turning away.

"Hey," he said, drawing me back. "You really don't want to tell me?"

I shook my head, refusing to meet his probing stare.

Long, quiet minutes passed, and I prepared for his anger.

"All right," was all he said, drawing my eyes.

He half smiled, seeing my surprise. Grasping my chin, he leaned in. "Stop expecting me to yell at you, puppy. I won't. You don't have to tell me. There is something I want to show you, though." Releasing my chin to step back, he asked, "Will you come?"

His large hand reached between us, probing for mine.

I already said earlier that my instinct with Ethan was to submit. I really did trust him that much.

So of course my fingers slid easily into his.

Seventeen

*E*THAN

HE WANTED DINNER FROM A CART. ON THE SIDEWALK.

Of all the things...

I gave it to him.

I was incapable of saying no to Fletcher. It was becoming a serious issue.

"I cannot believe this is what you wanted to eat," I said the second he bounced himself into the passenger seat of the Mercedes carrying a white Styrofoam container and clutching a small plastic bag filled with God knew what.

"You said I could pick!" he said happily, practically hugging the food against his chest.

Why are you so damn cute?

"That cannot be healthy," I said, refusing to give in to his adorableness to eye his choice with derision.

The scent of meat, oil, and—well, I didn't know what—wafted from the closed container.

"It has everything!" he argued, flipping the lid, releasing a puff of steam to reveal a huge plate of fried rice, piles of meat, and lettuce, all of it drenched in some kind of white sauce.

"Look! Protein, carbs… It even has vegetables!"

"Iceberg lettuce is barely a vegetable," I told him. "It has no nutritional value, and you might as well just drink water. And what is that sauce?"

"Flavor," he replied, dipping his finger in it to lick it off with a big sigh. "I like this. I haven't had it in so long," he said, looking lovingly at his plate.

And this was why he was always getting his way.

Leaning over, I closed the lid, tucking the tab in to keep it shut. "Well, close it up, then, so it doesn't get cold."

He smiled, and I swear I almost kissed the shit out of him right there.

"Are you sure you don't want some?" he asked. "I can go get you some."

"No, thank you. I'll grab something at home."

"I thought you wanted to show me something."

"We have time."

He didn't question me any further, and honestly, it made me feel the trust he said he had for me. Like wherever we were going, whatever I had in mind, was okay because I was with him.

The second we walked inside the penthouse, I dropped my keys on the table by the door and sighed. His massage had done wonders for my migraine, but I still felt like the pain was coiled and ready to strike.

"I'm going to go change. Just go ahead to the kitchen. I'll be there in a minute."

Heading upstairs, unbuttoning my shirt as I went, I peeled off the business clothes with relief, dropping them in the bin for cleaning.

In the bathroom, I washed my hands and face and ran a brush through my hair. The brush obviously loosened the style I'd had it in all day, taking away the hold of some of the product, but I didn't care. I wanted the day off me so it would only be me and Fletcher.

Back in the closet, I pulled on a black pair of jeans and a

cream-colored rib-knit Calvin Klein turtleneck sweater with a large black CK in the center.

Not wanting Fletcher's food to go cold, I hurried back downstairs, where I found him sitting on a barstool, swinging his feet while staring longingly at his plate.

"You waited for me?" Fondness saturated my tone.

"I didn't have to?" He complained.

Laughing, I backtracked from my path to the fridge to where he sat, leaning down to press a kiss to the top of his head.

He stilled, and I took the chance to grab the container and flip it over, sliding it under him. "Eat."

Not having to be told twice, he grabbed his fork, shoving a huge bite between his lips.

The sounds he made while chewing appreciatively did nothing to quell the exceptional desire I felt for him.

"Is it still warm enough?" I asked, turning from inside the open fridge.

"Yeah," he said, food stuffing his cheeks.

Reaching inside, I grabbed a container with the premade chicken salad Jane stocked for me and the container of balsamic vinaigrette to top it.

Still eating, Fletcher watched me drizzle on the dressing and grab a fork and two waters before sliding onto the stool beside him.

Leaning over, he glanced into my bowl and made a face. "A salad?" he declared. "That isn't gonna fill you up. You're huge."

Amused, I tilted the bowl to the side for him to look again. "It will fill me up. It has grilled chicken, avocado, some nuts, vegetables, even some feta cheese."

"It's cold."

"You don't like cold, do you?"

He shook his head. "I like warm food."

It reminded me of the other night when he said love

meant someone worrying if he was cold. *Did no one ever try and keep you warm?*

"Eat more," I told him softly, directing him back to his plate.

We ate in comfortable silence, occasionally mentioning something mundane, until both our containers were empty and he patted the belly he considered squishy.

"Are you still hungry?" I asked.

He shook his head. "I really appreciate dinner. It was really good, but didn't you say you wanted to show me something?"

Smiling, I glanced around to the large wall of windows, noting it was dark. "I think it's probably about time."

Following my gaze, Fletcher frowned. "For what?"

"Come on," I said, tossing his container and placing mine in the sink. "Let's go."

At the door, Fletcher stopped to put on his shoes, which he'd adorably took off, placing neatly by the stairs.

"Hey!" he said, noticing the sneakers I chose. "We match!"

His foot bumped mine when he put it close, showing off our identical footwear.

Reaching into a nearby concealed coat closet, I pulled out a couple jackets, draping them over my arm. He was wearing a hoodie today, but it was still cold out.

"Out we go," I said, gesturing ahead of me toward the open front door.

"Don't you need your car keys?" he asked, pointing at the dish where I'd dropped them earlier.

"Nope. Don't need the car where we're going."

"We're walking?"

I made a sound, closing the door behind us and heading toward a stairwell on the other side of the elevator.

"I thought we were on the top floor," Fletcher remarked, eyes wide when he saw the rising stairs.

"We are, but there's something more upstairs."

We walked a few flights up, Fletcher asking me with nearly every step what was up here.

Finally at the top, I pushed open the heavy door, motioning for him to go ahead. Both of us stepped onto the large, flat rooftop, everything in front of us dark but the city beyond alight.

"Wait there," I said, moving confidently through the poor lighting to find a small box. Opening it, I flipped the switch, and the area around us illuminated.

"Whoa," Fletch whispered with awe. "This is yours?"

I nodded. "The rooftop space came with the penthouse."

Moving forward, he took in the string lights looped around a wide section of space defining a sitting area with a few all-weather couches, chairs, and a large table in the center. A patterned rug decorated the cement floor, and lit-up lanterns in varying sizes sat everywhere.

"Is that a swing?" Fletcher exclaimed, bypassing all the decorations my designer probably worked hard for to zero in on a partially enclosed hammock swing filled with cushions. It swayed lightly on its chain when Fletcher touched it, eyes turning in question to me.

"Go ahead." I encouraged him, completely enchanted by the delight he found in the simplest things.

With a sound, he climbed in, the entire thing swinging wildly with the way he wiggled around.

The wicker material it was made of allowed me to see through, making out his frame as he shifted and crawled around.

"This is cool!" he exclaimed, his hand appearing out of the opening. "Come see."

As if I haven't seen it before.

I went anyway, bending at the waist to peer in at him. "Having a good time?"

As he patted the cushion beside him, his eyes were beguiling. "Will you fit too?"

We would be squished, but that didn't deter me. If anything, it made me more eager to try.

The swing bobbed and dipped when I gave it all my weight but recovered nicely to sway slowly back and forth.

Fletcher had his legs tucked up underneath him, his knees jutting out on either side.

I tried sitting the same way, but we both wouldn't fit like that, so instead, I pulled him into my center, settling him between my spread legs.

"We fit like this," I murmured against his ear.

"I bet you come up here a lot."

I made a sound, considering. "Not really, actually. It's usually late when I get home from work and I'm too tired to bother."

Sitting up, he glanced over his shoulder. "That's practically a crime. You have a view like this, and you don't even enjoy it." With a little harumph, he turned back, staring out at the glittering city skyline.

"Another version of the city I haven't seen before," he murmured, aptly taking it all in.

Tucking my arms around his waist, I drew him closer, making a low sound.

"We're so high up you can even make out some of the stars you can't usually see from the ground."

Following his gaze, I glanced up. "Make a wish."

"Wishes don't come true," he said, pulling his chin down to look out across the city once more.

"Who told you that?" I asked, jostling him a bit. Hearing that kind of pessimism from him made me upset.

"No one had to tell me. Life taught me."

"Fletcher—" I began, only to be rudely interrupted by a sharp, familiar whistle overhead.

Pop! Pop! Crackle. Shimmer.

The sudden, loud sounds startled Fletcher, and he cowered back into the swing. Into my embrace. Ducking, his arms came up to shield his head with his hands as small trembles quivered his limbs.

"Hey." I spoke quietly, pulling his elbow away from his ear. "It's okay. You're safe. Look up."

Slowly, he withdrew, wincing when more loud explosions filled the night.

"I got you," I vowed, practically wrapping myself around him. "Look, it's just fireworks."

I felt rather than heard him gasp, face turning up toward the sky as the exploding colors lit his features.

"Whoa!" he yelled, a grin filling the lower half of his face. "They're so close!" He pointed as red, green, and gold exploded, streaking the sky with shimmering colors.

"That's because we're up so high. It's why they're so loud too." I spoke right in his ear so I didn't have to yell.

A particularly large one burst overhead, gold dripping in shimmering streaks, the sound of it crackling and the scent of the powdery sulfur filling the air.

Eyes fixed ahead, Fletcher watched as more and more fireworks exploded, exclaiming at every new color and wrinkling his nose at the ones he didn't like.

"Look!" he yelled. "That one is the best!" His hand found mine, wrapping around the place where I held him.

My stomach flipped, and my heart stuttered. I could barely think because of the overwhelming emotions rolling over me and the feel of his hand clutching at mine.

"Ethan, look!" he demanded again, patting my hand impatiently.

I made a sound. "Awesome." I agreed, not really seeing. How could I pay attention to anything when he was this close?

Not even loud, bright explosions in the sky could compare.

I don't know how long they went on for. Frankly, I hoped they lasted forever. The more they lit up the night, the more he leaned into me, face upturned, hand still grasping mine.

The night was cold, but we were warm, the swing swaying slightly as the yearly show captivated the city.

When the grand finale finally began, the sounds and ferocity seemed to grow too much because he turned his face into the side of my neck, lips brushing over my skin.

Curling my palm protectively around his head, I held him close, offering him shelter and enjoying the way he fit so perfectly.

Eventually, the show died down, leaving behind curling smoke, making the sky gray instead of black.

Tentatively, Fletch pulled away from my neck. "Is it done?"

"I think so," I said, smoothing his hair. "Were you scared?"

He snorted. "No way. It was just really loud."

"You don't like loud noises much, do you?"

He shrugged.

Worried he might clam up again, I shifted the subject slightly. "They do this big firework show every year. Have you ever watched it before?"

Surprised, he glanced over his shoulder. "Every year?"

I nodded. "Every year on this day, at this time, for over twenty years."

His eyes went wide. "Really?"

"You've never seen?"

He shrugged again. "I mean, I guess I've noticed fireworks a few times, but I never knew it was on the same date and every year."

I nodded. The Grimms did seem like a world away. Maybe he really hadn't seen them. "This is what Henry came to remind me about."

Stiffening, he pulled out of my embrace, turning slightly between my legs to stare at me in the dim light. "He came to ask you to watch fireworks with him? Why?"

"He and his wife, Samantha, they're the ones who sponsor this every year."

"All of that?" he asked, pointing toward the sky.

"All of it. Every year."

"But why?"

"It's for their son. Today is his birthday."

Amazement lit up his face. "Woah. He must really like that."

A melancholy feeling stole over me, and familiar sadness I'd known almost my whole life filled me. "I'm not sure if he's ever seen them."

"Did he… did he die?" Fletcher asked, his expression worried, his tone apprehensive.

"No one really knows what happened to him. He was kidnapped when he was a baby."

The swing bobbed with the way Fletch jolted. Turning in a full one-eighty, his back going to the opening of the swing, he faced me completely, eyes wide. "Kidnapped?"

I nodded. "Stolen right out of his crib while he was sleeping. They say that when Samantha went to check on him and found him gone, her screams filled the entire Upper East Side."

"Kidnapping a baby sounds like something that would happen in the Grimms, not here in the rich district." Hearing his own words, his eyes widened. "Is that why they did it? For money? Did they want ransom?"

"There was no ransom note. No contact at all when he was taken. I heard—" I stopped. Just because I heard something didn't make it true.

"You heard what?" Fletch asked, leaning in.

"Just rumors," I murmured, eyes gliding over his features. He had a fine-boned face, wide cheekbones that narrowed into a small chin. "I shouldn't repeat things that probably aren't even true."

Grabbing hold of my sweater, he tugged the material as if begging. "But I want to hear."

Chuckling, I bumped his nose with mine. "Fine, but it's probably all gossip. I was just a boy when this happened, and I really don't remember much."

"Did you know the baby?"

"Sure. My family and their family are close."

Fletcher's head bobbed, his eyes asking me to go on.

"Some people whisper it was a crime of a woman scorned. That someone from Henry's past was so jealous he chose to marry someone else that she stole away his child to make him as miserable as her."

"Is that true?" he demanded, leaning in, completely enthralled by the story.

I couldn't help but laugh lightly. "I told you it was a rumor."

"Have you ever asked them if it's true?"

"I would never." I admonished easily. "Henry and Samantha were devastated when their son went missing. It was quite a media circus and a huge scandal here. They searched for the baby for years and years. Samantha was completely inconsolable."

"But they never found him?" Fletcher asked.

"They never did. The police think the person who took him left the country." Gazing over Fletch's shoulder, I looked into the still smoke-heavy sky. "Samantha was never able to conceive another child, and her only son was gone. Even after all these years, they've never given up hope he would be found. They set off fireworks every year on his birthday as a way to honor him, hoping that if by chance he ever saw, he might feel their love."

His little sniffle brought me around. Alarmed, I refocused, pushing away the sad tale to see him and only him. "Fletcher? Are you crying?"

"No," he whimpered.

"Puppy," I whispered, taking his face in my hands.

His damp eyes lifted to meet mine. "They must really love him a lot to celebrate his birthday when he isn't even around."

The emotion I heard in his tone, the unspoken meaning in his words, made me drop my hands from his face to slip them around his waist. "I don't think they will ever stop loving him."

"He's lucky, then," he whispered.

I frowned. Never once in the last twenty-two years did I ever think of that stolen child as lucky. If anything, I felt sad because he was robbed of the life he was meant to have. His parents were robbed of their child and cursed with a barren nursery. It seemed to me that the love they would always have for that boy was almost worthless because he would never know it.

But looking at Fletch now, feeling the energy flowing around him, seeing the way he gazed back at the sky almost longingly, and hearing the way he whispered that lost boy was lucky... I saw things from a completely different perspective.

Perhaps love in any capacity is a gift.

"When is your birthday?" I asked.

His eyes lifted, surprise lighting them for a moment. "Me? It's in February."

I made a soft sound. "And how old will you be in February?"

"Twenty-three."

"Such a puppy," I said, smiling fondly.

He rolled his eyes. "Am not."

"And how do you celebrate your birthday?"

A new mood permeated the air the second the question was out. I could almost feel him withdraw, become somehow smaller.

"Last year, my brothers got me a cake with candles," he

told me, smiling wide. It was an odd contrast to the emotions I felt swirling around us.

"What kind of cake?" I asked, humoring him.

"Chocolate!"

Laughing lightly, I petted his head because, really, I couldn't help it. "And what about when you were young? How did you celebrate with your parents?"

That feeling I'd felt? It quadrupled.

Fletch pulled away from my hand, averting his face. "Birthdays weren't really a big thing in my house."

"So no parties or cake… What about presents?" I asked, already dreading the answer but forcing myself to ask.

Lips rolling in on themselves, he clasped his hands in his lap. "No. We didn't do any of that. She said my birthday wasn't anything to celebrate."

I recoiled from his words, forcing myself not to strongly react. "Who told you that?" I demanded, unable to keep the harshness from my words.

"My mother."

Grabbing him by the shoulders, I gave him a light shake. "Are you saying you've never celebrated your birthday?"

He shook his head adamantly. "No, my bothers celebrate it with me. They have for three years now."

So he was nineteen when he started living with them.

With Fletcher, you learned as much from what he said as what he didn't say, and I was learning very quickly to pay close attention.

"Tell me what you want for your birthday this year. Name it, anything, and it's yours." I promised, wishing I could scoop up the entire world and hand it to him in the palm of my hand.

His nose wrinkled. "That's months away."

My nose wrinkled. "And?"

"And by then, I won't be working for you anymore."

My head tilted. Staring at him intently, I asked, "And you

think we are here right now, like this, because you work for me?"

A look of insecurity crossed his features. "We aren't?"

"I can assure you I do not kiss any of my other employees."

The way his throat bobbed with the force of his swallow drew my eyes and made my heart thud a little heavier than before. "T-then why did you kiss me?"

"You really don't know?"

He shook his head.

"Look at me."

Golden orbs lifted. Shy apprehension lit with a spark of hope. Oh, how I wanted to blow on that spark until it grew into flames of confidence.

"I like you, Fletcher. Not as an employee. Not even as just a friend. But more."

"More?"

"When you aren't at my side, I wonder what you're doing. I worry if you're hungry or if you got enough sleep. I want to buy you a new coat. The only reason I need to see you is because it's what I want."

His eyes widened the more I spoke, eventually so round I could see the white around his entire iris.

Brushing the pad of my thumb lightly along his lower lip, I whispered, "I want to kiss you all the time. Hold you. Protect you. I want you to be mine."

I felt his intake of breath with my thumb, body swaying closer to mine.

Wanting so badly to close the distance between us and crush my lips to his, I almost gave in. At the last moment, I resisted, clinging just enough to reason to hold off until I heard his reply.

"Yours," he echoed almost wistfully.

"Mine," I echoed back.

When our stares collided, the disbelief in his almost hurt

until he punctuated that look with words. "No one's ever wanted me before."

Screw reason.

The rough sound I made cut off abruptly when our mouths crashed. The aggressive way I went for him did not make my lips rough. Just the opposite, in fact. Cajoling and careful, I tugged his lower lip between mine, sucking and loving it with every fiber of my being. When it was fully lavished, I kissed him wholly, moving us together without once breaking contact. I couldn't tolerate distance in this moment, not even a breath of air.

Licking across his upper lip, I solicited entrance, and he opened with a moan of welcome. I loved the way Fletcher kissed back, fully present in the moment, fully present with every caress, but still yielding and soft, still allowing me to lead.

That trust he gave so readily was a heady thing, intoxicating me with the knowledge he knew I would take care of him. As our tongues danced, things I'd learned about him echoed deep inside me. How alone he'd been. How unloved and unwanted he'd felt. I thought of the coat he handed a stranger. How he cried for a kidnapped child he never met. How willingly he smiled despite it all and the almost child-like way he found joy in everything.

It was as though there were two people inside him, one broken and one still full of hope.

How could two such things exist in a single body? How could I make them both mine?

You could hear us breathing heavily before our lips even broke apart. The smacking sound when I finally released made me want to dive right back in.

My palm lay against the side of his neck. The frantic beating of his pulse pounded against my finger. "I want you." I said it again, almost desperate for him to believe me.

"Puppy, tell me you want me too," I rasped, still trying to catch my breath.

A silent moment stretched into two, and I began to panic.

"Fletcher." My thumb tapped the front of his throat.

Avoiding my gaze, he whispered, "But why would you want me?"

A strangled sound erupted from my throat. "Well, why wouldn't I?"

"I'm poor, clumsy, and don't have a job. My clothes are sloppy. I'm from the Grimms… and not even my own mother loves me."

"*Fletcher.*" I scolded him, appalled he would say such things about himself. Appalled that was all he thought he was.

His fingers pressed against my lips, stopping my words but also somehow squeezing my heart. "You're a prince. Rich. Famous. You live above the city," he said, gesturing to the sky. "You have a family name and business, and everyone loves you. You could have anyone you want. You shouldn't choose me."

"I am all those things," I said, making him huff at my arrogance. I laughed under my breath. "Listen," I implored, shaking him gently.

His nod made hair flop into his eyes, and my heart swelled so much from that simple thing.

"If you think I'm so wonderful, you should also know I have impeccable taste, and with it, I choose you. *You.* That means you must be pretty damn incredible."

"But I'm not."

"You are. And you make me feel things in here." Grabbing his hand, I put it against my heart. "Feelings I've never felt for anyone ever before. Emotions I didn't even think were possible. I don't care what clothes you wear or how much money you have. If anything, I like how simple you are. It's refreshing in a world of insincerity."

His brows wrinkled a bit at the last word, and I swore I fell even harder in that second.

"I like that you're clumsy because it gives me a reason to hold on to you. You do have a job. You enchanted me that day with your violin. Music practically pours out of your skin. And as far as your mother goes… well, I don't like her." *Which is a very polite way of saying it.*

The last of my words made him smile just slightly, like the idea of me denouncing that foul woman made him happy. Maybe I should have just said what I really thought of her then.

Too quickly, the secret smile faded, and a frown took its place.

"What?" I practically crooned, reaching to tangle my fingers with his. "Tell me."

"I just don't see how it could work."

"Do you like me?" I asked boldly.

The straightforward question made him gasp, and his fingers quivered lightly against mine. I wasn't a man to beat around the bush, but even I was a little unsettled by my own brashness. Well, not so much the fact that I'd asked, but perhaps because I was afraid of his reply.

If he said no, I'd have to let him go.

If he said no, the kiss we'd just shared would be our last.

Nerves bounced around inside me.

If he says no…

Fletcher

Every word Ethan spoke drew me deeper and deeper into whatever spell he'd cast. He said I enchanted him.

No. It was me who was enchanted.

Never in my entire life had anyone ever looked at me like he did. Like everything I was, was more than enough. Never in my entire life did anyone ever so boldly confess they liked me… that they wanted me.

No one has ever wanted me before.

No one has ever made me feel *wanted.*

But he did.

This perfect prince. He was literally everything I could never be. Strong, capable, insanely good-looking, and so sure of himself. Everyone respected him. Eyes followed him around a room. Not to mention he knew a lot of words.

And he smelled like Christmas trees. My favorite.

It seemed ridiculous he would be sitting here with someone like me. It seemed ridiculous there was a hint of doubt in his blue stare when he asked, *Do you like me?*

How could I not?

"Is this a dream?" I wondered aloud, twisting around to gaze out across the city from inside a swing we shared.

"If this was a dream, I wouldn't be on pins and needles

waiting for your reply." His voice was wry, not at all frustrated as his words might imply.

I turned back, taking in his strong jaw, smooth skin, and perfectly straight nose. I couldn't deny how he made me feel, even if I should. I just didn't know how.

"I like you," I confessed simply.

The blue of his eyes seemed to light up in the night, flames sparking to life and making my stomach feel funny again.

The hand wrapped around mine squeezed. "How do you like me?"

Heat suffused my cheeks, the tips of my ears burned, and I knew I was blushing like crazy. Ducking my head, I searched for a moment alone even though I was totally exposed sitting here in front of him.

"Puppy," he pleaded, using our linked hands to lift my chin.

"I want to be yours," I confessed, the words rushing out as I squeezed my eyes shut.

A moment of silence wrapped around us, and I squinted one eye open to peek at Ethan sitting there staring at me with this look in his eyes.

Is this what love looks like?

"Good boy," he praised, which maybe should have pissed me off, but I really liked it when I made him happy. I really liked being good for him.

The feel of his palm smoothing out my hair made me push into him, so comforted my eyes forgot they were supposed to be closed.

"So," he murmured, still brushing his fingers through my hair. Tingles of pleasure raced across my scalp, making my head swim. "You're mine now."

"You can kiss me now," I told him.

His teeth flashed, the warmth of his laugh shining on me like the sun. "You like kisses, do you?"

I blushed all over again, embarrassed.

Making a grumbly sound in his chest, Ethan brought me even closer, wrapping his legs around me so I was totally enclosed.

"I'll give you as many kisses as you want, puppy," he whispered, brushing his lips across mine.

Ethan's chest supported my weight as I clung to his broad shoulders, fingers deep in the thick material of his sweater as his tongue swept deep inside, brushing over the roof of my mouth.

My tongue wasn't as bold as his, tentatively licking into his mouth for a taste. He moaned with pleasure, and it made the lower part of my stomach tighten. So I did it again, and then our tongues were dancing together as though they heard a song no one else could.

Heaviness settled over my mind, my limbs growing weightless as I gave him more and more of myself, totally enthralled by the sensation of his mouth moving with mine.

I'd never felt like this before, never wanted someone so badly my pulse nearly screamed his name.

When I felt him easing back, I whined, clutching him even tighter, and he chuckled into my mouth, swiping his wide tongue along my lower lip and making me shiver.

"So responsive," he murmured, caressing my face with his heavy-lidded stare.

"You said as many as I wanted," I complained.

His laughter mixed with his breath as his lips brushed across mine once more, again, and then a third time.

"It's cold out here, and I left our coats by the light switch. We should go in."

"I'm not cold," I argued as a strong wind blew, swaying the swing and making goose bumps prickle beneath the hoodie I wore.

"Stay with me tonight."

My stare flew to his.

My body screamed yes. My heart nearly tried to climb out of my chest and into his. I wanted to stay. I never wanted to leave.

But…

But if I stay, will we do more than kiss?

My inexperience suddenly screamed in my face. He would be disappointed.

"I'm a virgin," I blurted out, then slapped my hand over my mouth.

Did I just say that out loud?

Tenderness washed over his face, softening the sharp angles of his bone structure and making my heart beat unevenly.

Tugging my hand away from my mouth, he nodded. "I know."

"How do you know?" I demanded.

"You said you never dated anyone before."

I pursed my lips. "So? Maybe I like to have one-night stands."

"Do you?" he asked, eyes sparkling with humor.

Why is that so funny?

"No," I grumbled.

"Good," he murmured, running a finger over my collarbone. Suddenly, I hated the hoodie between us. "I don't like the idea of anyone else touching you."

Nerves and excitement filled me, making it hard to know which was which.

"I'm not asking you to stay for sex," he stated, still caressing my shoulder. "I won't do anything you aren't ready for."

"But I like kisses." I didn't want him to forget.

His grin was quick and made my belly turn over. "Yes, I got that."

"Can I sleep in your bed again?" I asked.

"Only if I can hold you."

"Okay."

His caressing hand stopped, making me feel somewhat empty. "Be careful climbing out of the swing. Don't fall."

It took a minute to pull my eyes from him to back out of the swing. When I finally managed, he called out.

"Fletcher?"

Pausing, half in, half out, I gave him a questioning stare.

"Thank you."

I frowned. "For what?"

"Being mine."

I tried to hide the smile his words spread on my face as I climbed the rest of the way out, straightening to look out over the city again. It seemed to stretch on forever, glittering with golden lights and echoing with the sounds of urban life. Arms wrapped around me from behind, a small kiss pressed against my ear.

"C'mon, my puppy. Let's go to bed."

I didn't even look back at the view as he led me away. Why would I? What I walked toward was far more enticing than anything behind me.

Nineteen

ETHAN

I WAS ALREADY IN BED WHEN HE EMERGED FROM THE bathroom, freshly showered, wearing nothing but a pair of boxers and a Gucci T-shirt. The shirt was too big, falling almost to the hem of the underwear and swallowing his shoulders whole.

Clutching a white towel in front of him, he made a face, eyes finally landing on where I sat waiting. "Don't you have anything that isn't designer?" he complained.

Pursing my lips, I pondered the question. "I might have some GAP in the back of the closet."

He made a face. "That's designer too."

Not where I came from, but if he thought so, I wouldn't argue.

"Do you not like that shirt? Do you want something else?" I asked, ready to shove the blankets back to do his bidding.

"No," he said quietly. "I like it."

"Come here." I beckoned, patting the space beside me in the bed.

"Your shower is bigger than my bathroom at home." He rambled on, slowly coming forward. "I had hot water the entire time, even after you showered."

I frowned. "I would never shower first if there wasn't enough hot water left for you."

As he stopped beside the mattress, a look of uncertainty crossed his features, which only endeared him to me more.

"You don't need that in bed," I said softly, gesturing to the towel he still clung to.

He glanced down, seemingly surprised he still held it. Looking around for somewhere to put it, he glanced back at me helplessly.

Leaning forward, I snatched it, tossed it to the floor, and pulled back the covers. He gulped, taking in the tank top I wore, eyes sliding over my exposed shoulder and arm.

"Did you change your mind?" I asked, voice neutral, watching his reactions very carefully.

"No." He asserted, scrambling onto the mattress. His knee caught in the hem of the big T-shirt, making him tumble forward into my chest.

Hand splayed over my abdomen, he pushed up, eyes going wide at the exposed skin above the neckline. Hearing him swallow, I bit back a smile and looked down at him instead.

"Hi."

He blushed.

Laughing lightly, I leaned down, pecking a kiss onto his cheek. "Can I turn the light out?"

He nodded, so I leaned over to hit the switch, plunging the room into darkness. Turning back, I grinned wide, seeing how he rolled away onto his side, showing me his back. As I stared, his fingers spider-crawled toward the sheet at his hip to tug it up and over him, concealing everything but the top of his head.

"Are you scared of me?" I asked, lips still twitching.

Why is he so cute?

"No." His voice was muffled from the sheet.

"Don't you want a good-night kiss?"

The top of his head bobbed.

"Come over here and get it, then."

"Never mind," he called, burrowing even farther down into the blanket.

I couldn't hold my laughter back any longer, and it rang out in the darkness. Beneath the blankets, I slid closer, snaking an arm around his waist to spoon him.

Putting my lips right against his ear, I whispered, "You know when you slept here the first time, I was going to put you in the guest bedroom, but you clung to me so tight you only let me put you in this bed."

He gasped, practically elbowing my midsection with the way he turned. "I did not!" he argued.

"You did." I confirmed. "I guess you liked me even then."

"You tease me." His lower lip jutted out.

Closing the distance between us, I fused our mouths, swallowing down the small groan he let free on contact. Warm friction crackled as our lips rubbed together, the tip of his tongue cautiously bumping against mine, seeking more.

Palming his hip, I deepened the kiss while fighting the urge to roll him under me.

We kissed endlessly, his hand fisted in the center of my tank, gripping tight as if I might run off without him.

I wouldn't dare go anywhere without you.

His mouth grew heated, lips slick and swollen. Eventually, his tight grip released, fingers dancing restlessly against my chest.

I knew his body wanted things his mind wasn't ready for yet, and I knew if he grew any more daring, it would be an uncomfortable night for us both.

Gently but firmly, I eased him back, shifting so he wouldn't feel the raging hard-on inside my boxer briefs.

He made a sound of protest, eyes fluttering thickly to stare at me with dazed eyes. "Ethan."

"Go to sleep now, love," I said, voice hoarse.

The use of the endearment cleared his eyes, but then they clouded over again. "Kiss me again."

I groaned, glancing down at his plump, glistening lips. I wanted nothing more than to bury my tongue between them again. "I'll kiss you again tomorrow."

"Please," he whispered, eyes pleading.

"My little kiss monster." I groaned, dipping my head once more.

His contended sigh fanned out over my lips, his breath tasting faintly of mint and something sweeter. Surprisingly, he rolled from his back onto his side, bringing us chest to chest while his hand slipped into the hair at my nape to tug me closer.

Blood near to boiling, my arm wrapped around his waist, yanking him fully against me. I felt his nostrils flare when he felt the obvious bulge I was sporting. I thought maybe it would shock him enough to pull back.

It didn't.

He kept on kissing, rubbing against me like a cat.

He was hard too, and it only took a moment for his erection to meet mine, the friction so delicious that our lips broke apart, both of us moaning.

His head buried in my neck, the fingers in my hair tightened as he thrust against me again, clearly craving more.

When he found what he wanted, his opened-mouthed heavy panting brushed against my neck. God, he was sinful. Innocent and open, not realizing that literally everything he did made me want to claim him completely.

The amount of self-restraint I showed was frankly impressive, but if he thrust into me one more time, I might snap.

Catching his hips, holding them firm, I whispered his name.

He looked up from where he hid in my neck, but the

lustful haze wrapped around him probably hindered his sight.

"We have to stop now," I told him patiently, my own cock nearly screaming.

Blinking, his eyes cleared just slightly, teeth sinking into his lower lip. "I don't want to."

"What do you want?" My voice was strained. The urge to give in was so powerful.

"More." He beseeched, trying to thrust up again. "It hurts," he whimpered.

"All right." I soothed, smoothing a palm over his hip. "I'll take care of you."

His low whine filled the bedroom and sent my protective instincts into overdrive, his need the only thing I could focus on.

Pushing him into the mattress, my hand went between us to lightly brush over his throbbing length.

His back arched instantly, pushing his hips up, offering his body to my hands.

"Can I take these off?" I asked, tugging the boxers at the waistband.

He nodded instantly, but his quick assent did not make me happy. Releasing him, I planted both hands on either side of his body to stare down. "Look at me, puppy."

His eyes opened.

"Can I touch you? We don't have to have sex, but I can make you feel good."

"Yes, Ethan," he slurred, voice thick with desire and need.

Leaning in, I licked his lips, tasting those sweet words off his tongue before kissing across his jaw, over his ear, and then down his neck. His head fell to the side, offering me more access so I kissed and sucked a path down to the collar of the T-shirt, tugging the neckline away so I could suck his collarbone between my lips.

The action made his hips buck up, and I lowered mine a bit so his lower half brushed against mine.

The meeting of our clothed members made my forehead fall onto his shoulder, no longer able to kiss. Together, our hips rolled, cocks rubbing against the other.

Lips latching back onto his collarbone, I licked and sucked as our bodies moved together, making love as if the clothes weren't between us.

Moving down, I kissed across his clothed chest, feeling the way his fingers played in my hair as I moved.

When I made it down to his hips, I glanced up his body, noting the way his chest rose and fell heavily. "I'm taking these off now."

He lifted his hips in invitation, and I wasted no time peeling the boxers down his long, lean legs to discard them somewhere across the room.

His cock bounced up, nearly standing off his flat stomach, glowing in the darkness. Even though I considered Fletcher small, his manhood was not. It was much like his hands, like it waited for the rest of his body to grow into it. His girth was not as wide as mine, but he was strong and beautiful, the tip already glistening with arousal.

"You're so beautiful," I whispered, still taking in the part of him no one else had been permitted to see. His thighs were smooth and soft, his balls already drawn tight against his body.

A whimper above made me look up, my heart tumbling when I saw his flushed cheeks, heavy eyes, and thoroughly kissed lips. He practically vibrated with need and was looking at me to fulfill it.

"Don't you ever let anyone else see you like this," I growled, wrapping my fist around him, enjoying the low hiss from between his lips.

Every pump of my hand contracted his lower stomach, which was exposed because the shirt had ridden up his body.

Wanting to see more, I pushed the fabric up around his chest, taking in his narrow waist and soft belly. Pulse hammering with overwhelming love and lust, I leaned down to press a kiss beside his belly button.

He murmured something incoherent, and I smiled, kissing again, then leaning down to lick over the top of his sensitive head.

Both of us groaned, him from my tongue and me from his salty taste. Parting my lips, I sank down over him, my heated mouth enclosing his arousal, sinking until my lips nearly hit his base.

A strangled sound ripped out of him, his body bucking up off the bed. Using my hand, I pinned him down, dragging my lips back up his dick, only to slide back down again.

When his tip hit the back of my throat, my name fell from his lips, and my heart swelled. Pulling up, I swirled my tongue around his bulbous head, lavishing it with attention and making sure it was good and slick.

He was breathing heavy when I lifted my head, wrapping my fist around it again and sliding my thumb over his leaking slit.

Hands gripping the sheets at his hips, he lifted his head, blissed-out eyes finding mine. "Kiss me," he slurred, releasing the sheets to grab at me.

When I crawled up his body, we sank into each other, his kisses more eager than ever before. The salty tang on my tongue added another layer to the kiss as his arms slipped around my waist, asking for more of my weight, and I was in no mind to deny.

The second our bodies touched, we started moving together, hips thrusting, his hot, wet cock pushing up to find mine.

Fletcher tugged at my waistband, making an impatient sound.

My boxers joined his in the darkness, and then our overheated bodies met for the first time with nothing between them.

Gasping, my head dropped onto the pillow above his shoulder, an intense fog of need concealing us from the rest of the world. The silk sheets were cool compared to the burning temperature of our skin, the contrast only heightening my senses.

Pushing up with one arm, I made just enough room between us for my hand. His cock was silky against mine, still damp from my mouth, offering just enough lubrication for our throbbing rods to slide easily together with sweet satisfaction.

Grasping us both in one hand, I pumped slowly at first, letting him get used to the feel and rhythm of me. It didn't take long for his little whines to spur me on, quickening the pace and pressure I used. Heavy breathing and low moans were our only verbal communication as we rode a wave of connection and need, both rocking needily into my hand.

I loved the way he pulsed and throbbed, the strain in his body growing and growing until he was wound so tight I thought he might snap.

Despite the trembling of my arm that held me over him, I didn't stop, instead leaning into his ear to coax. "Come for me, puppy."

His breath hitched when he thrust up into my hand one last time. A beautiful low keening sound filled the room as white ribbons of his release shot out, decorating his belly and my hand. I worked him through his orgasm, riding the blissful wave alongside him as he strained and bucked, gasping in between with pleasure.

When his spent body fell limp against the sheets, I gazed down, seeing the mess he'd made of us both and feeling extremely proud but also very possessive.

"That's my good boy," I murmured, laying my lips against his dampened forehead.

He smiled softly, eyes fluttering when I lifted my head. "Now you," he said, thrusting lazily against my still hard erection.

"Don't worry about me," I said, leaning in to kiss him again, but he turned his face, denying me.

"You."

Already wound tight and holding myself back, his little plea and blissed-out state was all it took for me to acquiesce. Wincing a little when I shifted back onto my knees (seriously, my arm was numb), I shook out my hand, staring at him hotly while dragging my fingers through the pearly liquid all over his stomach.

Eyes widening in surprise, he watched as I swirled around and then wrapped the cum-coated fingers around my throbbing length.

Golden eyes flared. Even in the darkness, I saw how the action affected him, and a low groan vibrated my throat. "So silky," I whispered, my hand easily sliding along my shaft from his juice. "You feel good, love."

I saw his gaze avert. Even completely turned on, he was shy. Reaching for his hand, I wrapped it around my cock, making him gasp.

Before he could pull away, my hand covered his and started to move. "Help me," I murmured, leaning over him again to capture his lips.

The kiss was passionate, my teeth nipping at his lower lip as our hands sped up, bringing me to the very brink.

Breathing heavily, I dipped my head into his shoulder, and the second his fingers tightened, my own release spilled out all over our hands, mixing with his.

He kept pumping even when my hand fell away, staying with me, prolonging the pleasure because his touch was just that euphoric.

When I finally collapsed, my arms slid between him and

the mattress, hugging his frame so I could roll, draping him across my chest.

The only sounds in the room were that of our breathing as we lay in postcoital bliss, my fingers slipping beneath his T-shirt to drag lightly along his spine.

We hadn't even had sex, but I was more satiated than probably ever before. The way he responded, the sounds he made, and the way he just let go when I told him to… I was obsessed.

He was it for me.

It was him and only him.

"Fletch," I murmured, caressing down his spine once more. "Are you okay?"

When he didn't answer, all thought of my own bliss blew away, and concern took over. Hooking my hands under his arms, I lifted him a bit, his body like a rag doll when I looked into his face.

"Fletcher. Are you okay?" I repeated.

His eyes lifted, awe and fuzziness still in their depths. "I didn't know it could be like that."

"Good or bad?"

"So good."

I smiled, relief washing through me like a rainbow brightening up a stormy sky. "So you're okay."

Forehead wrinkling, he said, "How come it's never like that when I do it?"

A laugh burst out of me, bouncing around the room. "Puppy," I said, still laughing.

He scowled. "Seriously, E. How come it feels better when you do it?"

All the laughter died, and emotion clogged my throat. "E?"

He shrugged. "It just came out." Suddenly self-conscious, he averted his eyes. "Is it okay?"

"Oh, baby, you can call me whatever you want," I crooned, snuggling him into my chest once more.

He tried to wiggle away, but my arms were too tight around him.

"Baby?" he complained. "No way. Puppy is bad enough!"

"Puppy." I corrected, rubbing a hand over his hair.

Propping his chin on my chest, he gazed up. "Was I—" He paused, self-doubt befalling his features. "Did you like it too?" The second the words were out, he bit down on his lower lip.

He squeaked when I rolled, pinning him into the mattress with my body. Staring until his eyes reluctantly met mine, I smiled. "You were so perfect."

Hopeful eyes widened. "Really?"

"I promise."

A beautiful bright smile spread over his features.

I love you so much.

"Come on," I said, trying not to let emotion pull me under. "Up you go."

His arms closed around my neck when I stood and lifted him out of the bed. "Go where?"

"You made a mess of us. We need to clean up."

"You did it too." He accused me as I carried him to the bathroom.

I made a sound of agreement. "That's why I'm coming too."

It didn't take long to clean us both up and dress.

Just as I was about to tug on a fresh tank, his hand bunched in the material, tugging it away. "Can you leave it off?" he asked, voice small.

Smiling, I dropped it immediately, drawing him into my bare chest.

"Better?"

He nodded, cheek rubbing against my chest.

Back in bed, we settled under the blankets. This time,

Fletch didn't roll away, allowing me to tuck him into my side with his cheek pillowed on my bare shoulder. One of his long legs pushed between mine, tangling us together, making him sigh contentedly.

"You make me feel safe," he confessed quietly in the dark.

That seemed to be something very important to Fletcher and something he clearly wasn't used to.

"Go to sleep now, puppy. I'll keep you safe." I assured, tucking him just a little closer.

I always took care of what was mine, and Fletcher was most definitely mine.

Fletcher

Happiness was scary.

Scarier than being alone, more intimidating than misery.

I didn't really realize it until now. Until now, I guess I kind of just went along with life, accepting the things I had no power over, learning to live with things I didn't like.

Unfairness was just something to be endured, and not being wanted was my fate.

Being angry about it seemed like a waste of time, so instead of wallowing in the things I didn't like, I looked at things I did. I let the sound of my violin offer escape, the enclosed area of the subway be my hideaway. But I couldn't really say I was ever happy. Maybe before, I would have said I was.

Before I sampled what real happiness tasted like.

Before Ethan.

And now?

Now I was more afraid than ever before.

That was the about with being a misfit, about never really belonging anywhere or to anyone. It was hard to be afraid when you were already at the bottom, when there was nothing to lose.

Sure, after I met Neo and my brothers, things were better,

but something was always missing. There was always a sense of gnawing loneliness, a part of me always unsettled.

It had only been a few days since I'd sat on Ethan's rooftop and he confessed he wanted me. A few days of endless kisses, touches that made me lose my head, and for an entire lifetime of gnawing loneliness to begin to fade.

I did still feel like something was missing, but the darkness of that wasn't as black, almost like that feeling would eventually be swallowed up by Ethan too.

Now happiness didn't mean enduring.

Happiness meant the scent of Christmas trees all year round, pancakes, comfortable shoes, silky sheets, and blue eyes that looked at me like I was enough, no matter how empty I was.

And warmth.

So much warmth.

Suddenly, I had something to lose. No. Not something. *A lot.* I had so much I could lose. The weird feeling always in my stomach was back, but this time, it was worse than before —and this time, I knew the cause.

Love.

Fear.

Loving someone so much so fast and afraid they would turn out to be like everything else in my life: a disappointment.

I got attached to things easily. I was pretty tenderhearted, which I understood made me weak. Even still, I'd managed to protect myself, probably because if I hadn't, I'd already be dead.

But Ethan snuck in. I hadn't even seen him coming. He was in deep, deeper than anyone else had ever been. Which meant he had a lot of power.

What if it is too much?

What if he realizes what she *told me all along?*

That I'm nothing. Nothing at all.

"Are you sure you don't want to just hang at my place today while I'm at work?" I felt Ethan's sidelong glance from the driver's seat, but I didn't turn to meet his stare.

Gazing out the window at the grim part of the city, I replied, "No. I haven't been home in a while."

When Ethan said nothing, I spoke again. "You should have just let me take the subway. There was no reason for you to drive me all this way."

"If I let you take the subway, I wouldn't be able to hold your hand right now," he crooned, smoothly cupping his hand around mine.

My heart squeezed and an uncomfortable ache tightened my chest, but I didn't pull away. I couldn't. His affection meant more to me than probably anyone could ever know.

Even though it pained me, I still wanted it. Even if I was afraid, he would eventually take it away. I would accept it while it lasted.

And this was exactly why I needed to go home.

Without even thinking, I clenched my fingers around his.

How can he make me feel so scared but also so safe?

"What are you going to do today?" he asked, pushing our tangled hands farther into my lap.

It's like he knows I need him.

I shrugged, turning back to the window. The sky was dull, not particularly sunny and not particularly dark. The clouds were thick and grayish-white, hovering over everything with somberness. Wind blew, scattering leaves from trees I never saw over the scuffed sidewalks along with the occasional (okay, more than occasional) piece of trash.

The Grimms seemed like such a long way from where we'd just been. How can two places be so close yet so far apart?

"I'll come back and pick you up tonight when I get off work. Probably around seven."

"No," I said, genuinely wanting to say yes but not allowing

myself. I needed time. Time to think. To breathe. To learn how to endure this new fear.

Because really, that's what I would do. Endure. Because once again, I wasn't strong enough to walk away.

Surprised, Ethan whipped his head around to fully glance at me. "No?"

"Watch out!" I yelled, my entire body tensing, anticipating the collision from the sudden stop in front of us.

A series of movements happened all at once, Ethan graceful and calm despite my flinching anxiety.

His hand pulled free from mine. One steely muscled arm stretched across my chest, holding me back against the seat. The Mercedes braked hard and fast, still managing to make the abrupt stop smooth.

The brake lights of the cab in front of us disappeared because we were so close to his back end, but there was no crunch of metal or crash.

"It's okay." Ethan soothed. "Everything's fine."

I collapsed into the seat, his arm still stretched out like a giant shield. As I glanced at it, my chest tightened.

His first instinct was to protect me.

"I'm sorry I scared you. Are you all right?" he asked, reaching around to cup the back of my head.

My eyes tried to flutter closed, but I forced them to remain open. "I didn't think you saw," I murmured, watching the cabbie in front speed off.

His low chuckle was like a blanket, and when his fingers left my hair, I really wanted to complain for him to put them back.

"I'll always pay attention to anything around us that can do you harm."

I turned my head to stare out the window again, letting his words go without reply.

A few minutes later, we turned onto my street, the bar a welcome and familiar sight.

"Thank you for the ride," I said, fingers wrapping around the door handle.

"Not so fast." His voice left no room at all for argument.

Slumping back into the seat, I reluctantly looked up. Gentle blue eyes stared back, watching me with patience and care.

"You don't want me to pick you up after work?"

Yes. So much. "No. I'll just stay here tonight."

"Why?"

"Because this is where I live."

The air around him changed just slightly, and creases formed between his eyes. I knew he wanted to ask for more answers, and if he did, I might not be able to deny him.

Leaning over, I pressed a kiss to his cheek. His expression had changed to one of surprise and happiness by the time I pulled back.

"I'll see you later, okay?" I said, smiling as I opened the door to exit.

"Puppy!" he called, making me wince.

I knew I wouldn't get away that easily.

Rotating, I took my time lowering myself back into the open door. "Yes?"

"If you need anything, call me."

All the nervousness I felt vanished without a second thought. I smiled. The simple offer of him just being there made me feel so full. "Okay. Thank you."

He held out my violin case, reminding me I'd left it inside.

I took it, hugging it against my chest when I stepped farther onto the sidewalk so he could drive away.

When the shiny white Mercedes turned off the street, disappearing from sight, my anxiety came back tenfold, and I had to resist the urge to chase after his car to crawl back inside.

Instead, I went up to the apartment I shared with my

brothers, listening to all the locks slide free for them to allow me inside.

"Well, look what the cat dragged in," Earth said the second he saw me. His scowl was the same as always, but his eyes swept me from head to toe as I came inside.

"You knew where I was," I muttered. "It's not like I didn't call."

"We thought you abandoned us!" Beau yelled dramatically from behind his wall of computers.

"Whatever," I muttered, setting aside my violin case to drop on my knees to greet Snort who was lumbering around my feet, wagging his entire back end. "Hey, boy!" I said, rubbing his ears. The loud sound of his breathing increased, his underbite on full display. "Did you miss me?"

His entire stout body flopped onto the floor, offering me his belly to rub. The entire time, I felt Earth staring, the back of my neck prickling with awareness.

Moments later, the dog gave a loud sneeze, jumped up, and wandered off to his water bowl.

When I stood, I nearly fell back because there was a wall of two brothers standing side by side, glaring expectantly. They mirrored each other's positions, arms folded over their chests, feet apart. Earth's eyes were dark and fierce. Beau's eyes were green and not nearly as intimidating… but still, I was unsettled.

"Why are you staring at me like that?" I demanded.

"We're waiting for an explanation," Beau said, and Earth grunted in agreement.

"An explanation for what?"

"Why you haven't been home for days."

"I told you—" I began, but Earth cut me off.

"Yeah, yeah, we got the phone calls. We let it slide then, but you're home now and we want more than a flimsy excuse about a contract and a job."

Scowling, I reached into the fleece-lined hoodie I was

wearing for the envelope full of cash and a copy of the signed contract.

Earth's eyes narrowed. "Nice jacket," he said. "New?"

"It's Ethan's," I mumbled, remembering the way he refused to let me out of the apartment this morning without something warm over my long-sleeved T-shirt. It was gray and had some kind of thick, ultra-soft lining inside that felt like fur (he promised it wasn't real). Even the inside of the hood was lined with it, and the cuffs around the wrists were tight so it kept the cold wind from blowing against the skin on my wrists.

Now that I had some cash, I should go and buy myself a new coat and maybe some jeans that weren't too big. Then maybe Ethan wouldn't keep wrapping me up in his clothes.

But I kinda like it when he does.

No. You have to take care of yourself, Fletch.

"You're wearing his clothes now?" Beau commented, arching a red brow.

I ignored them both to pull out some money, hastily counting out what I owed. "Here," I said, handing the first stack to Earth.

Glancing between me and the money, he said, "What's that for?"

"Rent. I'm behind two months. Now I'm caught up."

"Fletch—" He began, but I halted whatever he would say.

"Take it, Earth. I earned this. Well, I will when I play at the event, and we all pay rent here."

He nodded once, taking the cash and slipping it into his pocket.

I felt better watching the money disappear like a weight I didn't know I carried was suddenly lifted off my shoulders.

Next, I counted out some more cash and handed it to Beau.

"You don't owe me any money," he said, backing away from it.

"I've been borrowing your clothes and shoes, and you put money in my pocket almost every time I leave this apartment."

"That's what brothers are for," he argued.

"You don't do that with Earth and Neo."

His face changed like he'd swallowed a lemon, but he didn't argue because I was right.

Reluctantly, he took it, holding it at his side like he didn't want to put it in his pocket.

"I'll get groceries for the house too since I haven't for a while."

"Why are you doing this?" Beau asked.

"Doing what? Acting like an adult?"

Both of them shared a look, then gazed back at me.

"I told you I'm not your responsibility, and I won't keep taking money from you. I got a job. I'm paying for my own way."

"And what happens when this job is done?" Earth challenged.

"I have more offers."

"You took them?" Beau asked.

"Not yet," I mumbled. *That scares me too.* "But I will."

I didn't like being afraid. Not at all.

"So you won't let us help you, but you'll wear designer clothes from Ethan and let him get you jobs," Earth deadpanned.

His words pierced me, stinging like an open cut caught in the rain. Why was it that everything I did was always somehow wrong? Why did I always seem to disappoint everyone?

My fist closed tight around the envelope I held, the crinkling filling the room. Filling my lungs with a deep breath, I stared straight at my dark-haired brother.

"Ethan didn't get me those jobs. *I* got them because I play well. I got them before I even started..." *What to say?* "Before I knew him. Ask Ivory."

Beau slapped Earth on the shoulder when he stood there stonily, staring without a word. He sighed. "I didn't mean to imply you couldn't get a job on your own. We all know how good you are at violin. You just... disappeared with that richie for days, and now here you are handing out cash like it grows on trees."

"I'm just paying what I owe!" I yelled, frustration boiling over. "You guys should understand that!"

"We do," Beau said, always the calmer voice of us all. "It's good you are settling what you owe. We just want you to know that if you need anything, you can come to us, okay? We're family."

Shoulders slumping, I stuck the envelope back into my pocket with a nod. "I know. Thank you."

My stomach grumbled, and I rubbed at it. I thought about going to the kitchen for a snack.

"Fletch," Earth said.

I forgot about food, and embarrassingly, I felt my lower lip wobble. Rather than let it betray me like that, I sank my teeth into it to make it stop.

"You know I'm just worried, right?" he said after a minute, his tone low and serious.

I rushed forward and hugged him, wrapping my arms around his waist. "I didn't mean to make you mad," I said against him.

"I'm not mad."

"Yes, you are," I argued.

"He's always mad." Beau compromised.

He was right. Earth was permanently grumpy.

"I'm not mad at *you*." He tried again.

I pulled back. "Really?"

He grunted.

I smiled.

The smile stretching my face didn't last long because he pinned me with another one of his piercing stares. "What's going on with you and Ethan?"

A little squeak left my lips, and I backed away from my larger brother. "Me and Ethan? Nothing. Why would you ask?"

"Even you aren't that clueless, Fletch," Beau added.

I gasped. "You're ganging up on me too?"

"You don't stay at some guy's house for days because of a job," Earth deadpanned.

"He's our friend!" I argued.

Earth lifted both eyebrows. "So you and him are friends?"

Well, not exactly. I was pretty sure friends didn't kiss like that, and they definitely, *definitely* did not get hand jobs from each other.

I didn't like to lie. I wasn't good at it and it seemed like a bother, but I wasn't sure what we were. Well, I wasn't sure I was ready to admit it.

I mean, hadn't I just practically run from his car because of it?

"I-I'm not sure," I stuttered in lieu of a direct answer.

"You know we don't care about that, right?" Beau said. I could feel his eyes follow me as I went to the couch to flop down.

"About what?" I wondered, confused.

"If you like him."

I blinked, still not really getting what he was trying to say.

Earth muttered something under his breath and flung out a hand. "If you're gay! We don't care if you're gay!"

My shoulders left the back of the couch, eyes wide. "I don't think I'm really gay. But if I was, why would you care?"

Earth groaned, and Beau laughed. "We wouldn't."

It never even occurred to me that they might care if I liked Ethan because he was a man. Why would they care if I didn't?

"So you don't like him?" Earth asked, his voice strained.

"Of course I like him."

"For the love of God…" Earth muttered, making Beau pat him on the shoulder.

"So you *like him* like him, but you aren't gay and you aren't sure if he likes you?" Beau surmised.

"Oh, no, he likes me. He told me."

The silence in the room stretched on. Both of them just stared at me until I felt an uncomfortable heat creep up the back of my neck.

"Please help us understand." Earth nearly choked, dropping onto the coffee table.

Beau stifled a laugh.

"Do you have to be gay to like another man?" I wondered. "I just like everyone. That's what I told Ethan."

Beau laughed again. "If anyone asks, just tell them you're bi."

I shrugged. *Why would anyone ask me that? I don't really understand the need to label it like that. I mean, if Ethan was a girl, would I have to tell people I was gay or bi? It seems stupid. Can't I just like who my heart picks?*

"So you and Ethan are dating," Beau announced.

I nodded.

"Why didn't you just say that?" Earth bellowed.

I winced. "You didn't ask."

"I need a beer," Earth declared, storming from the living room into the kitchen.

"It's not even eight a.m.," I whispered to Beau.

"He's been worried."

"I don't know why. Ethan's apartment is very safe."

"Not about your physical safety," Beau returned, but then he frowned. "But about that… Have you and Ethan…?"

Shatter!

The sound of glass breaking in the kitchen made both of us look up.

Earth appeared in the doorway of the kitchen, eyes wide and wild. "Did he touch you?"

I dove behind the tall back of the couch, cheeks heating like they were on fire.

"I'm going to kill him!" Earth roared.

Forgetting all about my mega embarrassment, I leaped up and over the sofa, rushing to stop him as he stormed toward the door.

"No!" I demanded. "Earth, no!"

Earth paused, and I kind of wanted to laugh because he looked like a charging bull. But I held it back because there was also a murderous sheen in his dark eyes, and I knew—we all knew—what he was capable of.

An announcement of murder from Earth was practically a promise.

"You promised no more bad stuff!"

"I promised no more jobs," Earth growled. "I didn't agree to not take out perverted rich dudes who take advantage of my little brother."

"He didn't take advantage of me!"

Earth's nostrils flared. "That makes it worse!"

Moving me aside, he went toward the door. I spun to look at Beau, who was looking more alarmed than usual.

"We didn't do anything!" I yelled.

Earth stopped, hand on the doorknob. "He hasn't touched you?"

"Well, I mean… we kissed."

Releasing the handle, Earth spun. "Is that all?"

Is that all? I giggled. Clearly, he'd never been kissed the way Ethan kissed.

My reaction did nothing to soothe his raging assassin.

"That's all." I promised.

Look, I said I didn't like to lie, and I wasn't that good at it. But this was do or die.

Literally.

Besides, it wasn't like we'd had sex.

Just the thought of it sent a rush of heat and blood down south. The unforgettable image of Ethan's silhouette hovering over me in the dark bedroom, his hands slipping over my skin, grabbing onto the neediest part of me…

"Fletcher!"

I snapped out of it. "Huh?"

"He hasn't taken advantage of you?"

I shook my head. "No."

It was the absolute truth because everything that happened between Ethan and me was totally consensual.

"Fine. I'll let him live. For now," Earth announced.

It was ridiculous he acted like he could decide… but still, I was relieved.

"Thank you."

Suddenly, everything we'd just talked about became more of a realization, and awkwardness descended over the entire apartment. I gazed around at some of the art Neo painted all over the walls, but really, I couldn't be distracted from this wild conversation.

Beau cleared his throat first. "Well, since it's already kinda awkward, I just want to say if you ever have any, ah, questions, you can come to me."

I felt my nose wrinkle. "About what?"

Beau sighed. "Sex."

My eyes grew wide. "You've had sex with a man?"

Earth started to laugh, true laughter that rang out through the room.

Beau choked, green eyes nearly falling out of his face. "Ah, no."

"Then how would you know anything?" I muttered.

Earth laughed again.

I don't know why he found this so funny.

"I can Google it," Beau mumbled, itching behind his ear, his face suddenly as red as his hair.

All three of us started to laugh, anger and awkwardness suddenly giving way to humor. When at last the laughter faded away, we all stood there in the middle of the living room, gasping for breath.

"So," Beau said, voice still kind of breathless. "Everything between you and Ethan is all good?"

Dividing my stare between my brothers, I lied again. "Yeah. It's great."

This lie was a little harder to pass off because it wasn't do or die. And because as far as Ethan was concerned, everything was all good. It was me with the problem, me who was afraid.

Twenty-One

Ethan

Something was going on with him, and it was affecting me. I wasn't used to other people's moods influencing mine or worrying about someone when they weren't in sight.

He said he wanted to stay at his place tonight. Just the thought of going home to a dark, empty penthouse was depressing.

After a few days of him bouncing around, exclaiming over everything, eating copious amounts of food, and clinging to me in his sleep, I was… well, addicted.

The genuine way in which he did everything made me feel as if I'd just woken up from a lifetime of slumber.

Which was likely why his morose mood in the car this morning clung to my clothes like bad cologne, lingering all day and invading my senses. *It seemed he was trying to put distance between us, as if he were pushing me away.*

I couldn't accept it.

The hands on the clock neared six, and I was almost done with the pile of work in front of me. After work, I would go to the Grimms and make him say again that he didn't want to come home with me.

I'd make him tell me why.

After completing the last report with focused precision, I

snapped the folder closed, letting out a breathy sigh. I already felt a bit lighter knowing I was going to go to him.

With Bree gone for the day, I tidied up my desk and was about to head out when my door pushed open, my father filling the doorway.

"Ethan!" he called jovially.

Attention snapping up, I gave him an odd look because he was using his "work" voice with me and it was after hours.

"Father?"

"It appears that we came at the perfect time. You just finishing up for the day?"

We? I nodded. "Yes, I'm on my way out."

"I have a surprise for you," he said, turning sideways to glance behind him.

What is he up to now?

"Sienna, honey, don't be shy. Come meet my son, Ethan."

The internal groan I let loose could have ruptured an organ. Maybe if it had, I would have been able to get out of this.

The look on my face must have reflected my inner thoughts because I got that parental death glare that promised unbearable pain if I didn't straighten up.

I didn't understand why that worked even when you were an adult.

Because you let it.

I really had no time right now for my painfully truthful inner dialogue.

Plastering on the well-mannered aura everyone knew me for, I watched as Sienna Pope gracefully stepped through the door.

I'd give my father credit. He definitely knew how to pick them. Sienna was a gorgeous woman, one that would definitely inspire jealousy and trips to the nip-and-tuck doctor for the women of the Upper East Side.

Except of course Ivory. Ivory White was the fairest of them all.

Sienna came close, though, with long, thick chestnut hair that waved past her shoulders, accentuating a California golden-hued complexion, warm-brown eyes, dainty nose, and high cheekbones that were expertly contoured and delicately blushed.

She was tall, probably around five feet seven—*around Fletcher's height*—with a long, slender build. Her attire was, of course, impeccable with a pale-pink tulle skirt that swished around her ankles. She also wore golden, strappy high-heeled sandals and a white lace top tucked in. The golden clutch in her manicured hand boasted an exclusive label on the clasp. Thin golden bracelets tinkled around her wrists, and golden rings adorned several of her long fingers.

"Ms. Pope," I said smoothly, coming around my desk. "I've been anticipating your arrival. If I had known it was today, I would have met you at the airport."

"Please, call me Sienna," she said, glossy lips parting to show perfectly straight white teeth. "And nonsense on the airport. You have better things to do."

"You take precedence over it all!" my father declared, stepping fully into the office behind her and giving me another look.

"You'll have to excuse me. I forgot my manners momentarily. You must be used to that by now, though, as I'm sure so many do the same upon first making your acquaintance."

So lame.

But also entirely expected of me.

Moving forward, I grasped her hand, bringing it up to press my lips against the back of it. "Such a pleasure to finally meet you."

Behind us, my father preened like a ridiculous peacock.

She laughed lightly, the bracelets on her wrist lending a musical background. "It's also a pleasure to meet you. Are you sure we aren't interrupting? Your father assured we wouldn't be, but I would hate to be a burden."

"Of course not. I was finished and about to leave. How was your flight? Are you tired from the travel?" Gesturing to the sofa close by, I said, "Would you like to sit down?"

She smiled. "Not at all. I got in earlier today and rested. So kind of your parents to allow me to stay with them."

"Your comfort while you are here is our top priority," I answered smoothly.

These conversations used to be so easy for me, and now, uttering this nonsense felt so superficial and fake. I was tired of that life. I wanted real.

"About that, I made a reservation for you at Empire. I thought it was a good way to introduce Sienna to New York City."

Dinner? Tonight? Right now?

Bitterness flung itself up the back of my throat, the flavor sour. How much longer was I going to allow this man to dictate my life?

"Does it have a city view?" Sienna inquired, her words punctuated by the slide of her hand into the crook of my arm.

My father practically cawed in delight, and I stifled a sigh.

"It has one of the best city views. It's one of our most exclusive restaurants," I replied, smiling down at her. It was also one where everyone went to "be seen," and clearly, my father wanted the entire Upper East Side to see me with her.

Sidling a little closer, she clasped her fingers a little tighter into my jacket.

It was wrong. Completely wrong. These were not the fingers I wanted to cling to me.

"I can't wait to tell Daddy all about it," she crooned.

My father smiled, a triumphant glint in his eyes. "Well, I'll leave you to it. Have a good time, and make sure you tell

Ethan all the places you want to see while you're here. He will make sure it happens."

I murmured an agreement as he left, holding back from spewing so many things.

So many truths.

But I didn't.

Not because I didn't ache to but because right now was not the time. It would be abrupt and rude. Sienna didn't know what she'd stepped into. She didn't know anything about me. Hell, she was probably her father's pawn too.

It seemed the least I could do was take her to dinner. It was no less than I would do for any client. That was what Sienna was to me, a client. Part of a business deal. She was also a means to an end to keep my father at bay.

"I've seen photos of you, but I have to say they really didn't do you justice."

I glanced down at her words. She was smiling, holding on to me while honey dripped off her tongue. It was that sticky honey that held her mask in place.

She might be beautiful, but she was just like everyone else in my world. Insincere and vacant. The glint in her eye, though… Perhaps she wasn't her father's pawn. Perhaps he was hers.

I laughed low, a fake sound she wouldn't recognize. "Well, I could say the same to you."

"We make a striking couple, don't we?"

I made a sound, alluding to agreement. I supposed, in a sense, she was right. We did make a visual pair.

But we were no couple and never would be.

Dinner was a blur I could barely recall after it was over. I flipped the switch to automatic, slipping easily into the man everyone knew and loved. I smiled, laughed, and entertained the woman across from me. We talked about family and her socialite life in California.

The only moments of real clarity I felt were when I gazed

out the massive windows into the city and thought of Fletcher.

Where are you right now? Are you safe?

After dinner, she mentioned a temporary art exhibit on display nearby. Naturally, I escorted her because being a prince meant I had to act like one.

We wandered through the open space, the hushed atmosphere a backdrop to the art. I found myself comparing it to Neo's more colorful, graffiti style and becoming bored. A particular sculpture of a bust caught my attention, and I paused in front of it, tucking my hands into my trouser pockets to stare but not really look. In my mind, I was seeing the smaller bust in my foyer and hearing Fletcher say a Spider-Man statue would be better.

"You like this piece?" Sienna asked, coming to stand beside me, slipping her arm through mine.

"It reminds me of someone," I replied, still gazing at it.

"Really? Who?"

I was prepared with a flippant, general reply, even turning my head to deliver it with ease, but with Fletcher filling my heart and my head, I changed my mind. "Actually, the person I like."

Her fingers tightened upon hearing my words. Interesting, right? She didn't let go. She clung tighter.

That should tell you a lot.

"You're involved with someone?"

I nodded. "Yes. I am. And I feel that a woman of your caliber deserves the truth."

"But your father…"

"My father doesn't know about this person. Not many people do. It's, ah, complicated. And frankly, private."

"Why?" She was almost demanding, instantly brushing off that I said it was private because, in her world, she was the exception to every rule.

I could have pointed this out in a scathing manner, but

what would be the point?

"It's new and something I intend to protect."

"So she's poor, and Daddy won't approve."

See? Calculating and smart. A woman not to be underestimated.

"I definitely do not call my father *daddy*."

"I know that I'm here basically as a bargaining chip. Our fathers want to do some archaic form of business and use their children as collateral."

I felt my eyebrow lift. "Is that a thing on the West Coast too?"

"It's a monied thing no matter where you live."

"Touché."

"But you intrigue me. You have for a while, which is why I planted the seeds for this meeting months ago."

I wasn't surprised. Not one bit. I was, however, a bit shocked to hear I intrigued her. "You're intrigued by me?"

"You let the richest heiress in the country slip out of your grasp and don't seem the least bit upset. You're the first man in a long time to not fall over himself to impress me, and during our first date, you tell me you already have someone and that person is *poor*." She said the last part as though it were a sinful secret, and that was when I decided once and for all I didn't like this woman in the least. Even her looks ceased to impress me.

Up until this point, she'd been tolerable, and I'd even felt the urge to be honest with her. She was a typical spoiled elite, a product of her environment, and that was fine.

We were all products of our environment. I didn't think this was her flaw.

Her flaw?

She implied Fletcher was somehow less than because his bank account was lacking. And that I would never forgive.

"This is not a date." I clarified, no room for debate in the words.

She smiled as though the denial somehow pleased her. "At first, I just thought you were handsome, and I like that you live on the other side of the country from my father. But now that we've met, I realize there is so much more to you."

"It's late. I'll escort you back to my parents' penthouse."

Her hand slipped around my bicep once more, and I had to grit my teeth to keep myself from removing it. The trip to my parents' building was short, and I told the valet to just keep my Mercedes up front because I wouldn't be long.

Doing my gentlemanly duty, I accompanied Sienna up in the elevator, walking her all the way to the large pristine white door with gleaming gold hardware.

Pulling out the keycard, I hesitated before engaging the lock. Turning back toward her, I began. "I would appreciate—"

She smiled indulgently, eyes gleaming with pleasure. "Don't worry, Ethan. I won't tell them that you are secretly dating someone they won't approve of."

Oh, I hated her words. Not only that, but they brought an echo into the back of my mind in the sound of Neo's voice. *I won't let you make him some dirty little secret.*

A sick feeling plagued the deepest pit in my stomach, expanding until my entire midsection roiled with turmoil.

"It's not a secret," I snapped, making her eyes go wide. Sucking in a deep breath, I didn't bother to tamper back my expression. Let her see who she was dealing with. "But it's also a private matter. I have the intention and the right to speak to my family myself."

When I held out the card to be scanned, the door beeped, the locks unlatching.

Grasping the handle, I turned back, regarding her. "I will honor my word and show you around the city. Please let me know if there is anything you want to see. I will also wait until you are on a plane to break the news to my father so things aren't uncomfortable for you."

"How chivalrous."

"Call it what you want," I said, my patience so thin it was about to snap.

I'd wasted a lot of precious time tonight that I could have spent with Fletcher.

"I always do," she purred, moving forward to enter the penthouse. Her entire side brushed along my midsection as she went.

I wanted to laugh that she thought that would entice me.

Before she was fully inside and I could shut the door, she turned back, dark hair falling around her shoulders and a glimmer in her gaze. "The way I see it, I have the rest of my stay here to convince you I'm actually the match for you."

I didn't hold back my laugh this time.

Leaning close, I looked straight into her conniving eyes. "I have no doubt you are used to getting what you want. But not this time, princess. This prince isn't interested."

I closed the door with an audible click, cutting off the view of her surprised expression.

As I went back to my car, I mulled over the evening. I didn't regret telling Sienna what I did. Even if I hadn't realized I planned to tell my parents about Fletch the second she was gone, the moment the words were out, they felt exactly right.

I wasn't embarrassed about Fletcher. I wasn't even worried if my parents would accept him. They would or they wouldn't.

I didn't care.

I was beyond that point. I was done living for everyone else. I was going to live for me now.

For Fletcher.

Still, a part of me worried I'd just made this into some kind of game to that West Coast piece of work, and games were her favorite thing to play.

Twenty-Two

Fletcher

I wasn't a glutton for punishment. In fact, I didn't like being punished at all. I tried to avoid it.

Yet here I was.

Walking through the gloomy day over gritty, littered sidewalks, past an alleyway I once hid in, and avoiding the bakery I'd stolen from.

I told my brothers everything was great. I wasn't sure they believed me, but even if they did, they probably didn't now. I didn't tell them where I was going, but I was sure they knew.

After I spent some time helping Earth with the bar, playing a video game with Beau, and filling the fridge with groceries, I still couldn't shake the feelings rattling around inside me.

It seemed some distance and time to think did nothing to calm my fear. If anything, I grew more anxious.

I missed him. His scent, the softness of his voice, his eyes when he looked at me. His touch. His lips. I craved his affection and kisses so much it left an ache inside me, making me wonder why I'd parted from him at all.

You know why.

Yes, because if it was this hard now, imagine how hard it would be in a few months.

So I pulled on my old worn-out coat, shoved my hair under a black knit beanie, and set out to a place I knew that would remind me of who I was and who I would never be.

The wind was bitter and the sun almost completely gone for the day. Though dirty, the sidewalk seemed to be the brightest thing out here this evening, but when I finally turned onto the street where I grew up, everything turned dark.

No stars shined overhead, the moon nowhere in sight. All that existed was me, the chilling darkness, and a row of dilapidated brownstones that were haunted not only by age but by everything they'd seen.

My nose was numb from the wind, my cheeks prickled with the last bit of feeling. Ragged pieces of the old homes banged against each other, rattling and clanking almost like warnings for me to turn back.

There was no use in turning back from the place I had always been.

Cold air pushed through the threadbare fabric of my pocket, making my fingers ache and curl closer into my palms. The hand curled around the handle of my violin case had gone numb a few streets back. If it wasn't for Ethan's jacket, which I had layered on beneath mine, the rest of me would probably be numb too.

Funny how he keeps me warm even when we're apart.

A small light lit up the front window of my destination. It shone through the broken slats of the old blinds that had been hanging there all my life. Another harsh wind whistled, cutting through the night as I crept around the side, fingers fumbling to open up the hiding spot for my precious instrument. Once it was tucked away, I trudged up the cement steps, letting myself into a place I lived but never really considered home.

The air inside was warmer, but not by much. Shuffling past the crooked, dark staircase, I stepped into the small living room, gaze going immediately to the small lamp on a table beside the couch.

Mother sat near it, a blanket covering her lower half. In her lap was a ball of yarn, and in her hands, she held two large needles.

"I need a refill," she said, not even looking up.

My eyes strayed to the empty glass on the coffee table. The TV hanging on the wall was on, but the sound was so low I couldn't hear it as I passed by on the way to the kitchen.

Most of the cabinets in here no longer had doors. They'd all fallen off long ago, except for one. And I went to it, opening it with a loud creak to see a large bottle of clear liquid sitting on a shelf.

I brought the vodka with me, pouring more than I should into her glass, then setting the half-empty bottle beside it.

"What are you making?" I asked, looking at whatever she knitted.

"Like you care."

"Guess I don't."

The needles fell into her lap, and she looked up, an echo of surprise on her face. "What did you just say?"

Maybe the unsettled way I'd been feeling all day made me brave. Or maybe I wanted to set her off. Whatever the cause, my eyes leveled on hers. "I said I don't care what you're making. You'll probably be too drunk to finish it anyway."

The blanket and yarn fell to the floor when she shoved to her feet. One fist clenched around one of the needles while the other rolled between the cushions of the couch.

"How dare you?" she crowed, voice crackly and low.

My entire body tensed, and I stared at the needle still in her grasp. Instead of using it like I thought she would, she slapped it on the table to pick up the cup and down almost all the liquid.

Before she could even swallow, she pitched it right at me, the thick glass smacking into my chest, remnants of the vodka splashing my coat and peppering my jaw with the strong-scented alcohol.

It bounced off, falling to the floor and shattering into a thousand tiny pieces.

"Look at what you've done!" She raged. "You're nothing but a nuisance. I wouldn't need to drink if it wasn't for you!"

Sniffing, I took a step back, shaking the glass away from my feet.

The room went silent for a moment, and then she spoke, eyes trained down. "New shoes."

I gave the shoes Ethan gifted me a cursory glance, thankful they didn't seem to be torn from the glass. Guess it was pretty useful for them to have spikes.

"Mine were worn out," I said, sidestepping the little bit of liquid on the floor.

Her eyes were that of a hawk's when they swept over the rest of me. "What have you been doing?"

"The same thing I always do. Working."

Her tongue jutted out, wetting her bottom lip. "Where's my money, then?"

Pulling my hand out of my pocket, I brought with it some cash. Taking a step forward, I held it out.

She looked at the bundle, her eyes slipping to the small patch of sleeve from my hoodie that was sticking out from under my coat.

Her eyes snapped up.

"Do you want it or not?" I said, gruff, motioning for her to take it.

With a hiss, she snatched the cash, dropping down with it in her lap.

"Clean that up." She gestured to the glass.

I thought about refusing, but suddenly, I was tired.

I want Ethan.

I bent and began plucking the shards of glass off the scuffed-up, worn wood floor. As I piled all the chunks into my palm, the pungent scent of straight vodka burned my nose.

A small hiss slipped from between clenched teeth when a sharp piece stuck my finger. Shaking it out, I watched blood well and begin to drip.

"Stupid. Can't even pick up some glass without bleeding." She griped.

"Why did you even have me?"

My question hung heavily in the air, silencing all her insults.

"What?"

Straightening from the floor with a handful of jagged shards, I repeated what I wanted to know. "If you hate me so much, why did you even have me?"

Her cheeks paled, turning her face ghostly compared to her dark hair. Her eyes, which were always glassy, turned a little dull.

"My father left because the idea of me was so gross, and you've hated me since. So why?" I challenged. If there wasn't anything at all about me she thought she could love, what was the point?

Her back straightened, demeanor turning even frostier than usual. "You think you can just question me and my life choices?"

"When it's about me, yes."

"You ungrateful, spoiled child!" she shrieked, the sound so piercing my hand involuntarily clenched around the glass. Pain stung, but I ignored it, walking into the kitchen to dump the trash, then stopping to run the bleeding cuts under the faucet.

When I came back, she was in the middle of the room,

clutching the vodka bottle and staring at me with malice.

"You know why I kept you?" She seethed. "Revenge. So that man would know there was a piece of him out there that he would never see. That the piece of him was being kept by me, the woman he hates!"

Confusion muddied my brain. "But I thought it was me he hated, not you."

Her eyes widened a bit but then narrowed all over again. "Get out!" She raged, shaking the bottle in her fist. "I can't stand the sight of you! You're nothing without him! Nothing!"

"You better make that money last because I won't be back for a while," I said, stomach churning as fresh blood welled from the cuts on my hands.

"Good!" she roared and, to my surprise, hurled the entire bottle of precious vodka at my head.

I ducked, and it hit the wall, exploding everywhere.

She was still screaming when I left the house, every part of me shaking. It took several tries for me to get the violin out of the hiding spot, and once it was, I didn't bother covering it back up. Instead, I left it wide open and hurried away, willing my knees not to give out.

Twenty-Three

Ethan

One phone call.

Two hours.

Four stops and three train changes.

Finally finding Fletcher?

Worth every minute.

The pressure release when the doors opened on the enclosed bullet-shaped car was nothing compared to the pressure release I felt the second I stepped onto the platform and heard his violin.

I didn't need my eyes to know it was him. I didn't have to wait for the crowd to thin to follow the sound his heart made.

The lighting was dim down here, harsh from the fluorescent bulbs overhead. There wasn't wind like on street level, but as the train closed up and departed, there was definite movement in the air. Even with the warm bodies bustling about, the temperature down here was chilling. The atmosphere wasn't as loud as I expected. The sound of his melody hushed everyone, even in the grittiest of places. Even in this dark, cold tunnel with tired faces, grumpy passengers, and worn-out tourists, there was a sense of life.

Tucking my hands into the quilted down jacket I wore,

breath puffing out in a white cloud, I walked, my eyes searching for him.

Emotion welled beneath my skin from the reedy, eloquent tune he played, which somberly wafted through the tunnel. He played a dark sound this night, a muted, mellow song that was underscored by a harmony of sadness and longing. It was the sound of pain but also of something else… *Longing.*

I sensed he was unsettled this morning when he got out of my car, but I didn't want to push.

I should have pushed. Maybe then, the melody wouldn't be so powerfully sorrowful.

Hands clenching in my pockets, I craned my neck, looking ahead toward a wide stairwell that led up to street level.

The music was louder. I knew he was closer.

A person passed up the stairs, and he came into sight, shoulders hunched in on the wooden instrument, back turned away to me as his entire body moved and swayed, creating the music wholly and not just with his hands.

My entire midsection clenched from my throat all the way to my lower stomach. He seemed to me like a thin reed billowing in the wintry night air while people passed by, maybe seeing his beauty but somehow overlooking every-thing else he was.

Did they not see his fragility? Hear the vulnerability in those notes? Did he not seem small to them as he hunched in, trying to be invisible even as everyone within earshot could hear?

I didn't know what ailed him most. I didn't know how he played with such hopeful sorrow. And honestly, I didn't care.

If he was shattered, I'd love every jagged piece.

If he was cracked, I'd try and fill in his spaces.

If the hope still flickering inside him needed fanned into a flame, I would be his oxygen.

It didn't matter to me what form Fletcher came in. It only mattered that he was mine.

A particularly powerful chord was struck, his frame arching into the billowing sound. Feet stalling out, I stood rooted in place, just watching, listening… appreciating what he was and even what he wasn't.

Emotion welled up inside me, pressing against the backs of my eyes. I wanted to run to him, but I also wanted to prolong this moment of essentially being invisible to him so I could selfishly take in every detail without him knowing.

The platform began to empty, not nearly as busy as it had been when the train emptied a few minutes ago. His back remained to me, his case open near his feet as he played. People would stop and listen, appreciating his talent before moving on. The hat on his head made him appear more melancholic because it hid the messy mop of hair usually flopping wildly about.

As he played, his body straightened, and I felt rather than saw his attention move outward, focusing instead on something else nearby.

It took a while to find what I thought might have caught his eye, the movement low to the ground and difficult to make out.

As I stared, a man in an ill-fitting business suit with a briefcase from the 1940s passed, nearly tripping and falling. His curse echoed to me because the music suddenly stopped.

Dropping the violin and bow, Fletcher rushed over to where the man had tripped, nearly being knocked over by the way he angrily stormed off, muttering something clearly nasty.

I couldn't hear, but I started forward, angry he would direct any of his ire at Fletcher.

Fletcher wasn't focused on the retreating man. Instead, he dropped to his knees, carefully leaning forward.

Was he hurt?

Did the man hit him and I didn't see?

Worry robbed my senses, pushing me forward at the same time Fletcher stood and turned.

Our eyes met over the distance between us, people rushing through our line of sight but never once breaking our stare.

His eyes widened with surprise, but then emotion filled them. An entire plethora of sentiments poured from those honey orbs. Pain, relief, happiness, desperation… need.

I wanted all of it.

Heart pounding, stomach fluttering, I opened my arms, offering him a choice. He hesitated only a split second, then rushed forward, burying himself into my chest as a shuddering breath moved through him.

I held him as tight as I dared, clutching around his waist and palming the back of his head. Despite the relief I finally knew at having him close, my heart still thundered wildly.

And standing there in the murky, arctic underground cave, I felt at home.

Meow.

A loud but muffled yowl broke us apart. But even as we both looked down, my hand reached out, curling around the back of his arm so he didn't go far.

A scrawny, dirty, and obviously loud kitten was clutched against Fletcher's chest.

"Is this what you ran over there for?" I asked, staring at the animal.

"That man practically kicked it and didn't even stop," Fletcher said, shifting it a little closer. His hand was massive compared to the small furball.

I wasn't really an animal person, but seeing the way he was staring at the pitiful creature softened my heart.

"I've seen it before." Fletch went on, stroking its filthy head. "Last time, it was with its mother and a few other kittens. She's the smallest and had a hard time keeping up. I guess this time she got left behind."

He shivered slightly, and I realized what a poor excuse for a coat he was wearing. Reaching down, I felt his fingers, gasping when I felt how icy they were.

"Come on." I cajoled, wrapping an arm around his waist. "Let's go."

"Go where?" he asked.

"My place."

"But I—"

"I'm not sleeping without you tonight, puppy." I cut him off.

He nodded once. "My violin."

I packed it up for him as he stood close by, eyes trained on me the whole time. I wanted to tease that, clearly, he wanted to come with me, but I didn't want to poke fun at his need.

Especially when that need was obviously me.

"Come on." I ushered him toward the stairs. We'd take a cab back to my place.

When he didn't immediately follow, I turned back.

Hugging the kitten a little tighter, he lifted his doe eyes to meet mine. "Her mother left her behind. I can't do that."

Like I would deny him. "Bring her along, then."

Light brightened his eyes, mixed with honest gratefulness I hadn't seen from almost anyone. "Really?"

"If it makes you look at me like that, then yes."

Rushing up the stairs between us, he threw himself into me for a hug. "Thank you for finding me."

I didn't think those whispered words were meant for my ears. But it wasn't my ears that heard them anyway. It was my heart.

"If you needed me, why didn't you call?" I asked, the hat preventing me from stroking his hair, so my palm settled against the back of his neck.

He shook his head, face rubbing against my chest.

The brakes of an approaching train squealed, and so I bustled him, the cat, and his case up the stairs, holding on to him even as I signaled for a car.

Inside the cab, I gave the address, and before I was even done, Fletcher was pressed against my side, his cheek resting on my shoulder. Gazing down, I watched him stroke the kitten who was clinging to the front of his coat for dear life.

"I won't abandon you," he murmured softly.

Heart pinching, I started to shift so I could pull him even closer into my side, but he sat up to speak to the driver. "Can we stop there a minute?" he said, gesturing to some sort of corner store.

It didn't look very reputable, and the quality of their items was probably poor.

"What do you need?" I asked as the cabbie swerved abruptly toward the curb.

"Meter's running!" he said, tapping the box on top of the dash.

The audacity of this man was why I preferred to drive.

Well, that and my car didn't smell like nachos and dirty feet.

"Here, hold her," Fletcher said, using his hands to pry the kitten off the front of his coat.

Appalled, I drew back. "Me? What for?"

"I need to go in there and get a few things for cats."

"I can call Jane—" I started to object, but he shook his head firmly. "It's late, and I'm already here."

I glanced at the small creature he held out.

"Meow," it complained loudly.

A pleading look crossed his face. "Please, E? I'll only be a minute."

"All right." I gave in, reaching for the animal.

Her claws sank into my arm immediately, but I didn't

complain because Fletcher was staring at me with a soft look on his face.

"Am I doing it wrong?"

He shook his head once. "She looks even smaller when you hold her." Without warning, he bounced forward, pressing a kiss to my cheek.

By the time I blinked, he was already out of the cab and hurrying into the store.

"Meter's running." The cabbie reminded me.

"I would never think otherwise," I replied as the cat climbed up toward my shoulder.

Startled, I grappled at the little thing, trying not to hurt her as I tugged her back down.

It meowed forcefully, and I frowned.

"He'll be right back." I assured her.

"Cats are extra," the cabbie said.

I rolled my eyes. "Naturally."

Of all the places I could have hypothesized I might end up tonight, sitting in a grungy cab, holding a stray kitten while waiting for Fletcher to shop in some uncivilized store was not even close to any guess I would have made.

The cat started wiggling around again, climbing up to my shoulder and poking me with its vicious claws, when Fletcher jogged back out to the cab, dropping all his purchases on the floor and scooting all the way across the seat until our bodies bumped.

"We can go now," he called up front.

The cabbie sped off, throwing Fletch back into me.

"Aww, she likes you," he crooned.

"I think this cat is having an identity crisis," I announced.

Fletcher's face grew serious. "Really? Why?"

"It's trying to sit on my shoulder like a parrot."

He smiled, a low giggle bubbling from his chest. "Come here," he cooed, scooping her back into his arms.

She settled there as though she belonged, making me feel

a ping of jealousy, but Fletch's light shiver made me forget quickly.

"I'm buying you a new coat, and that's final," I said, shifting so I could pull off my coat and drape it over him and the cat like a blanket.

"Warm," he whispered, snuggling into it and making my heart clench.

His eyes were heavier than before when they focused on me, taking in the fitted white dress shirt with black buffalo check on the inside of the collar and down the center where the buttons fastened. The top button was undone, but there was a black silk scarf covering my neck where it opened. With it, I wore black dress pants and designer leather ankle boots.

"You look fancy. Were you still at work?" he asked, eyes scraping over me once more.

I thought about the dinner I'd just endured. I thought about the sadness I'd heard in his music and the way his eyes clung to me. Now wasn't the time to tell him about Sienna. He was already exhausted enough.

"I had a business dinner." It wasn't exactly a lie. My time with Sienna tonight had been for business.

Father just hoped it would turn out to be more.

"Will you be cold without your coat?" He worried.

I nodded sagely. "Very. You'd better sit real close and keep me warm."

Releasing a worried sound from his throat, he pushed me against the seat, then proceeded to climb into my lap.

Shock rendered me silent as he wiggled and settled with a deep sigh.

"Are you warm now?" he asked, side curled against my chest, head tucked into my neck.

Oh, he is going to be the end of me.

His shyness was overruled by worry I might actually be

cold. He was clearly so needy for affection that he climbed into my lap to soak it in.

Heart tumbling, I hooked an arm around his waist. "Yeah, puppy," I murmured low. "I'm warm now."

The loud purring of the cat was almost interrupted when the cabbie glanced at us in the rearview.

I cut him off before he could even utter his nonsense.

"I'll pay it," I practically growled, hand curling into Fletcher's hip possessively.

His eyes snapped back to the road, and blissfully, he said nothing else the rest of the drive.

Twenty-Four

Fletcher

"This is completely unsanitary," Ethan declared as gentle sprays of water splattered around the kitchen sink and counter.

Warm water flowed out of the faucet, which was a really cool kind because you could pull it out and direct it anywhere you wanted.

Right now, I was directing it at the kitten.

"Aww," I replied, not even looking up at him because I was too focused on the tiny wet animal sitting pitifully in a puddle. "But look how good she is. She's not even trying to run away like most cats would!"

"Why would she run away? She probably doesn't like being dirty."

I smiled at his logic. He was probably right. As if to argue, the kitten gave a loud yowl that echoed through the entire kitchen. Scooping more water from the spray into my hand, I gently cleaned her neck.

Now that she was clean, her fur was much whiter than I realized. Both ears were gray, and there was a patch of gray fur on her nose as well. Her eyes were blue, and under the very wet fur, her skin was pink.

When I saw her stumbling through the subway terminal,

alone and dirty, my stomach clenched. No one paid her any mind as if her tiny size made her unimportant. When the man nearly crushed her underfoot and didn't even pause, I'd had enough.

Why were some so easily overlooked? So easily discarded?

I felt a sort of affinity to this slight kitten who'd been abandoned by its mother.

Nearing the end of her patience, the kitten tried to dart out of the sink. With a little yell, I let go of the sprayer, grasping her with both hands. My shirt was completely drenched.

Ethan made a sound, and I laughed, looking up as I clutched the soaked, frustrated cat while water sprayed everywhere.

"Are you having fun?" he asked, indulgence in his tone.

My laughter died, but a smile remained. "Yes."

Laughing beneath his breath, he tugged the beanie off my head, tossing it onto the island. When I frowned, he ran a hand through my hat hair, explaining, "I miss seeing this golden mop."

My nose was still cold from all the time I'd spent outside, and I reached up with a wet hand to rub at it.

Ethan's eyes went dark like a storm rolling over an ocean. Snatching my hand, he pulled it between us, staring at the small cuts. "Did that cat do this to you?" he demanded.

"Don't yell," I admonished, shrinking back a little before I could tell myself not to. "It wasn't her." I hurried to explain, not wanting him to be mad at the cat.

His expression turning soft, his chest moved with a deep inhale and exhale. Rubbing his thumb over my palm, he explained, "I'm not mad. I'm concerned. What happened here?"

Flashbacks to earlier this evening, of the broken glass,

splashing vodka, and sharp words Mother hurled, poured over me almost like it was happening all over again.

"Nothing," I murmured, tugging my hand away. "I just cut myself is all."

Dropping his hand, Ethan shifted closer. "You know you can tell me anything, right?"

The kitten flexed her claws, sinking them into my wet shirt and pricking my chest. Pulling her up gently, I motioned to the towel nearby. "Can I have that?"

Ethan tugged it close, spreading it wide so I could set her in the middle and dry her with the ends.

She let out a loud complaint, and I promised we were almost done. "Doesn't it feel better to be clean and warm? Are you hungry? I got you some food."

Ethan watched me quietly as I fussed over the animal. The weight of his eyes didn't make me uncomfortable. If anything, I felt comforted by his watchful gaze.

"You're soaking wet. You need dry clothes," he observed a short while later.

"I want to feed her first."

With a sigh, he grabbed a plate, a bowl, and a fork, managing to hold it all with one hand, and settled his other at the base of my spine. "Come on. You can feed her upstairs."

On the way, he grabbed the bag of things I'd bought, ushering me into his room.

Going over by the window, I dropped onto the floor with the kitten still wrapped up in my lap. She didn't stay long, leaping onto the floor beside me to lick at her wet paws.

Ethan handed me the bag, and I dug out a can of wet food and popped the top. The second the food was exposed, the kitten stopped licking herself and came close like she would eat it right out of the can.

"Wait a minute." I giggled as she climbed into my lap to get to the food.

Placing the plate on the floor, Ethan took the can of food

to scoop some out onto the plate. The kitten followed, gobbling it down like she hadn't eaten in weeks.

I frowned. "She must be really hungry." Looking up to Ethan, I said, "Give her more."

"If we give her too much too fast, she'll get sick."

While the kitten ate, I pulled out a small litter box and a small bag of litter. "You probably don't want this in here, right?" I said, glancing around the super nice bedroom.

He sighed. "Put it wherever you want, puppy."

"It's better to put it in here, because if we put it somewhere else, she'll be lonely when we're sleeping. She might think we left her." I reasoned.

Without another word, Ethan took the pan, setting it on the other side of the nightstand in front of the spectacular view, and filled it with the litter.

When he was done, he grasped my hand to tug me toward the bathroom. "Come on. You need to shower, and then I'll bandage those cuts."

Digging my heels in, I glanced at the cat. "But, but—"

"She's eating."

"She's gonna be cold."

"I'll get her a blanket."

"Why are you doing this?" I said abruptly.

He stopped and turned, surprise on his face. "Doing what?"

"Coming to find me. Letting me bring her here." In a smaller voice, I finished. "Taking care of me."

His palms were wide and warm when they settled on my cheeks, angling my face up. "Because you're mine. Did you forget?"

I tried to lower my face, but he wouldn't allow it. Instead, I closed my eyes. "You're going to change your mind," I whispered.

The hands on my face jolted before settling once more. "Is that what you think?"

I didn't say anything. I didn't open my eyes.

"Fletcher."

It didn't seem to matter how vulnerable I felt with him, how badly I wanted to hide myself away. The minute he commanded anything at all, I did it without delay.

Lashes fluttering open, I met his resolved stare.

"I won't ever change my mind."

I wanted to believe him so badly it hurt. My chest actually constricted in pain with the force of how much I wanted him, of how much I wished I could not be afraid.

"I'm scared," I confessed in a shaky whisper. "I'm so scared, but I still want to be here with you."

Bending down, he brought his lips to hover seductively close to mine. "Don't be scared, puppy, not of me."

Eyes drifting, my chin tilted up, quietly asking for a wordless reply.

His breath tickled my lips, his presence invaded mine, and the tips of our noses bumped softly. Heart hammering, I felt my lips reach for his, but he shifted angles, enticing me to follow. We hovered so close it was like being kissed without actually meeting lips. But then he was on me, and I was tumbling deep. Long, graceful kisses that melted my bones, mouths rubbing insatiably, and gentle sucking against my upper lip.

Knees like Jell-O, I filled my hands with his shirt, anchoring myself against his body and into his kiss. Strong arms wound around my waist, pulling me firmly into his solid frame. Stretching up, I sought more, and my feet left the ground, Ethan lifting me as if I weighed nothing at all, not once breaking the kiss.

As our tongues rubbed together, his scent and strength surrounded me while I molded into him, goose bumps rising along my skin. Kissing him was my favorite thing, something I never knew I couldn't live without. My whole life had been a fight, and survival meant never giving in. But, oh, just one touch of his velvet lips and submission was all I knew.

How heady it was to give up that struggle, to surrender my never-ending guard. Letting him consume me was relief in the best possible way.

The blood in my veins turned to desire. The cold I'd been plagued with burned away. Lifting my legs, I wrapped them around his waist. Grunting into the kiss, Ethan palmed my ass, grasping me tight in the new position.

Boldly, my arms wound around his neck, and my tongue dug deeper into him. Dizziness made me lightheaded. Instinct made me thrust into his muscular midsection.

Heavy breathing filled the room when the kiss broke, punctuated by my helpless little whine.

"You have no idea the kind of restraint you require." His voice was hoarse and deep.

"I never asked for your restraint."

"You didn't have to."

The throbbing length between me and his waist was making it hard to think, and I pushed into him again, wondering what it would take to get his restraint to snap.

The hands still holding my ass flexed, and then he started walking to the bathroom. "You shower. I'll get you some dry clothes."

"Ethan," I whined, dropping my forehead to his shoulder, wondering how he managed to stay so in control.

"I know," he murmured, stepping into the shower to turn on the spray before retreating.

The slow slide of my body against his as he lowered me, coupled with the feel of his not-so-soft shaft, made me gasp.

"I'm not as unaffected as you might think, puppy," he murmured, grasping my fingers and pressing them fully against his clothed steely rod.

"Shower with me."

His hot stare split between me and the running shower before he slowly shook his head.

"Please," I whispered. "I missed you."

A stricken look rolled over his face, which was quickly replaced with stark need.

"All right." He relented. "You go first. Let me get the cat a blanket like I promised."

I shed all my clothes into a heap where I stood and then walked into the massive white marble shower already steamy and warm from the multiple sprays.

A low groan rolled out of me as the heated water blasted my tired muscles. I didn't realize how tense I was until my body began to unclench with the liquid massage.

Above me, the rainfall showerhead sent steady but gentle drops cascading down, making me feel like I was standing in a summer rainstorm in the middle of a peaceful day. Sighing, I turned to the controls, edging up the temperature just a little, amazed when the water warmed instantly. Water drenched my hair, making it heavy, and dripped over my cheeks. Every drop seemed to make me tingle, my body already so sensitive and hyperaware from Ethan's touch.

Just when I started to wonder where he was, bare skin slid along mine as capable arms drew me back into his chest.

Pressing a kiss to my temple, he rubbed and stroked my bare belly, making my eyes droop.

Soap that smelled like him lathered over me, thick white suds clinging everywhere he washed. His hands were thorough as we rinsed, my chest finally coming around to meet his.

The wet strands of his hair were darker than usual, and drops of water clung to his eyelashes. Slight stubble shadowed his chin and upper lip, and tendrils of water raced over his chest, teasing erect nipples.

Fascinated, I reached up, brushing the pad of my finger over one of the tight buds, loving the way his body contracted with the simple touch. Braver, I did it again, this time giving it a light pinch.

Glancing up, my eyes asked for the permission I was too shy to voice, and he pushed farther into me, offering himself for whatever I wanted to do.

The second my tongue lapped at the wet nipple, he moaned, hand pushing into my wet hair to encourage me. This time, I drew the pebble into my mouth, working it with my lips.

He'd done this to me before, and I thought it felt amazing. Judging from the sounds he was making now, I would assume he did too. Wanting to make him happy, I sucked and lapped at him again and again before moving to his other nipple to do the same.

Just having him against my lips made my lower stomach knot with need and a hunger I didn't understand gnaw at everything inside me.

I want more.

Reaching for the shampoo, Ethan began washing my hair, but I wanted to taste more of him. I started to kneel, trying to slip free of his hold, but he caught me, making a sound.

Eyes wide, I glanced up, biting into my lower lip. "You don't want me to?"

He moaned. "Oh yes, yes, I want you to. But if you do that now, I won't last."

Before I could say anything, his lips were on mine, kissing me senseless as his fingers massaged the shampoo into my hair.

I don't know how long we kissed, but eventually, his hands fell from my head, dragging down my spine and over the curve of my hips.

Our dicks bumped together, both of them slick and throbbing. Moving against him in search of more friction, I noticed the way his fingers practically crawled over my rounded ass, moving to the spilt down the middle.

The second fingertips parted my cheeks, the kiss broke, and my forehead fell against his chest.

"Fletch?"

"More," I answered, wiggling a little in invitation.

"That's my good boy," he murmured, fingers dipping into the crack, slipping along my most private area.

Totally turned on that I pleased him, I latched my lips onto his pec, sucking lightly, drinking in some of the water that slipped between him and me.

When his finger met the tight ring of muscle of my hole, I automatically tensed. He didn't shove in or even back away. Instead, he circled the muscle again and again, creating a rhythm I found insanely soothing. Water trailed between my open cheeks, the warm cascade plus the gentle ministrations of his finger relaxing me.

When the finger slid away, I made a disappointed sound, honestly surprising myself. Just minutes ago, I was tense with worry, and now I wanted more.

"Patience, puppy," he whispered, the promise in his tone making me shudder.

The finger trailed lower, down my perineum, to tease the underside of my sack. Lips latched back onto his chest, my fist clenching against his side.

Slowly, he dragged back up, my tight hole jerking with surprise when he met it once more. When he peeled my cheeks farther apart, a rush of water coated me. Then the tip of his finger breached my entrance.

My breath caught, body going tense. I was tight, the intrusion shocking. My fist unclenched only to clench again, but this time around a handful of his muscle.

"So tight," he murmured, just holding his finger in place.

I whimpered, not sure if I liked this or if I wanted him to stop.

His lips brushed the top of my head. "Relax around me, sweetheart."

I tried, but the sensation was so new I wasn't sure I succeeded. He murmured praise anyway, moving just slightly as he spoke, pushing just a little deeper as my body began to loosen.

Water poured over us as I clung to him, ass jutting out under his attention. My dick was still hard and wanting, which convinced me that what Ethan was doing, I clearly liked.

Carefully, he slid out, making me gasp and look up.

His eyes were dark, pupils dilated, when he gazed down, water trailing over his lips.

"Why'd you stop?" I asked.

"You didn't want me to?"

I shook my head.

"Let's finish and go to bed," he said, the words like a delicious promise.

Stomach buzzing, heart pounding, I scarcely paid attention as we finished up in the shower. My hole still tingled from the little he'd played, and I was both anxious and apprehensive about what it would feel like when all of him breeched me.

"What are you thinking?" he asked, clearly noting my silence.

Dropping my eyes to his impressive girth, I swallowed. "Is that going to fit?"

He laughed, hand automatically going to his erection to stroke. "It will."

With my teeth sinking into my lower lip, heat pooled in my stomach, watching him touch himself. "It's going to hurt."

Releasing his shaft and taking my chin in his hand, he stared levelly into my eyes. Even with the clear passion swirling in their depths, there was sincerity as well. "All you have to say is stop. I'll stop no matter what."

"Really?"

"I promise. And I won't be mad. I won't yell. I'll stop immediately and hold you."

A wave of emotion pummeled me, knocking down all the butterflies in my stomach, making me feel overwhelmed and heavy. Breathing ragged, I would have dropped against the shower wall, but he caught me instead.

This.

This was why I submitted to him so readily. Why I felt so safe letting him have all the control. Because I wasn't really giving up anything… just letting him take over for a while, and having that made me feel free in a way I never had before.

Heart still shaking, body overwhelmed, and lashes heavy with water, I stared. "No one's ever been like this to me."

"And no one else will," he said, ferocity breaking into his tone. "No one will ever love you like me."

My breath caught.

Love.

Did he know what he said? Was it just a slip of the tongue?

Reaching around, he shut off all the sprays. Moments later, a heated towel wrapped around me, and his wide palms rubbed along my covered arms.

We dried in silence, my limbs still shaky and nerves still raw. Occasionally, I would sneak long glances at his sculpted, naked frame.

"We're gonna get you some clothes to keep here," he said, holding out some of his for me to use. "So they fit you better."

I took them, immediately setting them aside. "I don't want clothes."

He frowned. "You'll get cold."

"I want you to keep me warm."

The towel he was using to dry his hair slipped down, catching on his shoulder. A flash of something dominant and delicious burst in his eyes, making my spine tingle with anticipation. But even with heavy need pulsing all around us, he assured me. "We don't have to do this tonight."

"I want to."

I'd spent the entire day trying to get some space, trying to reconcile my fear, hell, even seeking out abuse, thinking maybe I could spare myself pain later… but all it did was lead me back here. Was he the cause or the answer?

My fear or my safety?

My pleasure or my pain?

It seemed Ethan was all of those things to me, all of them in a single man. Perhaps none of them could exist without the other.

Our towels landed, abandoned, on the bathroom tile, lying in a heap just like our clothes. Hands entwined, he led me into the bedroom, which was only lit by the sparkling city beyond the window.

We moved, two bodies as a single silhouette, toward the massive bed with welcoming silk sheets. As I climbed onto the mattress, I spared a glance for the kitten, seeing her curled up in the center of a plush blanket that Ethan had folded to make more cushiony. The plate of food nearby was empty, and she seemed content in her makeshift bed.

All thoughts of her vanished when Ethan moved beside the mattress, golden skin highlighted by the moon.

Anticipation curled my toes, and I opened my arms to welcome him.

Twenty-Five

I'VE NEVER WANTED TO GIVE SO MUCH OF MYSELF TO ANYONE. Hell, until now, I didn't realize I even had this much to offer. People always seemed to only desire my status, power, and money.

Fletcher was different.

He wanted *me*. My attention. My touch. The comfort of my presence. It was like this misfit saw things no one else bothered to look for, and it was those things he valued most.

And right now, he was giving me something he'd never given anyone before.

Rights to his body, an invitation into his heart.

Maybe I didn't know a lot of details about his past, but I knew this was a big deal, the trust he was holding out. Trust I would cherish.

As I slipped into the bed beside him, the cool sheet settled over our bare bodies, enclosing us in an intimate shared space.

My heart thumped so heavily my ribs felt bruised, and my stomach quivered. Buzzing emotion soared through my veins, and the weight of delicious responsibility settled over me when those doe eyes innocently looked for me to lead.

Possessiveness had my palm curling around his bare hip,

sliding him through the distance between us until our skin met, making the back of my neck tingle.

Words seemed superficial at this point. The emotions welling between us meant far more than any words ever could. It was in this moment that actions would speak louder than words, so dipping low, I fused our mouths together.

Like Velcro, we fit together, mouths fastening like two halves of a whole. Gliding eagerly against each other, tongues reaching and swirling while his hand closed around my bicep to squeeze. Tugging him flush against me, I deepened the kiss, exploring every part of his wet mouth, lapping him up and swallowing him down with a thirst that would never be quenched.

Tasting him was like the first sip of a freshly made beverage or the first taste of your favorite dessert. The first taste was always the most satisfying, the most delicious. His flavor never diluted, no matter how many times I licked, sucked, or tugged his lips between mine. He exploded relentlessly across my tongue every single second, making it hard to think or breathe.

I was filled with desire to consume, to satiate this ever-growing need I felt for him.

His teeth sank into my lower lip, nipping and then settling a little deeper. My lashes lifted so I could stare with hazy eyes in surprise.

Oh, my little kiss monster loved to kiss, but rarely did he ever grow bold.

At first, I feared I'd somehow been too rough and this bite was retaliation, but when our eyes met, I saw the cloudy haze in his, accompanied by a little naughty glint.

I started to smile, and he bit down again, pulling my bottom lip out away from my face. Knowing he was watching, wanting to know if his little game was okay, I groaned deep in my throat, thrusting against him so he knew I approved.

After nibbling another moment, he released, following up the bite with a soothing lick of his tongue.

My eyes fluttered closed again, and I deepened the kiss once more, rolling so he was beneath me. I loved when he was under me like this, how I covered him completely, keeping him all to myself.

We were both already painfully hard when our dicks thrust together. I could feel the warm slick of precum on us both, making it all the easier for our throbbing shafts to slide along.

A shudder moved through him, breaking the kiss. The sound of our lips unsealing echoed through the quiet bedroom. Gazing down, I took him in, finding a boy with flushed cheeks, swollen lips, and half-lidded eyes. His hair was still damp, falling in his eyes, and his chest rose and fell with uneven breaths.

"Is my puppy okay?" I murmured low, not wanting the sound of my voice to break whatever it was that filled the air.

Instead of answering, he looped his arms around my neck and used my body to pull himself up, pressing his face into the side of my neck. The familiar feel of his slick lips caressed my throat, grip slackening as he moved down to my chest, lingering above my pounding heart.

Completely unnerved by the intimate reply, I swallowed thickly, trying to regain some composure as he fell back into the pillow, looking up and puckering his lips.

Forgetting all about composure, I dove in, kissing him all over again but dragging my lips over his jaw and down his neck.

Little whines floated above my head as he stretched to give me even greater access.

"Mine," I growled, latching on and sucking deep.

His body arched off the mattress, a perfect opportunity for my palm to fit against the small curve of his back. Holding his body against mine, I sucked until I knew there would be a mark, then moved down to suck another at his collarbone.

He whimpered and moved restlessly, hands gripping me tight. It seemed as though he wanted to be owned just as much as I wanted to own him, which made the dominant part of me roar with delight. Finished with my task, I proudly stared down at the marks I'd left on him, satisfaction tattooing itself on my heart.

Despite me holding him so tight, his hips thrust, seeking friction and moaning a bit when he found it. We moved together seamlessly for long moments, my lips closing over his nipple to suck.

The hands that had been gripping me fell onto the bed, his body bending over the palm placed at the curve of his spine. He was like an offering of the sweetest kind, completely pliant and boneless in my hold.

Trusting me to give him pleasure and take nothing he didn't offer.

I love you.

My heart beat to the tune of those three words as I continued to kiss down his narrow waist, carefully pulling my hand from his back to lay him out under me to devour.

His gasp of surprise tightened my balls when I swirled my tongue around his belly button, then dove in, wetting the dip in his body, offering a preview of what it might be like to feel my tongue invading other places he possessed.

My name was a mere echo floating up to the ceiling while his fingers tangled in my hair. I chuckled huskily when he pushed me down, wanting my tongue somewhere else.

"Patience," I muttered, kissing his pubic bone and then slipping around the proudly erect cock to sink my teeth into the soft flesh of his inner thigh.

Gasping, he opened his legs wider, body arching up once more.

So responsive. So sensitive.

All mine.

Settling between his spread thighs, I sat up, allowing myself the pleasure of staring down at his languid body. Kiss marks littered his neck and collarbone, and a new one darkened his inner thigh. His waist was damp from my tongue, and his lower belly was slick with precum.

In the center of it all was his manhood, stiff and throbbing, the head already flushed and swollen.

Another incoherent sound came from above as he reached to grab himself as if the pressure of waiting was too much to bear.

Intercepting his hand, I wrapped mine around it, keeping it from grabbing his erection.

"Ethan," he half whined, half demanded.

Chuckling, I brought his hand up to my lips, sucking two fingers into my mouth, swirling my tongue to wet both digits.

His eyes widened, teeth sinking into his lower lip.

I sucked them deeper, making sure they were good and slick before pulling his hand down, directing it to my aching dick.

A hint of shyness crossed his face, his eyes skirting away from mine.

My heart squeezed with his cuteness, and I wanted him even more. "Play with this for a minute," I instructed, rubbing his wet fingers along my shaft to make it easier for him to pump me.

His hand tightened immediately, his shyness no match for desire.

I sagged back onto my haunches, letting myself get caught up in the blissful feeling of him working me.

He was a little clumsy, which oddly made me love it more. Knowing he was learning with me, that he'd only ever been like this with me, made me weak.

As he stroked my length, I reached into the bedside table

for a bottle of lube and a condom, bringing them back to lay near his hip.

His eyes followed the items even as he pumped my cock, hand stuttering a bit.

"I'll stop whenever you want." I reminded him, sincerely meaning it.

Eyes flashing up to mine, he jutted his tongue out to wet his lower lip. Pushing up, he leaned in, holding my cock out like a treat.

I made a sound of protest, but his fist tightened, eyes pleading, and I relented.

The first few licks were small like he was sampling a new flavor of ice cream he wasn't sure he would like. I held my breath. With every lick, the feel of his lightly textured tongue was a combination of heaven and hell against my throbbing dick.

After a moment of licking, his head lifted, and I forced my stare down.

"I like it," he announced before taking me fully into his mouth and making mine fall open with a wordless scream.

My God, he went from little kitten licks to sucking me deep as if he might starve without it.

My stomach jerked, the muscles spasming as he drew back only to plunge down again.

"Puppy," I begged, my voice strained and weak. Pushing his shoulder lightly, I tried to dislodge his lips from my cock.

I felt his big eyes look up my stomach, past my chest. I watched him lick over my head, swiping across the slit and making me shudder.

Pulling back, I denied him more access, at the same time reminding myself he clearly had no idea the effect he had on me.

"Lie down," I said a little more roughly than I intended.

He lay back obediently, and goddammit, that made me even harder.

"Good boy," I crooned, moving over him, caging him in.

"I like it when you say that," he confessed, refusing to meet my stare.

Ah, so someone's got a praise kink, I thought, filing that information away for later.

"Yeah?" I crooned, cupping the side of his face to press a quick kiss on his nose. "Well, it's true. You are my good boy."

His body moved restlessly, clearly ready for more. As I slid down, I thought of how accepting he was in the shower, how he seemed to like the way we played.

He sighed thickly the minute my fist wrapped around his shaft. I spent a few minutes pumping him, making him moan before reaching for the small bottle of lube.

Not wanting him to tense up, I leaned down, taking him into my mouth. The sounds he made covered up the snap of the lid, and I didn't think he noticed as I coated my finger.

Pulling back, I dribbled a little more on my hand, warming it between my fingers before wrapping the slick digits around his hot rod.

His body bucked up, and I pushed his thighs wide.

"Feels good," he mumbled.

"I know," I said, his pleasure becoming my own.

As I worked him, my other hand slipped over his thighs, caressing his sack and down his perineum. When my slick finger circled his hole, I felt his body tense just slightly, so I did exactly as I had in the shower, massaging the sensitive area until he was accustomed to my touch.

Taking him back into my mouth, I slipped in the tip of one finger, and a little moan left his throat.

My heart was hammering, nerves bunched tight. I wanted so badly for this to be good for him, but in all truth, I'd never done this with a virgin, and because I was always the "top," I didn't know exactly what he might be feeling.

Add that I'd never before been so worried about someone

else's pleasure, so willing to forgo my own to make sure he was taken care of.

Fletcher didn't have a lot of consideration in his life. His needs almost never came first. I was hell-bent on changing that, on being that for him. Even if it meant a painful dick and a case of blue balls.

I knew the more relaxed and loose I could get him, the much less painful this first time would be.

So I settled in between his thighs and worked slowly, using generous amounts of lube to slide my fingers in and out.

By the time I made it to two full fingers inside him, he started to move a little, testing what it was like to push down on the pressure my fingers provided. He was tight and hot. The way his channel squeezed my fingers made me want to come right there.

I wanted to add a third finger, but before I did…

"Ahh." Fletcher gasped, hips bucking up toward the ceiling. "W-what was that?"

"That's your prostate. Feels good, right?"

"Do it again."

Smiling, I curled my fingers against the bundle of nerves I'd found, applying just the right amount of pressure.

He gasped and thrashed again as pleasure rippled over his limbs, lifting his skin with goose bumps.

"How'd you do that?" He panted, legs moving restlessly.

Chuckling, I added more lube and then carefully inserted another finger.

He made a sound, his legs going tense. "Ah, I don't—"

Stilling my hand, I didn't thrust deeper or pull out. Instead, I held still, allowing him to adjust to the intrusion. "Do you want me to stop?"

He was quiet a moment. After another heartbeat, I started to retreat. "You did so well," I praised. "I'll let you come now, and then I'll hold you."

He shoved up on his elbows, whole face a mask of blissed-out pleasure. Reaching down, he caught my wrist, stopping me from pulling all the way out. "No." He panted. "Don't stop."

"I don't want to hurt you."

"You aren't." He promised, eyes sincere. "Just… kiss me."

I moved up, latching onto his lips, tongue slipping into his mouth. He settled back down, sighing into the kiss, wiggling a little to remind me to keep going. After another minute of kissing, I did, pushing in all three fingers.

His body accepted me, and I rewarded him with a stroke to that magic gland, and he broke the kiss with his shudder.

"More." He panted.

I did it again.

He groaned, the sound of his pleasure making me huff.

"I want you now."

I hesitated, knowing that my dick was much wider than three fingers. Putting my forehead against his, I whispered, "I can't promise it won't hurt at first."

"I know. I'll take the pain if it's you."

A broken sound filled the space between us. My heart literally fell from my chest. He owned me. Completely.

With a shuddering breath, I left his body and smoothed a condom down over my seriously aching cock. I felt his eyes watching as I added too much lube to myself before adding even more to him.

His shaft had started to soften, clearly in anticipation of pain, so I bent, taking it between my lips to suck gently, feeling it harden anew.

When the tip of my head met his slick hole, I paused. Our eyes meeting in the dark.

Planting a hand on either side of him, I kissed him deeply, languidly, putting all the reassurance I possessed into the kiss.

With the first push, I slid about halfway in, his nails

sinking into my side. Panting, I held myself there, our lips no longer kissing but still together.

"More," he whispered, and so I pushed the rest of the way in, seating myself completely into his body.

A sound vibrated his throat, and his nails dug so deep into my sides I was sure there would be marks. Gazing down into his face, I noted his watery eyes and pursed lips.

"Puppy," I murmured, stroking the hair off his forehead. "Such a good boy for me. I'm all the way inside you now. You took all of me so well."

He made a sound, and I smiled, pressing a kiss to his temple. "That's my good boy."

The effort it took to not move, to feel his incredibly tight channel clench around my throbbing rod, was almost torture, but I withstood the desire to thrust and pound into him because no matter what I was feeling right now, he felt more.

Another minute ticked by as I peppered his eyelids, nose, and cheeks with soft kisses, whispering words of praise between each brush of my lips.

Eventually, the grip on my sides loosened, and his breath fanned across my face. "You can move now."

"Are you sure?"

He nodded.

I slid out, then pushed in again, this time both of us groaning. I moved slowly at first until his body started to respond, moving with me, his ass pushing down to meet my thrusts.

The room filled with the sound of lube squelching between our bodies. Moans and pants bounced off the walls, and then I found his prostate.

A high-pitched whine erupted, Fletcher silencing it with a slap of his hand over his mouth.

Stopping mid-thrust, I tugged his hand from his mouth.

"No," I said a little more sternly than I'd spoken previously. "Don't cover your sounds. They're mine."

"B-but—" He started to protest, but I thrust against that sensitive bundle again. "Oh God," he moaned.

Angling a little deeper, I pushed in again, this time wrapping an arm around one of his thighs.

His moans and gasps became a song my hips danced to, my dick pulsing with the need to come so desperately that spots began swimming in my vision.

Reaching between us, I stroked his dick, using my thumb to spread the pearly liquid over his tip, dragging it down the vein running down the side.

His whole body tightened.

"Oh God, I need—" The sound of his desperation was punctuated by the slapping sound his hand made on my arm.

"That's it, my good boy. Right there," I said, teeth tight as I began hammering more ruthlessly into his prostate. My hand sped up to match, and then he was coming, white ribbons of release spurting out across his lower belly and even going as far as his chest.

His entire body writhed and shuddered, mouth open but no sound coming out. I slowed a little but kept stroking him inside and out, working him through the entire orgasm before he collapsed, completely boneless underneath me.

The last stroke of my hand made him wince, and I knew he was likely nearing the zone of oversensitivity.

Pulling my hand away, I leaned down, pressing a kiss against his chest, then one on his cheek. "Okay?"

"My whole body tingles," he slurred.

I chuckled, pleased he was pleasured.

My own dick jerked inside him, reminding me of my own desperate need. I drew back, starting to slip out, but his legs wrapped around my hips, pushing me all the way back in.

I groaned.

"Inside me, E."

I was in no headspace to argue, a low growl all I could manage as my hips started pumping. It didn't take long, already at my limit and easily pushed over by staring down at his release decorating his chest, blown-out pupils, and love bites adorning his neck.

The only warning I gave was a low shout and the stiffening of my body, and I thrust deep one last time, shuddering into the side of his neck as my cock jerked and jerked inside him.

As I came, Fletcher's arms wound around me, holding me tight as I emptied into his body.

Eventually, I came down from the high, limbs weak, forehead damp, and, frankly, slightly dizzy. Pushing up, he winced, and I frowned, making sure to be extra careful when pulling out.

Gazing down between his thighs, I wished it wasn't so dark so I could see the condition he was in, wanting to make sure I wasn't too rough.

Pulling off the condom and tying it off, I lay down beside him, tucking my arm around his side to nuzzle his cheek. "How do you feel?"

"Mmm," he grunted.

Patiently, I nuzzled his cheek again. "Fletcher, I need you to use your words."

His head turned toward me, and a smile filled his face. "I'm really good, E. That was… It's even better than kissing."

Pride and relief swirled inside me, making me smile. "How much do you hurt?"

Turning his head, he buried his face into my neck. "Maybe just a little."

I didn't want to take away the bliss we both felt, but I knew the importance of aftercare because, truly, it would set the tone for the next time we did this.

I wanted to ensure he was comfortable before, during, and after because, honestly, all of those things worked together to create an experience that was pleasurable to us both.

Pressing a kiss to his forehead, I started to slide out of bed.

A sound of distress followed me, along with his grabby hand.

"I'm not going anywhere, puppy. I'm just cleaning us up."

"Don't wanna."

Laughing beneath my breath, I said, "I'll take care of you."

Before I could retreat, he reached out for me. I gave him my hand.

"Ethan?"

"Hmm?"

"I'm really glad you're my first."

My heart swelled, but then I climbed back on the bed, hovering over him with intensity that made his sleepy eyes widen.

"I'm glad I'm your first too, puppy. But you need to know that I'm also your *only*."

The alarm that originally sparked in his widening eyes faded fast, and a languid smile warmed up his small face. "My only."

"Don't you forget it." I warned.

"I won't," he said, still smiling. Laying a hand on my cheek, he whispered, "My only prince."

My heart was still fluttering when I stepped into the bathroom.

Twenty-Six

FLETCHER

THE SPLASH OF WARM WATER AND THE FEEL OF IT ENVELOPING me made me sigh.

"Lean back," Ethan murmured, gently pulling my naked body to rest against his chest.

I winced a little, my back and lower body stiff in ways I hadn't known before, but then Ethan was there, taking all of my weight and gently splashing the bathwater up over my chest and shoulders.

Despite the little bit of pain I felt down there, I was completely relaxed, satiated deep in my bones. I knew it would hurt some, and I wasn't wrong, but the pain only lasted a moment whereas the pleasure still lingered.

I didn't know it could be like this between two people. I didn't know how overwhelming it would be to have him inside me, to feel him move within. He'd been careful and patient, building and building the tension even though I felt the effort of it make his arms tremble.

No one ever cared about me that much before.

No one ever thought about me first.

I was in love with him.

Irrevocably so.

I loved him so fast and so fiercely that I couldn't be sure

the pain I felt wasn't from that rather than the pain of him penetrating my body.

"Hey." His gentle voice broke into my thoughts. "What's going on in that head?"

Ignoring the protest in my body, I turned, climbing into his lap, wrapping my legs around his waist.

Looping my arms around his neck, I pillowed my cheek on his shoulder. When his arms didn't instantly close around me, I wiggled closer, wanting to be surrounded by him completely.

A small sound vibrated his chest, his arms enclosing me tight.

I sighed dramatically, nosing against his neck.

"Fletch," Ethan said, gently stroking my back. "If I hurt you, you have to tell me."

"Please don't leave me," I said, the words jumping out before I could stop them.

His body stilled. The hands stroking me stopped.

When he tried to peel me back, I clung, making a desperate sound.

"Why would I leave you?" he asked, cupping the back of my head.

I shrugged. *Because everyone leaves. Because you're too good for me.*

"Didn't I just tell you back there that I'm your only? I'm not going anywhere."

"Even if you leave, you'll still be my only," I whispered.

It was true. He'd won my heart. My loyalty and my trust. In my world, that was almost impossible. The only people to have ever done that before were my brothers and Ivory.

But even this was different… deeper somehow. I let him inside me. Just thinking about him leaving made it hard to breathe.

This time, Ethan peeled me off his chest, refusing to let me cling.

"Look at me," he demanded, and automatically, I listened. "I will not leave you. You're mine, but I'm also yours."

My heart lightened a little. "You're mine?"

"Oh yes, puppy. All yours."

I sniffled, diving back into his neck.

"All yours," he crooned, holding me tight.

Emotions pummeled me as I clung to him. His reassurance kept me anchored. I felt like this day had lasted many weeks, but instead, everything happened all at once.

I couldn't regret it, though. I couldn't find any ounce of remorse inside me for everything that led me here, to his arms, to his bed.

He let me sniffle a little longer, whispering soothing words, stroking my back, and pouring gentle cascades of water over me until he finally lifted me away.

He washed us both in quiet, my hungry eyes eating up his face, memorizing his features.

Every so often, he would smile and kiss me.

Did I mention I liked kisses?

I was disgruntled when he left me in the bath to soak while he changed the sheets on the bed. Soon enough, he was back and lifting me out of the tub, supporting my weight while I got dried. My legs were still weak and shaky from sex, my lower back and, ah, behind sore.

When I was dry, he pulled one of his T-shirts over my head, then swept me off my feet.

"What are you doing?"

"You can't walk yet."

"I can too!" I argued even though he was right.

The bedside lamp was on, the curtains drawn closed. The kitten was still sleeping on the blanket, her fur fluffy now that she was dry.

After setting me on the bed, Ethan grasped one of my ankles and started to spread my legs.

"Hey!" I said, trying to shake him off.

"I need to look at you."

My entire face and neck burned. "You do not."

His blue eyes leveled me with a humorous stare. "So you'll let me put my fingers and my cock in you, but you won't let me look?"

"You don't need to look," I hissed, face on fire. Then I noticed the tube of cream in his hand. "What's that?"

"It's for you. I want to take away as much soreness as I can."

My heart melted a little at the thought.

He used it to his advantage and pushed my legs apart.

I made a sound, but he shushed me. "Hold still."

Grabbing a pillow, I pulled it over my face while he stared. He made a soft sound, and then a second later, he said, "I'm touching you."

His finger with the cream wasn't cold as though he'd spent time warming it between his fingers. I winced a little when he spread it around but then relaxed because it felt kind of good. After applying just a bit more, he pulled away.

My knees fell together, and I listened to him move around. Then the pillow was plucked from my face.

"All done."

I felt myself blush even more.

He kissed me softly and then switched out the light.

We settled together in the bed with him folding his body around me protectively.

"Ethan?" I asked, into the night.

"Hmm?"

"Was I okay?"

He was quiet a moment, making my stomach twist.

"Like, did you like it?" My questions echoed into the silence.

Gentle hands tugged me onto my back. His blond hair and face hovered over me in the darkness. "I'm sorry I made you wonder, sweetheart. I loved it. Every single minute of it. You were so perfect, and I already want you again."

My toes curled in the blankets, and my stomach tumbled, a soft smile pulling my lips. "That's good."

"C'mon then, let me hold you. You need to sleep."

Meow. The tiny sound resonated from beside the bed.

"Oh!" I said, pulling out of his embrace to stare down at the glowing white kitten.

Meow.

"Are you lonely?" I asked her.

Ethan sighed loudly, sliding out of bed on the other side. All he wore was a pair of tight boxer briefs, and it totally distracted me when he bent to scoop up the tiny kitten.

I thought he would put her back on her blanket, and it made my chest ache a little.

But he didn't.

He set her on the bed, right against my body.

Feeling my surprise, he laughed low. "You won't be able to sleep unless you know she's okay."

"Thank you," I said quietly as the kitten began to purr.

Back in bed, Ethan slid up behind me once again. "Come here, my puppy and my kitten," he said, spooning around me and the kitten who was lying in a ball against my stomach.

I'd never in my entire life felt so complete.

Twenty-Seven

Ethan

Responsibility was not new to me. I'd grown up in a world where it was pretty much assigned at birth along with your last name and bank account.

I never minded much. The responsibilities I had in life were things I could handle easily, perhaps *because* I'd known them from birth.

The responsibility of love was completely different.

Lying in bed with Fletcher curled into my side and a tiny fluffball somehow using us both as a mattress, I realized I never knew love. Not like this.

Love in my world was different. Somehow cold and less emotional. While I knew my parents loved me, they always seemed a bit distant as though I wasn't just their son but a trophy of sorts. They'd given me a wonderful life full of every advantage, but the more I thought about it, the more I realized their kind of love felt limited.

But him... *Fletcher*. Emotion pummeled me whenever he was near. Every feeling, every moment was heightened with him, everything seemed so... endless.

I discovered quickly there was no limit to the depth of my love for him. Just when I thought I'd maxed out, he'd do something to push me deeper.

Last night was… overwhelming. Exhilarating. Unlike anything I'd ever experienced before.

The way he looked at me, the way he bowed beneath my touch. Complete trust. Complete faith.

He inspired wild and deep emotion I could literally feel coursing through my veins. And with these unbridled feelings came a new type of responsibility, one that wasn't easily handled.

In a way, I felt like I was stumbling around in the dark, and while I wasn't afraid of the dark, I was afraid now.

What if I let him down? What if being in unknown territory made me stagger? What if these overwhelming feelings acted like heavy fog, making it hard to see the right way?

Suddenly, the responsibility of bearing someone else's heart was so much more terrifying than handling my own. I loved his more than mine, and I didn't want to let him down.

If the feelings I had last night standing inside an art exhibit with Sienna were weighted enough to confess I was already with someone, then this morning, they were tenfold.

I didn't regret at all telling her. If anything, I was relieved. But I did regret agreeing to wait to tell my parents until she was gone.

It made me feel like a coward, but a coward I really was not.

Or was I? Is that why I'd never told my parents I was gay? Was I afraid it would be beyond the limits of their love?

No. Yes. *Fuck.*

Yes. I guess part of me thought they wouldn't accept me. They were very old-school money who cared very much about image. *No.* I didn't really care because if they did turn me away, I would be fine. I had plenty of money and connections of my own.

But I saw no reason to rock the boat.

Until now.

For Fletcher, I'd drain an entire ocean.

Keeping an arm anchored around Fletch, I snatched my cell off the charger to shoot a brief text to Bree. *I'm coming in late. Reschedule my morning.*

Then I shot off another text to my trainer. *Can't train this AM. I'll make it up tomorrow.*

The thought of a more punishing workout than I normally did was intense, but not as intense as the need to stay in this bed.

Bree: *Are you sick? Migraine? Do you need me to come over?*

Trainer: *I'll be there earlier than normal tomorrow.*

After sending a brief agreement to the trainer, I typed another message to Bree.

Everything is fine, just need the morning off.

When that was done, I scrolled through my contacts and found the one I needed, sending off another message.

After relaying a fourth and final message to Jane, saying I didn't need her this morning, I replaced the phone on the nightstand and rolled to cuddle Fletcher.

I never thought I'd be the kind of guy to cuddle anyone, but now imagining not doing it with him made me ache.

Though still asleep, a small sound vibrated his throat, his cheek rubbing against my bare chest. Absentmindedly, my fingers stroked his hair, lips pressing a kiss to the top of his head.

Long fingers spider-crawled over my abs, making them ripple under the whispering attention. Languidly, he continued exploring, tracing the contours of my muscle, circling my belly button, and tracing the waistband of my boxers.

It didn't matter that he was probably half asleep. It didn't matter he was just innocently exploring my body… It turned me on. Desire I carried only for him ignited, chasing all my conflicting thoughts to the back of my mind.

"Your heart is beating faster." His voice was scratchy and

heavy with sleep. Just the tone sent tingles racing over my scalp.

"Because you're touching me," I murmured, fingers departing his hair to caress his ear.

Lifting his cheek, Fletcher pressed an open-mouthed, gentle kiss to where he'd just been lying over my heart. The tender action caught my breath. All I could do was stare.

"I missed you a lot yesterday." He confessed, face turned up but eyes unable to settle on mine. "I tried so hard not to, but I just…" He buried his face in my neck.

Cupping my hand around his shoulder, I gave it a light squeeze. "Just what?"

I hung in limbo, the unexpected words so sweet they instantly created a craving for more.

"I just really wanted you," he whispered.

"I just really wanted you too."

His head lifted. "Really?"

I made a sound. "Why else would I ride around on a subway searching for you?"

"I ran away."

"And I followed," I echoed. "I will always follow no matter where you go."

The room swelled with chemistry. His lower lip disappeared into his mouth where he sucked just enough to make it glimmer when he let go.

Golden eyes dropped to my mouth, and his entire body swayed closer, silently asking for what he wanted.

It was a gentle meeting of lips at first, languid and easy with our tongues reaching out at exactly the same time. His mouth was slick as though he'd been salivating for this kiss, his mouth anticipating mine.

A low moan deep in his throat had me pulling him closer, the kiss turning more demanding. His eagerness endeared me as if he forgot to be shy when our mouths were fused. He kissed with abandon, retreating only when he wanted me to take control.

Rolling, I pinned him under me, my fingers slipping beneath the T-shirt to stroke over his chest and belly.

His small cry when I plucked at his hardened nipple had me back on his mouth again, slashing my lips over his with ownership I hoped left him branded.

Hands went everywhere. Hips started to thrust. The drag of his fingernails down either side of my spine made me shudder.

He was hard and hot against my stomach. I felt his heat even through his boxers. Pulsing need and the insatiable urge to claim took over, and it wasn't until he whimpered that I realized I had his underwear pushed down and his leaking cock in my hand.

A very low swear dropped from my lips as I tried to rein in some control. I wanted to take him again so badly, but it was just too soon. I didn't know his condition this morning, and I wouldn't risk hurting him by having sex again.

"Don't stop." He urged, thrusting into my fist.

How I adored his flushed cheeks, rumpled hair, and seeing those marks I'd left all over the side of his neck.

At this point, stopping wasn't physically possible, the need between us just too strong to deny.

The sound of alarm he made when I moved off him to the side made me smile. "Easy, puppy. I know what you need."

So pliant, I thought proudly when I was able to move him into position with barely any effort at all.

With Fletcher on his side, I spooned behind him, bringing our bare bodies flush. A low hiss filled the room when he wiggled back into my erection, making my toes curl.

His ass was round and soft. The warmth against my dick made me shudder.

Reaching around, I grasped his length, enjoying the way it

jerked in my hold. Giving it a few light strokes, I relished his body arching with a sinful moan.

"Good boy," I crooned, nipping his ear and smoothing the light bite with my tongue. "You're my good boy."

His breath huffed out at my praise, his hand reaching down to encircle my wrist.

He writhed restlessly against me. His whimpers and wiggles made me near insane. When I released his throbbing length, he tried to pull me back, but I denied my hand.

"Be a good boy." I warned with just a bit more demand in my tone.

He went still, though I felt the need making him quiver. As a reward for his obedience, I kissed his shoulder before sliding my palm between his legs.

Glancing over his shoulder, he gazed at me in question.

"We're gonna do it like this because I don't want to hurt you."

"You won't," he whined, tempting me with his round, bare ass against my groin.

I made a stern sound, and his teeth sank into his lower lip, big doe eyes looking to me for forgiveness.

Unable to resist, I laughed low in my throat, leaned down, and kissed away his worry.

"I'm gonna use your thighs," I whispered, adjusting so my throbbing cock was sandwiched between his smooth, warm legs.

The pressure of that alone made me groan as I thrust against him.

He made a low noise, thrusting back against me, offering more friction. Two of my fingers pressed against his kissable lips, tapping for permission. "Suck."

Lips parting immediately, he tugged both my fingers in, wrapping his tongue around them.

Groaning, I thrust again, the feel of him around my dick

and my fingers a sinful combination. "Make them wet," I murmured, hips snapping forward again.

He worked my fingers so well I briefly considered pulling them out and replacing them with my cock, but I decided to save that activity for another day. Feeling my fingers good and saturated, I pulled them away, only to have his tongue chase after them.

"Kiss." I beckoned, and he came eagerly, our mouths molding together only to break apart when my wet fingers slid along his still-hard dick.

His head fell on the pillow, body arched again. Anchoring him close, I began stroking him to the rhythm of my thrusts, both of us panting and moaning in tune.

When his body went taut, I thumbed his slit and tightened my grip around the sensitive area near his head.

He came undone that instant, his hot, pulsing dick spilling all over my hand and the sheets.

He was still pulsing when my own thrusts became sloppy as I chased the orgasm just barely out of reach... *There.*

With a low shout, I came, pumping into him even as I jerked, making a mess out of his perfect thighs.

At last, we both came down from the high, our bodies sticking together with sweat and release.

I felt the rapid rise and fall of his back against my chest, and I gently released his cock to hug him into the center of my body.

"Good?" I asked against his ear.

"Mmm." His head bobbed. One of his hands found and curled around one of mine. "Next time, I want you inside me, though."

My smile was fast and wide. When I gave him a loud kiss against his neck, he giggled. "I have to make sure you're okay before I'm inside you again."

"I told you I'm okay," he demanded, laughter gone from his voice.

"Not until I'm sure."

"I know my own body." He scolded, pushing into a sitting position.

His wince was not missed by either of us. Face falling, a sheepish expression took over.

I sat up, pulling him into my arms, offering to take his weight. Very gently, I caressed his lower back.

"Maybe I am just a little sore."

Kissing his temple, I smiled. "How about a shower and breakfast in bed?"

Pulling back, he asked, "Don't you have to work out? Go to the office?"

I shook my head. "I don't, and I'm going in late."

His eyes went round. "Really?"

"I'd rather be here with you."

Launching forward, he flung himself into my chest, arms winding around my shoulders to squeeze. I couldn't help but laugh. The pressure in my heart was almost too much to bear.

Slipping out of bed, I considered pulling on the boxer briefs but decided against it, choosing instead to just walk around to carefully place the kitten on the floor before reaching down to lift Fletch into my arms.

The tiny animal rubbed against my ankle as I cradled him against my chest.

"I can walk," he protested, but it was weak considering the way he snuggled in close.

I carried him into the shower, turning on all the controls before standing him out of reach of the spray.

When I was sure he was, in fact, steady on his feet, I ruffled his hair. "I'll shower off in the other bathroom and then bring up breakfast."

"Why in the other bathroom?" He complained.

Dragging my eyes up and down his naked, lean frame, I

let my stare linger on the love bites I'd littered over his pale skin, feeling the sudden urge to create even more.

Ears red, Fletcher glanced down and gasped. "Did you do that?" he said, pointing at the mark on his stomach.

"Mmm." I agreed. "And this one." I pointed to his inner thigh, then up to his collarbone and neck. "These too."

His hand slapped over his neck and the other on his thigh. "Ethan!"

A warm, throaty chuckle rose around us with the steam. Sliding closer, I leaned down so we were eye level. "You wear those marks so prettily, my good boy," I crooned. All the embarrassment on his face shifted into something much hotter. "You wear them so good that if I stay in here for a second longer, I'm gonna mark you up even more."

His little shriek was punctuated by the way he splashed over the floor to hide under the spray. Water dripped over his nose, cascading over his chest when he finally looked back.

I winked.

He flushed.

We both knew damn well he'd let me mark him up all over again, and both of us would enjoy it.

Twenty-Eight

FLETCHER

"I'M CALLING HER GWEN," I ANNOUNCED WHEN ETHAN LET himself into the bedroom a short while later.

"Gwen?" he asked, halting partway across the room, hands filled with treats that made me realize how starved I was.

"Is that *Kismet?*" I jumped up, racing over to reach for the familiar paper cup.

"Ah-ah." He scolded, holding it out of reach. "What first?"

I crooked my finger for him to lean down. Instead, he just lifted an eyebrow.

"I'm sore." I pouted.

Tenderness filled his entire face, and my heart performed a summersault. Bending at the waist, he lowered, turning his cheek in my direction.

Smiling in triumph, I bounced forward, lips smacking against his freshly shaven cheek.

Truth? I really wasn't that sore. I just wanted to see if he would come to me.

Kiss delivered, he handed over the *Kismet* cup, the unmistakable scent of their rich hot chocolate hitting my senses and making me drool.

Tilting it to my lips, I took a big drink. Whipped cream and chocolate burst over my tongue… and so did pain.

"Ow!" I wailed, pulling it down. "Hot!"

Making a sound, Ethan set aside everything to grasp my face and tap his finger against my lips. I was instantly transported to when we were in bed just a little while ago and the way I'd sucked his thick fingers into my mouth.

His deepening expression told me he knew exactly where my mind went, but instead of playing, he cleared his throat and tapped again. "Let me see."

I stuck my tongue out. He studied it.

Leaning in, he kissed it quickly before declaring, "You'll be okay. Be careful."

The next sip I took was much more cautious and also under his watchful blue gaze. Dropping down on the floor, legs tucked beneath me, I stroked down the kitten's thin back.

She was gobbling up the plate of food I'd given her when I'd finished showering.

"Gwen?" Ethan asked, turning back to the paper bag he'd set aside. "Kind of an odd name for a cat, don't you think?"

"No!" I declared, completely offended. Leaning forward, I stroked her again. "Just ignore him, Gwennie. He doesn't know."

"C'mon, off the floor so we can eat."

"I'm eating with Gwen." I sniffed, turning my attention to the incredibly rich, warm hot chocolate.

I really expected him to argue. To use that commanding tone, I seemed to be unable to deny.

He didn't. Instead, he sat down, mirroring my sitting position.

I nearly gaped as he sipped at his drink, which was probably coffee without enough creamer.

Noting my unbelieving expression, he smiled. "I told you, puppy. Anywhere you go, I'll go too."

I took another sip so it would keep me from blurting out words I felt but wasn't ready to say.

"So why not Mittens or Snowflake or Fluffy?" he asked as if telling me he would follow me all around was just some passing comment that didn't make me want to blurt out how much I loved him.

But it was a good distraction.

Making a face, I lowered the mug. "Lame," I muttered. "Don't you know who Gwen is?"

"Should I?" he asked, eyes thoughtful and cup paused partway to his lips.

I held out one hand palm up. "Spider-Man's first love?"

"I thought Spider-Man was in love with Mary Jane."

Smacking my forehead, I made an insufferable sound. "But before Mary Jane, there was Gwen. She died."

He frowned. "I don't recall that."

"You haven't seen *The Amazing Spider-Man?*" I practically yelled.

Gwen stopped eating and looked up.

"You're going to give her a stomach ache." I scolded Ethan.

"My apologies," he told the cat. Then to me, "The last Spider-Man I saw was with Tobey Maguire."

I was completely offended, and I shook my head sadly.

"And I saw him in one of the newer *Avengers* movies."

"You missed the best two *Spider-Man* movies made. Andrew Garfield made the best Spider-Man ever."

"And Gwen was in those movies?"

My head bobbed.

"Well, if we're going to have a cat named after her, I guess I need to watch them."

We. If we *are going to have a cat.*

A feeling of homesickness washed over me, making my arm wrap around my middle. I stared at Gwen, unblinking, grip on the paper cup a bit tighter than before. This wasn't a feeling I knew very well, and it was a feeling I didn't really like. I'd only known it once before when I stayed at the Christmas tree stand I worked at last year for two nights.

It was somehow foreboding and wishful all at once. Wishful because I wanted to be here with him, and when he talked that way, it made it seem like he wanted it too. But the insecurity in me couldn't completely let go, and it whispered not to get too used to this because he would eventually realize I wasn't good enough.

"Fletch?" His voice was accompanied by gentle fingers just beneath my chin. Blinking, I looked away from the kitten to Ethan who slid closer to me.

I offered him a small smile.

"How about we have a talk?"

Without waiting for me to answer, he straightened, picking me up off the floor to head toward the bed.

"But it's messy!" I fussed.

"I changed the sheets."

Eyeing the bed, I noted it did seem freshly made. "How many sets of sheets do you have?" I wondered.

His smile was quick. "Not enough if we're going to be making a mess of them every night."

"Every night!" I gasped, neck and ears on fire.

He paused, holding me at the side of the bed. Tilting his head to the side, he asked, "Oh, are you tired of me already?"

He was teasing, but I didn't like the words. They hit a little too close to home.

Averting my gaze, I spoke low. "It's you who's gonna get tired of me."

His gentle noise brought my chin up, but it was the sincerity in his blue gaze that held my attention. "I won't."

After setting me in bed, Ethan retreated to get the large brown bag with the Kismet logo on the side.

Scooting toward the center and leaning against the headboard, I asked, "How did you have time to change the sheets, shower, and go to Kismet for breakfast?"

"The sheets only took a moment, and I had Kismet brought to us." Ethan tugged the lid off a black container and handed over a huge croissant filled with eggs, bacon, and cheese.

Once it was in my hands, he set a white paper sack beside me with a giant blueberry muffin inside.

"Ooh!" I exclaimed, propping the sandwich in my lap to pull out the muffin and take a huge bite out of its top. A little groan of satisfaction broke free around my chewing.

Smiling, Ethan settled beside me, tugging up the blankets before leaning over to brush a crumb from my lower lip. After another huge bite, I held it out to him, but he shook his head. "Eat some of your sandwich. It has protein."

I took another huge bite of the muffin. It was the best muffin ever.

Ethan's container was filled with scrambled eggs mixed with some vegetables and other stuff. He did have some bacon, though, so that made up for the veggies.

We ate in comfortable silence before Ethan set aside his fork. "Do you want me to lift the blinds so you can look out over the city?" Palming the little remote, he aimed it toward the windows.

Laying my hand over it, I pushed it down. "No."

His expression turned quizzical. "I thought you loved the view."

"I do. But right now, I'm looking at you." I admitted, feeling shy.

The remote disappeared, and the blinds stayed shut, hiding us from the rest of the world. Leaning into the space between us, Ethan kissed me slow and soft.

Hints of his coffee, my hot chocolate, and blueberry flavored the kiss, but it was still distinctly ours. The way my stomach fluttered and dipped, the way my head buzzed emptily, and the unmistakable way his tongue slowly twisted with mine as though he didn't care if we ever untangled.

It didn't matter we'd had each other last night and then again this morning. Need still thrummed between us, clinging in the air, sticking to my skin, and making me melt just a little closer into his lips.

As we disconnected gradually, his shuddering breath fanned over my damp lips while his palm cupped the side of my neck. "You have no idea what you do to me."

"I might have some idea," I whispered, bumping my nose against his.

"I just want to protect you from everything. Even from me."

Pulling back, I bounced my eyes between his. "What do you mean?"

"I want to tell you some things about me. Will you listen?"

My head bobbed.

He swallowed thickly, moving his plate aside. "I probably should have said something before we… well, before last night."

Nerves coiled in my stomach, and fear slammed into me so hard I rocked back, nearly knocking over my cup.

"Ah!" I fussed, lunging to catch it before it spilled. The container on my lap slipped free, though, landing on the sheets. I started to tremble, a mass of nervous energy and dread settling onto my shoulders like the heaviest of weights.

"I-I spilled it." I worried, tucking the cup into my chest and reaching for the upturned container.

"Hey, it's all right," he crooned, taking care of the mess in a second flat. When he reached for the cup, I surrendered it, suddenly sorry because now there was nothing left to do with my quivering hands.

"Why are you so scared?" His voice was gentle as though he were talking to a frightened animal. I wouldn't lie and say it wasn't soothing, because it was. The next thing I knew, I was in his lap, my back supported by his chest, his back against the headboard.

I felt surrounded by him with his cheek pressing against the side of my head and lips close to my ear. "Calm down, puppy. I'm not gonna say anything that terrible, okay? It's all right. I'm here."

I knew he could feel me shaking. It didn't matter how stiffly I tried to hold myself. The trembles still came. His large hand stroked my hair, and the feel of his breath against my ear was soothing.

"I'm not going anywhere, puppy." He reassured me.

"But you said—"

"I said I can't keep my hands off you, and that's why this conversation is coming after I've already had you." His words were a bit sheepish, and hearing him put it that way made me calmer. "I feel like I've done everything backward with you. Not at all the way I should."

"I don't understand," I whispered, my rigid limbs giving up their fight and allowing me to surrender against him completely.

"It's because I'll take you no matter what. It doesn't matter if you don't want to talk about your past or about her." I sucked in a breath, but he moved on. "I don't need to know everything there is to know about you because, to be honest, it won't change how I feel. I want you no matter what. But I realize that probably isn't the case for you."

Gasping, I twisted around to stare at him, incredulous. "Yes, it is!"

His smile was a bit sad, and it made me want to hug him. "But I should have told you."

"Told me what?"

"My parents don't know I'm gay."

Oh. Was that what this was about? All the worry I'd felt just moments ago drained away, leaving me relieved yet worn out. I shrugged. "Okay."

Ethan's eyes widened. "Okay?"

"I kinda already figured most people didn't know. I mean, up until last year, everyone thought you were with Ivory. But I guess I thought maybe your parents knew, the people closest to you." But then I thought back to when I'd met his father and made a face. "Well, actually, no. Your dad is scary. Are you worried he'll hate you?"

A funny look crossed his features. "Partly."

Sadness enveloped me because I knew what it was like to hope for acceptance even when you knew you wouldn't get it. "It's okay," I told him quietly. "You can tell them when you're ready."

"Really?" he asked, the relief in his tone too great for him to conceal.

"Yeah. I understand." For once, I wondered if maybe having a parent who never cared was better than having one who only cared when you were who they wanted you to be. The hovering possibility they could take away their love at any moment was probably crippling.

"There's something else."

I looked up, inner meanderings forgotten. There was something in his tone. Something I didn't want to acknowledge but definitely couldn't ignore.

"What?" My voice turned timid. The anxiety I thought was gone reappeared, churning my stomach almost like a warning or a venomous snake waiting to strike.

I was tired of talking. I wanted him to kiss me instead.

"My father is trying to set me up again." As he spoke, I noticed the way he watched me very carefully.

My eyes widened. "You mean like with a girl?"

"With a wife."

"He wants you to date a married woman?" I demanded, completely offended. "I know you're rich, but that's not right!"

Ethan laughed and ruffled my hair, but I moved from the touch to scowl.

Still chuckling, he lowered his hand. "No. He wants me to get married."

My mouth formed an O.

"He seems to think my lack of finding anyone who interests me is the perfect reason for a marriage of convenience."

I blinked. I didn't know what that meant.

"For money and for business," Ethan explained. "Like with Ivory."

He reads me so well. He pays such close attention.

The warm thoughts left me cold. Cold because we were talking about his impending marriage. And if he got married… *What about me?*

Suddenly, I was pummeled with insecurity, fear, and doubt. Instinctively, I pulled in on myself, tucking my knees closer against my body and scooting back for some distance between us.

I got attached.

I shouldn't have gotten attached.

Now I knew why he wanted to tell me before we had sex.

I probably wouldn't have slept with him...

A distressed sound brought my head up as he reached for me, but I jerked back, denying us both.

It hurt. It hurt to think last night was not only our first but our last.

You're disposable to him, Fletcher. You aren't anyone's forever.

He said he was your only... but he never said you were his.

The whispers were savage and sounded so much like *her* in the back of my head that it sent me scrambling back until there was no more mattress, and I dropped onto the floor with a yelp. Echoes of pain shot through me, reminding me all over again of last night.

A night I might never have again.

"Fletcher!" Ethan rushed around the end of the bed.

The second he was within arm's reach, I held out my hand. "No. Stay back."

Face pale, he lowered his hands but didn't back away. "I won't touch you. But please just keep listening. *Please.*"

I made a sound kind of like a scoff. I hoped it sounded uninterested and pissed off. In reality, it was me groaning because I couldn't run. My legs felt too weak.

"He flew in a socialite from California. Her father could be an ally in business. She's staying with my family, and he's hoping we'll hit it off."

Dread was a heavy emotion. It was like an anvil that could anchor you at the bottom of the sea. And I could do nothing but sit here. Sit here and drown in the ache his words created within me. "You met her."

He made a strangled sound, sinking to the floor. "He brought her to my office yesterday. I, ah, I took her to dinner."

Sudden anger gave me strength. The immense hurt I felt took a back seat, and I embraced the heat. Shooting up, I felt daggers stab from eyes. "You met your future wife yesterday and then came home and slept with me?" My voice was fierce.

"No!"

"It's a little late to lie," I spat, turning toward the door to leave.

You let him fool you, Fletch. You let him convince you that maybe, just this once, you were good enough. Stupid. Stupid boy.

Mother's laughter rang out in the back of my ears. I flinched, trying to get away from the sound.

Strong arms locked around me from behind. I bucked and struggled, trying to get free. "Let go!"

"No. Listen to me!"

Why should I keep listening? Every single word you say hurts worse and worse. I expected better from you, Ethan.

In the end, you're just like everyone else.

"I said let go!" I roared, stomping down on his foot.

He grunted but didn't loosen his hold. In fact, his arms shackled me tighter.

"You're hurting me," I whined pathetically, but sadly, it was true.

He let go instantly, and honestly, that just hurt worse. Did the idea of physically hurting me bother him?

No. You just aren't worth the fight.

No one wants you. You're worthless.

A sob caught in my throat, burning and robbing me of breath, but still I forced it down. I would not cry in front of him. I would not let him know just how badly this was killing me.

Wrenching away, I fled, flinging open the door and running as if my life depended on it.

He shouted my name and begged me to come back. The sound of his pounding feet giving chase was like the heavy beating of a drum.

It wasn't until I was in the elevator that I looked back.

"Fletcher!" he exclaimed, rushing out of the penthouse.

I hit the button a thousand times, willing the doors to close quicker. His eyes were wild, his mouth set. In his haste, his strong frame knocked into the fancy table with the huge vase of flowers. It crashed to the floor. The sound of it shattering was deafening.

Ethan didn't even pause but charged through the broken glass, water, and scattered flower petals, trying to make it to me.

"Wait." His voice was strangled, and he reached out a hand.

But it was too late.

The doors eased shut, redrawing the line between us that never should have been erased.

Twenty-Nine

ETHAN

GLASS AND CRUMPLED FLOWER PETALS STUCK TO THE BOTTOM of my feet. Wet footprints trailed behind me as I dragged myself up the stairs.

I'd run out of the penthouse, shouting onto the street. People stared and made wide arches around me as they walked, but I didn't care.

All I cared about was Fletcher.

"Fletcher!" I roared, pounding up and down the sidewalk, searching desperately for his retreating frame.

He was fast, somehow an expert at escape.

I searched and searched until my nose ran from the cold, my eyes watered in the wind, and my dirty, bloody feet were numb. Even then, I paced down close-by alleyways, shouting his name, desperation clinging to my vocal cords.

He was gone.

Somehow he'd slipped away no matter how earnestly I searched.

I let him down.

I did the one thing in this entire world I never wanted to do.

The hurt in his eyes was something that would haunt me

the rest of my days. The way he stared at me as if I were a stranger was not at all the way he'd look at me last night.

This was why I hadn't wanted to tell him about Sienna.

This is exactly why you should have told him sooner.

I should have held him down. I should have let him punch and kick and scream. I should have ignored his proclamation that I was hurting him because at least he would still be in my arms.

Now he was… gone.

Running the streets with no shoes, no coat, and a shattered heart.

If only he'd let me finish. If only he'd have listened.

This isn't his fault.

No. It wasn't. It was mine. His trust was misplaced for a reason. His panic and doubt had obviously been learned.

I wanted to be his exception.

But now I was just like everyone else.

In the bedroom, a tiny mewling sound hit me in the chest. The small white kitten stood impossibly small and thin, staring up at me with questions in its eyes.

I sank to my knees in front of her, and after a moment's hesitation, she strolled close. Her fur was soft against my knee, but she didn't purr. Instead, she stared with wide, curious eyes, asking me where her savior went, why I chased him away.

My fingers stroked over her back, recalling the way Fletcher's had done the same. Leaving me behind, Gwennie —as Fletch called her—walked to a pile of fabric I hadn't noticed before.

My T-shirt. The one Fletcher slept in last night. The one he'd been wearing when I made love to him this morning.

A rough sound ripped from my throat, and the base of my skull pierced with sharp pain.

I watched the kitten do a little turn in the center of the fabric before curling up in a ball.

Ignoring the migraine threatening to overtake me, I pushed to my feet.

"I'll bring him back," I told the kitten. "This is where he belongs."

Thirty

Fletcher

I WASN'T TOO GOOD AT SCHOOL, BUT I DIDN'T SO MUCH MIND going. The buildings were old, but they were warm, and the ladies in the cafeteria always gave me extra mashed potatoes. Cold air didn't seep in around the windows, and the teachers never yelled.

I never really did my homework, but this year I would try.

I liked it when my teacher smiled at me. It didn't matter if I got all the answers wrong. She smiled anyway. Her smile was like the sun. Bright.

Yesterday when I'd come to school with missing buttons on my coat, the teacher sewed new ones back on. They were different colors and sizes, but I didn't mind. She buttoned me up before I walked home, telling me to make sure I stayed warm.

Today, we spent all morning working on crafts. The teacher told us to make something for someone we loved.

My mom wasn't as nice as her, and she didn't ever smile. But I loved her anyway because she was my mom, and she was the only person I had.

I wanted to see her smile. I thought maybe if I made this gift for her, I might finally get to see it.

I worked all morning, gluing popsicle sticks together, skipping snack time, and getting glitter all over my jeans and hands. When I was done, I showed it proudly to my teacher.

"Wow, Fletcher! That's the most beautiful snowflake I've ever seen!" she said.

Pride welled in my chest. For sure, this would make Mom smile!

"Do you think my mom will like it?" I asked, hope making my heart flutter.

"Absolutely. She will love it."

My teacher even helped me wrap it up with red tissue paper and tuck it into a little brown bag.

I clutched it the whole way home, anticipating Mom's face when she saw the gift I made just for her.

It was okay if she was grouchy a lot, and it was okay if our house wasn't as warm as school. She didn't really like me much, but maybe this would change her mind.

I left my backpack by the front door the second I walked in.

"Mom!" I called up the stairs. "Mother!"

The house stayed quiet, and I glanced into the small living room.

"Mom?"

A few seconds later, she appeared out of the kitchen, a small glass clutched in her palm. "What is all this racket?" she yelled. "What the hell do you want?"

"I made this for you at school today!" I beamed, holding up the bag.

She seemed surprised. "You made something for me?"

I nodded vigorously. "Open it!"

She put aside the glass and turned toward me.

I bounced from foot to foot as she opened the sack, pulling out the bundle of red paper. Holding it in her palm, she pulled the edges back, and even in the dim lighting of our living room, the glitter I'd applied so meticulously sparkled.

"What is this?" she asked, staring down.

"A snowflake!" I exclaimed. "I put all the sticks together, I painted it, and I even made it sparkly."

She glanced up at me. "You did all this?"

I nodded proudly. "I made it just for you. Teacher said to make something for someone that we love."

Something in the room shifted. The excitement I'd felt dimmed. My tummy felt a little funny, and I waited for her reply.

Mother's lips curled in a snarl, her brows slashing over her eyes. "Someone you love," she spat.

"That's you, Mom," I said, still hopeful.

She threw back her head and laughed. It wasn't at all a happy sound.

Her body was stiff, her shoulders rigid. Eyes flashing at me, she looked back at the snowflake. "You used too much glue here, and you missed a spot with the paint."

I bit down on my lip.

"And this glitter," she spat. "I hate glitter! So shiny and sparkling, pretending to be pretty when, really, it just gets every-where and never goes away!"

"I did my best," I said, hope extinguishing as though it hadn't even been there.

"Of course you did!" she wailed. "That's why it's worthless! Because you are worthless!"

I recoiled. "I-I'm s-sorry."

The red paper drifted to the floor as she held up the snowflake and snapped it in two.

I gasped. "Mom!"

"It's hideous!"

The delicate wood snapped again, glitter raining down to the floor.

"I don't want your love. I don't want it! No one wants you!" She threw one of the broken pieces at her feet.

Tears welled in my eyes, and I tried so hard not to let them fall. The last time I'd cried, she made fun of me for a week.

Crybaby. Crybaby. Wah-wah-wah.

"I just wanted to see you smile."

"If you wanted me to smile, you should never have been born!"

My hands went to my tummy. It didn't feel good at all.

Throwing the rest of the snowflake on the floor, she stared with a cold look in her eye. "What's that on your coat?"

I glanced down at the multicolored buttons. "N-n-nothing."

"Don't tell me it's nothing! I can see it's something. Where did you get those buttons?"

"T-t-teacher sewed them on."

A wild noise ripped from her throat, and she rushed me. I stumbled back, falling onto the floor, and she was over me, ripping at my coat.

Ping. Ping. Ping.

The sound of buttons hitting the floor and rolling away was louder than even her yell.

Closing my eyes, I waited until she was gone to roll onto my side and curl into a ball.

"Being warm is a luxury I will never allow!" she wailed.

I waited for her to take her glass and go back to the kitchen. Long minutes passed, and I finally rose to my knees.

Broken popsicle sticks lay on the floor. The glitter was no match for the dark and dirty floor.

I stared at the snowflake I'd lovingly made as cold air prickled through my buttonless coat.

I would never see her smile. I guess you couldn't smile at something you didn't love.

THE MEMORY OVERWHELMED ME, SLAMMING INTO ME LIKE A sucker punch. The bitter flavor of my childhood splashed up the back of my throat like acid, bringing with it the taste of blood. I stopped bringing her gifts after that day because I knew it wouldn't matter what I brought. Nothing would make her love me.

My entire life was filled with moments like these, reinforcing the idea that I had no value and there was nothing remarkable about me to love.

The only thing that kept me going was something deep inside that never completely went out. It didn't matter how cruel or cold she was or even when she managed to snuff out the flickering flame.

Hope always reignited. It always offered just a tiny bit of warmth to get me through the coldest of days. Sometimes it came to me in sleep, in the melody of a violin, a sound that swirled in my head for days.

I'd looked for more of that feeling my entire life, never thinking I would find it but searching just the same.

Life got better when I found my brothers, bringing hope that perhaps there was a place for me somewhere in this world. But it wasn't until Ethan that I thought perhaps someone could love me the way I craved so badly to be loved.

Just thinking of him made me stagger, shoulder scraping against a rough brick wall. I blinked, finally taking in my surroundings.

The alleyway was unrecognizable, a place I hadn't been before. I'd run and run from Ethan's building, not even seeing the direction in which I escaped. It hadn't mattered where I ended up as long as I got away.

Tingling cold prickled my feet, and I glanced down, seeing I wasn't wearing any shoes. I'd rushed out with only the clothes I was wearing and nothing more. Tiny cuts probably cluttered the bottom of my feet, but they were nothing compared to the gashes in my heart.

The sob I'd been holding in finally ripped free, reverberating through the alley, echoing with loneliness I was all too familiar with.

As I sank down the wall, the rough brick scrapped through my shirt, stinging my back the way my feet already stung.

Collapsing in on myself, I wrapped my arms around my knees, giving in to the urge to cry.

"I thought you were different," I whimpered. "Why did you make me love you if you wouldn't love me back?"

Wiping my face with my shirt, I huffed out a breath, staring through tear-blurred eyes. "Why won't anyone love me?" I asked no one at all. "Why am I never enough?"

Crumbling again, I sat and sobbed, stuffing my fist into my mouth to muffle the sound. When undeniable longing to be safely wrapped up in the scent of pine and for a familiar voice to whisper that I was a good boy clutched at my heart, all I could do was weep harder.

Thirty-One

ETHAN

BANG! BANG! BANG!

My knocking on Ivory's door was not gentle. It was insistent and demanding.

"Sir." The bodyguard always standing outside cautioned me.

My stare slanted to him aggressively, and his eyes widened with surprise.

Bang! Bang! Bang!

A heavy hand dropped onto my shoulder, tugging me away from the wood. "You should leave."

I spun, knocking his hand away and shoving with all my strength. He rocked back, stumbling until he slammed into the wall.

The door swung open, Neo filling the space.

Shoving past him, I rushed into the apartment. "Fletcher!" I roared, racing into the living room. "Fletch!"

"No one invited you in," Neo intoned, voice hard.

I swung around, ignoring his wide stance. "Where is he? Is Fletcher here?"

I yelled his name again.

Neo advanced. "You think I'd tell you where he is? After what you've done?"

Hope sparked inside me. "So he is here?" I shoved by, heading toward the hall to search the rooms myself.

Neo caught my shoulder, spinning me around.

"Get off!" I growled, shoving him back.

He wasn't nearly as clumsy as the bodyguard.

"What is going on?" Ivory exclaimed, rushing into the room, her blue eyes wide and worried.

"I'm here for Fletcher."

"Fletcher isn't here," Ivory told me.

"You said he was!" I yelled, jabbing a finger at Neo.

"No. I said I won't tell you where he is."

Surging forward, I grabbed a fistful of his shirt, rushing until both of us collided with the wall. Neo didn't seem surprised or even afraid. He just stared with glittering black eyes.

Ivory yelled something behind us, but we paid her no mind.

"Tell me where he is."

"I told you not to make him your dirty little secret."

I snarled, baring my teeth. "I didn't."

Neo laughed in my face, making the hand in his shirt tighten.

"I swear to God." I swore, voice menacing and low. "If you don't stop playing games and tell me where he is—"

A new glint came into Neo's eyes. "You haven't seen it?"

"Seen what?" I spat.

A folded-up newspaper was inserted between our snarling faces. I blinked, focusing on the photo on the front page.

With a choked sound, I forgot all about Neo, dropping him to grab the paper, the edges wrinkling under my grip.

"What the hell is this?" I roared.

Neo jabbed the black-and-white photo with the same aggression I felt. "That? That's you doing exactly what I told you not to do!"

I stared down at the front page of the socialite section, which featured a large photograph of me and Sienna at dinner last night.

The Upper East Side's New Royal Couple?

The smile on her face was that of a hungry cat catching her mouse.

And me? My smile was the same one I always wore at events I never wanted to be at.

Fake.

I wadded the entire paper into a ball and threw it across the room where it hit the wall and bounced off.

The fucking press!

"What's the matter, Ethan? Pissed off you got caught dipping your fingers in the cookie jar one too many times?"

Incensed, I grabbed Neo again, slamming him against the wall. "Did Fletcher see this?"

A hint of doubt crossed Neo's dark stare. "Isn't that why you're here?" The force in my hold went slack, and Neo shoved me back, straightening off the wall. "Why are you acting like you've never seen that until now?" He pointed at the crumpled paper.

"Because I haven't!"

"You haven't looked at the paper today?" Ivory said, her voice incredulous.

"I was busy."

Neo did not like whatever he heard in my tone and lashed out. "What the fuck did you do to him?" he roared, his fist accompanying the words with a blow to my jaw.

My head snapped back, pain exploding through the left side of my face. Straightening, I turned my head, rubbing my jaw.

"One's all you get." I warned him.

A light-colored aura bloomed out around his huffing frame. I really didn't have time for a migraine right now.

But I deserved one.

I deserved all the pain the world handed me right now, and that was exactly why I hadn't taken any medication.

"If he hasn't seen you out two-timing him around the city, then why the fuck are you here?"

"You really don't know where he is?"

"I thought he was with you!" Neo spat.

Worry crashed into me all over again, and I felt my heart strain under the pressure. "I have to find him."

If he sees that photo after this morning...

"Call Earth!" I demanded. "Call him and see if he's home."

"He's not." Both of us spun around to Ivory who was holding a cell a short distance away from her ear. "Earth said he hasn't been home since yesterday morning."

The sound of muffled shouting through the line echoed through the room, and I rushed forward, grabbing the phone.

"It's Ethan. Fletcher ran off this morning, and I can't find him. He's alone." My voice cracked, and I sucked in a deep breath. "Please help me find him."

"What the hell did you do?" Earth yelled, but I dropped the phone back into Ivory's hand.

"Ethan?" she whispered, voice low and afraid.

"I'm sorry," I whispered miserably. "I'm so sorry."

"If this isn't about that, then what the hell is it about?" Neo demanded.

"He hasn't seen that." *That I know of.* "But I told him about her this morning. I was in the middle of trying to explain, and he freaked out and ran off." I pushed a hand through my hair and glanced up at the ceiling. "He's not even wearing shoes."

Neo advanced again. "I told you he's not a game. I warned you what would happen if you hurt him! How dare you play with him behind closed doors and then take your shiny beauty queen out on the town?"

"It's not like that!" I roared, suddenly completely incensed that everyone was assuming the worst of me.

"Sure as hell looks that way to me," Neo spat. "

His face snapped back with the rest of his body when I plowed my fist into his chin. Chest heaving, I shook my fist out while Ivory gasped, rushing between us like she was going to shield Neo.

Lip bleeding, Neo quickly moved so that she was behind him out of my reach.

I rolled my eyes. "I would never."

"That's what you said about Fletcher too."

My fists balled up again.

"Please stop!" Ivory wailed, her hands curling around Neo's shoulders from behind. "Family doesn't fight each other like this!"

"He's not my family!" we both snapped at once.

"Well, you are both Fletcher's!"

That sucked the fight right out of me. I sagged, feeling utterly exhausted. "I have to go. I need to keep looking." I started forward, but Neo grabbed me back.

"Leave him alone."

Shaking off his hold, I crowded his face, my blue eyes boring into his black ones. "I will never stay away from him. I don't want that… West Coast Barbie, and I never will."

"Is that why he ran off when you told him about her?"

My teeth gnashed. "I told him she was in town, but he ran off before I could tell him that I told her I wasn't interested."

Neo's eyes flickered. He swayed back just a little. But then he was crowding my face all over again, and we were squaring off. "It doesn't matter. The damage is done."

I shoved him back, storming out of the penthouse and past the bodyguard.

"Ethan!" Ivory yelled, rushing out into the hall after me.

I stopped and turned, not wanting to take my anger out on her. "I love him," I told her, the sound broken and weak.

"I know," she whispered, understanding in her caring gaze.

"Please call me if you find him," I implored. *"Please."*

He wasn't at my place. He wasn't here or at Earth's.

Where are you, Fletch?

Somewhere. He was somewhere, and I would find him.

Thirty-Two

FLETCHER

I SAT IN THAT ALLEYWAY, TUCKED INTO MYSELF, SQUEEZING MY knees as though I could hold myself together.

How ironic I held myself together while, internally, I fell completely apart.

The cold made me numb, tears dried on my cheeks, and eventually, the sky grew dim.

I wandered through the streets until I was too weak to walk anymore, and I hailed a cab to The Rotten Apple.

Upstairs, I tried the knob, not even alert enough to be surprised when the door was unlocked. I stumbled in, Beau shooting up from wherever he was, rushing forward.

"Jesus, Fletch! We've been worried sick!" He produced a cell phone I didn't even know he had and pressed it against his ear. "He's home."

"When did you get a phone?" I asked vaguely, dropping onto the end of the sofa.

Snort jumped up beside me, wagging his tail and whining. I patted his head, thinking of Gwennie and how I'd just walked out.

She probably thought I'd abandoned her.

Tears welled in my eyes. I thought I was done crying. I

thought I'd dehydrated even my reserves. I guess when it came to Ethan, my tears were limitless.

"We all got phones when you moved out."

I made a face. "I didn't move out."

"Well, you haven't been here."

"I'm sorry." I wallowed. "Do you want me to leave?"

I started to stand, but Beau pushed me back down, and Snort plopped into my lap. "No! Of course not! You're our brother. We've missed you."

"You did?" I looked up, focusing on my green-eyed friend. He looked like he always did, like he lacked sunlight, beanie tugged over his hair.

"Duh."

"Where's Earth?" I asked, glancing around.

"Out looking for you."

"He is? Why?"

"Because Ethan and Neo called here hours ago out of their minds because you were MIA."

Just hearing his name made me wince in pain.

"You okay?" Beau worried, leaning down. "You look like shit."

"Nothing new."

He frowned. "What happened?"

"I don't want to talk about it."

"Was it the photo? It was the photo," he asked and answered himself.

"Photo?" I asked. "What photo?"

Alarm spread over his face, and his throat cleared. "Uh, nothing."

"Beau!" I snapped, my voice hoarse but still getting my irritation across. "Tell me! Stop lying."

Sighing, he scooped up a newspaper off the coffee table. My nose wrinkled. We never read the newspaper around here. Earth said half the news was fake.

I didn't know about that, but I didn't like to read unless it was about Spider-Man.

We never got to watch The Amazing Spider-Man *together.*

The door slammed open, hitting against the wall with a loud bang. Snort jumped up with a bark, and Beau straightened.

"Where is he?" Earth bellowed.

His heavy footfalls hammered across the floor, stopping in front of me. He sighed loudly, a few expletives filling the room. "I've searched half this goddamn city for you! Where were you?"

"I don't know," I answered.

All the anger left him, and he sighed tiredly. Rubbing a palm over his face, he sat on the coffee table in front of me. "I'll just kill him."

"No!" I yelled, jumping up off the sofa so forcefully I winced. My legs and feet were *so* weary.

But my heart?

It was the weariest.

"That's not even funny!"

"I wasn't joking," Earth deadpanned. "I told him not to mess with you. He didn't listen."

Jolting forward, I grabbed the front of Earth's shirt, my fingers aching with the force of their clench. "If you do anything to him, I'll leave and never come back."

I admit it wasn't much of a threat considering no one cared much anyway. But my brothers did, and this was all I had to threaten them with.

So sad the only thing I have is myself.

Earth sucked in a breath, dark eyes staring at me incredulously. "You protect him even after today?"

"Yes," I said, voice fierce.

Ethan hurt me. He hurt me so intensely. But I loved him anyway.

It is my fatal flaw. Loving people who don't love me.

"All right. I won't touch him."

I gave him a little shake. "Promise?"

"I promise."

I let go, falling back onto the couch.

"So, ah…" Earth asked, "What happened?"

"I don't want to talk about it."

"That might fly with Beau, but it sure as hell don't with me. We've been traipsing all through this city, searching for you, worried sick, and I want an explanation."

"How'd you know he said that to me?" Beau asked.

Earth rolled his eyes.

Both their stares turned to me. I crossed my arms over my chest. It only took a minute for me to buckle under their weighted glares.

"He's getting married."

Beau leaned toward Earth. "I thought it was just dinner," he whispered out of the side of his mouth.

"What?" I asked, confused.

Earth crossed his arms over his chest. "He's getting married?"

"To some woman his father brought here from California. I'm sure she's rich and beautiful." *Sienna.* Even her name was perfect.

"And he told you this?"

I nodded, sinking a little farther into the couch. I was so tired my body quivered. I was cold and dirty, and I just wanted to sleep.

"You told us just yesterday that he liked you." Beau scowled, folding his arms over his chest like Earth.

"Turns out I'm not very likable."

"That's not true!" both brothers yelled at once. Snort barked.

"What did Ethan say exactly?" Earth asked.

"It doesn't matter!" I yelled, tired of thinking about it. Tired of feeling it. "I'm cold."

Beau grabbed a blanket and draped it over my body.

Sighing, I slid onto my side, tucking my legs up onto the cushions.

Pounding footsteps sounded out in the hall, and I realized Earth didn't even close the door to the apartment.

"Fletcher!" Neo yelled, rushing inside.

I raised my hand so he could see it over the back of the couch. "Here."

Rushing around, Neo dropped onto the table right beside Earth. "Where have you been? You okay?"

Ivory crouched down beside the sofa, bringing her head level with mine. "I was so worried."

"I didn't hear you come in," I told her.

"That's because Neo sounds like a buffalo."

I giggled.

Ivory's eyes softened at the sound. She reached out, brushing the hair off my forehead. My throat tightened because it reminded me of when Ethan did the same. "I'm glad you're okay," she whispered.

"Thanks."

"Are you hungry?" She worried. "Thirsty?"

I shook my head. All I wanted to do was sleep.

"I'm really grateful to have you all," I said suddenly, my heart aching. "Thank you for letting me be here."

"We're family," Neo declared. "We'll always be here for you."

"This is your home," Earth added.

"Can I get a cat?"

"No," Earth demanded.

"But if I can't bring her here, Ethan might not keep her." I worried, wringing my hands under the blanket.

Earth sighed insufferably. "Fine. But if Snort eats her, it's not my fault."

"You always give in to him," Neo quipped.

"Do not," Earth argued.

"Do too," Beau sang.

Ivory laughed. "You totally do."

I looked at Neo and Earth sitting side by side on the coffee table and smiled. "This is closest I've seen you two in a long time."

Both men flushed, glancing at each other out of the sides of their eyes.

"You should come around more often," Earth muttered.

"Maybe I will," Neo replied.

I smiled. Today had been super shitty, but I guess if it got Neo and Earth on the path of being as close as they used to be, then it was worth it.

Ethan's face swam before my eyes, and pain pinched my stomach. Curling a little tighter in on myself, I squeezed my eyes closed.

Even with all the hurt, I missed him. I craved the comfort only he'd ever been able to provide. I hoped for sleep, exhausted enough that it should have been easy to grasp.

But it wasn't. This couch no longer felt like a bed, and the missing scent of pine was disturbing.

I left my eyes closed, though, because letting them all think I was asleep was better than being asked questions I didn't want to answer.

"Where did he get a cat?" Beau whispered into the room.

"I should call Ethan. He's been worried sick," Ivory said.

My eyes almost sprang open at that.

Ethan was worrying about me? Beau said that he and Neo had called before. Was he looking for me? Why?

"Don't you dare!" Earth intoned.

"Let him worry," Neo spat.

Earth made a sound. "We finally agree."

"How can you say that, Neo? You saw him earlier. He was practically out of his mind." Ivory fretted.

I worried my lower lip, clutching the blanket a little tighter around me. Images of Ethan running through the broken glass to the elevator, begging for me to stop, assaulted me.

I started to tremble anew.

Maybe I should have listened to him, at least let him explain.

"You can't call him," Neo whispered fiercely, his voice near the kitchen. "Look at him! Ethan did this, and I won't let him near Fletch again."

Silence descended on the small apartment as I prayed for sleep to pull me under.

Thirty-Three

ETHAN

IT DIDN'T MATTER WHERE I SEARCHED. THE RESULT WAS always the same.

Nowhere to be found.

I searched the Upper East Side. I searched Central Park. I searched everywhere between my world and his.

As I nudged the Mercedes down yet another nefarious-looking alley, my stomach tightened, hoping I would find him, hoping I would not. I didn't want him in a place like this. Grungy, cold, and dark.

Worry gnawed away at my insides, feasting on me like earthworms in a fresh pile of dirt. Tendrils of anxiety wound around my heart, making my fingers shake with the desire to call the police. If I couldn't find him on my own, I would hire people who could. Time was ticking away, and the longer he was gone, the more afraid I became.

If anything happened to him… I'd never be able to live with myself.

A wave of nausea rolled over me, momentarily making me heave. My head throbbed so intensely as though someone were hammering away at my skull. Occasionally, spots swam before my eyes, and my vision was slightly blurred.

I hadn't had a head rager like this in a long time, but I

didn't care. All I cared about was finding Fletcher, making sure he was safe, and telling him the rest of what I wanted to say.

As day gave way to night, I started to think it might not change anything, that the damage had already been done. What if I irrefutably spoiled something between us? What if he wouldn't be able to forgive me even after I explained?

I should have told him I loved him.

I should have shouted it even as he ran away.

Beside me, my cell went off, making my heart leap and then sink. It had been going off all day. Hour after hour. The first handful of times, I'd been on top of the ringing, thinking it was finally Fletcher or at least news of him.

It never was.

It was my father.

Bree.

My father again.

I didn't show up for work. Everyone was probably freaking out. I couldn't think about that now.

I should have just told my father the truth from the beginning. My hesitation caused all of this.

You hesitated to protect him.

Yeah, how'd that work out for you?

The phone went off again, and I glanced down. A strangled cry filled the car, and I slammed on the brakes, stopping dead center in some sketchy alleyway.

"Ivory!" I practically yelled into the line. "Fletcher?" I demanded, heart nearly pounding out of my chest.

"He came home. He's at Earth's with all of us," she said, her voice oddly low.

Relief stole over me, and I folded in half to lean on the steering wheel. "Oh, thank God." I moaned. "Is he okay? Is he hurt?"

"I have to go," she whispered. "I just wanted to tell you where he is."

"Ivory, wait—"

The line went dead.

Groaning, I tossed the cell in the passenger seat and revved the engine. Due to the narrowness of the alley, I had to back the entire way out onto the street. I did so in record time, tires squealing when I turned out onto the main road.

Barely even braking, I fired down the street, turning the corner to speed toward the lit-up sign of The Rotten Apple.

I parked in a no-parking zone right in front of the bar. I practically dared that bozo Fig to show up. Squinting against the fluorescent lights in the hallway beside the boisterous bar, I jogged up the steps, taking three at a time.

I could feel every pound of my heart in my temple, and my stomach roiled uncomfortably. I pushed it all back, staring down at the black Christian Louboutin's on my feet. Fletcher's were in the car.

I didn't pause at all at the door, instead grasping the handle and flinging it wide.

Bang! It smacked against the wall in my haste. Somewhere in the room, a dog barked.

"What the fuck?" Earth snarled, jumping up from wherever he was sitting. When he saw me, his eyes narrowed. "Who forgot to lock the door?"

"Oh, hell no!" Neo spat, appearing from another room, charging right at me.

"Where is he?" I demanded, eyes scanning the apartment.

The longer I went without laying eyes on him, the wilder I became.

"Get out!" Neo slammed into my chest, shoving like he was some kind of human bulldozer.

Planting my feet, I refused to budge, hauling back and shoving hard, sending him flying back onto his ass.

Ivory gasped, and Neo swore, jumping right back up to charge me again.

"Back off." I warned even as I readied for the hit, preparing to give another of my own.

"I'm here!" a familiar voice shouted, a golden head popping up from behind the sofa.

Forgetting about Neo, I turned toward the sight, entire body sagging in relief.

Neo's fist bounced off my cheek, knocking me into the wall.

I didn't even flinch. My eyes never once left Fletcher. At one point, he turned into a blurred mess, but even so, he was the best sight I'd ever seen.

"Neo! No!" Fletcher exclaimed, jumping over the back of the couch to rush between us.

Laying a hand against Neo's chest, Fletcher said again, "No. Please."

"Puppy." The word ripped out of me, so raw that, at first, I hadn't even realized it was my own voice.

He stiffened, turning slightly, sneaking small glances and looking away.

"I've been so fucking worried."

He made a small sound, a sound he always made when he wanted my touch. Immediately, I pushed off the wall, blinking back the spots to go to him.

"Like hell you will," Earth said, suddenly right there, inserting himself and keeping me from filling my arms.

"This doesn't concern you." I snarled, looking at the hand he pressed onto my shoulder.

"I think that's my line," Earth deadpanned.

"Good heavens, can't anyone have a conversation? Snarl, snarl, growl." Ivory admonished. "That's all you men do."

Earth cocked an eyebrow. "You called him, didn't you?"

Ivory sniffed. "Yes, I did. He has a right to know."

"*Princess*," Neo intoned wearily, "I said not to call him."

"You're not the boss of me," she retorted.

During all this ridiculous conversation, I watched

Fletcher climb over the back of the couch and disappear. His feet were still bare and dirty with cuts.

Completely appalled, I shoved Earth back, ignoring his shout of surprise. "Did no one look at his cuts? Did no one give him clean clothes or a shower?" I demanded, rushing over to stare down over the back of the couch.

My heart turned over, and I let out a small sound. He looked so small buried under that blanket, mop of hair sticking out everywhere.

"He was sleeping." Beau defended. "He was about ready to fall over from exhaustion."

"Why isn't he in bed? Why is he on the couch?"

Everyone was silent for a moment. The blanket pulled down a bit, and I was rewarded with the flash of Fletcher's face.

It was blotchy from crying.

My puppy had been crying.

"This *is* my bed."

More spots swam before my eyes, but this time, it was out of anger. Despite the migraine and the sensitivity to sound, I started to yell. "You let him sleep on the couch? You didn't even give him a bed? What the hell kind of place is this?"

"The kind that doesn't hurt him." Earth challenged.

The breath whooshed out of my lungs.

I deserved that.

But I also deserved to make it right.

Stalking around the sofa, I bent down and pulled Fletcher into my arms. He shouted in surprise, but I didn't miss the way his arms automatically looped around my neck.

Even with the blanket draped over him, he was cold to the touch.

"Why are you so cold?" I demanded. "Why is he so cold?" I shouted to the room.

"Put him down," Neo said, menace dripping from his tongue.

"What are you doing?" Fletcher asked, his voice wobbly and timid.

"We need to talk."

"You already said everything," he answered, turning his face away from mine.

"No. You ran away before I could tell you everything."

"I heard enough."

"You heard him. Put him down," Earth demanded.

"Please," I practically begged. "Please just listen. Then I'll leave if you still want me to go."

Fletcher didn't say anything. He even denied me his stare.

Aching inside, I tried again. "I searched for you all day. Everywhere. Gwennie misses you."

He sucked in a breath and turned to face me. "Did you kick her out?" He worried, eyes wide.

Great gods, I love him so much.

"Who's Gwennie?" Beau whispered loudly.

"Probably that damn cat," Earth muttered.

"What a lovely name for a cat," Ivory added.

Despite the sideshow going on around us, I stayed focused on Fletch. "I would never kick her out. I promised her I'd bring you home."

He sniffled. "She's probably hungry."

"I told Jane to feed her."

"Who's Jane?" Beau whispered.

"His house manager," Ivory whispered back.

"Oh, for the love of God!" I moaned. "Everyone, out!"

"This is my house!" Earth commanded.

This was absolutely ridiculous. I was beyond exhausted, and all I wanted was to explain. If they wouldn't get out, then I'd just explain to everyone. Let them hear. It didn't matter who listened as long as one of them was Fletch. "I told her about you."

Fletcher's body stiffened, the arms looped around my

neck jolting in surprise. "What?" he implored, staring up at me with wide eyes.

Eyes that were tired. Eyes that had cried too many tears.

"I told Sienna about you," I said, voice gentle but loud enough for everyone to hear. "I took her to dinner, and I told her I was already involved with someone and there was no chance at all for us. I apologized that she came all this way because of my father, and I told her that as soon as she left, I was going to tell my parents about my relationship."

"Y-you told her about me?" Fletcher asked.

Despite the fatigue in my entire body, I tightened my arms around him. "It felt so wrong not to. There was no way I could pretend."

"That explains the photo," Beau commented.

Fletcher gasped. "The photo!"

I groaned. "You saw it?"

Fletch shook his head. "No, Beau was about to show it to me, but Earth came home, and I forgot."

I turned a cold stare to Beau.

He shrugged. "He asked."

"What is it?" Fletcher wanted to know.

"Someone took a photo of Sienna and me at the restaurant and posted it in the newspaper."

Fletcher's eyes turned downcast, and I feared what I'd said wasn't enough.

"Why'd you even take her to dinner?" Neo asked.

"Because my father made us a reservation and brought her to my office. It seemed honoring my father's promise of dinner was the least I could do. I didn't want to go." Gazing at Fletcher, I implored him to believe me. "And I found you right after."

A light-pink blush spread on his cheeks, and I knew he was thinking about the things we did last night.

"You're the only one I want," I whispered.

He didn't say anything, so reluctantly, I gently put him

down on the sofa. It infuriated me to no end that this was where he slept. That he didn't have a bed of his own.

I felt him watching me as I pulled away. I hoped he missed my arms as much as I missed him being inside them.

"Neo said not to make you my dirty secret." I spoke loudly, gazing at Neo with the line. "And I never once thought of you that way. But I have kept our relationship from my parents, from my colleagues. I just… I want so badly to protect you. I don't want anyone to hurt you, and the moment I tell people, the less control I will have."

"Oh, Ethan." Ivory sighed.

I knelt in front of the couch, the edge of the coffee table digging into my back. Reluctantly, I rested my hands in Fletcher's lap, tapping gently on the blanket covering him. "I should have told you sooner. I'm sorry. I don't want anyone else. Only you."

Silence draped over the room, but the only silence I didn't like was from the boy in front of me, the boy still refusing to meet my gaze.

I waited for what felt like forever, practically holding my breath.

No reply came.

Crestfallen and completely gutted, I wasn't sure what else I could do.

"You said your piece." Earth's voice cut through the thick quiet. "Time to go."

With one last lingering glance at Fletch, I sighed. When I stood, I swayed a little on my feet, dizziness getting the better of me.

Fletcher gasped, reaching out to grab my leg.

I glanced down at where he held.

"Are you okay?" he asked, eyes ripe with concern.

Just knowing he worried made my heart skip a beat, but I wouldn't play it up to my advantage. I didn't want Fletcher if I had to manipulate him.

"I'm fine." I promised softly. "Just a headache."

His forehead wrinkled. "A migraine?"

Unable to resist, I brushed the hair out of his eye. "Don't worry about me, puppy. I'm fine."

Hesitantly, I reached down to pull his hand off my leg and tuck it into his lap. "If you need anything at all, I'm here."

Walking away was the hardest thing I'd ever done.

In fact, the realization I was going to have to leave him here tonight made the idea of telling my parents I was gay seem like a piece of cake.

Neo was at the door when I approached. He opened it, but I was happy to see he seemed a lot less gleeful about it than ten minutes ago.

"Please take care of him," I said quietly.

Neo nodded.

"He has cuts on his feet. Please—"

"Ethan?"

His timid voice gave me tunnel vision as everyone else in the room faded away. Turning back, my heart thumped unevenly at the sight of his eyes staring at me from the back of the couch. "What, puppy?"

"Can I come home?"

All the butterflies in my belly caught fire and turned to ash. I swallowed the lump of emotion suddenly blocking my throat and blinked back the tears rushing to my eyes.

A rough sound ripped out of me, and I practically ran back to the couch. The blanket slid off his body when he stood, offering me a shy smile.

I couldn't say anything because emotion stole my voice. Instead, he tapped my shoulder so I would turn, and he climbed on my back.

Relief unlike any kind I'd experienced before flooded my limbs and loosened my aching heart.

"Are you sure about this?" Earth asked, frowning at Fletcher.

"I'll call you all tomorrow. Maybe you can come over." Fletcher leaned into my ear. "Can they come over?"

My voice was hoarse when I spoke. "Whatever you want, puppy. You can have anything you want."

"See you tomorrow, then!"

"Fletcher—" Neo started, but Ivory shut him down.

"Let them work it out, Neo." Her voice was every ounce the commanding heiress she was born to be.

I carried him out of the apartment, giddy excitement making me jittery. My car was still in the no parking zone, but there wasn't a ticket or Officer Fig in sight. Once Fletcher was in the passenger seat, I shrugged off my jacket, leaning in to drape it over his frame.

He caught my hand when I pulled back.

I leaned back inside, meeting his stare.

"I ran away again."

"That's okay. I found you."

Thirty-Four

FLETCHER

HE CHOSE ME. A CHOICE I DIDN'T EVEN ASK HIM TO MAKE, A decision he made on his own.

A decision he would have told me about this morning if I'd given him the chance.

I should have listened. I shouldn't have run off so fast.

Running away had become my ultimate defense mechanism, a habit that would be hard to break. It was so easy to believe I wasn't good enough, so easy to let that menacing voice rule my brain.

But there was one thing clearer than ever before: She would never rule my heart.

Even when my mind screamed I was worthless, my heart still whispered to love. Even when her evil voice resonated inside me, screaming that no one would ever love me, my heart whispered, *He will.*

I felt his anguish tonight before I even looked over the back of the couch. His desperation tainted the air. It felt like an earthquake inside my heart.

The moment I looked at him, my heart whispered again. *See, I told you.*

Even when my brothers tried to chase him away, he didn't back down. I was completely in awe of this side of him, a side

I'd not seen before. Yes, he was always strong and protective, always capable and sure. Tonight, he'd been all of that, but he was vulnerable too.

Not only did he explain to me but to my family. When they refused to leave, he just told them too. Despite how strong and confident Ethan was, he was also just a man.

Human just like me.

A prince. But an imperfect one.

"I can walk." I protested for the third time.

Glancing over his shoulder, he made a sound. "You aren't wearing shoes."

"I would be if you'd let me put them on in the car." *He carried my shoes around all day because he knew I'd run out without them.*

"Your feet are dirty."

"I can walk."

"I want to hold you."

I nuzzled the back of his neck, smiling at his words. Despite the exhaustion in my body, suddenly, my heart felt suffused with energy.

The elevator dinged open, and I held my breath, thinking of the broken glass and flowers I'd left in my wake. Everything was completely clean, the table empty.

Ethan must have felt me staring because his voice was soft as we went to the door. "Jane cleaned it up."

Embarrassment and awkwardness assailed me. The thought of Jane knowing what happened earlier and the way I ran off made me want to hide.

"She's not here." Ethan's voice was quiet as he let us inside. "And I told her I bumped into the table because I was on my phone."

I said nothing, appreciative of his thoughtfulness but still reliving the last time I was here.

"There she is," Ethan said, stepping into the bedroom.

Gwen meowed loudly, her tiny body rushing over to the

door. I dropped onto the floor, holding out my hand for the tiny kitten.

"I missed you!" I told her, stroking her soft fur. She started purring immediately, rubbing against my side. "I'm sorry I just ran off like that. It wasn't your fault. I hope you weren't upset."

I continued stroking and talking to the cat, fussing with her blankets and making sure she had enough food.

A short while later, Ethan appeared above us. "She's happy you're home."

Home.

I knew I'd called it that earlier, but the truth was it would still take some getting used to. I realized now it wasn't that I didn't trust Ethan, but I didn't trust myself.

I didn't trust that I was good enough. I didn't trust that I was lovable. And until I learned, I might always be fearful it could all just disappear.

The air in the bathroom was slightly steamy and humid as Ethan led me toward the tub filled with warm water.

"Wash up, okay?" He spoke gently, making my toes curl against the tile. "Make sure you clean your feet good, and when you're done, I'll see if they need bandaged up."

My stomach dipped because it sounded like he wasn't going to stay. "What about you?"

"I'll be in the other room. If you need me, yell."

I watched him retreat. Every step he took made me more anxious than the last.

"Are you mad at me?" I called, my words chasing after him.

He made a shocked sound, spinning back. "Mad? Why on earth would I be mad at you?"

"Because of before, of how I acted."

His eyes never left my face as he came back, the distance between us blissfully disappearing. "I am not mad at you. I was never mad. You ran off because of what I did. Because *I* hurt *you*. You didn't do anything wrong, okay?"

"Then why are you leaving me in here?"

An exasperated look filled his eyes. "I'm just trying to give you some space. Today was a lot. I-I'm not sure how you're feeling."

"I don't want space. We had it all day."

He groaned, reaching out to cup the back of my neck. "I don't want it either."

"Stay."

Grasping the hem of my shirt, he tugged, and I lifted my arms so he could peel the clothing off my body. His eyes surveyed my bare chest and arms as if he were taking inventory, making sure I was really okay.

As he hooked his fingers in the waistband of my pants, his eyes asked for permission. Settling my hands over his, I pushed them down, peeling away everything on my lower half.

His eyes were heavy. Tension and desire swirled in the humid space. Every touch against my skin felt electric as if I were a live wire about to shoot sparks.

When he was also bare, we sank into the hot water, the gentle waves lapping against our skin. Settling between his thighs, I lay against him, sighing in relief.

Cascades of water poured over me, his big hands lazily washing everywhere he could reach. The cuts and scrapes on my feel stung, but the feeling was secondary to everything else.

Lifting my head, I reached up to stroke my finger across his forehead. "How's your head?"

"Not as bad as before," he murmured, eyes drifting closed as I continued to stroke.

Water splashed lightly when I sat up fully to press my thumbs against his temples to massage in gentle circles.

He hummed appreciatively as I continued the ministrations.

"Did you take medicine?"

He hummed again. "Yes, just a little bit ago."

"You should have taken it sooner."

His eyes opened. The deep flash of blue colliding with mine made me shiver. "I couldn't think about that. All I could think about was you."

I frowned, feeling incredibly stupid for running off this morning, for letting my self-doubt cloud the way he made me feel. "I'm sorry I didn't listen."

Reaching up, he cupped my wrists gently, pulling them down to rest on his chest. "I'm sorry I didn't tell you sooner."

I nodded, wanting to ask something. Wanting to hear it one last time. But I was afraid.

"Hey," he murmured, tipping my chin up with his hand. "If there's something, just say it. Anything."

I swallowed, drawing in a breath. "You really don't love her… right?"

A rough sound bounced off the bathroom walls, punctuated by the splash of water and the feel of it waving against my sides. "

Taking my face, he held it firmly, blue eyes spilling over with emotion, imploring me with truth. "How could I possibly love her when I've given my heart to you?"

My lower lip trembled. My heart seemed to swell. "You did?"

A beautiful smile lit his tired eyes, and he nodded. "Oh yes, Fletcher. You own me. Heart and soul. I could never love anyone else because I am so in love with you."

Shock rippled through me. Shock and awe. My hands clamped around his wrists, holding on while he held me.

"W-w-what did you say?" The stutter was a complete tell of my surprise.

His eyes softened. "I love you, Fletcher. I love you so goddamn much."

My breathing hitched. The world went dull around me. Everything ceased to exist. All that remained was those words, those beautiful words no one had ever said to me before.

A tsunami of emotion crashed over me, filling me until there was no room left beneath my skin, and my feelings spilled out, streaking my cheeks with tears.

A tender sound filled the room. The pads of his thumbs swept away the wetness. "Puppy."

More tears trailed down my cheeks when I finally found the courage to look back into his eyes. Even through the watery gaze, I could see love reflected there. I could feel it in his fingertips.

He means it.

"No one's ever said that to me before."

Shock rippled over his features, followed by sadness and disbelief. "No one?"

I shook my head. "Not even *her…* not even my own mother."

"Milly?" he whispered.

Squeezing my eyes closed, I nodded.

More tears fell as his lips fluttered like butterfly wings over my damp cheeks and nose. My chest squeezed so tight I had to gasp for breath, the overwhelming emotions pummeling me still.

"I love you," he whispered against my skin.

A broken sob left me. I lifted my lips, seeking his. We met no more than a second later, kissing without caution, devouring each other as if we were starved.

He stood, bringing me with him, my legs winding instantly around his waist. We continued kissing as he stepped out of the bath, our lips still fused as he draped us with warm towels.

I shivered and clung to him, not because I was cold but because I was so entirely overwhelmed.

When he pulled back, I made a sound of distress, trying to follow.

He clucked his tongue, making my eyes lift, my breath catching all over again. The glowing blue embers in his stare nearly scorched me from the inside out.

"It's just us, okay? No one else allowed."

"Just us," I echoed as my back hit the wall. His hand cradled my head as his mouth slanted over mine again and again until the only thing that definitely existed was us.

His love for me.

My hands turned greedy, moving to explore his bare skin and sink my nails in.

Disconnecting our mouths, he dipped his head to suck one already sensitive nipple into his mouth.

I cried out, arching into him, digging my hands into his hair, demanding more.

He sucked and nipped until it was swollen and nearly sore before traveling to the other one and leaving it in the same state.

Desperation tinged the air. Need made me blind.

"Ethan, please," I whimpered, moving restlessly against him.

Carrying me to the bed, he laid me out, his large frame blocking out every other sight. Our kiss this time was sloppy and full of desire, his hard, naked body rubbing against mine.

I sighed even as we kissed, his weight delicious, the scent and feel of his skin exactly what I needed. Reaching into the nightstand, he pulled out a small packet and a now-familiar bottle. A small expression of doubt crossed his eyes as he glanced between me and the bottle. I put my hand over his, silently telling him it was okay. That I was okay.

The soreness in my body was no match for the gnawing

need to have him inside me again. I didn't care if it would hurt. I would die if he didn't do it.

He wasted no time, warming the lube between his fingers, our combined moans of satisfaction ringing loudly when he finally pushed the dripping digits between my legs.

Despite our desperation and the fervor in our kisses, he worked me open slowly, thorough in his touch. His mindfulness of my body added another layer of sweet desperation to the way I felt for him, to the way I needed him. He used so much lube I felt slippery and drenched, but it was a feeling I honestly loved and would welcome again and again.

Lips unlatching from my neck, he left behind a stinging sensation I knew would be another mark, a mark I wholeheartedly welcomed. Ethan leaned down to kiss me, only to halt hovering just above my lips.

Gazing up in hazy confusion, I watched him smile.

The fingers inside me curled against that sensitive spot, and light exploded behind my eyes. Vibrating in pleasure, he stroked me again and again until I thought I was going to come from just his fingers.

"That's my good boy," he crooned, pulling his fingers out of my body.

I whined because it left me feeling so empty, because I wanted him where he belonged.

"Look at me." He beckoned, voice hoarse and deep.

"Where else would I look?" I practically slurred. "You are literally the only thing I see."

Possessiveness sparked in his eyes, as well as a predatory flame. In response, my thighs spread wider, and I bit down on my lip.

"I love you, Fletcher." He said the words at the exact moment he thrust in.

I cried out, body burning as I stretched around his steely rod. The combination of pleasure and pain was heady, and my cock jerked in excitement.

Holding still, he hovered above me, his swollen lips brushing against my ear. "Thank you for coming home."

Wrapping my arms around him, I tugged, asking for his weight, sighing when he gave it.

And then we were kissing again, and he was moving, filling me up in a way I'd never been filled before. Filling me up in a way I knew no one else ever could.

Thirty-Five

*E*THAN

*A*RE YOU WORRIED HE'LL HATE YOU?

His question taunted me. The verbal answer I'd given was vague.

The honest answer inside me was absolute.

No, Fletch. I'm worried he'll hate you.

I was worried that old-school, old-money elitist would snarl in derision because I loved someone who was poor. Someone who could offer me nothing but his love.

To my father, love wasn't that valuable.

To me, it was priceless.

And yes, I worried he would be appalled by my heart who loved a man more than it could ever love a woman. He would assume because it was a man I loved, that, again, our love wasn't as valuable.

In my father's eyes, Fletcher wouldn't make a pretty trophy on my arm at balls, dinners, or in the press. On the contrary, I didn't want a trophy, but if I did, Fletcher would be the most beautiful one I could hold. He was the ultimate prize I could ever win in this life.

I always knew my father and I were different, but I didn't realize until recently just how truly opposite we were. Maybe I never noticed because it never really mattered.

Until now.

I feared he would make me chose. And I would. The choice wouldn't be my parents. I would choose Fletch time and again.

They might hate him for that. Might blame him for the "sudden" change in my desires and wants when, in reality, this was who I was all along. This was just a part of me I never chose to show them.

I could not, would not, abhorrently refused to let Fletcher suffer the consequences of my actions. He did nothing at all to deserve derision. And if they hated him for such petty things… then I would hate them.

I didn't want to hate my own family, but without a doubt, I knew I would.

Regret swarmed me, stinging like a thousand bees. I regretted the choices I'd made to keep pieces of myself private. It never seemed like a big deal before. In the beginning, it was more out of shock. The realization I could be gay was something I wanted to be sure of. I wanted to know that part of myself before I allowed anyone else to.

And when I did choose to explore that part of me, I mostly kept it abroad, out of the prying eyes of the press, away from the elitist gossipmongers. I was content that way, basically having my cake and eating it too. I explored that part of myself with Preston, no strings attached, and I kept my life intact here as well.

I always thought those things made me smart. I never considered it might make me a coward, not until recently.

Now that damned word echoed in the back of my mind, constantly taunting, making me feel like I was less than who I pretended to be.

I'd never been so hard on myself. The torment was maddening.

A soft sound, the feel of a smaller body cuddling close, chased away those dark thoughts. Short golden strands of wild hair fanned across my chest. Plump pink lips were slightly parted, the feel of his steady breath tickling my bare skin. Long fingers curled around my bicep, clinging even as he slept.

My heart tumbled, stomach flipping as possessiveness so fierce rose inside me that my fist tightened against the sheets.

No, I wasn't afraid my parents wouldn't accept me, but not accepting Fletch? I would never tolerate that.

The need to protect him was so fierce it kept me quiet these last couple weeks. He changed me so profoundly, altering the very way I was built, and I needed time to live in it. To revel in this new world he created within me, to absorb the overpowering feelings I never knew I could feel. It wasn't that I was ashamed or embarrassed. I was so insanely overwhelmed by him that I needed time to have him to myself.

That time was running out, however. And after seeing his stricken reaction to even the thought of Sienna being around made that startlingly clear.

Oh God, the look in his eyes. The broken, let-down pain.

"Never again." I vowed quietly, stroking his hair. "I'll never make you hurt like that again."

My hand stayed buried in his hair even when his head lifted. Blinking slowly, his dark lashes lifted, tendrils of sleep clinging in his gaze. Even in his sleepy stupor, he smiled at me, owning my heart, slaying my soul.

Massaging the pads of my fingers into his scalp, I watched his eyelids droop.

"You can sleep a little longer," I told him, completely soaking in the delicious feel of his weight against me.

I canceled with my trainer again, this time telling him the migraine left me slightly sick, which really wasn't a lie. I'd worked out with a migraine hangover before, but the truth was I wanted every moment I could get this morning with Fletch.

"You have to get up soon. I don't want sleep our time away," he murmured, thoughts clearly aligning with mine.

I made a sound, ready to indulge with whatever he could ask. "What do you want, then?"

His eyes turned shy, round cheeks suffused with pink. I watched his teeth sink into his lower lip, then release.

"Tell me what you want, puppy." I cajoled, running my fingertips down his spine.

I loved the way he shivered under the touch.

"Say it again."

My fingers paused, settling in the middle of his back. Of all the things he could have asked for, of all the things I was more than willing to hand over, it was this he wanted?

How am I going to survive him?

I didn't make him wait. I never would. These words would be available to him at any moment's notice.

"I love you."

His face ducked into my chest, and I felt him smile.

Gently but firmly, I pulled the strands of his hair, lifting his head so I could look into his face. "I really love you. So much."

Emotion swirled in his gaze, overtaking his entire face. And then he was crawling up my body, movements clumsy and endearing, lips latching onto mine and pulling me into a kiss that robbed us both of breath.

I don't know where we tumbled, but we went there together, sinking into each other like it was the last place on earth.

When finally we broke apart, Fletcher sucked in a deep breath and then pecked one last kiss against my lips.

My little kiss monster.

"If we don't get out of this bed, I'm going to have you again." I half growled, half groaned.

He bobbed his head like he was hoping I'd do just that.

"Stop being so cute," I said, pecking the tip of his nose

with a kiss. "Your body needs a break."

He whined when I slid out from beneath him but uttered no word of complaint when I carried him into the bathroom to shower us both.

"Ethan?" His tentative voice made me pause as I was soaping up his back.

I hummed, inviting him to go on.

"How did you know Milly was my mother?"

The loofah fell out of my hand, and instead of pulling him around, I slipped forward, pushing between him and the wall to stare into his face.

"I guessed. Seems like you have a pretty complicated relationship with your mom, and the only other name I'd heard mentioned was that one… I thought they might be one and the same."

"She doesn't like me."

Water dripped off his nose, rivulets tracing over his ears. His downturned face hid his expression, but I didn't have to see his face to feel the stark pain he emanated.

My heart clenched at how small and vulnerable he appeared. He'd refused to speak about her before, so now that he was, I wanted to tread carefully.

I also didn't want to scoff and deny what he said because, just judging from the things I'd seen and snippets of talk I'd heard, he was likely telling the truth.

What a moronic woman. An evil villain in this city.

She must lack a heart to not love someone like him.

"It doesn't matter anymore," I said gently, drawing him into my arms. "I'll love you enough for both of us."

"I don't want your parents not to like you because of me."

His words were hollow. Aching. Incredibly perceptive.

I pulled back, but he refused to look up.

"Look at me," I ordered.

His eyes lifted.

"Good boy," I murmured, stroking the flesh of his earlobe.

Just that minuscule praise softened him noticeably. "I choose you. Over anyone. Anything. People who don't like you don't matter to me, and I'm begging you not to let them matter to you."

"You don't know what it's like to have someone hate you. Someone who is supposed to love you."

My heart cracked. Swallowing down the lump of sickness lodged in my throat, I blinked, trying to rein in my thundering heart. "You're right, puppy. I don't, and it kills me that you do. I can't take that hurt away from you or erase the scars it's left. But I can love in spite of it. I can promise I won't ever hate you, and I will always be by your side."

"Don't make promises you can't keep."

Not really sure how to reassure him, I did something I hadn't ever done before. The moment I did, he drew back slightly, dividing his gaze between the pinky I held between us and my face.

"What are you doing?"

"They don't pinky swear in the Grimms?"

He made a face. "I highly doubt they pinky swear in the Upper East Side either."

I shrugged. "They do it on TV."

He giggled. The sound was pure and innocent and made tears spring to the backs of my eyes. His pinky hooked around mine, and we stood there under the spray while I sealed my vow.

"Always by your side," I whispered, holding my thumb up.

He blinked, confused, and I lifted his thumb, then pressed the pads of both together. Pinkies entwined, thumbs pressed together, I leaned down and kissed them.

"Stamped and sealed," I announced when I was finished.

He giggled again.

We finished washing in comfortable silence, his mood not nearly as heavy as before. It just made me all the more determined to make his future better than his past.

Villain

Red soles.

The brand-new black shoes he wore were adorned with unmistakable red soles. It was a signature design the stupid boy probably didn't even know.

But I did.

Knowledge from long ago still branded my brain. Not like a tattoo, more like a scar. Though I was a far cry from the world I'd once forayed in, it was a past life I would never, ever forget.

How could I?

That life was the reason for the one I lived now.

There was definitely something different about the boy when he stepped into the house that night. At first, I didn't think much of it. But his boldness grew until it was hard to ignore, and the flash of red on the bottom of his feet caught my eye. The hem of the designer hoodie that peeked out from beneath his threadbare coat was impossible to miss.

He smelled of money, of a new sort of arrogance, which made him think he could ask questions and try to trip me up.

Did he know something?

No. He was too stupid for that.

Still, I couldn't shake the feeling something was going on.

Something I wouldn't like. I'd hidden that child away for over twenty years, practically in plain sight.

No one would dare look for the son of an elitist in the slums. It was impossible for them to even comprehend.

But now I found myself worrying their paths might somehow cross.

This wouldn't do. No, not at all.

All my years of sacrifice would be for naught. And his years of torment were far from over.

I hope you die wondering where your precious blood went. I hope you die knowing the reason you lost your son was that he didn't have the right mother.

I couldn't shake the vision of the red soles, of the feeling those were a warning I needed to heed.

The air outside was bitter, its icy fingers reaching into the cloak I wore to brush over my cheeks and the tip of my nose. A stark craving for vodka ate away at my insides.

That stupid boy even wasted my stash, and now I had to go out to buy more. How I hungered for the flick of the alcohol's fire, to feel it burn a path all the way to my core. Alcohol was the only heat hot enough to mask the frozen soul inside me.

The aromatic scent of yeast flooded out an open door ahead, accompanied by the annoying jangle of a bell. The wintry air blasted me, bringing with it the slightly sweet aroma, making my stomach growl.

Before the door to the bakery closed, I slid in, folds of the heavy cloak flapping around my ankles. Inside was brighter than the sidewalk, the bright lights accented by the glowing counter displaying a bountiful presentation of bread and sweets.

The aisles were lined with other staples and things people thought went well with bread. Honey, jam, and different spreads. Things I never bothered to buy. Packaged rolls, loaves, and cookies sat in baskets, and people stood around the counter across the small shop, gossiping as if they had nothing better to do.

People were the same no matter what social circle they walked in. All of them gossiped, whispered, and pretended. All of them played games and lied.

The only difference between the Grimms and the Upper East Side was that the people dressed, ate, and lived better.

"Is that all you want today, Martha?" the man behind the counter asked, packing some stuff into a bag.

"That'll be it for today," she replied. "Just add it to the tab."

Another woman standing among them scoffed. "Just add it to the tab," she mocked. "You get a real thrill outta saying that every day, don't you, Martha?"

Martha took the bag, making an uppity sound. "You act as if I haven't earned the right."

My eyes rolled as I stepped behind one of the displays, listening to their petty dribble.

"You hardly earned it. A boy stole a loaf of bread out of your bag, and you threw a fit. If it wasn't for the richie coming in to save the day, you'd be eating days-old bread like the rest of us."

My ears perked up at those words. *A richie... here in the Grimms?*

"I was a victim just like our fine baker," Martha said, and I peeked around to see the man behind the counter nod.

"Never seen anything like it. That man marched into the police station with his fancy clothes and monied accent. Just his presence alone had Fig shaking in his boots. I knew that boy Neo had connections with that Ivory White, but I had no idea the little guy knew one too."

The little guy.

Fletcher.

Moving along the racks, I slithered until I was closer to the gossip, not wanting to miss a single word.

"Is it really true? The heir of the Abbott group really

walked in and bailed him out?" Another shopper appeared from somewhere in the store, clearly also listening.

The baker made a sound. "As true as can be. Gave me a handful of cash and has been paying the tab for Martha since. Paying for all she can eat for the whole year!"

The heir of the Abbott group... Beneath the cloak, my hands curled into themselves. My upper lip curled, and a bitter taste coated the back of my throat.

"I've seen that white Mercedes in these parts a few times now," someone added. "Fig better think twice before he keeps trying to haul in that boy. Ethan Abbott threatened with his lawyers, and we all know it's not an empty threat."

"Money," the baker spat. "Buys you out of all kinds of trouble."

"It also buys you bread." Martha cackled, the rattling of her bag loud in my ears.

Out of the corner of my eye, I saw her walk toward the exit. Clearing my throat, I stepped forward. "Excuse me."

Martha turned, a wary expression crossing her features.

I pushed back the hood, ignoring the tremble in my hands. *I really need a drink.*

The moment my identity was revealed, Martha relaxed. "Milly. Haven't seen you in a while."

"Been busy," I said. "Did I just hear you talking about Ethan Abbott?"

Her eyes widened, and a little bit of a gleeful glint came into her conniving gaze. "You mean you don't know? It involves your own son!"

"If I knew, I wouldn't be asking," I snapped.

The glee left her eyes, replaced with caution. Caution she would do well to entertain.

"Well?" I demanded, drawing the stares of the others standing up front.

"It was your boy," she explained. "Fig caught him stealing from me and the baker. Dragged him into the station, and that bigshot from the Upper East Side came and bailed him out."

"Ethan Abbott?"

She nodded. "Knew it was him right away. See him on TV all the time."

What is Fletcher doing tangled up with Ethan Abbott? How in God's name did they meet?

"Don't you have something to say to me?" The entitled snap brought my attention back to Martha.

"What?"

"I said your son stole from me. Aren't you going to apologize? He's been running these streets for years, causing trouble, taking everything he can get his dirty hands on. You should have raised him better."

How dare she? How dare this insignificant wretch pass judgment on me?

When I stepped forward, she stepped back. I stepped again, but she was frozen in place. My glare unwavering, I leaned in, keeping my voice low and controlled but achingly cold. "You're lucky I didn't *do better* at raising him, because if I had, he would have struck you dead and emptied your pockets before relieving you of your bread."

All the color seeped from Martha's know-it-all cheeks. Her eyes flashed with horror, and the bag in her hand suddenly was hugged against her chest. "You're an awful woman," she whispered.

I smiled.

She escaped quickly, the door unable to close because it was caught by the blowing wind.

Feeling the eyes of the others behind me, I rotated, meeting their stares. They glanced away, going back to idle tasks they weren't even bothering with to begin with.

Reaching down, I grabbed a packaged muffin that was sitting in a basket with others just like it. The wrapper crinkled loudly, filling the pungent silence.

"Put this on the richie's tab too," I said, teeth sinking into the pastry.

The man at the counter didn't argue, and I left through the still-open door, not once looking back.

Ethan Abbott.

Red-soled shoes. Designer hoodie. A pocket full of money and a sudden display of backbone…

Fletcher, Fletcher, what have you been up to?

Thirty-Seven

FLETCHER

THE PLACE WHERE THE BALL WAS BEING HELD LOOKED LIKE IT belonged in a fairy tale. Everything was sparkling and brand new, and the rooms were wide-open, grand and glittered with gold touches. I knew it was a hotel, but really, it felt more like a castle.

I mean, sure, I knew Ethan was rich. I even thought of him as a prince. But lately, I thought less about that because, to me, he was more.

He had become the first thought in my head in the morning, my last thought every night. His kiss echoed across my lips, and his scent lingered on my skin. He was warmth and comfort, reassurance and strength, control in a chaotic world, order in the mess that was my heart.

While I knew my brothers loved me and we shared a bond no one else could touch, Ethan was different… He was more.

I was still scared to love him, but I was also scared not to. Scared that one day I would wake up and realize this had all been a dream.

What a beautiful dream Ethan was, and as I stood inside this massive ballroom, the glass dome ceiling framing the already darkening sky while polished marble stretched beneath my feet, I couldn't help but feel like Sleeping Beauty.

If this was a dream, I hoped to never wake up.

"Agh!" a dramatic voice called from the second floor above. "The sound just floats up here, swirling through the air with romantic perfection!" The coordinator, whose name was too fancy to remember, made a kissing sound into the air. "Bellissima!"

Lowering my violin and bow, I glanced at the man sitting nearby at the piano. "Is that good?"

The man snickered. "Very."

The coordinator walked dramatically along the carved-stone railing above, his hand trailing the cool stone as his oversized pants swished with every step. His hair was slicked down, making it look wet, and the ends of the scarf tied at his throat trailed behind him like there was an invisible wind only he felt.

He descended the wide stone and marble staircase slowly, as if he were on TV. "The upper crust of this city is going to go gaga over this!" he practically squealed.

My stomach grumbled, and I had a sudden craving for pizza. We'd been rehearsing for hours. For days. I didn't mind so much. I liked to play my violin, but I was tired. I'd never rehearsed for anything so much in my life. Usually, I just played what came. I played with no plan or organization.

Apparently, I couldn't do that when there were other musicians hired to accompany my playing, so we'd made a setlist and had been rehearsing nonstop.

"Now," the coordinator declared, stopping where we were stationed toward one side of the ballroom. "I think this is the perfect setup. The music carries beautifully, and you are still in sight of everyone but won't be in the way."

"Does that mean we're done for the day?" I asked, hopeful.

"My job is far from done," he quipped but then waved his fingers. "But you can go. Everything is set. Play like this tomorrow night, and the crowd will be eating out of your hands."

I didn't want anyone to eat out of my hand, but I didn't say that. I just packed up my violin and grabbed the coat Ethan insisted on buying me.

It was light-gray wool with a big hood that spread over my shoulders when it wasn't up. It had lots of buttons and deep pockets that kept my hands warm.

It was a lot different than the puffy black coat Ivory had gifted me, but I liked this one too. I liked it because Ethan had chosen it, and when I put it on the first time, his eyes went soft and he'd said, "This will keep you warm."

The cell phone in the pocket was also something new. Again, I carried it at Ethan's insistence. I didn't think I needed one, but when he told me he wanted to be able to hear my voice at any moment, I couldn't possibly say no.

And honestly, after the way I ran off the other day, I knew me having it made him feel better.

Sometimes I called him in the middle of the day just to see if he would answer. He did.

Every. Single. Time.

After buttoning up my coat, I pulled out the phone, checking the time. Despite the long day, we'd actually finished a little early. Ethan wasn't due to pick me up for another hour. Deciding not to wait, I tucked the phone away and grabbed my case.

It wasn't a far walk to his building, so I would just go to him.

As I stepped out from inside the golden glow of the hotel, night enveloped me, and cold wind blew down the sidewalk. It wasn't quite winter here in the city, but the weather didn't seem to care. As soon as the sun sank behind the city, the temperatures dropped and the wind turned biting.

Tucking deeper into my coat, I grimaced at the way the cold seeped through my shoes, nipping at my toes. I was going to have to buy a pair of boots, something I'd never had the money to do before. I'd do it one day when E was at work because if he knew I wanted boots, he'd insist on taking me shopping, and I'd end up with a pair that cost more than I made off this entire job.

Just like the wardrobe he'd bought along with my coat.

At first, I refused the extremely pricey items, having only agreed to a coat. So he relented and took me to Sak's Fifth Avenue like it was some kind of compromise. And of course, a lot of my new clothes were from Reflection, Ivory's label. I couldn't possibly say no to anything that would support my sister.

Oddly, I didn't feel guilty for the things he'd bought. Maybe I should have. But he looked so happy giving them, and his eyes lit up every time I got dressed. I didn't see dollar signs when I looked at them. All I saw was love… All I felt was him caring about keeping me warm and comfortable.

And honestly, I liked the clothes. They fit. I even had a shirt with Spider-Man on it.

My nose numbed as I walked, the violin case slapping lightly against my leg. Sounds of the city echoed between the buildings, steam rose from street grates, and the scent of food stalls on the sidewalks competed in the air.

My stomach rumbled again, but I ignored it, wanting to wait to eat with Ethan.

An odd tingling sensation crawled up the back of my neck. Hairs standing on end, I shivered, reaching up to tug the coat closer around my neck.

A few more steps and the odd feeling still lingered, making me glance over my shoulder. The man walking a few paces behind me glanced up but then back down at his phone. Cabs whizzed by, a car with squeaky brakes. Nothing seemed out of place, but I couldn't shake the feeling.

The feeling of being watched.

The ominous notion followed, making me glance around

warily every few yards but never seeing anything amiss. The sky seemed to grow darker, the city colder, and I let out a sigh when the Abbott Group building came into view.

Just before heading inside, I stopped and rotated, giving one last glance, eyes lingering on the shadowed intersection down the block.

Nothing.

My breath puffed out in a white cloud as I turned my back on it all to head inside. The second the warm, lit-up foyer closed around me, the muscles of my neck relaxed a bit, and I stepped into a waiting elevator to head up to Ethan's floor.

Just as the elevator doors began to close, a familiar shadow of black seemed to appear. I pushed off the wall, rushing forward, eyes trained through the shrinking opening. Something sinister squirmed inside me. The golden doors shut, blocking off whatever it was I thought I saw. Collapsing against the wall, I trembled with anxiety, mind churning with uneasy thoughts.

It couldn't have been.

No way.

You're just tired and nervous for tomorrow night.

It definitely wasn't her.

"It couldn't have been," I muttered to myself. "This isn't her world."

It's not yours either.

I felt the color drain out of my face. The efforts I made to calm myself were clearly not working. The elevator dinged open, and I all but ran out, nearly tripping in my haste.

A few people looked up, but I rushed by without care. Bree's desk came into view, and when she looked up, I tried to smile.

"Hey, Fletcher," she said warmly. She was always that way with me. She never seemed to care that I wasn't rich like the rest of them.

Normally, I would have stopped to talk or even ask if Ethan was busy. But not tonight. Tonight, all I could think about was laying eyes on him, running right into his arms.

"Oh, Fletch—" Bree's voice seemed so distant behind me. So unimportant that I didn't even pause.

Grasping the handle like a lifeline, throwing the door open wide, I rushed inside. "Ethan—"

Shocked faces turned toward my haste, and I stood there shaking, realizing Ethan was not alone.

Thirty-Eight

ETHAN

I MANAGED TO AVOID MY FATHER FOR A FEW DAYS. I PUT HIM off by finally answering one of his many calls to assure him I was fine and my absence from work that day was due to a horrible migraine.

I didn't use the migraine card, well, *ever* with him. Because honestly, I knew he saw my "headaches" as a weakness. And honestly, I considered them a weakness too, even if my specialist declared they absolutely were not. I usually didn't discuss them with anyone besides Bree, who basically had to know about them in case something came up.

It wasn't a complete lie. I did have a heinous migraine the day I missed work. That just wasn't the reason I didn't come in.

I kept the call short, claiming I had a mountain of work and several conference calls, which was true. I was extremely busy with the ball tomorrow night, making sure my work was done and spending as much time with Fletcher as I could. It was selfish, but I wanted a little more time with him. I was ready to tell my parents. I was ready to do whatever I had to do to make sure Fletcher knew he was most important.

It was still worrisome. After his reaction to Sienna, I was

sincerely concerned that any less than a positive reaction from my parents would send him spiraling again. I wanted more than anything to give him something stable.

But deep down, I knew I couldn't do that if we built what we had on a rocky foundation. And that meant drawing lines, not just in his world but in mine.

Even knowing this, I still stalled, hoping we could get through the ball and Fletcher's performance without anything else causing undue stress. But when my office door sprang open with my father filling the frame, I knew we wouldn't make it.

I could no longer look at my father in the eye and pretend. Actually, I could. I just wouldn't.

"I'm going to have to call you back," I said into the phone, leaning forward to hit a button, instantly disconnecting the call. My eyes flicked up to my father. "I was in the middle of a business call."

"Well, apparently, barging into your office is the only way we can get your attention these days," he intoned.

Surprise drew me up when my mother stepped in, her blond head only reaching that of my father's shoulder.

"Mom," I called, moving from behind my desk to greet her. "I wasn't expecting you."

Elizabeth Abbott never came to the office unless she had to show up for some work or charity event. She'd only been in my office maybe a handful of times.

"I've been worried sick, Ethan. You haven't come by or called, so I came to you." Her blond hair was down around her shoulders, and a thick nude-colored headband with pearls and a generous knot at the top adorned her head. Her eyes were green, my blue ones having come from my father. Her cheekbones were high, her nose narrow, and the makeup she wore accentuated her flawless skin. She was on the taller side, probably around five feet seven, with willowy limbs and a graceful walk.

Her pantsuit was cream-colored, tailored perfectly, and overtop she wore a camel-colored long coat with fur around the collar and breast. She was very obviously a beauty. Her kind but not-gullible reputation in the Upper East Side preceded her.

She and my father made a striking match, and their personalities complimented each other well. When I was a child, I often thought of them as good cop-bad cop, my father being the "bad" and she the "good." Even still, mother was very much an Upper East Side elitist, and people knew she was no one to tangle with.

"I'm sorry for making you worry, Mom," I said, leaning down to kiss both her cheeks. "Have a seat." I offered, leading her to the sofa.

"Bree?" I called, and my assistant appeared instantly as if she'd been hovering nervously in the doorway.

"Yes, Mr. Abbott?"

"Could you get us some tea please? And also, please send Chancellor a gift as an apology for the abrupt end to our call."

"Tea isn't necessary," Mother said, turning to glance at Bree. "But thank you, dear."

My brows furrowed. "Are you sure?"

"We're here to see you, not drink tea." Father spoke gruffly, sitting next to my mother.

I nodded at Bree. "Just the gift for Chancellor, then."

She nodded and left, closing the door behind her.

"So what brings you all the way here?" I asked, sitting in a chair close to the sofa.

Father made a rude sound. "As If you don't know. You won't answer my calls, you're always in a meeting, and I draw the line at making an appointment just to see my son!"

"I just spoke with you a few days ago." I pointed out.

"To tell me you were too busy to talk."

"Your father said you had a migraine that caused you to

miss an entire day of work. Why didn't you call me? I would have come. I would have brought the doctor."

"I didn't want to worry you, Mom. And I'm fine. I took medicine and slept it off."

"Well, you do look healthy," she mused, her shrewd eyes roaming every detail of my face. "Actually, there is something a little different about you," she added. "You're glowing." She turned toward my father. "He's glowing. Don't you think so, Adrian?"

"Chandeliers glow, Lizzie, not men," he quipped in his usual gruff manner, but his tone was softer, and the use of the nickname only he was permitted to use totally negated any of his disagreement.

"It's the tie," I said, slightly amused. "Glitter," I explained further, gesturing toward the shimmering necktie around my neck. It was a navy-blue custom-made piece that caught the light and reflected like crushed diamonds. I'd paired it with a brown suit and a light-blue dress shirt.

"Hmm," mother hummed, not agreeing or disagreeing.

"Now, about you avoiding us…" Father cut right to the point.

"I told you. I've been busy."

"And I told you that this week was not a week for that. Sienna says you haven't answered any of her calls either. What kind of behavior is that? How do you expect to win her favor when you ignore her this way?"

"I don't want her favor," I said, keeping my voice even. "Something I told you more than once. Something I told you before you flew her across the country."

"Now just one minute! We agreed that you would court her, that—"

A frustrated sound burst from my chest, and I shoved up, pacing to the other side of the room. "No! *You* agreed. You pushed and needled and insisted, and I just didn't put up a big fight. And that's on me."

"What do you mean?" Mom asked, her eyes following my movements.

"All my life, I've been the dutiful son. The trophy on your mantel. I've always done what's expected of me, never made a fuss when you asked for something. I wanted to be the son you could be proud of, but that's not all I want anymore. I don't want to be who you want. I want to be who I am."

"I don't understand," she reiterated, dividing her gaze between me and my father.

I sighed. "I know it's hard to understand something that is likely out of your norm."

"Son, did Sienna do something? Did something happen between you the other night?" My father pressed.

Behind my eyes hurt, and I pinched the bridge of my nose, letting out an insufferable sigh. "This has nothing to do with Sienna!" I burst out. "I'm not interested in her. I never will be, and I told her that. So if she's acting like she's surprised I haven't answered her calls, then it's just her ego taking a hit."

My parents gasped. "You told her you weren't interested? Why on earth would you do that? You know who her father is. You know her family name," Father hollered.

"I don't care!" I exclaimed. "Why does everything have to be about money and names, reputation and status? Aren't you exhausted? Don't you ever just want something because it makes you happy?"

"Ethan," Mom intoned, her voice surprised but also holding a note of sadness.

"I'm sorry to do this now. Here. I was hoping to put it off until after the ball, but here you are… and here I am."

"You're tired. Perhaps the UK deal, the ball, and everything else has been too much at once." My father excused my behavior. "Once everything is in order, you will feel more composed. You can rest—"

"I'm not tired, Dad." I cut him off. "I'm gay."

The silence that followed was deafening. So absolute that it was almost eerie. Even the pounding of my heart didn't ring in my head. The declaration lay between us like a thick layer of snow that had fallen upon the city.

I watched their faces go from blank to confusion until their eyes lit with some sort of realization.

"W-what did you say?" My mother spoke first, her words breathless.

"I'm gay. I don't like women. I prefer men."

My father shot to his feet. "That's impossible!"

"Why?"

The question caught him off guard. Flustered, he turned to my mother as if she might have an answer.

"What about Ivory?" Mom asked, voice neutral.

"Ivory was a choice that *you* made. You and her father matched us before we were barely out of diapers. We went along with it because it was easy. And because, for me, going along with it was easier than telling you that the son you loved to brag about was gay."

My father went to the drink cart, pouring himself a scotch.

"But Ivory found true love, and in a sense, her discovery set me free."

"Free?" Mom echoed. She was far more composed than my father. And much less shocked. Vaguely, in the back of my mind, I wondered why.

I nodded. "I didn't have to be her prince." *I was able to be someone else's.* "I saw how happy following her heart made her."

"No," Father said, the liquid in the bottom of his glass sloshing. "Ivory chose another man, a man of much lower breeding, and it upset you. Rightfully so. And the shock of that made you question everything, and now you have this silly notion that you're… you are…"

"Gay," I supplied. "And rejection didn't make me gay,

Father. Furthermore, I can't be rejected by someone I never really had. I've known this part of myself for a very long time. I just kept it private, at first out of respect to myself but then out of respect to you."

"You didn't tell us out of respect?" My mother's hand went to her throat, fingertips fluttering there like butterfly wings.

"I saw no reason to create scandal and upset you. But I can't do that anymore."

"Why?" Father asked, downing the last of the liquor.

So he would prefer me to just be someone I'm not to avoid scandal?

"Because I met someone. Someone I love very much."

Mother made a soft sound.

Father's glass made a sharp clicking sound when he set it down. "A man."

"Yes." Clearing my throat, I went on. "So I would appreciate it if you would stop trying to create business deals based on my relationships. In fact, don't try to set me up at all. I'm not available. I won't ever be, and I will *not* have the person I love hurt by these charades." *He's already been hurt enough.*

Silenced enveloped the room once more, and it gave me a chance to take stock of myself. For all the time I spent worrying about this moment, of thinking how my life could be split in two, I was calm.

Suddenly, I wasn't worried about their reaction, their raised voices, or even their judgment. I didn't care. *I am sure.*

Sure of my feelings. Sure of my heart. Sure in my resolve to ensure Fletcher knew where he stood in my life.

"I quite understand that this is probably a shock. I also understand that you are probably embarrassed. If you want to sever ties with me, I will understand. I know you have your reputations to uphold."

Distraught, my mother surged up from the sofa. The

clutch she'd been carrying fell from her lap onto the floor. Leaving it, she rushed across the room, reaching out to grab my hands. "Ethan, is that what you think?" She worried. "You think that your father and I would disavow you to save face?"

"Yes," I said boldly. "That is what I think."

Tears rushed to her eyes, and she fell against my chest, wrapping her arms around me. She was almost the same height as Fletcher, but hugging her felt entirely different.

"Oh, my son! What a terrible mother I've been. Raising you to believe I cared about our stature more than you." Sniffling, she pulled back. Even though she cried, her makeup wasn't smudged at all. Lifting her teary eyes, she cupped my jaw with her hand. "I don't care if you're gay, Ethan. I'm so sorry you thought I would. You're my son, and I love you."

Surprise pinched my heart, creating a stinging sensation throughout my entire chest. The emotion I thought I didn't feel came rushing over me, threatening to push me under. *She is accepting me.*

Blinking, I focused on my mother. "You don't care?"

"Great gods, no! I only want you to be happy. Besides, there are lots of gay people nowadays. Our new neighbors in the Hamptons are a gay couple who moved in from California. They wear matching sweaters."

I didn't know what to say. How to react.

"Do you wear matching sweaters with your mister?"

I blinked. *My mister?* "Shoes," I muttered automatically, then jolted in surprise.

Mom laughed, hugging me again. I stood there completely still, trying to comprehend this conversation. My mother acted like being gay was trendy.

"Mom," I said, finally getting my wits about myself. Pulling her back, I held her at arm's length to regard her seriously. "This is not a phase. Being gay is not a phase. Do you understand that?"

"I'm rich, not stupid."

"Sometimes it's the same," I muttered.

Her green eyes burned jade. "Ethan Theodore Abbott, did you just imply that I'm stupid?"

"Not you, Mother. Of course." I hurried to assure her.

"And if I am not as accepting?" Father said, his voice filling the room. "If I tell you that my only son, my heir, being gay is an embarrassment to me, then what?"

There it was. The expected. The reason I'd kept my personal life personal all these years. This was what I'd prepared myself for, so strangely, his words of rejection had less impact on me than the words of acceptance my mother offered.

"Adrian!" My mother swore.

"You had your turn, Lizzie. Now it's mine." His voice was devoid of the softness he used earlier when speaking to her, but his eyes never left me.

Turning fully to face him, I straightened my suit jacket and lifted my chin. "Then I'm fully prepared to choose."

"And your choice?" He challenged

"Will not be you."

Mother's gasp behind me barely registered as my ears filled with the deafening roar of adrenaline as it spiked through my veins. The beat of my heart tripled, and my breathing turned rapid. But I stood there calmly while rage nearly ripped me apart inside, remaining picture perfect on the outside.

My father maybe thought he could intimidate me, make me back down from any choice he did not approve of. Abandoning the drink cart, he stalked forward, our eyes never once straying from the locked battle they waged.

He must have forgotten that I inherited my resolve from him.

"Just like that?" he asked.

"Just like that."

"And should I not be offended, then, that you would turn

away from your blood so easily? From the people who gave you such a life? From this entire empire you are due to inherit?"

"Should I not be offended that you would turn your own blood away because his heart doesn't beat the way you want it to?"

His nostrils flared, eyes flashed.

"You and Mother might have given me life, sir, but it's not yours to dictate. It's mine to live."

"Adrian! Ethan!" Mom called. "Enough of this!" The anxiety in her voice was undeniable, but neither of us turned or backed down.

We stood there measuring each other for an undisclosed amount of time, until, finally, one of us relented.

His hand pushed between us, and my eyes dropped to look at the offered peace. Lifting my stare, I found his once more. He nodded briskly, emotion I rarely saw shimmering in the depths of his gaze. "All right, son. I admire a man who knows his own mind."

"Seriously?"

"Yes. You've lived many years being a son we can be proud of. Now it's our turn to be that kind of parents."

I didn't want it, but emotion rushed to the backs of my eyes, and I couldn't swallow past the sudden lumps in my throat. Sliding my hand into his, we shook on it, which honestly was as close to a hug as we'd ever come.

But it was enough for me. In fact, it was more than I expected.

Clearing my throat, I drew back, putting a little distance between us, trying to get a little air. The muscles in my back were tense, and I could feel the pressure at the base of my skull. For as "unemotional" as I'd been at the start of this conversation, it was clear I'd been under stress.

My body was now reacting, my mind slowly catching up.

"I, ah, I apologize for pushing Sienna on you. I—"

Is my father apologizing? Adrian Abbott *very* rarely apologized. But whatever he was about to say was abruptly cut off by the loud rattling of the door handle and the way it burst in.

Frantic, Fletcher stumbled in, pale cheeks and wild eyes searching. "Ethan—"

The clear anxiety radiating from his every pore put me on high alert. My instincts to protect roared front and center.

"How dare you just barge in here?" my father barked fiercely.

Fletcher's eyes blew wide as he stumbled back, his violin case falling at his feet. "I-I-I'm sorry. I—" He stuttered, clearly not knowing what to do as he stared at the people in my office.

"Fletcher," I called, and his honey-colored eyes fastened back on me instantly. The second the weight of my stare settled on his, I felt a little part of him relax.

"Excuse us for a moment," I said to my parents, not taking my eyes off Fletch.

A shocked expression crossed the older man's face, and then came the anger. "Excuse me?"

"Fletcher has just come from the hotel. I need to speak with him a moment," I said, straining to hold on to my patience.

"We are in the middle of something important, and you would dare interrupt that for… well, for that?" He tossed his hands out at Fletch, who actually flinched.

I had a sudden vision of Fletcher rushing out of my apartment days ago, and just that brief memory made my gut clench. Patience completely snapped, I rushed toward Fletcher, using my body as a shield to offer him a bit of reprieve.

Curling around his upper arm, my fingers squeezed just enough to get his attention. There was no mistaking the anxiety in his eyes, an expression that was also underscored with fear. I felt him trembling, and I couldn't help but wonder what made him this way.

"All right now," I crooned ever so softly, leaning down so it was only him that could hear. "I've got you. You're okay."

His hand wrapped around my forearm. The grip he had on me was so much stronger than the one I applied to him.

"I-I shouldn't have just burst in," he said, unable to keep his voice hushed like mine. He was too worked up. Too nervous. "I j-just…" His eyes strayed to the area above my shoulder, looking in my parents' direction, unable to see them but still aware they were there. His voice dropped so low I had to strain to hear. "I needed you."

Everything under my skin turned soft and pliant. If he wanted to, he would be able to reach out and mold me into the exact shape and size he wanted.

He needs me. Something scared him, and he did what his instincts always insist upon. He ran. But this time, he ran to me.

I wanted to pull him in. I wanted to crush him close until I felt his body mold with mine. I wanted to wrap around him and offer protection and safety from anything and everything.

Behind me, my mother shifted. "We'll wait outside."

"The hell we will!" my father bellowed. "This is ridiculous. You, boy," he intoned, stepping forward to see Fletcher, "get out."

A low rumble vibrated my chest. The hand on my forearm squeezed but then let go. A cloud of resolve surrounded me. Even with its force, I was steady. Rotating, I caught Fletcher's hand even as it fell away. I wasn't letting go.

Sliding down his arm, my fingers found his, tangling together and holding tight. He gave one surprised tug, but a quick, pointed look over my shoulder made him still.

My father's footsteps paused when my eyes flicked back to him.

Charged, poignant silence echoed through the room.

Fletcher's fingers were cold and quivering in mine. I wanted to tuck them in my pocket, but first, I had something to do.

"This is Fletcher. I told you about him a few moments ago."

Father's brows drew down in consternation, and confusion clouded his face. "You said nothing about him. We were talking about—" He stopped, eyes widening. A look of complete shock stole over his face.

Adrian Abbott looked at the man at my side with renewed interest, his stare slipping down to where we held hands. Fire was glowing in his gaze when he looked back up.

Fletcher yanked his hand free of mine, taking a timid step back. "Ethan," he whispered, overwhelmed and probably confused.

I turned my back to my parents, softening my stare toward him. "No running today. You stay here where you belong. At my side."

Fletcher's eyes darted toward my parents, then back to me.

"Trust me."

Even though there was doubt in his stare, worry creasing his forehead, he nodded, stepping forward to erase the distance he'd created when he pulled away.

Leaning down, I let my lips brush his ear with my low murmur. "That's my good boy."

When I turned back to my family, his hand slipped beneath the suit jacket, fingers bunching in my shirt at the small of my back.

"You can't possibly be saying that—"

"That's exactly what I'm saying," I announced, my voice cool and steely. "Fletcher is who I love. And you would do very well to remember who I said I would choose."

His hand jerked in the fabric of the shirt, pulling it out a little from the waistband of my slacks.

"Fletch," I said, turning just enough to see him but not

enough to dislodge his killer grip. I offered him a smile. "These are my parents, Adrian and Elizabeth Abbott."

"You've got to be kidding me," Father muttered.

I raised a brow.

"Hello, Fletcher. It's wonderful to meet you," my mother said, coming forward. Her smile was soft and accepting, though her eyes roamed eagerly over the man still tucked half behind me. "I complimented Ethan on his happy glow earlier, and he tried to tell me it was his tie, but I think the real reason is you."

Fletcher shifted to stand at my side, his hand still buried under the back of my jacket.

"Ethan always glows," he told her. "Even before he met me."

She smiled, eyes soft. "Well, I suppose you have a point."

"Maybe he gets it from you," Fletcher said, his voice shy but easily heard.

My mother was obviously delighted by this. She smiled brightly, and I could practically feel Fletcher's ears turning red.

"Aren't you a charmer?" she crooned.

"He has a bear on his shirt!" Father snapped as though he were disgusted.

Fletcher stepped a little closer into my side.

"It's Moschino." My mother and I defended it at the same moment. In my world, you could wear anything as long as it had a hefty price tag.

"Is that a designer?" Fletcher bemoaned, tugging on my shirt. "I told you nothing expensive."

"But it's cute," I argued, glancing down at the definitely designer sweater with a big teddy bear on the front.

A repulsed sound ripped from my father. "You bought that? Of course you did. Does he even have anything to his name? You hired someone off the street just because he could play a violin, and now look!" He fumed. "He's attached himself to you like some kind of urchin. A street urchin, Ethan." Throwing his hands up, my father's cold stare drilled into Fletcher. "Look, rat, I don't know what kind of games you've been playing with my son, but he's not your ticket to riches."

Fletcher's hand slipped from under my coat.

"Dad!" My voice was like a lightning bolt through the room, causing even my mother to flinch. "Were you not listening before? I said watch your words. Watch your tone. I will not tolerate you degrading him. And if this is the way you feel, then you can leave. Now."

Father blinked. "You seriously would pick him over us?"

"I already have."

Fletcher sucked in a breath. I could feel his shock and upset. Reaching out, I anchored an arm around his waist, tucking him close. It wasn't so much for comfort. It was to ensure he didn't bolt.

"I can accept the fact that you aren't interested in women. But this? Declaring you're in love with some riffraff off the street! It's borderline ridiculous. Have some sense, Ethan. At least find a-a man with some breeding and—"

"Get out," I intoned, releasing Fletcher to take a threatening step forward.

My father's words fell away, and his mouth hung in shock.

"I said get the hell out!"

I never yelled at my parents. Not ever. Yelling was below us.

Not today. Not ever again.

Blood boiled in my veins, making me itch with heat. I could scarcely see past my anger and the arrogant, uppity attitude my father dared display.

At first, I thought maybe I'd been wrong about the way my parents would react. After all, they originally accepted my confession.

But no. It was as I feared.

My father couldn't accept the fact that I would dare love anyone he deemed unworthy.

"It's not Fletcher who's the unworthy one." I spat the words, advancing on the older man. "It's me. I might have money, but he gives me things money can't buy. He doesn't need a name to be worthy because he's already invaluable. I don't expect someone like you to ever understand, so go. And don't ever darken my door with your ignorance ever again."

My father stormed out, slamming the door against the wall so hard I was sure everyone on the entire floor heard.

Mother stood in the middle of the room, dividing her gaze between me and the door. Tears shimmered on her lashes. "Ethan, he's just—"

"I don't care," I said, unable to keep the coldness in my tone when I spoke to her. "Just go."

Her eyes slipped back to Fletcher, and I stiffened. Noting my immediate reaction, she pulled away and swept from the room.

Chest heaving, I stood there trying to calm my racing heart as anger still lit up my veins. Bree scurried into the doorway, wincing in apology as she grabbed the door and gently pulled it closed.

It was silent, but the room was not quiet. Too much raw emotion overwhelmed the atmosphere. My ragged breathing seemed to bounce off the walls.

I knew Fletcher probably needed me. I was sure he was likely shocked by what just happened on top of whatever sent him running here to begin with.

I just needed a moment, just a brief second to catch my breath.

And then I would make sure he was okay. I would—

Slim arms wound around me from behind, linking at my

waist while a body pressed along my back. His cheek nuzzled against me, and one hand flattened on my stomach.

The breath whooshed out of me.

He hugged tighter.

The room finally went quiet.

It turned out it wasn't Fletch who needed me in that moment. It was me who needed him.

Thirty-Nine

FLETCHER

WE SAID NOTHING IN THE MERCEDES ON THE WAY TO ETHAN'S place.

We said nothing in the elevator.

Nothing as he unlocked the front door.

The moment we stepped into our safe haven, with the door shut and locked, all the unspoken words found their voice.

"You told your parents," I said, still trying to process what I'd walked in on. I knew Ethan was going to tell them. I had no idea it would be today. No idea the panic threatening to choke me would no longer seem important when he boldly stood in front of me and declared his love.

How effectively he smeared that line drawn between our worlds. How easily he acted like it didn't even matter. I knew it wasn't easy, but he made it look like it was.

I really admired Ethan Abbott. I felt it all the way down to the soles of my feet. He was honorable and humble. He was not weak but brave.

At first, I'd stood there scared and afraid, desperately wanting to flee. But his strength was my anchor. It gave me courage. Next time, I didn't want to stand behind him. Next time, I hoped to be strong enough to be beside him.

I loved him.

I loved that he was willing to shield me, willing to say all the things I wasn't while never making me feel less than for not being ready.

I might have money, but he gives me things money can't buy. He doesn't need a name to be worthy because he's already invaluable.

His words burrowed deep inside me, next to my deepest, secret insecurities. Hate cannot chase out hate. Only love can. His love was shining a light on the dark insecurities inside me, making them seem smaller than I ever realized them to be.

"Yes," he said simply, dropping his keys on the table and rubbing the back of his neck.

"They don't mind you being gay. It's me they don't like."

His head shot up, eyes fierce as though he were ready for an argument. An argument to keep me.

The corner of my lips tipped up. My heart swelled so much that it put pressure on my ribs. "I'm not going anywhere. Even now when I run, it's in your direction I turn."

A rough sound ripped from his throat. I felt it in the pit of my belly. He rushed me, but I was ready, leaping into his arms, tangling my limbs around his upper body. I breathed in deep at the juncture of his neck, his scent flooding my senses.

"I wish you didn't have to choose," I whispered, sadness enveloping some of my swollen heart. I was beyond grateful for his love, but to be truthful, it cost him a lot.

"Fletcher…" He beckoned, his voice rough but sweet. I looked at the sincerity shining in the blue depths of his stare. His emotion was so strong it nearly stole my breath. "I can live without anything, anything but you."

I melted into his lips, sighing into the kiss. It seemed like weeks since he'd kissed me last and not just this morning. It felt like, since we'd met, we'd crossed oceans and continents together, nearly drowning, sometimes getting lost. But fate always steered us back.

The muscles in his upper body flexed as he carried me up the stairs. We kissed endlessly as if he didn't need air, as if I was all the oxygen he could need. The way his wide, skilled hands cupped my ass as he stepped into the bedroom made me hungry for things food could never satisfy.

I shuddered when he slid me down his body, my limbs already weak and quivering in anticipation. I swayed when he let go, which brought his hands right back to anchor my hips. Lifting my chin, I asked for more kisses, which he instantly gave while carrying me to the edge of the bed.

Dizzy with passion, need thrumming beneath my skin, I watched him strip off his suit, revealing inch after delicious inch of his smooth skin. The broadness in his chest was comforting, the definition to his abs sexy as hell. Narrow hips, long, muscled legs, and at the center of it all, a cock that was already flushed with a glistening tip.

Completely entranced by his physical assets, I drew him closer, licking my lips. Breath hissing in anticipation, he slid his fingers through my hair. Warm saltiness bloomed over my tongue when I licked across his bulbous head. His fingers tightened against my scalp, and I swallowed him down, taking his impressive length as far as I could. I did it again and again, plunging down his length, taking him so deep my eyes watered.

He tasted delicious. Having him against my tongue was better than any meal. His moans gave me confidence to reach into my hair where his fingers were already tangled to gently tap his hand, telling him to take control.

With a deep intake of breath, he thrust, making both of us groan. The way his abs contracted as he used my mouth made my stomach flutter, and I stared up his body, watching pleasure play over his features.

The high points of his cheekbones were flushed when he

glanced down, our eyes colliding. His pupils blew wide when he saw my lips stretched around his cock, and I felt it jerk against my tongue.

In a smooth, quick move, he pulled out of my mouth, his large body crawling over me to back us onto the bed. His weight was warm and strong, reassuring and safe. He was everything I never had, everything I always wanted. Ethan did something no one else had ever done.

He loved an unlovable. He made a misfit feel like he belonged.

He claimed me in front of my family and in front of his.

Emotion pummeled me, making my breathing hitch.

Plump, slick lips unlatched from my skin, and a blond head lifted. "What is it, puppy?" His voice was tender, his eyes incredibly soft.

"You won't leave me, will you?" My voice was hoarse and unstable from everything swirling around inside me.

He smiled, dropping a kiss to the tip of my nose. "I won't ever leave. I'll always be at your side."

He thought I was asking a question, but in truth, I was really just thinking out loud. I knew his answer before he even gave it. But it was nice to hear that I was right.

Dipping his head, he kissed across my jaw and down my neck to suck and bite in a way I knew would leave marks.

"I have to perform tomorrow." I gasped, intending to push him away but only managing to pull him closer.

"Good," he growled against my neck. "Let them see. Let everyone see that you belong to me. You're *mine*," he intoned, latching on again.

I arched up into the sensations, skin stinging where he marked me, the air brushing against the heated skin as he kissed down my body. When his lips got to my belly, his kisses turned into gentle caresses, and the tender licking of his tongue raised goose bumps on my skin.

"I love you so much," he whispered, peppering me again with kisses.

Heart fluttering, my legs spread wider in a silent invitation. His tongue dragged down my throbbing length, eliciting a broken moan from deep in my throat. As he sucked, his fingers circled my rim.

"Yes," I whimpered, completely overwhelmed by sensation. Completely overwhelmed by him.

When I was drenched with lube, Ethan slipped one finger inside me, pushing past the tight ring of muscle into my channel. I moaned, hips lifting off the bed, finally having part of him inside me.

He didn't move right away, instead holding his finger still to give my body a chance to get used to the intrusion, but I was beyond that and so needy I started to move. "Please, Ethan." I practically sobbed, wanting more.

Soon, I had three dripping fingers thrusting, stretching my tight walls and nudging against that sweet spot I never knew I had.

"The sounds you make are music to my ears." Ethan's voice was thick with arousal.

"I want you," I said, making a grabby motion with my hands.

He laughed low. "So cute," he murmured as his fingers slipped out and he moved from between my legs.

"Ethan?" I worried, pushing up onto my elbow.

"Shh." He soothed me, settling next to me on the mattress. "I'm not going anywhere. I'm right here with you."

"Please don't leave me," I whimpered, vulnerability spilling out.

"Never," he vowed, reaching for me. "Come here. Come closer."

I climbed into his lap, legs automatically wrapping around his waist. When our chests pressed together, a contented sigh escaped me, and I snuggled in, clinging to him like a koala.

"You like that?" he murmured, caressing my ear with his lips.

"So much," I confessed, loving how I could feel his heart beating against mine.

Large, warm hands grasped my ass, pulling my cheeks apart and making my breath stall. Gentle fingers circled my stretched hole like he was making sure I was still soaked with lube.

I gasped and pulled back when I felt his thick head nudge my entrance. This was the first time he'd entered me like this, the first time I'd been on top.

"Okay?" Ethan asked patiently and pressed a brief kiss to my mouth.

Intrigued, I nodded, tightening my arms around his shoulders.

He pushed in slowly, the movement punctuated by our low moans. Despite the way his arms shook with the effort of moving slowly, I sank down easily. All the preparation he'd done enabled my body to stretch around him perfectly.

A low curse stumbled from his lips, and his forehead dropped to my shoulder. "You take me so well," Ethan practically purred. "Squeeze me in all the right places."

The sensations of him being inside me like this were indescribable and intense. His praise only made the experience that much more overpowering.

"You're in so deep," I whispered.

"It's this position," he whispered back. "Does it hurt? Want to change?" He worried, muscles tensing to flip us over.

"No! Stay. I like this…" I said, wiggling my hips a little and then dropping my chin onto his shoulder. "I feel so full." *So happy.*

There was something completely intimate about this position, me sitting in his lap while he was buried deep. Our skin touched everywhere, hearts pressed together as his arms and legs wrapped around me tight.

Cupping the back of my head, his fingers stroked my hair. "Oh, my beautiful one," he whispered, wrapping me in his arms.

Love swelled up inside me, bubbling up and nearly bursting out. I was wholly overwhelmed by him, totally blown away. Holding in my words and feelings suddenly started to hurt as though keeping them in was costing more than letting them out.

"I love you," I whispered, knowing in my heart it was safe to tell him so.

The fingers in my hair stilled, and I felt his breathing pause. Drawing back, Ethan searched my eyes almost like he was afraid to believe what he'd heard.

I smiled. "I love you."

Unexpectedly, tears rushed to his eyes, shimmering like diamonds and making me wonder why I'd ever been scared to say it out loud.

I didn't see the tears fall, but I tasted them as we kissed. The salty tang across my tongue made me lick a little deeper into his mouth.

Eventually, kissing wasn't enough, and all the emotion between us needed somewhere to go. Grasping my hips, he thrust up, making me tingle with pleasure.

Against his ear, I nipped at the flesh and whispered, "Again."

He thrust up again, and I gasped. He didn't stop there, thrusting into my body again and again. All I could do was cling to him and marvel at having him so deep. Head lolling on his shoulder, I latched on to suck softly and moan against his dampened skin.

Groaning, Ethan cupped the back of my head, pushing me a little harder against him. Still holding me, he rocked up, and I bit into him, ecstasy rolling over me.

"That's it," he murmured as I continued to suck and lick.

With a particularly powerful thrust, he pushed into my most sensitive place, and my head fell to the side with a deep gasp.

My leaking cock was trapped between us, and I started to thrust, finding friction against his body as a familiar tightening sensation in my lower belly made my movements turn desperate.

"That's my good boy." He encouraged me, giving one last powerful thrust against my prostate, pushing me over the edge.

I came hard, my release smearing all over both of us as I clung to his shoulders, panting and shaking, half out of my head.

His voice sounded far away when he yelled my name, but I felt him pulsing inside me, the feel of his warm release painting my insides as my body clenched around him, milking everything he had to give.

Once our breathing returned to normal, Ethan shifted, and I made a sound, clinging desperately, not quite ready to let him go. "Stay," I whispered.

His chuckle gave me butterflies and so did the way he held me close. "There's nowhere else I'd rather be."

Forty

Ethan

He loves me. He loves me not... *He loves me.*

I felt like I'd had some kind of breakthrough with Fletcher tonight. I didn't realize how much of a burden it was to keep him to myself, how it played into his insecurities. But now there was nothing between us. Our families knew where we stood.

I wasn't stupid. I knew it wasn't over. The way I left things with my parents earlier today would have to be smoothed out. And I might have to pack up my office. Regardless, I wouldn't back down. I meant everything I said to them today, and if my father couldn't accept Fletch, then I couldn't accept my father.

I hadn't wanted to do that in front of Fletcher. I wanted to protect him from that ugly scene. But oddly, it seemed to push us closer instead of the way I assumed it would rip us apart.

Even now when I run, it's in your direction I turn.

Hearing those words was almost as good as hearing him say he loved me. One night. Two confessions that would live inside my heart forever. Somedays, I doubted I would be enough, that maybe I wasn't good enough at getting things money couldn't buy.

But after tonight, he made me feel worthy. Worthy in a way I'd never felt before.

Yes, the day was hard. Yes, I felt regret over the reaction of my parents.

But this love was worth it. Fletcher was worth it.

If I'd been overprotective before, I would be fiercely scrupulous now. The roaring alpha inside me demanded to protect what was mine. Perhaps that was why I felt so unsettled even after tonight. Even now as I held him in my arms.

I couldn't forget the way he'd burst into my office, pale and shaking, a wild, afraid look in his eyes. I knew it was her even without him having to say. Her name lingered on my tongue; her presence clung in the air like a bad odor not even a good candle could eradicate.

I didn't want to, but I had to ask. It was required in order to know what I needed to protect him from.

When I dragged my fingertips along his spine, he stirred a little, making a sound of pure contentment. I almost didn't ask, but that damnable alpha in me let loose a great growl. "Puppy," I said gently, my voice barely disturbing the lazy quiet.

"Hmm?"

"Will you tell me what happened earlier, why you rushed into my office like that?"

"We finished rehearsal early, so I decided to walk over."

"And then what?"

His chest rose and fell with his great exhale. He was silent as though he were trying to decide if he was ready to talk. "I don't want you to think I'm weak."

With a sound, I tried to pull back so I could look into his face, but he resisted, clutching me closer and pushing farther against my shoulder.

Relenting, I settled back into the headboard, holding him close. If he felt safe talking to me like this, then this was what I would give him.

"Why would I think you're weak?" I questioned, lightly rubbing a slow circle over his back.

"Because she scares me."

It felt like someone reached into my chest and squeezed my heart. It felt like those words had tried to rip it right out of my chest. Such a short sentence, but it was a declaration that seemed to cost Fletch so much.

A broken sound vibrated my throat. My fingertips slid up his back and into his hair.

"If she scares you, there's a reason. It's because you're so strong, and deep down, you know you should be afraid."

He was quiet a moment. Then, remarkably, he pushed up, palms resting against my chest. Golden eyes blinked, passion still lingering, along with surprise. "Really?"

I felt myself nod. "Fear isn't weakness. It makes you strong. Those that say they don't have fear are the ones who are weak."

His head tilted. "Are you ever afraid?"

"I was afraid all these years to tell my parents. But I did today. Know why?"

"Why?"

"Because you gave me courage."

Surprise filled his face, as did doubt. "But I'm not strong."

I brushed the hair from his forehead and smiled. "Oh, puppy. You are. You're stronger than you know."

Drawing his lip under the sharp edge of his teeth, he worried the still thoroughly kissed flesh. "I thought I saw her today. Following me on the street and then into the Abbott building."

I did my very best to keep myself relaxed. Having him this close meant controlling my reactions. I didn't want him to tense up or make him worry and stop talking.

"Milly, your mother?" I questioned lightly.

He lay back against me but thankfully kept talking. "But it's silly. She wouldn't be all the way on this side of town.

Why would she? She has no idea about you or my job. She's not interested in me anyway."

"But you saw her?"

He shook his head against my shoulder. "No. I mean, I saw someone. Like a familiar flash. It was more… I *felt* her. Whenever she's around, I always get…"

"Panicked." I finished when his words trailed away.

His arms tucked around my neck. My heart turned over. His clinginess was so endearing to me.

"Fletcher, has she ever hit you?" I had to know.

His head bobbed.

I bit down on the inside of my cheek. Anger so intense filled me that spots swam before my eyes. I thought back to when he'd flinched from me, how that flinch was probably a learned behavior to avoid being struck. *Did she hit him when he spilled things? Did she punish him physically when he was just a little boy?*

Sickness wormed inside me. Just the mere thoughts of him enduring such heinous treatment made me want to vomit.

"Mostly, she would just yell and scream and throw things at me."

Angling my face down, I looked at him lying across my chest. "She threw things at you?"

"The last time I saw her, she threw a bottle of vodka at me. It shattered everywhere."

This time, I couldn't stop the physical reaction. My entire body jolted, my hands digging into his hips. "When was this?" I demanded, tone undeniably harsh.

His silence was poignant, body tense. I expelled a breath, trying to gain some composure. "I'm not mad at you. Please tell me."

Finally, he peeled himself off my chest, keeping his gaze trained down. "The night we found Gwennie."

I sucked in a breath, grabbing at one of his hands. "All

those cuts on your hands." I recalled, gazing down at the marks that had since all healed. "Those were from her?"

"Sort of."

Again, my body jolted, but this time, he winced.

Forgetting about my anger, all my focus zeroed in on him. "Did I hurt you?"

He shook his head. "Just a little sore." His voice was sheepish.

I was still seated inside him even though I'd since gone soft. It seemed he found reassurance with this position, and I wasn't about to deny anything he wanted unless I thought it might be hurting him.

I moved to pull out, but he made a sound of alarm, bearing down. "No, wait!"

I halted and cupped his face. "I love being inside you, puppy. I do. And I know it makes you feel safe."

His face flamed as he tried to duck out of sight.

I made a stern sound, stopping his retreat. "I need to pull out now. You're going to be too sore. And we need to clean you."

He made a face, clearly not understanding. His innocence would be the death of me.

"I forgot a condom," I said honestly. "By the time I remembered, I didn't want to pull out."

He blinked, little mouth forming an O. I wasn't sure if I should be offended or impressed with myself that he didn't notice.

"I'm sorry," I said sincerely. This was on me. This was my responsibility to make sure he was taken care of when we had sex.

"Is that why it felt so good?" he murmured, making me look up.

He wasn't upset. Not even a little. If anything, he just seemed... curious.

"Doesn't it always feel good?" I mused.

"Of course." His eyes rolled. "But this time was… different. A little *more*."

All I could do was nod. I could feel my lower belly tingle, and if he didn't stop looking at me like that, I was going to grow full-on hard and take him again.

"I promise I'm clean. I get tested regularly. I'll get tested again to prove it. I've actually never forgotten before…" *That doesn't make it okay, Ethan.* "And I won't forget next time."

Again, still doesn't make it okay.

"You've never done it like this with anyone else?"

"Never. Just you. Only you." I vowed.

"What if I don't want you to use one next time?"

The internal beatdown I was indulging in quieted. My cock twitched. Even though I wanted to shout a hell yes, I didn't. This was something I wanted to let him think about. "We can talk about it."

Without waiting for his reply, I lifted his body, slipping out. I couldn't help but stare, captivated as the rush of my release followed.

Feeling the warmth, Fletcher looked down, seeing the smear on his thigh.

I grimaced. "It's messier without a condom." *I'll have to make sure he's clean.*

His eyes lifted. Even shy, they settled heavily on mine. "I like it."

A light moan vibrated the back of my throat. How was I supposed to get out of this bed when my cum was literally dripping from his body, dampening his thighs while he looked at me with those innocent Bambi eyes and told me he liked it?

"I think you like it too." He spoke, and I followed his stare down my stiffening length.

"You have no idea," I practically groaned.

Before I knew what he was doing, he was back in my lap,

angling my cock against his hole and sinking down in one smooth motion.

I fell back against the headboard, shivering as he sheathed me with his body. He was still warm and pliant, his body still slick from the lube and my release.

With a sigh of contentment, he leaned forward, tucking his arms between us, cheek on my shoulder. "You're right. I feel safe like this."

My heart felt bruised under that soft concession. How anyone could make me feel equal parts of love and lust, I might never understand. "You're always safe with me."

"Mmm," he hummed. "Being this close puts me at ease."

My hips thrust up, making our breathing catch. He was so warm and welcoming, so accepting of everything I gave. "I love you."

"I love you too."

Giddiness ran through my heart, and for the first time in my life, I felt truly whole. "I hadn't even realized I'd been missing pieces of myself until you came and filled them."

"I always knew I had missing pieces," Fletcher replied, making me realize I'd spoken out loud. "I never expected anyone to love me."

How could anyone not love him?

"I don't want you to see her anymore," I declared, the words just bursting right out. Despite my obvious arousal, it was clear I couldn't just forget about what we'd been talking about. It had taken Fletcher so long to open up even just a little. I still had more to say.

He went rigid against me. Between us, his fingers curled in.

"But she's my mother," he whispered, vulnerability making his voice weak.

A flash of a memory of Earth and Fletcher arguing outside the police station came over me, and I realized this was likely a fight Fletcher had before.

But I didn't want a fight, and despite how dominant I sometimes could be over him, I did not seek to control his life.

"Fletcher."

His silence was clear.

But what broke me down was that despite his clear unhappiness with my request, he was still on top of me. I was still inside him. He made no move to pull away.

It gave me an inkling of hope. It made the trust he had for me palpable because maybe, just maybe, he understood I was speaking out of love.

Brushing my fingers through his hair, I spoke. "Family doesn't get a free pass, puppy. No one does. I know she's your mother, and I know that makes her your family. But sharing blood with someone doesn't give them the right to treat you like this. And sadly, sharing blood doesn't automatically equal love. You don't have to endure her abuse. It's *your* life. *Your* choice. You don't have to allow her in. You can walk away. They say you can't pick your family, but I think you can. You get to choose who you allow in your life, and I love you so much. I only want good people around you. People who won't hurt you."

Silence fell between us, and so did something damp.

A tear.

He was crying.

A hollow ache settled in my stomach as I wrapped my arms around him. I wasn't sorry for the things I said because I'd meant them. When I thought about what he endured his entire life, I wanted to find that witch and make her pay.

But I couldn't because that would hurt him too.

"Your parents have each other. If I leave, she'll be all alone." His voice was small.

My heart tightened. He was so… pure. How he could still have love, empathy, for a woman who did nothing but abuse him all his life was almost unimaginable.

It just proved how beautiful his soul truly was.

"Maybe you'll both be free."

After a while, he said, "I don't know."

"You don't have to know right now. And whatever decision you make, I will support you. I won't get mad. I won't yell, and I won't leave."

He lifted his head. His cheeks were damp. "Really?"

Chest caving in, I wiped the wetness away, hoping he could see every ounce of love I felt in my gaze. "It's your choice, and I love you no matter what. Thank you for listening to my point of view."

A small smile lit up his face.

"Can you promise me something, though?"

Smile dimming, wariness crept into his eyes. "What?"

"The next time you go see her, don't go alone."

He frowned, clearly not expecting this request. "I don't want you to see where I came from."

"I don't care where you came from."

He made a face. "That's easy to say when you're rich."

"Fletcher." I warned.

His teeth sank into his lower lip, and then his hips rotated. Pleasure distracted me, momentarily making me forget my thoughts.

When awareness washed back in, I scowled. "Are you trying to distract me?"

He giggled.

"You little brat," I growled, flipping us so I was pressing him into the mattress.

His chin lifted, asking for his favorite thing.

I pulled back, arching a brow. "Promise me."

The playfulness left his eyes. His lip jutted out in a pout. "I won't."

"It doesn't have to be me," I said, though the allowance cost me some peace of mind. "You can take one of your brothers. Even if they wait outside. Just don't go alone. If she hurts you, I can't guarantee what I will do."

He thought it over a minute, then nodded.

I smiled, feeling much lighter than before. "Promise?"

"I promise."

"Wanna pinky swear?"

He shook his head and puckered his lips.

"Kiss monster," I teased, dipping my head and giving him a hell of a lot more than a single kiss.

Forty-One

THE ENTIRE KITCHEN WAS FILLED WITH THE SCENT OF cinnamon, maple, and vanilla. The earthy sweetness of the syrup and the savory melted butter swirled together on my tongue, mushing together with fluffy pillows of the homemade breakfast Jane had generously set in front of me.

I gasped, closing my lips just before any of this good bite fell out.

"Is something wrong, Master Fletcher?" Jane asked, turning from across the kitchen.

Lowering his coffee, Ethan eyed me with mild concern.

"I just realized something!" I punctuated the announcement with the shake of my fork.

Ethan's smile was amused. "And what is that?"

"Waffles are much more considerate than pancakes."

Jane's light laughter rang up toward the ceiling, and Ethan's smile turned into a full-on grin.

"Do tell," Jane prompted, pulling another perfectly shaped waffle from the iron she was using. I didn't know that you needed an iron to make waffles. I thought you just got them in the freezer section at the grocery store.

"Well, when you pour syrup on a pancake, it slides right off and goes all over the plate. But waffles, they have little cups! They hold the syrup for you." Jabbing my fork into a new bite, I shoved it into my mouth and sighed. "It's like the perfect bite every single time!"

"That is much more considerate," Ethan mused.

I brought a bite up to his lips. He went to shake his head, but I huffed. "It's only one bite. Your perfect abs won't even notice."

Eyes twinkling, his lips parted, and I pushed the bite into his mouth. He chewed, and I knew the moment the flavors burst over his tongue because his eyes rolled back a little.

"See? Perfect."

"Much better than egg whites and vegetables."

I held up another bite. He pursed his lips. I batted my eyes, and he surrendered. Giddy, I licked the syrup off the fork, watching him chew.

"When my abs disappear, I don't want to hear any complaints."

"Like I'd complain about any part of your body. It's perfect." I fussed, turning back to my food.

A poignant pause crowded the room, and I looked up. Jane was staring at us. A flaming blush rushed to my cheeks. I'd forgotten she was there.

I didn't dare look at Ethan, worried he would be upset. His throat cleared, and I set down my fork. But before he spoke, he ran a hand over the back of my head, flooding away my worries with reassurance.

"Jane, I think I should make it clear that Fletcher is not just a friend. For lack of a better term, he's my boyfriend. When he stays here, it's not in the guest bedroom. In fact, he's going to be moving in."

I gasped. "What?"

Ethan glanced at me, unbothered. "You stay here every night anyway. Might as well make it official."

"But I already have a home."

His eyes flashed. "A couch is not a home."

I made a face. *He is never going to let that go.* "You didn't even ask me," I muttered, staring down at my lap. Did he think he could just tell me what to do and I'd do it?

Reaching over, he grasped the edge of the stool I sat on, the legs made a screeching sound when he dragged me right up beside him.

"Fletcher," he sang, voice soft and sweet. It was the exact tone that always melted me, the tone that only he had ever used with me.

Don't cave, Fletcher! Don't cave!

"I love you, and I want you here with me all the time. I don't want this to be my home anymore but ours. Will you move in with me?"

My heart was thundering. My ears felt hot. And the waffle I had just eaten was jumping around in my stomach like it was on a trampoline. Truth was this already felt like my home. Anywhere Ethan was felt that way. *Don't cave!* "What about Gwen?"

"Gwen already lives here."

"How much is rent?"

He made a sound. "I own this place. I don't even pay rent."

"I can't just live here for free."

"It's not free."

I sucked in a breath, finally looking up to meet his eyes. Why did they have to be so blue? "Then what's the cost?"

"Your heart."

My lips pressed together. I did my very best to hold in the giggle and my smile. "You already have that."

Ethan leaned close, so close our noses practically bumped. "Then I guess you're qualified."

I nodded.

He drew back, hope sparking in his eyes. "Is that a yes?"

"Okay."

Without even getting up, he swooped forward, pulling me

from the stool to transfer me into his lap. He leaned in to kiss me, but this time, I remembered Jane.

"Jane!" I yelled before he could make contact.

Ethan straightened, looking to where Jane stood. "I understand this may change things. You may not want to be employed by—"

"Posh!" She cut him off, waving a spatula in front of us. "I knew about you two from the minute I met this one," she said, pointing at me.

"You did?" I asked, surprised. "Are you psychic?"

She laughed. "No, I just have eyes."

"So you'll stay on?" Ethan asked.

"Who else will make waffles in the mornings and help take care of Gwen?"

Gwennie really liked Jane.

"Thank you," Ethan said, his arms tightening a bit around my middle. "I, ah, I appreciate your professionalism."

She made a rude sound. "Ethan Abbott, of all the things. After all these years, this isn't even about professionalism. I thought we were at least friends."

"Family!" I exclaimed. "Jane is family."

Her gaze turned a little sentimental, and she smiled at me. "Such a sweet boy." She looked at Ethan. "Much better than any of these well-to-do hoity-toities in the Upper East Side."

"What's a hoity-toity?" I wondered.

"Family," Ethan said softly. Then, "I'll give you a raise. After all, there will be more to manage here with more than me in residence."

"My considerate pancake is getting cold." I worried, staring longingly at my plate.

Ethan laughed, and Jane pushed the plate in front of me. "Eat up. You need all the energy you can get for your performance tonight."

Nerves coiled in my stomach, but I ate anyway because it was too good to waste.

After breakfast, Ethan went to change, and I played in the living room with Gwennie. She was already looking a little bigger, and her ribs didn't stick out as much. The vet we took her to said she was fine, she just needed to gain some weight, and then he poked her with a bunch of needles.

I laughed when she leaped on the string I dragged across the floor and then again when she abandoned it to pounce on a ball with a bell in the center.

Ethan stepped into the living room, stealing my attention with the way he looked. He wore a fitted suit jacket in some kind of small plaid pattern in the colors of gray, navy, and black. Under the open jacket was some kind of black button-up sweater with a low, gray-trimmed neckline that showed off a black and white polka-dot tie. The pristine white collar of his dress shirt seemed to make his skin appear sun-kissed, and his blond hair was brushed off his forehead but still looked a little mussed.

The black pants he wore were fitted, and I stared at his lean hips and the way the belt hugged his waist. The left lapel of his jacket held a gold and red pin, and a white and black patterned handkerchief poked out of the pocket.

I glanced down at the Spider-Man T-shirt and jeans I was wearing. We really didn't match at all. In fact, I wondered what he saw in me.

He made a sound, cutting off my thoughts. "I love you just the way you are. I have to dress like this for work."

I rolled my eyes. "You look like this all the time."

"Would you prefer I dress another way?"

"No! I would never ask you to change. I love you the way you are." It still felt funny to say the L-word, but the way his eyes lit up when I did made it much easier.

My body bumped against his, my hands curling into the lush fabric of his fancy jacket when he pulled me into his body. His eyes glowed, drawing me in as if he'd cast some sort of spell upon me. "And I love you the way you are."

The low timbre of his voice brushed over my nerve endings, making them fizzle, making my stomach dip. I felt a blush bloom over my cheeks, and even though I really wanted to, I couldn't look away.

"Don't I embarrass you?"

He blinked, evaporating the spell instantly, leaving me floating away like whatever tethered me had suddenly snapped. A small purr vibrated the back of my throat when his large hands curled around my hips, anchoring me against him, grounding me once more. "You could never embarrass me, Fletcher. Not ever."

"But—"

"No buts." His fingertips squeezed my hips. "Clothes do not make the man. His heart does."

"Even in your world?"

"In *our* world, you have the most beautiful heart of anyone I have ever known. What you have," he said, pointing his finger against my heart, "is something that no amount of money can buy. And something not many are even born with."

"My heart isn't that impressive."

"Oh, but it is." He assured me. "To be honest, I wonder how it's stayed so pure and loving considering everything you've endured."

"It's probably the music."

His brows furrowed. "The music?"

"Mm." I agreed, pulling away to lift Gwennie into my arms. "Whenever things got really bad, sometimes I would feel music inside me, and it would give me hope."

Ethan watched me a moment, a funny expression in his eyes. Then he nodded. "The sound of your soul."

"Huh?"

Gwennie's claws dug into my shirt, stabbing me in the chest, making me wince.

Ethan took the kitten out of my arms, tucking her into

his. He was so big and broad, dressed boldly in his suit, but I couldn't help but smile as he held the tiny, squirming kitten.

"When I heard you in the park that day, I felt like I was listening to your soul."

I didn't really know what to say, so I said nothing at all.

"Tell Gwen bye," E said, holding her out for me to pet.

"Bye," I echoed, patting her head. Ethan set her down beside her toys and caught my hand. "Come on. You're due at Ivory's, and I'm due at the office."

DESPITE THE FACT THAT HE HAD TO GET TO THE OFFICE, HE insisted on walking me up to Ivory's door.

"I still don't know why they need almost the entire day to dress me for tonight," I whined as we walked down the corridor toward her massive front door.

The guard glanced our way, then away, probably recognizing us.

"I know I said clothes don't make the man, and it's true. But sometimes in business, appearances do matter."

I nodded, understanding. "Your parents will be there, right? I'll be sure to dress nice."

He halted, turning to face me. "I did not ask Ivory to get you a suit because of my parents."

"Well, that's good because your parents don't like me. It won't matter what I wear."

"Puppy—"

I held up a hand. "Don't bother telling me I'm wrong, E. My own father hated me so much he left before I was even born."

His eyes widened, then narrowed into half-moon shapes. "He left?"

I nodded. "He hated me so much he left. My mom was so angry I chased him away and she was stuck with me."

"Fletcher, this is not true."

I frowned. "It is. She's told me that more times than I can count."

"Listen to me," he said, quiet yet urgent, his fingers firmly grasping my shoulders through my coat. "He couldn't possibly have hated you—a baby who wasn't even born yet. Maybe he was afraid or—" His lips pressed together into a fine line. I saw the unspoken words in his eyes, felt that he was holding back.

"Or what?" I demanded.

"Or maybe it was your mother who drove him away." He finished, eyes flashing with something I couldn't quite call anger. Whatever it was made my stomach hurt and made me wish Ethan would never look at me that way. "In any case, he couldn't have been much of a man if he did flee that damnable woman and leave behind his defenseless child."

I used to wonder about my father a lot when I was a kid. What he was like, how he looked. Why he didn't like me. I never really thought that maybe it was her he didn't like. She was always so adamant that it was all my fault.

But Ethan's words stirred a weird feeling inside me, something that bloomed into a memory. "You know, the last time I saw her, she said something kinda confusing."

"What?"

I lowered my gaze.

With a soft sound, Ethan lifted my chin with the backs of his knuckles. Everything about him radiated warmth and assurance. "You don't have to tell me, but you can if you want to."

"I asked her why she even had me," I whispered. "You know, since she hated me so much."

He made a strangled sound and pulled me in, pushing my cheek against his chest. "Just the mere thought of you not being here is too painful to bear." Suddenly, I was pulled back, my face pressed between gentle palms, and wide, imploring eyes stared solemnly into mine. "Thank you for enduring all those years. Thank you for keeping yourself safe until I could find you. You did so well, love. So well."

My lower lip wobbled. "You say really nice things, E."

Maybe it was because I was clearly getting emotional, or maybe it was because we were standing in a hallway, but he pulled back, offering me a small reprieve from all the knots he always tied me in.

"What did she say?" he asked, his eyes still caressing my face.

I frowned, recalling. "She said she kept me so he would know part of him was being raised by someone he hates." I glanced up. "Why would she say that? She always said he hated me, not her."

"Was she drunk?"

My mouth fell open. "How did you know?"

An angry bolt flickered through his stare. "Because you said she threw a bottle of vodka at you."

I nodded. "She drinks a lot."

"Could have been the alcohol talking." He reasoned, slipping an arm around my waist so we could walk to Ivory's door. "This is a heavy topic for the middle of a hallway. And you don't need the stress today. How about we talk about this later? As much as you want."

"Okay." I agreed. But really, there wasn't anything else to say.

"I'm sorry I can't be with you all day, but it's a busy time."

I huffed. "I'm not a baby, Ethan. I can take care of myself. I don't need Ivory to babysit me either."

"So I'm your babysitter now and not your sister?" Ivory exclaimed from the doorway.

I hadn't even heard it open.

"Of course not!" I called, rushing over to hug her. She laughed, a light, airy sound. Leaning into her ear, I said, "But I gotta give him a hard time, or he'll get a big head."

"Duly noted," she whispered back.

"Telling secrets?" Ethan inquired.

"Yes, and I shall take them to my grave," Ivory announced.

"Where's Neo?" I asked, heading into the penthouse.

"He had to run to the gallery. His showing is approaching, so he's been busy, but he'll be back soon." Her attention turned to Ethan. "Are you prepared for tonight, Ethan?"

"Of course. Just a few last-minute things to check on. I expect everything to go smoothly."

"I'm sure it will, and I'm sure the entirety of the Upper East Side will be gossiping about it for days to come."

Nerves coiled in my stomach. Being reminded I would be playing in front of basically everyone in this fancy world made me feel sick.

And well… so did knowing I was essentially defying Mother's wishes by doing so also made me extremely anxious.

I never want to see one of these in your hands again! EVER! The angry yell echoed in the back of my head, and it took everything inside me not to wince.

"I have to get going," Ethan announced, making my stomach drop further. "I'll put this here for you, puppy." He continued, showing me where he set my violin case.

With the case aside, he came forward, smoothing my hair and leaning down.

My lips tapped his cheek automatically. "Bye," I echoed.

Surprise made me giggle when he popped a kiss to my nose before straightening. "I'll see you later this evening."

When he disappeared out the door, my heart clenched, and I rushed after him. "Ethan!" I called, hurrying into the hall.

He stopped halfway to the elevator, rotating on his heel. When he saw me there, he opened his arms.

"Close your eyes," I told the bodyguard, who dutifully did as I asked.

Then I ran the distance between us, leaping up into his arms, wrapping around his upper half.

My heart instantly felt lighter, my worries less pronounced.

"Missing me already?" he asked softly.

I nodded.

"I love you."

I nodded again.

Leaning around me, Ethan gazed toward the bodyguard and then back at me, smiling. "Come here."

I leaned in, lips already parting so he could sweep his tongue inside, kissing me the way I craved. I was breathless when he pulled back, his taste still lingering on my lips.

"Love you," he whispered again before gently setting me on my feet. "If you need anything, just call."

When I stood there staring, he chuckled. "Go on, then. I'm not leaving 'til you go."

Bouncing forward, I kissed his cheek once more, then raced back into the apartment.

Forty-Two

ETHAN

I SCANNED THE LENGTHY CONTACT LIST PROGRAMMED INTO MY phone. A name and number I hadn't used for a while pulled up on the screen.

The line rang twice before it was answered.

"It's Ethan Abbott. I need you to do something for me."

"Go ahead."

"Find out everything you can about a woman in the Grimms. Milly Brown."

"I'll contact you when I have a report."

"I'll pay double if you're quick about it."

"Pleasure doing business with you, Mr. Abbott."

I disconnected the call and slid my phone back into my coat. It was hardly a pleasure, but ensuring this insufferable cow did nothing else to hurt Fletcher was of utmost importance.

And also, I was suddenly very curious about the so-called father who'd abandoned him.

Forty-Three

Fletcher

"Pink!"

"Blue!"

"Pink!"

"Blue!"

I stared unblinking at Ivory and my self-proclaimed fairy godmother as they had quite the argument over the color of the tie I would wear tonight.

I had no idea that choosing a tie was such serious business until I met people from the Upper East Side.

Honestly, I'd never even worn a tie.

Well, okay, I wore a clip-on one once. It was oversized and had four-leaf clovers on it for Saint Patrick's day. I wore it at the Rotten Apple because someone dared me to.

But it was a tie, so it counts.

"His jacket is midnight blue, sweet child. The lighter blue tie would complement that superbly," Marco, Ivory's stylist—and I guess now mine—insisted.

"Blue is a very nice choice." Ivory agreed. "But the pink silk would be an eye-catching contrast to the blue velvet."

The small raven-haired beauty and the tall man with flawless deep-chocolate skin rotated toward me at the exact same moment. Their expectant stares made me swallow nervously.

"Which one do you think?" Ivory asked.

I kind of wished they'd go back to arguing and forget I was standing here. "Uhh…"

"Now look, we've scared the poor child."

"I'm not a child."

"It's just a figure of speech, darling." Marco clucked his tongue. "Of course you aren't. No child could snag the most eligible bachelor in all of New York!" Marco leaned in. His dark eyes were lined with something that enhanced their natural brown shade. "I positively must know," he whispered with a flourish. "How good of a kisser is Ethan?"

"Marco!" Ivory gasped.

Marco rolled his eyes. "Please. If you'd have told me, then I wouldn't have to ask this little cupcake."

Cupcake? But then the rest of his words caught up to me. Swinging around, I focused completely on Ivory. The burn of jealousy heated my lower belly, making me feel unnaturally grumpy. "You kissed Ethan?"

Ivory's red lips fell open. Closed. Her blue eyes shifted to Marco accusingly.

Marco made a sound and spun toward the rack of clothes they'd just been arguing over seconds ago.

Of course she did. I mean, after all, they had been bequeathed… No, *betrothed*. For a long time, they were supposed to get married. I hadn't thought about it until just now, but they probably kissed lots. Held hands… *Had sex*.

The heat previously in my stomach rushed through all my limbs, making my ears grow hot. I loved Ivory, but this… I did not like this. I didn't like thinking of Ivory in Ethan's bed, between those silky sheets, his body blocking the rest of the world from her vision.

I squeezed my eyes closed, toes curling against the floor as the urge to run came over me. I wanted out. Away from these feelings, away from the hurt that these thoughts conjured up.

"Fletcher." Ivory's voice was concerned and soft.

It made me even more upset. Ivory was perfect. The fairest of them all. There was no way I could ever compete with that. Insecurity slammed into me. I tried to reason with myself, but it laughed in my face.

I spun to flee, but Marco stepped into my path.

Fairy godmothers were supposed to be dainty and magical. Marco looked like a wall I wouldn't be able to get around.

"Wait!" Ivory rushed forward to take my hand. "It's not at all what you're probably thinking."

"You have no idea what I'm thinking," I retorted, not meeting her eyes. A pang of guilt hit me because she was my sister and had always been kind to me. But then I had another vision of Ethan's large hands floating over her skin, and I got upset all over again.

"Ethan and I..."

A rough sound ripped out of my throat.

"Our relationship wasn't like that. We weren't... physical."

My eyes shot up to hers. "You weren't?"

"No. There was never that kind of attraction between us."

My head tilted. "You never kissed him?"

Her lips pressed together, and my stomach fell. "Yes. But only a handful of times. And those times only confirmed that we were not attracted to each other."

My chest was tight, my foot bouncing restlessly on the floor.

"But it never went beyond that. It was never anything more. And he most certainly never, not even once, looked at me the way he looks at you."

I glanced up. "Really?"

She giggled. "Most assuredly."

Marco made a sound, rejoining the conversation. "I can

second that. I've never seen that cool, composed man look lovesick until you."

A small smile played at the corners of my lips.

"And I can tell you…" Marco shifted closer, gesturing toward my neck. "I've never had to match concealer to Ivory's neck to cover up a slew of hickeys he left behind."

The sound of my palm slapping against my neck filled the room. Embarrassment burned my cheeks, but I also burned with something else. Satisfaction. Just remembering the marks on my neck (and places they couldn't see) lifted my confidence.

"Don't be upset," Ivory implored sincerely. "Ethan and I have never been anything more to each other than friends."

"I'm not mad. Thanks for telling me," I said, exhaling most of the jealousy I felt. Looking at Marco, I gave a small smirk. "Ethan uses a lot of tongue when he kisses. And sometimes he growls. He's very possessive, and I like it."

Marco squealed.

Ivory's mouth dropped open.

Glancing at the two ties they'd been arguing over, I chose. "Pink. It's Ethan's favorite color."

"I think my soul has left my body!" Marco declared. "And I also think Ethan isn't the only possessive one."

Maybe he wasn't. Maybe it felt good to let people know he belonged to me and me alone.

Clucking his tongue again, Marco guided me toward a chair. "Let's get you all done up so you can knock the socks right off your prince at the ball."

Forty-Four

ETHAN

Despite the endless amount of tasks throughout the entire day, the daytime hours seemed to crawl by. I checked my clock and phone more times than I cared to admit.

Waiting. I was reduced to waiting until I would see Fletcher tonight, left wondering what was taking the private investigator so long.

Sure, I'd only called him hours ago, but I expected results quickly. The more time that passed, the more uneasy I became.

It didn't matter the day was filled with things to focus on. In the back of my mind was the memory of Fletcher's pale face and wild eyes. The whispers of the truths he finally told me and his palpable fear when he thought she'd been following him.

Maybe he didn't think she would be creeping around the Upper East Side. Maybe he didn't think she cared enough about him to figure out where he spent his time these days.

I flat out refused to operate on what-ifs and probably-nots. Knowing what I knew about that damnable woman now and the abuse my love had suffered, leaving anything up to chance was not something I was willing to do. I was willing to trust his instincts, and if they told him she was lurking, then she probably was.

I wanted to know her whereabouts. Now. I wanted every last detail about that woman so I could do whatever was needed to keep her away.

I was dressing in one of the brand-new suites of the hotel we were opening tonight because it seemed much easier to do so here than fight with city traffic just to go home and change. I was unzipping the garment bag my tuxedo was in when my phone rang.

Forgetting the suit, I picked it up to stare at the caller ID. It wasn't the PI but someone better.

"Puppy," I said affectionately into the line.

"I look stupid," Fletcher announced into my ear. "I don't look like you in a suit."

A wide smile broke over my face, and for the first time all day, I felt at ease. "You must look better."

He made a rude sound. "I look ridiculous."

"You do not!" Ivory said from somewhere close by.

"And it's uncomfortable," he muttered.

"You'll get used to it." Neo assured him, also somewhere close by.

"Where are you?" I asked, feeling a ping of jealousy they were with Fletcher and I wasn't.

"Stuck in traffic."

"You should have gotten ready here," I murmured, regretful.

"What if I'm late?" He worried, voice small.

"You have plenty of time to get here. And even if you are, it's okay." I could feel his nerves through the phone, the electricity of them practically reaching through the line with a shock.

"Don't be nervous." I spoke softly. "You're so talented."

"But I'm not used to playing in front of crowds."

"You play in the crowded subway station all the time." I reminded him.

He made a rude noise that I found adorable. "This is different."

"It is." I allowed, not wanting to invalidate any of what he felt. "But I believe in you. And I'll be here the whole night."

He was quiet, but his energy was very different from just moments ago.

"Are you smiling?" I asked.

"Maybe."

"I love you."

"Me too."

Bree started knocking on the suite door, and I sighed. "I have to go, but I'll be waiting for you."

"'Kay."

After seeing to Bree, I dressed in a traditional but modern black tuxedo with a black and gold paisley printed silk tie. The sleek black boots I wore had a bit of a heel, so I stood even taller than my already impressive height.

The massive ballroom on the ground floor sparkled with all its brand-new finishes and golden details. Everything was in place. The staff was organized, and the piano player accompanying Fletcher was already filling the air with song.

Bree was dressed in a light-blue gown, her blond hair pulled up, accentuating a long, graceful neck. My assistant really was a beautiful woman, but she didn't seem to realize it. She also seemed rather nervous, which was something I didn't often see from her.

"Bree, you look lovely this evening," I told her when she stopped at my side.

"Thank you," she replied, demure. "Just trying to represent you and Abbott Group to the best of my ability."

"Yes, well, you are exceptionally good at it."

She flushed, which made me smile. "Don't be so nervous.

We've had many of these events before. It's just par for the course."

Really, all the work was done now. All that was left was to stand around smiling and shaking hands. The elite were incredibly predictable and socially boring. Everyone would laugh and interact while showing off their money and accomplishments, inwardly judging everyone that stood nearby.

I would be guilty of this as well. And I couldn't help but feel exhausted by it, knowing that the people I would have to fake it around the most tonight would be my own parents. The scene in my office yesterday was definitely not resolved, but I wasn't fool enough to think they wouldn't be here.

This was an important work and social event. My parents not showing would practically be scandalous as well as bad for business. Tongues would be wagging for weeks and stock prices in Abbott Group could take a hit.

So no matter how derisive I felt toward my parents, I would pull on my fake smile and charming laugh and act like our family was exactly as everyone wanted to believe: a picture of modern royalty.

And maybe we were modern royalty after all because, like all the other royals we'd come to know, underneath our shiny crowns were secrets and unrest. I might put on an act for tonight, but that didn't mean I didn't believe everything I'd said last night.

A light touch on my arm brought me out of the internal reverie, and I gazed down to Bree motioning for my attention. "Fletcher is here."

And with those words, my false bravado and fake smile were forgotten. Under the wide, ornately designed flower arch, Ivory and Neo moved forward, looking exactly like the royalty I'd been thinking of.

Ivory would hold every eye tonight in the scalloped hem red lace gown that floated across the floor as she walked. Her black hair, red lips, and blue stare would captivate everyone within close proximity, much to the frustration of the man on her arm.

Neo was dressed in a classic black suit, black vest, and a black tie with a red plaid design. His midnight hair was brushed back, and the air of arrogance I always thought he carried with him dared anyone to say that he didn't belong at Ivory's side.

They made a handsome couple for sure, likely to be the most talked about, most watched couple in attendance tonight.

However, it wasn't them I was interested in.

It was the man who walked in behind them, his silhouette causing a slew of butterflies to erupt in my waist the second he came into view.

His footsteps stalled under the archway bursting with white roses and green ivy, eyes skimming the room as if he couldn't care less about the posh decorations and fancy attendees. He was looking for only one thing… and the second his golden eyes found it, they didn't look at anything else again.

The wide space between us became irrelevant when our stares locked, saying everything lips and words never could, making up for all the hours we'd been apart.

Great gods, he looked unbelievable. In fact, I blinked more than once to make sure he was really there. Fletcher might call me a prince, but *he* was my fairy tale, one I never believed would come true.

His normally unruly hair was neat and parted at the side, styled to lie in a style that wasn't sleek but straight and slightly fluffy. The light-brown strands were newly trimmed around his ears and neck, which only accentuated how his chin tapered into a narrow point. Maybe it was the lighting in here. Maybe it was the shine to his hair, but his eyes were straight gold, purer than anything even nature could create. They stared at me from under groomed eyebrows and impossibly dark lashes resting atop wide cheekbones that burned with his natural blush.

His long, slim body was outlined by straight black pants and a midnight-blue velvet blazer that highlighted his narrow waist and broad shoulders. The tie was pink, my favorite color for a tie, but seeing it around his neck inspired wild thoughts of grabbing the silky length, wrapping it around my palm, and using it as an anchor so he couldn't get away.

"Mr. Abbott."

My eyes never left him. I stood there drowning in everything he was.

"Mr. Abbott." Finally, Bree's voice broke in.

"What?"

"People are staring." She warned.

"Let them."

Pushing off my heel, I moved forward, stopping only when the distance between us was barely anything at all. "You're wearing my favorite color," I murmured, letting him see the hunger I burned with.

"Is this your favorite color?" he asked innocently.

Tongue sliding over my teeth, I leaned in toward his ear. "I want you in that tie and nothing else in my bed tonight. Understood?"

I felt his shiver, and I truly considered pulling him up to my suite right then and there.

"I'll think about it." His response was much more ambiguous than his body's reaction.

Drawing back, I studied him incredulously with a single eyebrow arched. "You dare to disobey me?"

"Maybe I need to be punished."

The sharp intake of my breath was not quiet. I felt fire burn in my eyes, and I hoped it scorched him. "Teasing me like this in public is very dangerous, puppy. Be careful what you ask for."

His ears were scarlet, a clear indication he was feeling shy, yet he didn't back down.

The alpha inside me roared to get out. "Later." I vowed.

His eyes skirted away, and his teeth sank nervously into his plump lower lip.

"Hey," I said softly, making an effort to rein in some of the crazy sexual tension that just exploded. Reaching out, I relieved him of the violin case he carried and straightened. "You look beautiful," I whispered.

Happiness shone in his eyes, but then he frowned. "I'm not supposed to look beautiful."

"Well, that's what you are to me."

He tried to suppress his smile, but I saw it anyway.

"Ethan!" Ivory called, she and Neo stepping into the conversation. "This place looks incredible."

"Well, if you think so, it must be true." I smiled, leaning in to kiss her cheeks. She made a small sound and pulled back, slipping her hand between us.

A beat of surprise rippled through me, but I recovered, as any gentleman would, to lift her hand and kiss the back of it. "You look exquisite as always."

"Thank you." She smiled, glancing over the suit she had custom made for me. "As do you."

"All thanks to you."

Neo yawned. "The whole night is gonna be like this, Fletch. Everyone gawking at each other's clothes and complimenting them. But then when they walk away, you will hear them mutter something rude under their breath."

"Neo," Ivory admonished.

"Tell me I'm wrong, princess."

"Well, not entirely."

"Earth! Beau!" Fletcher called, making all of us look up.

The two men approached, both looking out of their

element in suits and walking under the huge archway of flowers.

Earth was dressed all in black, his Asian features sharp and solemn, black hair combed back from his face. Beau's suit was deep forest green, a color that had to have been chosen by Ivory because it played off his green eyes and red hair perfectly. Red hair that was shockingly *not* covered by a beanie.

"I didn't know you were coming!" Fletcher said, bouncing from foot to foot.

I knew his instinct was to hug them, but he held himself back.

"I told you I invited them," I said. "They definitely want to hear you play."

Earth looked like he'd swallowed a frog, but Beau was much more generous. "Wouldn't miss it. Not every day we get to see you play for this fancy crowd."

Fletcher swallowed heavily, eyes skirting around to the room that was starting to fill with guests.

"Ivory sent the suits. Thought it would be rude if we didn't use them," Earth said.

"You like being rude," Ivory quipped, and Earth made a face.

"Thank you for coming, Earth," Fletcher said, this time not holding back and wrapping his arms around Earth's waist for a quick hug.

Earth's eyes softened, and I suppressed a laugh. No one was immune to Fletcher. Not even big, bad, scary Earth.

My parents chose that moment to step into the ballroom, almost as if they wanted to prove that there was, in fact, people immune to him.

My gaze collided with my father's, and his narrowed when he saw who stood beside me. Turning away from them completely, I placed my palm on Fletcher's lower back. "Come on. You should get started."

"You shouldn't argue with them tonight," Fletch whispered as we walked toward the piano.

Disappointment twisted my middle when I realized he'd seen my parents. "I won't," I answered. "You should know that if you see me smiling and getting along with them, don't think I've somehow forgiven them. Neo was right earlier. Everyone here tonight is fake to some degree."

"Okay."

"Just focus on playing and don't worry about anything else."

I watched him efficiently unpack his violin, which, to be honest, looked like it had seen better days. But when I offered to get him a new one, pure offense twisted his face as he plainly declared he had a bond with his violin and he would not be replacing it.

The second he started to play, no one would notice the state of that instrument anyway.

"Do you understand?" I asked when he still said nothing.

His eyes finally lifted to mine. "Don't worry, E. I'll play no matter what tonight. I promised. I'll do my best and not embarrass you."

Concern hit me, making my face wrinkle. "That's not what I meant," I said, laying a hand on his arm. "I'm not worried about you embarrassing me. I just don't want you to worry about my parents."

"I—"

"Ethan!" a familiar voice called, making me look up.

Henry and Samantha made their way toward us, and though he called out to me, Henry was looking at Fletcher.

Removing my arm from Fletch, I straightened, offering it out to Henry. We shook, and then Henry did the same with Fletcher.

"I've been looking forward to tonight. I'm anxious to hear you play."

Fletcher's cheeks flamed, and his head ducked.

"Ah, you've had her a while." Nonplussed, he continued.

Fletcher looked up at that, raising the violin between them. "For many years. I'm sure she's not as beautiful as the one you use, but—"

Henry lifted his hand. "I completely understand. My most favorite violin, I've had for over twenty years. So many fond memories and attachments to that instrument. She looks a lot like yours. It adds character and depth of sound. People don't quite understand the bond you can form with your instrument."

"That's what I told Ethan!" Fletcher said enthusiastically. "He didn't believe me."

"Yes, I did," I argued.

Henry laughed, but so did his wife, Samantha.

All of Fletcher's attention turned to the petite woman with dark-golden strands. His eyes marveled a bit, and fresh pink bloomed over his cheeks. The look on my lover's face accompanied by the sound of Samantha's giggle hit me like a right hook in the side.

Recovering, I cleared my throat. "Fletcher, this is Samantha Cossgrove, Henry's better half."

"Hello, ma'am," Fletcher said, voice timid.

"It's wonderful to meet you, Fletcher. Henry told me about meeting you. He's very excited to hear you play. So am I. Violin is an important thing in our family."

Fletcher nodded, inching closer to my side. On instinct, I put my arm around his waist, hovering my palm at his side. I didn't think anything of it until I saw both Henry's and Samantha's gaze drop to where I held him.

Obviously noticing as well, Fletch stiffened and started to pull away. I didn't allow it, my hand settling more firmly at his waist.

It was not my intent to create a buzz or even a scandal here tonight, but I also refused to act as if anything I did was wrong. Fletcher had clearly needed my assurance, and I would give it under every circumstance.

"Well," I said, drawing everyone's stares once more. "Fletcher has to start playing, as guests are rapidly arriving. How about I show you a few of my favorite features of the hotel?"

"That would be lovely," Samantha said. Glancing back at Fletcher, she smiled. "I hope we can speak again later."

"Sure."

The couple moved off to the side, offering me a moment with Fletch, who glanced up, nerves clear in his stare.

"Just play like you always do. Pretend you're in the subway or in our living room. Play for me tonight, okay? Not for anyone else."

"Okay, E."

I wanted to kiss him. I wanted to lean in and allow my lips to linger on his forehead. I wanted to stroke the velvet of his jacket with my fingertips.

Instead, I tucked my hands into my pockets, feeling an irrational sort of anger strike through me.

"Ethan?" He seemed confused, worried even, as he picked up on my mood.

A choked sound broke out of my throat, and I told my "good breeding" to go to hell. Leaning in, I pressed a brief kiss to his forehead, feeling him stiffen under me in shock.

"Ethan," he hissed. When I pulled back, he glared. "People will see."

"I don't care." My voice was mild. "I refuse to hurt you in order to offer comfort to people who don't even matter."

Let them be uncomfortable. Let them be scandalized.

"You weren't hurting me."

"Well, I guess denying myself was hurting me." I realized that probably made me sound selfish. Refocusing on Fletch, I asked, "Did I make you uncomfortable?"

He shook his head, smiling.

"Play well, my love. I'll be listening to every note."

Fletcher turned toward the pianist, violin in hand, and I stepped toward the Cossgroves, who, to their credit, pretended they hadn't seen.

"Shall we get some champagne first?"

"Please." Samantha agreed.

From across the room, I saw my parents gaze in my direction. I avoided it, not quite ready to pull on my mask of pretend.

Halfway toward the hand-carved, one-of-a-kind bar, Fletcher started to play. Warmth pooled in my belly, my limbs loosened, and the tension I'd been carrying around all day released me.

A quiet hush rippled through the room, momentarily silencing all the conversations taking place. I smiled secretly, knowing without even looking that everyone had stopped to stare.

His talent preceded him, and the sound of his soul was unlike anything else in this world. I soaked it in for long moments, filling a well that had been steadily going dry. When I was reenergized, I turned back to my guests.

"About that champagne…"

But they weren't interested in a glass of bubbly. In fact, they had all but forgotten I was there at all. The couple stood side by side, staring through the mingling guests in the direction from which we had just come.

The set of their shoulders, the energy radiating around them, prickled over my skin, lifting the hair on my arm. Curious, I stepped around, looking at how intently they stared.

Mesmerized. Moved. Practically in tears.

A lump formed in my throat, and a weird, ominous feeling pressed close.

I watched them stare at Fletcher, something akin to

longing shimmering in their eyes. It was almost as though they were as affected by his playing as me.

Almost as if it were familiar somehow.

I realized something as I stared at them. The reaction I had when Samantha laughed just moments ago. Her giggle.

It sounded just like Fletcher's.

Forty-Five

FLETCHER

I DIDN'T KNOW HOW LONG I PLAYED WITHOUT LOOKING UP. Something I loved about the violin was the ability to get lost in it, to see and hear nothing else.

The nerves I'd felt melted away. At first, I imagined playing only for Ethan, and then eventually, even he fell away until it was just the music.

The moment I came back, though, the urge to look for him was there. The need to see his face and hopefully pride shining in his eyes. I might have challenged him earlier, declaring the need to be punished, but truly, above all, I wanted to be his good boy. I wanted him to be proud of me.

Maybe because no one had ever been proud of me before. No one had ever so easily told me that I was good.

Or maybe I just had a weird fetish that only E could unearth.

Maybe it was both.

The ballroom was full of guests now. It was easy to assume everyone had arrived. My eyes skipped through all the well-dressed elitists, avoiding any of their stares, and I tried to tune out all their conversations and laughter.

As I sought out Ethan, an uncomfortable feeling tickled

deep in my throat. It was followed quickly by sharp panic, making my hand squeeze painfully around the bow.

Not again. Please not here. Not now.

I took a deep breath, exhaling through my nose, trying to calm my over-the-top nerves. Even with the effort, the prickling, uncomfortable feeling sat crouched inside, heckling me. All these fancy people, this violin in my hand, it all became stifling for a brief, terrifying moment.

You are to never, ever play again!

I squeezed my eyes shut, willing her horrible voice and memory to fade. A moment passed, and I resumed searching for Ethan, his visual even more important to find.

Out of the corner of my eye, something hovered. I spun, following the shadow. But when I turned, nothing was there. Just glistening stone pillars, hand-carved wood trim, sparkling floors, and people I didn't know.

"Fletcher!" a voice called from close by. I spun, wishing it was Ethan, knowing it wasn't.

It was Henry and his wife. They made their way through a few couples, eyes and smiles intent on me. Samantha looked beautiful in a white and gold gown. Henry dressed in a deep-brown suit with a bowtie to match.

They were very nice people, but they made me feel weird. They made something inside me churn uncomfortably. The feeling was almost painful and most definitely confusing. When she laughed earlier, it was like an echo, like my own laughter being played back to me. And the way they stared... It was like they were looking for something they could never find. Something that made me feel really bad that I didn't have.

"I have to say I am impressed!" Henry boasted the second he was within earshot. His smile beamed, and his cheeks were slightly flushed. "I knew you'd be talented because Ethan declared it, but, my boy, I never expected such passion!"

My boy. Holding the violin in front of me, I smiled. "I'm very honored that you liked my playing."

"Truly, we didn't just like it. We loved it!" Samantha extolled, reaching out her hand.

I pulled back just slightly, suddenly so uncomfortable with the idea of being touched.

"Oh, I apologize. I don't know what I was thinking," she said, dropping her hand immediately.

I felt bad. The look on her face was one I knew well, and I didn't ever want to cause that kind of feeling in anyone. Especially someone who'd been so kind to me. "No," I rushed to say. "It's okay. I'm sorry. Sometimes when I play, it takes me a few moments to, ah, come back to reality." I tried to explain. "I think you just startled me."

"Henry says that sometimes too." She nodded encouragingly.

Awe had me looking at the older man. "Really?"

He chuckled. "Of course. Sometimes playing is like an out-of-body experience."

I nodded. "I've always been drawn to play. Even when I wasn't supposed to."

They both frowned. "Not supposed to?" Samantha asked.

"Oh. Uh. Well, my mother didn't like the noise."

Just the mention of her brought a sensation of something sinister… of eyes watching me that I couldn't see.

"Your mother doesn't like you playing the violin?" Henry asked, surprised.

My eyes flitted around, seeking out the cause of that feeling. Looking for someone who could be staring. "Well, ah…" I began to stutter.

"Where are you from? I don't think Ethan ever mentioned." Henry pressed again.

Their intense gazes, coupled with their invasive questions and the eerie feeling of someone stalking me from the shadows, was almost too much. The urge to make an excuse and rush off was so great that I opened my mouth to give some defense.

But a noticeable hush fell over the room.

I turned from the couple to focus on the wide staircase that gleamed under the glittering chandeliers. A woman descended the staircase, and the way people watched, you might think she was the queen of England.

Except she was younger.

And much more beautiful.

She wore a long gown in a saturated pink. The neckline plunged between her breasts, showing off skin that looked like she'd just stepped off the beach. The gown gathered at the waist and then fell in waterfalls of pink all the way down to brush the stairs. One shoulder had a large bow perched on the top, the other shoulder bare.

Her chestnut hair was pulled into some elaborate style at the base of her neck, and tendrils fell around her pretty face.

I couldn't help but stare. She was easily the second-most beautiful woman in this entire room. Second, of course, to Ivory. Everyone watched her even as the conversations started up again. She smiled at everyone but not exactly at anyone. Her eyes moved swiftly around the room, searching for someone like I'd been searching for Ethan just minutes ago.

"Sienna really is quite beautiful," Samantha said to her husband.

That name pierced my chest. "What did you say her name was?" I asked, not looking away.

"That's Sienna Pope, the woman Ethan—" The second she said his name, my eyes cut to her. She stopped speaking, pressing her lips together.

Turning back, I watched Sienna step off the stairs, immediately welcomed by two people waiting for her. Ethan's parents.

So this was the girl Ethan's father wanted him to marry.

This was the woman he flew all the way across the country because she was a suitable wife.

Oh my God, she is beautiful. Even more beautiful than I imagined. It hurt to look at her. Even now. Even knowing everything Ethan said, knowing he told his parents he would never date her.

How could he choose me over someone like her?

You're nothing! The voice echoed in my head. *Unlovable.*

I jolted when a hand slid against my lower back, nearly dropping my violin and bow.

"Careful." Ethan cautioned.

I spun, staring at him, wide-eyed.

Concern flickered briefly in his eyes as he looked into mine, but then he buried it to hold out a crystal glass filled with water. "I thought you might be thirsty."

"Oh, you didn't have to do that. I could get it on my own," I said, slightly breathless.

"I wanted to," he said, gently taking the violin from me to hand over the water. I took a small sip, eyes straying back to Sienna. She was laughing at something someone was saying, her teeth so white they were blinding.

"You were right, Ethan. This young man is incredibly talented," Henry said.

"I heard a few people already saying they wanted to hire him," Samantha added.

I could feel Ethan's palm hover at the base of my spine, not touching me but almost.

Her dress was pink. *Pink.* It couldn't possibly be a coincidence. Did she know pink was Ethan's favorite color? Did she wear it for him to try and win him over?

She wore pink better than I ever would.

As if she could hear my inner thoughts, she glanced at me. I nearly peed my pants, but her eyes didn't linger. They went to Ethan, where they stayed.

She leaned in, speaking to Ethan's father. Adrian and Elizabeth Abbott both looked up.

The trio turned, heading in our direction.

Forty-Six

Villain

Well, well, well, what do we have here?

Was fate at work? Was the universe trying to right the wrong that I committed?

Or was that boy just incredibly lucky?

What were the odds he would stumble into the very world he was snatched from? That Ethan Abbott, of all people, would take an interest in his miserable life?

I would laugh if I wasn't so infuriated.

How dare this child? How dare he unravel twenty-two years of vengeance and sacrifice. At first, I suspected that perhaps the jail incident was just a favor because of that girl, Ivory White. Perhaps she asked Ethan to bail him out because of her connections with that vagrant Fletcher called a brother.

But as I spied and lurked, following that unsuspecting fool all around the Upper East Side, I learned it was far more. That somehow Fletcher caught the eye of the city's richest man. How he came and went from the Abbott Group without care. No one batted an eye at his presence, as if they were already used to it.

Oh, how I laughed at first, realizing that the son Henry

still placed on a pedestal was even worse than I could make him. *Gay.* Their long-lost precious heir was gay.

Not only that, but the most eligible bachelor in New York was too.

Oh, to see the faces of those uppity, snobbish fools when they learned that truth. The coup was almost too much to ignore.

I could blackmail them to keep quiet. I could sell the gossip to a magazine. Either way, it would be a big payday, and I could take my bounty and disappear. Fletcher and his father would never learn of his paternity.

No. This went beyond money. No money could offer the satisfaction of keeping an heir from his throne. Of making an arrogant king live in a barren kingdom. His suffering was worth more than money. I wanted that man to rue the day he betrayed me.

I wanted him to die while his pleas for forgiveness fell from his tongue.

And it was all about to be ruined!

Ill-contained fury tried to burst from my pores every second. My palms would bear permanent marks from my fingernails stabbing into the flesh. I'd seen that boy carrying around that case. The rage at just seeing it in his hand made me want to murder.

I told him never to play that violin!

My God, the time I'd caught him playing, I nearly killed him then and there. Flashbacks had come over me of what once was, of broken promises and lost love. The rage I'd flown into had been of epic proportions, and I thought he'd learned.

I should have known he hadn't listened. I should have been harder on him as a boy.

If I had, I wouldn't be standing here in this sickeningly upscale ballroom, watching him play as if he'd been playing for a lifetime.

God, he looked like his father when he played. The way his body bowed and moved to the music almost like he *was* the music and not merely the vessel who played it. My vision turned blurry, and my stomach heaved.

I had to flee for a while. The familiar burn of the vodka singeing my throat as I gulped was the only thing that kept me sane. Flashback after flashback from years ago rolled over me, and I dumped more vodka into my system.

The violin stopped, and I slinked back into the shadows of the ballroom. What I found brought me to my knees. Everything around me darkened. The glistening gold tones of the room turned ash gray. The thorns curled into my heart sank deeper, fresh blood dripping like a leaky faucet. The withered and tortured soul that was imprisoned within my shriveled heart turned to stone, then crumbled to dust.

It turned out that little piece of humanity still buried deep within me had made a difference. All these years, that tiny battered thing kept me human.

Humanity that was now swallowed whole by a wicked dragon who'd been lying in wait. Here I stood, flames of vodka emitting with my harsh breathing as I watched Henry and Samantha Cossgrove standing before their unknown child, fawning all over him, looking at him as if he'd hung the moon.

This was not supposed to happen.

NEVER SUPPOSED TO HAPPEN!

Betrayed by the father… and now by the son.

With my humanity gone and pure, unfiltered hatred the only thing giving me life, my plan for the past twenty-two years no longer seemed enough. It was far too lenient.

They had taken my life.

An eye for an eye.

And so I would take theirs.

Forty-Seven

ETHAN

"Ethan," my mother crooned as she approached with my father and Sienna in tow. Why that woman stayed in New York even after I'd told her not to bother was beyond me.

Clearly, she was determined to try and win me over, but really, shouldn't all of the ignored voice messages and calls have put her off? The fact that I went back on my word about showing her around the city didn't seem to faze her at all.

Frankly, any respect I had for her went down several notches. Was she so eager for a wealthy match that she would forgo her own pride and proper treatment?

Obviously, because here she was clinging to my parents like they were indeed a happy family, and Fletcher was standing beside me, watching. The look on his face when I'd approached earlier now completely made sense.

"Mother," I replied smoothly, leaning down to kiss her cheeks. How easy it was to put on the cloak of society. To slip into the role I'd lived in all these years. "You look stunning. Thank you for coming tonight."

"As if we would miss it." She preened.

"Father." I acknowledged him. "I hope you find this event up to the Abbott Group standards."

"Well done." He allowed, sipping at his drink. "Well done indeed."

"Ethan," Sienna purred, clearly unhappy at not being acknowledged. Stepping forward, she curled her hand around my forearm, leaning her scantily clad chest against my side. "This hotel is absolutely stunning. And this ball! It puts all the ones I've attended in California to shame. I'm so honored to be here as your guest this evening."

The audacity.

A sour taste coating my tongue, I cleared my throat so I didn't choke and peeled her hand off my arm, stepping back so she was no longer touching me. "Well, the *Abbott Group* is honored to have you here as our guest," I emphasized, politely letting her know she was no guest of mine.

Her glossy lips pursed just slightly, but I turned away, dismissing her. Sliding an arm around Fletcher's back, I glanced down, shooting him a look, which he refused to meet.

"You remember Fletcher. He's the headlining violinist this evening," I told my parents, including Sienna in my sweeping gaze. I gazed at Fletcher gently, encouraging him to step forward.

"It's nice to see everyone this evening. I hope you enjoy the music we will play." His voice was stiff but polite.

"Of course we will. I've never heard a better violinist." I praised him. Looking toward Henry, I grinned. "No offense to you, of course, Henry."

Henry laughed jovially. "I might have accused you of being biased, but after hearing him play tonight, well, I understand."

Fletcher laughed a little under his breath, and I smiled down at him, giving him a sly wink.

I could feel the ice from Sienna's stare, but I refused to even acknowledge her.

Thankfully, my mother stepped in to steer the conversation. "It's nice to see you, Fletcher. You play beautifully, and your suit looks like it was made just for you."

"That's because it was." A new voice joined the group.

Everyone turned as Ivory slipped forward, Neo mere steps behind her.

"I had it made especially for him," she said, gazing at Fletcher with pride.

"Pink is a rather bold choice for the tie," Sienna offered, her words polite but the intentions anything but.

"Pink is my favorite color for a tie. I wear it all the time," I said coldly.

Sienna laughed. The fake sound made my back teeth gnash. "Well, you are an exception to the rule, Ethan. You can wear pink. But other men…" She eyed Fletcher. "Pink wears them."

I stiffened, at my limit of pretending she didn't exist. Her cattiness astounded me, and I swung in her direction to tell her just that, but Fletcher's hand tugged the hem of my jacket, quietly asking me not to say anything.

"Mr. and Mrs. Abbott, how lovely to see you." Ivory drew all eyes to her. She was very good at playing the society game. In fact, I would wager she was the best. "It's been too long."

My parents greeted her warmly as they always did as Sienna stepped forward.

"Ivory White," she said, already measuring up the woman in red. "Your reputation precedes you even all the way out in California."

"Hello, Miss Pope. It's lovely to meet you. I must say I didn't expect to see you here tonight."

"Well, with you off the market, Ethan needed someone of equal status to be on his arm."

Fletcher stiffened, and I made a rude sound, ready to cut in.

"You are not nor will ever be on Ivory's level," Neo retorted.

There was a collective quiet gasp from the people standing with us, and truly, I'd never liked Neo more than right this moment.

"And who are you?" Sienna asked, turning her full gaze to him.

"This is the one who took me off the market, as you said." Ivory's voice was smooth.

"Charming," Sienna murmured, tipping her glass of champagne to her lips.

"I should get back to playing," Fletcher said, turning away from the group to go back toward the piano.

I left everyone behind to walk along with him. "Fletcher…"

"It's fine, Ethan," he said, his voice betraying him.

I caught his arm, and he stopped, eyes bouncing between mine.

"She's very beautiful."

"Maybe on the outside. But inside, she's heinous."

His smile was sad. "Your parents like her."

I took a small step closer. "Remember I told you not to worry about them tonight."

He nodded. "I'm going to use the restroom and then get back to playing. I'm supposed to be working."

"Puppy…"

"I know you love me," he whispered, cutting off whatever I might say.

Yes, he knew. But would he forget? His insecurities were not lost on me. They stemmed from many years of being told he wasn't enough. I worried that his internal dialogue might be louder than mine.

Ignoring the room, I caressed his fingers with mine. "I do. So much."

Emotion swam in his eyes. "Go back to your ball. I'll see you in a little while."

When he walked away, I still felt uneasy.

FLETCHER

I found Marco in the crowd, his dramatic presence easy to locate. The moment I caught his eye, he excused himself from whoever he was talking to, and we moved together to the large hallway outside the ballroom.

"What's that look, cupcake?" he asked, sipping his champagne.

"Did you bring the blue tie?"

His eyebrows rose. "Blue tie?"

As if he didn't know. "You brought it, right? Is it in your jacket?"

Draining the rest of the champagne, he set the flute near a massive flower arrangement and dipped his hand into the interior of his white jacket. Seconds later, the familiar blue silk was in front of me.

Gripping the knot at my neck, I tugged, untying the perfectly entwined pink fabric.

Marco made a sound. "What's gotten into you?"

"You were right. Blue looks better." I huffed, peeling off the offending pink to crumple it in my fist.

"But you said pink—"

"I know what I said," I snapped, turning up the collar on my dress shirt. "Can you help me?"

Looping the blue tie around my neck, he silently went about adjusting it.

I felt bad. I was mad at Sienna, the people in this place… and honestly, myself. Maybe even a little at Ethan. I wasn't mad at Marco, but he was the one I took it out on.

"I'm sorry," I said, looking up from under my lashes at the ebony-skinned man as he concentrated. "I didn't mean to snap at you."

"It's her, right?" he said, a knowing tone to his words.

"Who?"

His eyes rolled. "Sienna." He flung out his hand with a dramatic flair. "Descending the stairs like she's some kind of princess in a fairy tale, all dressed in your man's favorite color." He made a rude sound. "Acting like she be claiming him for her own." His tongue clucked. "Someone should tell her that if she were in a fairy tale, she wouldn't be the princess. She'd be the wicked stepsister."

"She said that I wasn't good enough to wear pink."

The knot on the tie slid up so tight I nearly choked.

"Oh, cupcake, I'm sorry." Marco fussed, loosening it. "My temper got the better of me. Of all the nerve! And look at you out here taking it off. Don't let her win."

"I'm not." I confirmed. "But I refuse to wear the same color she is."

I knew Ethan loved me, but I was still jealous. And despite what I said to Marco, her veiled insults hurt my feelings.

But I wouldn't run. I would stay. I would do the job I vowed I would do. It didn't matter that I was nervous. That I felt like I was being watched. It didn't matter Adrian Abbott wouldn't even look at me and that Sienna looked perfect standing at Ethan's side.

Finishing up, Marco stepped back to pat me on the shoulder. "Fresh as a daisy."

"Thank you."

"Anything for you," Marco purred.

I started back to the ballroom, but Marco caught my hand. Spinning back, I looked at him curiously.

"Just remember you're the one going home with him tonight."

I nodded swiftly, smiling.

Letting go of my hand, Marco grabbed my cheek to pinch it. "There's that smile. Now go on, go wow me some more with your musical talent."

As I headed back into the ballroom, a tingly feeling crawled up the back of my neck. Snapping my attention up, I watched a figure disappear around the corner ahead. Despite the way my stomach dropped and the fear pulsing through my veins, I changed direction to run toward it, careening around the place I'd seen it disappear.

The hallway was empty. Well-lit with no shadows for something sinister to lurk in.

Chest heaving, I scanned the vacant space before turning back. No one was there. So why did it feel like I was definitely not alone?

Forty-Nine

I HAD NEVER BEEN MORE EXHAUSTED WITH HIGH SOCIETY THAN I was tonight. A shame that it came with a majestic ball that we'd been planning for well over a year. The pretentiousness felt heavy, the laughter sounded fraudulent, and the praise for this impressive opening seemed phony.

All I could do was stand here and play the game. A game I was so good at.

A game I never realized I despised this much until now.

Truth was maybe I wouldn't dislike it so much if I felt like I wasn't a puppet, my strings being pulled by the elitists so I would perform to whatever song they played.

I didn't want to perform anymore.

I wanted to dance to a song of my own choosing. A song only Fletcher could play.

The expressions of the people I stood with shifted. Knowing smiles curved over their made-up faces, and gleaming approval nearly chortled from their throats. Before I could turn to look, something slithered around my forearm, and the brush of silk dragged along my tuxedo jacket.

Suppressing a deep urge to shove her off, I schooled my features into a polite mask, coolly glancing down. "Sienna."

"Ethan, I missed you."

I hated the way she said my name, a cross between a sigh and a whine. It grated my nerves and so did she.

Would she never get on a plane and fly back to the other side of the country? Great gods, I was beginning to think even that wasn't far enough away.

"Please excuse us." I spoke to those standing there watching us. When we turned, I looked for Fletcher, gazing across the room to where he played.

He'd been playing for quite a while now with no break at all. People were incredibly impressed by him, his talent unmistakable, and the triumph of me being able to book him made his entertainment all the more appealing.

He didn't appear tired at all, his concentration focused somewhere else, clearly beyond this room. In this moment, I was slightly glad because he wouldn't have to be subjected to the vision of me speaking with this she-devil dressed in pink.

I knew he'd been lying when he said he was fine before. Fletcher was not fine.

The blue tie around his neck was definitive proof. He'd been hurt by this catty, spoiled heiress's remarks, words she'd just flung out carelessly with no thought for whom she might harm.

"You haven't danced with me all night." She pouted.

I looked at her like she had twelve heads. She might as well have. And all twelve of them were bonkers.

"I am not dancing with you."

"But what will people say if you do not?"

"Probably a lot more polite things than what they will say when you drag me to the dance floor and I proceed to accidentally drop you on your behind and step on your hem to rip your gown."

"You wouldn't."

"Try me, little girl. Try me."

Whatever she heard in my voice convinced her because

she veered away from the dance floor toward the bar. "A drink, then."

I started to pull my arm from beneath her talons. I would have to burn this jacket. She'd touched it far too many times. Too bad. It was a nice piece. I was sure Ivory would understand.

"So why didn't you tell me that the destitute girl you're dating is, in fact, a man?"

I gave her a mild, unsurprised look. "Figured it out, did you?"

"From all the way across the room. You really should learn to hide the way you look at him."

"I would never," I said, completely appalled.

"So?" She pressed. "Why didn't you tell me?"

"Because it doesn't change the fact that I'm not interested in you."

Her eyes flashed, and she removed her arm from mine. Near the bar, she grabbed a flute of champagne from a server's tray and turned to face me. "You know if you're going to bring home a man, the least you could do is choose one with impeccable breeding and an impressive bank account."

"How's that working out for you?"

She lowered the glass from her lips, eyes narrowing. "At least I'm not so desperate to bring home the help."

If she were a man, I'd probably deck her. But she was a "lady," so I had to settle for sharp barbs and mockery. "No, you just continually show up where you aren't wanted and make catty, unflattering comments that show off the ugliness all that Botox and fake tanning tries so hard to hide."

"My tan is not fake," she hissed.

I smirked. "No? But your boobs definitely are. And honestly, they could have done a better job."

She lifted her hand as though she would smack me. Thinking better of it, she drained her glass, thrusting it at the first waiter she set eyes on. Turning back, her eyes were cold and calculating. "You would seriously choose that over this?"

Why did people keep asking me that?

I sighed heavily. "Go home, Sienna. Find some poor sucker in L.A. who's impressed with your daddy's name, because if you stay here, I'll ruin you."

"Not if I ruin you first."

I lifted my eyebrow. "And how will you do that? Tell everyone I'm gay? According to you, all they need to do is look at me to figure it out."

"I'll tell your father."

I laughed. It was an honest, loud laugh that drew a few stares. "He knows."

A flicker of doubt shone in her eyes. I chuckled again, making it dim further. "Did he encourage you to come tonight? Is that why you're still here? Let me guess. He spoke to you last night, told you to show up tonight in my favorite color and give it one last try. The old man probably thought I would regret the way he stormed out after I told him."

She didn't say anything. In fact, she was finally beginning to look embarrassed.

I leaned in. "Even if I wasn't completely in love with Fletcher and was straight as your hair fresh from the salon, I still wouldn't look twice at you."

"Good-bye, Ethan. Let's never see each other again."

"Finally something we can agree on."

She spun to leave, but I caught her upper arm, turning her back. Her low gasp floated between us as I tugged her a little closer. I smiled at a couple walking by and then lowered my mouth to her ear.

"If you so much as look in Fletcher's direction on your way out, California won't be far enough away. Do you understand me? You'll have to move to another country to get out from under the scandal I will bury you under."

Her entire body tensed, her arm nearly vibrating under my grasp. "Let go."

"Do you understand?"

She relented. "I understand."

I let go, and she stepped back. I smiled. The fake transformation was so complete that confusion glazed over her stare. "It was so good seeing you, Ms. Pope. Please give your father my warmest regards and send my blessings to your mother."

She blinked, then recovered to plaster an equally fake yet convincing smile on her painted-on lips. "I most certainly will."

She left via the closest exit, and damn, it was so satisfying to watch her go.

The satisfaction lasted maybe three seconds because another well-dressed issue stepped right into her place.

FLETCHER

W**HEN THE MUSIC STOPPED, A FEW PEOPLE APPROACHED,** offering praise and business cards for jobs they'd like to hire me for.

I smiled and nodded, thanking everyone for their kindness. My attention was divided, caught between the musical world I'd just come back from, the people in front of me, and the vision of Ethan disappearing out of the ballroom after some man.

A man I hadn't seen before.

Rationally, I knew that meant nothing. This room was filled with people Ethan knew I had never seen before. But this felt different somehow. Perhaps it was the set of E's shoulders or the way I instantly disliked whoever that unknown man was.

Or maybe it was the fact that I still felt tendrils of unease curling around my feet in an attempt to shackle me down with anxiety.

When the last person drifted off, I turned to tell the piano player I was taking a short break, but the man was already gone. Apparently, he needed a break too.

We'd been playing for hours already. The pads of my fingers were sore. After this short intermission, I figured we would only need to play one more set before we would be able to finish for the evening.

I was ready to go, ready to be alone with Ethan. The Cossgroves materialized from a group, heading toward me, making my stomach bunch tight.

Inclining my head, I smiled, then headed off in the opposite direction. They were very nice people, but every time they approached or I noticed them watching me perform, my insides squirmed with discomfort.

Curious, I went in the direction I saw E go, toward one of the exits that led out into the wide hall. The massive double doors were thrown wide, and the air coming inside the ballroom was much cooler. Anger and something further slammed into me the second I had one foot in the hall. The intensity in the air was accompanied by Ethan's voice, which was so harsh that I froze in place.

He never spoke to me like that. Not ever.

"What are you doing here?" he demanded.

Swallowing thickly, I backtracked into the doorway, out of sight. Ethan's back was to me, but the man he was speaking to would see me if I stayed in place.

"Aren't you thrilled to see me?" The man beamed.

I drew back, not expecting the almost whiny tone the man used. Nose wrinkling, I finished up that observation with a stray thought. *Obviously, he's not thrilled. Can't you hear it in his voice?*

"Why didn't you tell me you were coming?"

The man's brow creased as if he finally realized Ethan was not happy.

Why? Why didn't Ethan want to see this guy?

"When your father called and said he would be coming to close the deal, I was so disappointed," the man explained, taking a small step toward E.

Ethan's shoulders stiffened, but he didn't move.

"It's been so long since I've seen you," he purred, reaching out to stroke his tie.

Shock rippled through me, making my hands tighten at my sides and my mouth drop open. How dare he touch Ethan?

"So I told your father since you couldn't come to me that I would come to you. I asked him not to say anything. I wanted it to be a surprise. So surprise!"

The man was larger than me but not as big as Ethan. He practically smelled like money, so it was clear he was someone from Ethan's inner circle. His suit was deep gray, tailored to his frame, and his shoes were so shiny you could likely see your reflection in them.

But what irritated me the most—besides the fact that he acted very comfortable with Ethan—was his tie.

It was blue.

The same shade of blue as the one I was wearing.

"I don't like surprises," Ethan said, drawing my eye. "You should have called."

"I've never needed to call before."

"Because I was always the one to come to you."

My stomach dropped. And wherever it landed, it took my heart with it. A dull roaring sound filled my ears as I watched them, trying to make sense of what they were saying.

All the conclusions I was leaping to made me want to puke.

"Exactly. And it was time for me to come to you." His voice was smooth like butter. He spoke intimately even though he just used words like everyone else.

He stepped even closer, reaching out his hand again. I bit down on my tongue, and the metallic tang of blood swept over my taste buds.

Ethan knocked away the approaching hand. "Don't touch me."

The man rubbed the back of his neck. His hair was blond

like Ethan's and trimmed short. Making a show of looking around the empty hallway, he smiled. "Relax. No one is out here. No one will see."

My lungs nearly burned from lack of oxygen, yet I couldn't convince myself to breathe.

"I'm serious, Preston."

I searched my memory for the name, for any information I might know. There was nothing. I didn't know this name or this man. But Ethan seemed well acquainted with him.

A low ringing cut through the hall, the sound coming from inside Ethan's jacket. He ignored it, choosing to stay focused on the man instead.

"What's the matter, lover?" Preston crooned, shifting closer without taking a step. "I thought you missed me."

Lover.

The breath I'd been holding whooshed out of me in one great exhale as if that word, that single word, poked a giant hole inside me.

This was Ethan's lover? Ethan was having sex with this man?

But what about me? He said he didn't want anyone else.

Did he lie?

My hand pressed to my stomach as I doubled over just slightly.

"There you are."

The familiar voice made me shoot up, the hand dropping from my sick middle.

Earth's eyes narrowed instantly. "What's the matter?"

"Nothing!" I said, trying to keep my voice quiet but making it sound squeaky instead.

Earth glanced at Beau, who was walking beside him, and they shared a look.

"Something is definitely wrong." Beau confirmed.

"You spying on someone out there?" Earth asked, starting past.

Catching him by the arm, I pulled him back. "Wait!" I hissed, pressing a finger to my lips.

Intrigued, Earth and Beau leaned out the door to see Ethan and that blue-tie-wearing homewrecker.

Both my brothers' faces darkened, and Earth's mouth pulled into a flat line. "Who is that?"

I shrugged. "He called Ethan his lover," I whispered. Then unable to stop the surge of unwanted emotion, my eyes filled with tears.

Beau cursed under his breath.

"I'll kill him," Earth spat and charged forward.

"No!" I yelled, grabbing the back of his suit.

It didn't stop him. He just kept barreling forward, pulling me along with him as though I were on a pair of skis.

"What on earth?" Preston gasped.

I felt rather than saw the second Ethan spun and spotted us. I didn't look to meet his penetrating stare. Instead, I focused on the back of Earth's coat, which I was still holding.

"You jackass!" Earth roared, charging forward.

I let go of his jacket, stumbling back into Beau. Earth swung at Ethan, who dodged the fist as if he'd done it a thousand times.

"Earth, stop!" I called.

"Security!" Preston wailed, ducking behind Ethan and wrapping his arms around his waist.

Hurt quaked inside me like a massive earthquake. Seeing that this man would automatically assume Ethan would protect him. Seeing someone touching what I thought was solely mine. Seeing that Ethan would even allow it.

"How dare you?" Ethan spat, and I wanted to die.

Is he mad Earth is threatening his lover?

I turned to go, but Beau caught my arms and forced me back around.

"I said never touch me," Ethan spat, flinging Preston off him to step away. "And you," he said to Earth, chest rising and falling with heavy breath. "Would you mind explaining why you are trying to clobber me?"

"As if you don't know," Earth grumped.

Ethan's full stare swung to me. "Fletcher."

"Who is that?" I asked, straightening away from Beau.

"This is Preston Willshire. He's a business acquaintance from England."

Oh, he had an accent. Was that why his voice sounded that way?

I didn't like it.

Preston made an unhappy sound, and Ethan shot him a look, making him shut up.

"I heard him call you lover." I lifted my chin. "Is he?"

"No," Ethan replied instantly, not once looking away from me.

My heart unclenched a little, and I fought the wobble in my chin.

"I know you want to keep things private, but I flew all the way from England to see you, and you will deny me like this?"

"Shut up," Ethan spat.

He came forward, but I froze him with a glare. He stopped halfway between me and Earth, his shoulder dropping a little. "Preston and I used to have a relationship of sorts."

Earth made a scoffing sound.

"What kind of relationship?" I asked, a sinking sensation already pulling me down.

"Ah, maybe we could talk about this somewhere else," Ethan said, glancing around.

"Answer the question," Earth intoned darkly.

Ethan sighed. "We were friends with benefits."

Preston gasped. "Friends with benefits? Used to have? Were?" He repeated all the offending words Ethan had said.

"Don't act surprised. You knew what we were," Ethan said, voice cold.

"I didn't know it was over."

I felt my eyes widen, and I whispered, "You never broke up with him?"

"There was no relationship for me to break off," he said gently.

"He seemed to think there was," Beau pointed out.

"Who are you people anyway?" Preston asked, taking on a haughty tone. Reaching up, he smoothed his blue tie and then glanced at mine with derision.

I hated ties.

"This is my boyfriend whom I love and asked to move in with me."

Beau made a noise and looked at me. "You never told me that."

"I've been busy," I retorted.

"Must be pretty convenient to have a lay in different countries. You got one in France too?" Earth asked, voice lazy.

I made a sound.

"I don't have a *lay* in every country," Ethan said, gritting his teeth. "I only have Fletcher. I only want him. I haven't seen Preston in months. Certainly not since I got involved with Fletcher."

"Don't lie, *lover*," Preston said, his voice smooth and sly.

Oh God, that word. The horrible images it conjured up. My stomach roiled, and I found myself grateful it was empty because, if it wasn't, I'd already have emptied it on the shiny floor.

Ethan's face went dark. The kind of dark I'd only ever seen Earth pull off. It scared me, made my heart pound.

"Ethan," I squeaked, starting forward.

But he was already looking at Preston who also had noted the look on his face and was recoiling rapidly.

"I-I-I—"

"Lying is not becoming, Preston," Ethan nearly growled. "And it's also very dangerous. You know full well what I am capable of, so I advise that you do not push me."

"Who says he's lying?" Earth asked, not even blinking at Ethan's wrath.

"Me!" Preston confessed. "I was lying."

"Who to believe?" Earth practically sang.

My voice was shaky, but I spoke up. "I heard them earlier, before they saw me. I heard Preston say he hadn't seen Ethan in so long."

Earth grunted, glaring at Ethan. "Lucky bastard."

"I think it's best if you go," Ethan told Preston. "Thank you for coming all this way to sign the papers. I will be sure my father meets you in the offices tomorrow to finalize everything. Despite the way our, ah, personal relationship has ended, I can assure you that I will respect the business deal as the professional that I am."

Preston's mouth dropped open. Closed. His brown eyes swung to me, assessing, glaring... judging.

Ethan made a sound, shifting between us to block me from sight.

I felt Preston glare even though Ethan stood in his way. "What's he have that I don't?"

"My heart."

The silence that followed Ethan's declaration was poignant. It filled the air until those shiny shoes of Preston's clicked across the floor as he left.

"Make sure he leaves," Ethan ordered.

I thought my brothers would laugh in his face. No one ever told them what to do. Especially Earth. Surprisingly, they retreated after Preston quietly, doing as E had asked.

"I'll be right back," Earth mumbled to me as he passed.

When they were gone, the space between Ethan and me

turned awkward, the distance seeming much wider than the few feet it was.

"Why didn't you call out to me? Tell me you were there?" Ethan asked, voice soft.

"Why didn't you tell me you had a lover?" My voice was not nearly as soft as his.

He stepped forward, reaching out. I stepped back, denying him.

"It was before I met you. I saw no point in bringing it up."

"Well, maybe if you'd said something, I wouldn't feel like this right now," I said, suddenly so tired.

"This is why I said nothing. I was trying to prevent you from being hurt."

I snorted. Reaching up, I ripped at the blue fabric at my neck. "It always hurts worse when the words come from someone who isn't you," I said, giving a final yank to undo the tie.

He stepped forward. "Fletcher."

The silk made a swishing sound when I pulled it from under my collar, but it was soundless as it hit the floor. "Do you know what it's like?" I spat. "To walk around this ballroom as a misfit in your world, watching hungry eyes follow you, watching beautiful women press up against you and vie for your attention? To hear a man who is almost as beautiful and probably twice as rich as the women call you his lover?"

He made a sound, but I stepped forward, silencing whatever he might say.

"Have you ever imagined someone else rising over me in bed, blocking out the entire world so the only thing I saw was his face? Not yours. Someone else's. Have you ever imagined someone else's fingers sinking deep into my heat and me moaning a name that isn't yours?"

"*Fletcher…*" His voice was stricken, and pain flashed in his eyes.

"That's what it's been like for me tonight. Seeing all these people your father approves of throwing themselves at you. And what do I do? I stand at the side of the room and disappear into my music so I don't have to feel the hurt. So I don't have to keep asking myself when you will eventually realize everything she said is true and abandon me."

Shock reverberated through his eyes, mixing with the pain. His fingers dug into the backs of my arms, and his breathing was ragged. "I will never abandon you. I don't want anyone but you."

Inside his jacket, his cell phone began to ring. And ring.

He ignored it.

"But so many people want you," I whispered, filled with an incredible ache. Lifting my eyes, I let him see the terrifying vulnerability that I couldn't seem to get rid of. "How do I compete with that?"

A broken sound left his throat. My body was crushed into his. He held me tight, his palm pressing my head into his chest. The sound of his heartbeat was thunderous and intense. I could nearly feel it pound against my cheek.

"You don't have to compete, sweetheart. You never have."

The phone started ringing again, and I pulled away. "You'd better get that."

"I don't care about the phone," he spat, reaching out to take my hand.

"I have to go finish my job." I tugged free.

"Forget the job."

I turned back, eyes flashing. "No, I gave you my word. I promised I would play tonight no matter what. I might not have much, but I am a man who honors his commitments."

"And after?" he asked, insecurity lacing the words.

"I don't know," I whispered, turning to walk away.

"Fletcher!" he called, rushing after me, catching me in the doorway to the ballroom.

I was tugged around. Warm, oversized hands cupped my face, and he swooped down, capturing my lips in a heated kiss. Completely shocked, I gasped, and he used the opportunity to invade my mouth, to climb into my body and take over my senses.

Everything fell away, including my hurt and doubt and the gut-wrenching images of him with another. All that remained was the feel of his tongue rubbing mine, his taste bursting in my mouth and my body turning pliant against his.

I don't know how long we kissed, but when he gently pulled back, my eyelashes fluttered. The soft golden light of the room created a halo around his head, and his eyes stared lovingly into mine.

"I love you," he rasped, and even if I wasn't in his arms, those words would be an embrace all their own. "You are my one true love and no one else. I won't let you get away. You're mine and mine alone."

"Okay," I said dumbly.

Hey, you try and speak when someone kisses you silly.

And in front of an entire ballroom, no less!

Oh. My. God.

We were in the ballroom. Well, in the doorway. I blinked, trying my best to reach beyond this little bubble. I listened for laughter and music. For clinking glasses and busy waiters.

There was nothing.

Not a single sound.

Thinking perhaps I was still just swept up in only Ethan, I turned my head.

Everyone was staring as if someone had hit pause on the entire room.

Even the people who couldn't possibly see us were quiet and unmoving, the entire room cast under some kind of sleeping spell.

My eyes went back to Ethan, and his palm rubbed the

back of my head. "Y-you kissed me in front of everyone," I whispered.

"I had to let them know who I belong to."

"Mine," I echoed.

"All yours."

"But what about—"

He made a noise, dipping his head and kissing me once more.

"No one else matters," he murmured against my lips.

This time, low murmurs began making their way through the room, bouncing up to the very high ceilings, circling the fancy chandeliers.

"We'll work it out, okay? Together."

"Okay."

He smiled the kind of smile that made the corners of his blue eyes crinkle. My heart tumbled in my chest.

"I love you." Then to the person standing closest, he said, "I love him."

My face flamed. Surely, it was on fire.

"Go on, then," he said gently. "Go finish playing so we can go home."

As I walked, people parted automatically, creating a private path for me to travel. I thought their eyes might feel intrusive, that the words on their tongues would be sharp like barbs.

I didn't feel their stares or even their words, which, frankly, were probably everything I thought they were.

All I felt in that moment was the tingle on my lips and the music in my heart.

ETHAN

THE PHONE IN MY JACKET KEPT RINGING. IT WAS SUCH AN interruption to the fluttering of my heart.

Ignoring the obvious stares and shocked murmurs, I pulled it from my jacket to silence the incessant ring.

"What?" I barked into the line without even checking the caller ID.

"Abbott, thank God."

The familiar voice reminded me I'd been waiting for this call, and the anxiety in his tone made the fluttering of my heart turn to something much more frantic.

"What is it?" I asked, immediately heading back out into the hallway, pressing a finger against my free ear to muffle any background noise.

"I ran the background check as requested."

"Yes. Yes," I hurried to say. "And?"

"And technically, Milly Brown does not exist."

"What do you mean?"

"I mean, legally, there is no one in this city by the name of Milly Brown."

"But I know her."

"You know someone using that name."

"Then who is she?" I demanded, frustration bubbling up.

"I had someone go into the Grimms and locate her. It was fairly easy. Apparently, the locals there think she's scary. My man has been following her around since late this morning."

"And?"

"And he was able to obtain a photo. I ran it through my system, which uses facial recognition. I have to say the results are… shocking."

Nervous, I spun, looking through the doorway and into the ballroom. Fletcher was near the piano, violin already tucked against his shoulder, music pouring from his pores. I breathed a sigh of relief.

He is okay. As long as he's okay, then everything else will be too.

"Just tell me." I spoke urgently, pacing down the hall for more privacy.

"She resembles someone who disappeared from this area about twenty years ago. Emily Bronwin."

Emily Bronwin… Why does that sound familiar?

Emily Bronwin…

Realization dawned. I gasped.

"She was the prime suspect in the kidnapping of the Cossgrove child. It was assumed she fled the country," the investigator said.

"You're telling me…" I stuttered, my brain trying desperately to make sense of what he was saying.

I looked back in Fletcher's direction. He couldn't be…

My mother said she wanted my father to know that a part of him was being raised by someone he hates.

Great gods!

"Ethan!" the man yelled in my ear.

My attention snapped back. I hadn't even realized I'd drifted away, that I'd wandered around the corner. Sweat was gathering between my shoulder blades. My stomach sloshed wildly about.

Impossible…

"Ethan! Please listen to me."

"I'm here," I said, my grip tightening on the phone.

"I realize this is a bombshell, but that's not the most important thing right now."

"It's not?" I asked, not realizing I should be bracing myself for something more.

"My man has been following her all day. You need to know where she is right now. You need to be warned."

"Well, my God, man, spit it out! Where is she?" I yelled into the line.

"She's at your hotel. She's inside that ballroom… with you."

A loud roaring filled my ears as the phone slipped out of my hand.

She's here?

"Listen to me. I'm not sure how you've come to be involved with her, but if she really is this kidnapper, she's highly dangerous. She's also a roaring drunk. You need…" His words kept going, but I stopped listening, the chaos in my mind drowning out everything he said.

Milly Brown, aka Emily Bronwin, was here right now. Emily, the woman who kidnapped the Cossgroves' child and disappeared into the night with him.

Fletcher was that son. He—he wasn't a misfit after all. He was the Upper East Side's missing prince.

Overwhelmed by every emotion, my hands shook, and my heart raced. I had to get to him. If she was lurking around, then there was no telling what she would do to keep her secret safe.

"Fletcher," I whispered, turning to run.

As I did, something heavy smacked into my head.

Momentarily blinded, I swayed on my feet as the world spun around me. Grasping for balance, I grappled at air before dropping onto the floor in darkness.

Fifty-Two

FLETCHER

I GOT LOST IN THE MUSIC AGAIN. DESPITE THE UTTER CHAOS surrounding me, despite the stares and curiosity trying to knock me off this stage, I was pulled under.

The music that always lived deep inside me, always there to remind me that hope was never completely lost, flowed up and out of the place I normally kept it hidden until it coursed through my limbs. Much like the sun, it chased away the darkness, providing warmth and light, giving me a reason to bloom.

I succumbed to it wholeheartedly, feeling compelled like never before.

The sheet music in front of me turned into nothing but a prop. The pianist, unable to keep up, eventually stopped trying. I played as I loved to, doing what came most naturally, and let the music be my guide.

This melody was wholly mine, the one that kept me going when life tried to bury me deep. I didn't know where I'd learned this song. It was always just part of me. Perhaps it was the sound of my soul, as Ethan often said. Why else would I know it so perfectly? How else could I play it without ever having been taught?

I swayed with the heavy chords, bent with the melancholy

notes, and then rose like a flower blooming under the shining sun when the tune turned cheerful. Swelling with emotion, my fingers moved over the chords, my arm smoothly navigating the bow. This song was like my calling card, a defining piece. When I felt like I was lost and alone, it would lift me up, whispering that out there somewhere, someone loved me.

Embracing everything I felt, I played on, oblivious to the stares of wonder, the awed expressions, and the whispers of sensation. I didn't play for them anyway. I did it because if I didn't, everything I was would be lost.

From out of nowhere a shadow passed over the sun I felt, dimming its light and bringing a chill. The insidious way it wrapped around me made goose bumps lift on my arms and the hair on the back of my neck stand at attention.

The wicked intent was so strong it burst into the world I was so enraptured in, tugging me out and slamming me back into reality. Light flickered beyond the ballroom like a light-ning storm in the middle of the night.

Standing just beyond the doorway, in the center of that tempest, was a familiar figure draped in black. The cloak seemed to move with wind that wasn't there. Perhaps it vibrated with the intensity of her maliciousness. The over-sized hood shielded her face, but I didn't need to lay eyes on it to feel the unrelenting hate focused entirely on me.

I played harder, muscles burning, shoulders aching as if my beautiful melody could combat the darkness lurking at the edges.

It only seemed to make her more incensed as she reached up ominously to pull back the hood, peeling away the concealment to reveal her hollow features brimming with malevolence.

The ear-piercing sound the bow made when it scratched against the violin was that of nails on a chalkboard. The remnants of the song echoed through the quiet room as my chest heaved from the effort, and I stared at the woman whose figure had not disappeared.

She wasn't a figment of my imagination. Those feelings of being watched had not been in vain all along. It was her. Lurking. Creeping. Proving herself as the villain I'd thought her to be.

She'd come for me. I wasn't sure why, but she was here nonetheless.

Shattering glass broke the spell she'd cast, making me jolt and glance away. The entire crowd was silent, everyone collectively drawing breath.

A wail followed just behind the shatter, and I spun toward the sound.

Samantha Cossgrove swooned into Henry's arms, her chest heaving heavily, her lashes fluttering wildly.

"Alexander," she whispered, lifting her head, which appeared to weigh a thousand pounds. "Alexander."

I don't know why, but the name was like an arrow piercing my lung, the organ deflating like a tire and making my chest cave in.

Holding his wife, a very pale Henry stared at me, incredulous. "H-how did you know that song?"

The low rumble of thunder shook the room, and rain began pounding the skylight above. Glancing back as the storm rumbled the night, I watched Milly tug the cloak up over her head, hiding her face once again.

Like a shadow, she slithered out of the doorway, disappearing down the darkened hall. She didn't say a single word, but I heard her nonetheless…

Come to me, child. Come to Mother.

Shouts erupted when I ran, but I didn't look back. Gripping the violin, I rushed after her as she stepped out an exit door, becoming part of the storm.

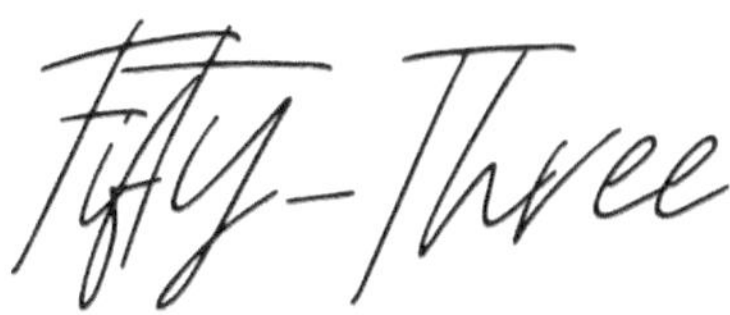

*E*THAN

DULL PAIN MADE ITS PRESENCE KNOWN BEFORE I EVEN OPENED my eyes.

"Ethan!" a rough voice insisted, but the hands shaking me were even rougher.

I groaned as my eyes fluttered, feeling heavier than ever before.

"He's waking up," another voice said.

The faraway sound of glass shattering broke into my stupor, and my eyes shot open.

"What the hell was that?" Beau said, his red head turned toward the ballroom.

The hands gripping the lapels on my jacket tightened, and my upper half was hauled off the floor.

What was I doing on the floor?

"Goddammit, Ethan, wake up right now, or I'm gonna put you out forever." Earth threatened darkly.

Awareness rushed in, and the dull ache in my head turned sharp. Wincing, I pushed it away as I took control of my own body.

Milly is here. Fletcher is in trouble.

"Fletcher!" I called, scrambling up to my feet.

"Whoa," Beau said, reaching out to steady my swaying frame.

Smacking his hands away, I looked imploringly at Earth.

"What the hell happened?" he demanded.

"Fletcher is in danger," I said, already starting away.

Earth grabbed my arm, yanking me back. "We took the trash to the curb."

I puzzled his words, then realized he thought I was talking about Preston. "Not him!" I yelled, shoving his hand off me. "Milly is here. She's after him!"

Adrenaline spiked among the three of us, and they required no more explanation.

"Find Neo," Earth told Beau as we rushed around the corner, stuttering at the darkness in the hallway.

Banging into the ballroom, I hollered Fletcher's name. When I didn't see him by the piano, I yelled again. "Fletcher!"

"He ran out of here a few moments ago," my father said, materializing from the crowd. If I'd been more in control of myself, I'd have realized his pale face and wide eyes were an indication of things to come. "What in the hell is going on?"

Not wasting time, I ran off down the hallway, not even sure where I was going.

A howling wind blew, banging open a door leading into an alleyway outside. Pelting rain slanted inside, the back of the door already drenched.

"This way!" I yelled, charging forward, well aware that Earth and the others would follow my voice.

There wasn't much light to lead the way because the outside was equally as dark as the hall. I went headfirst out the door, regardless of the torrential downpour and the icy-cold raindrops that felt like stabbing swords.

Blinking against it, I lifted my hand as the wind tore through my hair and water soaked my clothes.

"Fletcher!" I roared down the alley, my voice unable to echo in the downpour.

A dim streetlight flickered to life about halfway into the depth of the dead-end alley. The light was not a hopeful sign but a grim way to highlight a sight that could only be found in nightmares.

"No!" I roared, the protest ripping from the very depths of my core, so pungent I swear I felt my vocal cords tear.

There, ensconced in the dingy, orange-ish glow, was a man I loved more than my own life, drenched in rain but soaked in hate.

Three men dressed in the concealment of black surrounded him, delivering blows that I worried he could not withstand. But even in my doubt, he remained on his feet, giving back as good as he got, shaking off the exhaustion of a fight he could never win.

I ran forward, the pounding of my heart, the heaviness of my breath all drowned out by the sick sound of flesh smacking against flesh and the grunts of pain that somehow made the dim light seem even dirtier.

Fletcher's head rocked to the side when a well-placed fist caught his adorably rounded cheek. Red tinged my vision as his head snapped back, and he recovered to bury his foot in the attacker's middle.

The man went down, but the other two jumped him, one pinning him against the unforgiving brick wall while the other pulled back his fist to deliver a blow.

A sound I'd never made before ripped free, abusing my vocal cords once more, and I leaped between my life and the one who sought to end it, catching his fist in mine and squeezing until I heard the satisfying sound of small bones crunching under the pressure.

The man wailed but stayed on his feet, so I knocked him down. He hit the pavement with a grunt, and I buried my heel in his ribs, making him curl into himself.

Spinning, I grabbed the man who'd pinned Fletch to the wall by the back of the neck, yanking him back as he yelped.

Fletcher charged forward like a bull, ramming into the man's middle.

When I let go, he crumpled to my feet.

"Fletcher!" I gasped, starting forward.

"Watch out!" he yelled, pushing me out of the way. The blow meant for me landed on him, making him stagger sideways to fall onto one knee.

Raging, I grabbed the man who'd gotten back up and poured every ounce of the daily training I'd endured into making him wish he'd stayed down.

My entire body burned. Knuckles met flesh. Bones knocked against mine. I punched and kicked and buried my fist so deep into his middle I was sure his organs would bear the imprint of my hit for years to come.

He passed out before he even touched the ground, and I watched him fall with only mild interest.

Earth, Beau, and Neo charged down the alley as I turned toward Fletch.

"Stop right there." Her voice was low, unwavering, and full of the wicked storm that waged around us.

"What do you want?" Fletcher called over the loud pounding of the rain.

Blood smeared his cheek, dripped over his lip, and darkened the front of his white shirt. His hair was no longer soft and fluffy but plastered against his head from the weight of the water.

His eyes weren't glistening gold but filled with shadows and locked on the woman who'd stolen him as a child and raised him in hate.

"Why are you here?" he roared.

My skin crawled just having this villain near him. My skin crawled knowing he'd had to live with her all his life. A brief flash of him as a tiny newborn came over me, and I wanted to scream.

Ethan, meet Alexander. You two are destined to be great friends.

My shoes splashed over the ground as I rushed to put myself in front of his person. I might have been a child twenty-two years ago, but I was a child no more. I would protect him.

Slam!

Pain radiated through me, vibrating my organs and making me rock.

"No!" Fletcher screamed, the tortured sound the only thing strong enough to bring me back.

Numbly, I glanced down at where the woman had struck, the force of her swing only made more intense by the force with which I'd been rushing to Fletch. In her bony, darkly veined hands, the woman grasped his violin, the very possession he held most dear. It was the weapon she'd swung at me, the mere intensity of the hit snapping the strings.

The hood was blown back from her head. Dark curls waved wildly in the wind like poisonous snakes had formed a vile nest on her crown. Her skin was so pale it was nearly translucent, her eyes sallow and her cheekbones sunken. She appeared far older than I knew she likely was, her haggard appearance brought on surely by the hate she lived with every single day. Rain streaked her skin, plastering the dark fabric against her thin frame.

Just looking at her made my stomach tighten. The insidious energy she nearly choked on tried to strangle me as well.

I gazed at Fletch, momentarily struck. How had he survived this?

How?

Fletcher rushed across the distance between us, plastering his back against my front. The way he held out his arms wide, trying to create a bigger shield, was something from which I might never recover.

"I told you never to play this!" She snarled, anger vibrating her voice. "I told you this was forbidden. *I told you!*"

Fletcher winced and shook, but he refused to move from in front of me.

"And then you come here to a place you do not belong, you insipid, lying brat!" Her chest heaved as my palms curled around his sides to shift him out of the way.

"Don't move!" she wailed, banging the side of the instrument on the pavement. The splintering of wood punctuated her order.

"No!" Fletcher wailed, rushing forward as if he would retrieve his violin.

My arms wound around his waist, hauling him back, refusing to let him get close.

"I told you no violin. I told you to never, *ever* play that song!" She smacked the violin on the ground once more.

"Why?" Fletcher screamed. "Why do you hate me so much?"

"Why?" she intoned, her voice suddenly dropping to an almost impossibly audible level.

The sudden change in her demeanor was alarming, far more than her violence moments ago could ever be. Holding on to Fletch, I slid a look to Earth, Beau, and Neo who stood nearby, watching with shock.

It seemed not even Fletcher's brothers knew how toxic this creature was.

She paced forward, and I shoved him back, stuffing him behind me so she would have to go through me to get to him.

The brothers all lunged forward, but she held up the broken, ragged instrument like it was more destructive than a gun.

They faltered, staring between me and the woman, watching as she slowly advanced.

I felt the tremble in Fletcher's legs, in his entire body, as he pressed against my back. He was soaked and cold, mentally abused far deeper than his physical injuries could ever show.

"I hate you because you are not mine!" Her voice rose in hysterics with each word she screamed.

The great quivering in his body silenced for a moment as he peeked around me to stare at the woman he'd thought his mother. "I'm not yours?"

"Emily."

The new voice was familiar but oddly so foreign, as if it had reached through the past and made roots in the present.

The madwoman froze. Her entire body went still. The broken pieces and strings of the violin she clutched swayed when she turned to face the man this all began with.

"It is you," Henry said, staring through the dark and raging rain. His clothes were soaked through, and as I gazed around, I realized this alley was packed with people, with the elite who, for the first time in my entire life, had forgone their appearance and comfort to charge out into precarious weather for the sake of morbid curiosity.

I couldn't even blame them for staring, for this was a twenty-two-year-old scandal unfolding before their very eyes. Up until now, it had only been whispered about in the secrecy of homes and read about in old newspapers.

"Do you have any idea what you've done?" Henry asked, stepping closer. "You stole my son. You ripped him from his home. You took away his childhood, his life."

"And what of you?" she bemoaned. "Tossing aside a woman who gave you everything, who bled herself dry until the only thing that lingered in her veins was the love she had for a man who betrayed her!"

"I didn't betray you. I—"

"Lies!" she screeched, her voice so piercing that the crowd took a step back. "You made promises of love and marriage, and then you ripped it all away to give to a more suitable woman, someone befitting the Cossgrove name, someone who could never compare to me!"

"I fell in love with Samantha, Emily. I never meant to hurt you."

She laughed and laughed. The evil, vacant sound stopped as abruptly as it began. "Well, I meant to hurt you. Tell me, Henry. How was it all these years, knowing your only son was out there, knowing he was being raised by someone you deemed unworthy to mother your child? How did it feel to listen to the so-called woman you love wail in pain day after day because the crime she committed was birthing your son?"

The hands that had been resting on my back suddenly slipped away. Fletcher stepped out around me, face pale and lips wobbling. "Y-you aren't my mother?"

Both Henry and the woman turned to stare. Henry's eyes were wistful, filled with pain. And Milly… Well, my gentleman's handbook was not equipped with words to describe her brand of crazy.

"Alexander!" A new voice cut through the night. "Alexander!"

The crowd parted, and Samantha rushed through. She was clearly unstable on her feet, but determination shone in her eyes.

She stopped when she saw him. Not even the rain could hide the tears on her face. "Oh my God," she wailed. "It is you. My son."

Fletcher stood shocked as the blond woman started forward again.

"He's mine!" Milly wailed, lifting the violin to attack.

Everyone rushed to form a wall in front of Samantha, blocking her from reaching Fletcher and also being attacked.

"The police are on their way!" my father announced, stepping through the crowd.

"No!" Milly screamed. "This isn't over. You can't have him. No one can!"

In a burst of energy, she rushed Fletch, violin lifted above her head, both hands preparing to swing the broken instrument.

I stepped forward, planning to block the blow. Milly's eyes glinted, more than happy to go through me to get to him.

Completely panicked, Fletcher let out a wail. "Ethan, no!" Throwing his body into mine, he knocked me to the side.

An awful sad chord filled the air when the violin struck its target. The hollow, broken wood thumped heavily against Fletcher's head, smacking him sideways into me.

I caught him, both of us going down, my body cushioning his fall.

The woman, still enraged, cackled maniacally and raised the wood again, staring down at both of us. Wrapping my entire body around him, I rolled, using my body as a shield, and waited for the blow… a blow that never came.

Milly landed next to me, her head smacking off the drenched pavement, and then lay there prone.

Staring around, I saw Earth standing there shaking out his fist. His upper lip curled in derision. "I always did want to coldcock that bitch."

Sounds of sirens filled the city as the dirty, dim alleyway began to fill with flashing lights of red and blue.

Forgetting everyone around us, I worried over the man still wrapped protectively in my arms. The man who took a hit intended for me.

"Fletcher," I said, sitting up while still cradling him in my arms.

My shirt had blood on it, a fresh red stain that spread quickly over the white fabric, the color diluted in the rain.

"Fletcher!" I said again. Despite the urgency in my entire body, I held his head gently, turning it to see the gash.

A broken sound left me, and I pulled him tighter into my chest. "We need an ambulance," I yelled, drawing his brothers and Ivory close.

"Hang in there, puppy, okay?" I said, hunching over his body, trying to buffer the rain. "Wake up."

His lashes remained heavy on his cheeks, cheeks that were all too white.

"My son! Let me see my son!" Henry burst through the group, dropping to his knees and reaching for the one I held.

"Don't touch him!" I snarled, the sharp tang in the words a vicious promise to anyone who dared to disturb him.

Henry drew back, eyes wide. "Ethan..." He tried to reason.

I felt my blue eyes flash. "If you touch him, I will kill you."

"Okay." Neo interrupted, pulling Henry up by his armpits. "Take a step back."

"But that's—"

"Now is not the time, buddy," Earth added, stepping alongside Neo.

Fletcher made a small noise, and I forgot about everyone else.

"Fletcher?" I worried, swiping some of the blood and rain off his cheeks. "Puppy, can you hear me?"

"Mmm." His eyes fluttered, but the effort to lift his lashes was far too great. The absence of those honey-colored irises was truly gut-wrenching. "Ethan," he whispered.

A sob ripped through my chest. "I'm here. I'm here. You're going to be okay. Just rest. I love you."

The tiniest of smiles curled his lips. "Love," he murmured and then went silent once more.

Fifty-Four

THE BRUSH OF WARM LIPS BROUGHT AWARENESS. THE WEIGHT of them settling a little more firmly made butterflies erupt in my belly. It was those butterflies that encouraged me awake because, really, all I wanted to do was sink deeper into his kiss.

A small sound floated between us, and my eyes fluttered as he lifted his head.

"True love's kiss," I whispered, smiling. "I knew it existed."

Ethan's arm came down to gently rest above my head, caging me with his warmth and scent. Gentle fingers brushed over my forehead, and azure eyes gazed at me with relief.

"Thank God you're okay."

An echo of pain shot through my head and was followed by other whispers of aches, letting me know they were there.

Frowning, I tried to gaze beyond the very enticing view of Ethan's face. "Where am I?"

His eyes darkened. "The hospital."

Memories from the ball assaulted me.

Chasing her *out into the alleyway, being jumped by men she'd hired to take me down.*

"She didn't think I'd be able to fight back," I murmured,

recalling her shock when I held my own against the three men coming at me.

"What?" Ethan asked, and then I remembered him charging into the fight.

My entire body jolted. I recoiled in pain, but I pushed on, grappling for his face, eyes widening when I took in his black eye and the lump on his forehead. "Look at you!" I wailed. "You're hurt."

His large hand swallowed mine. "I'm fine." He promised, pulling mine down to tuck it under the blanket.

"You have bruises!"

His eyes narrowed. "And you are in a hospital bed."

Reaching up, I fingered the bandage on my head. "How long was I out?"

"All night," another voice replied. It was Beau, and he said those words around a massive yawn.

I glanced over, and my mouth fell open. "You guys are here?"

All of them were. Neo, Earth, Beau, and Ivory. They were stuffed onto a small sofa and a couple of uncomfortable-looking chairs. Their ball attire was gone. They'd changed at some point into dry and comfortable clothes.

My eyes rushed back to Ethan, noting that he, too, had changed. Gone was his dashing tuxedo, and in its place was a sweatshirt and matching pants.

"I know I said no designer, but you could have done better than a hospital gown," I muttered, glancing down at the garment I wore.

"Of course we're here," Neo said, rising from the couch to stand at the other side of the bed. "How ya doing, kid?"

"I'm not a kid."

"Yes, you are," all three of my brothers said at once.

I huffed. "I fought off three men last night! Can a kid do that?"

"They would have taken you down eventually," Earth muttered darkly. "I oughta kill them."

I didn't bother to tell him not to. I was too offended he thought I was weak. And I didn't really like those men anyway. They tried to beat up Ethan too.

I glanced at Ethan. "You saw me, right?"

He nodded, eyes filled with pride. Gently stroking my hair, he said, "I saw. You held your own until we could come and help you. You did so well."

I preened under the praise and glanced back at Neo with an *I told you so* look.

Neo rolled his eyes. "You spoil him," he told Ethan.

Ethan made a rude noise. "So sue me."

I snickered because if anyone tried to sue Ethan, his lawyers would eat them alive.

Neo opened his mouth, and Ivory materialized beside him. "You will not." She admonished, stopping whatever he might say. "Now tell your brother he did well."

Neo grumbled beneath his breath. Ivory elbowed him, and I smiled.

"You did good, Fletch," Neo said dutifully, but then his eyes and words turned more sincere. "But I always knew you could. You survived in the Grimms all these years. We might give you shit, but we know you're tough."

I beamed. The cut in my lip didn't even burn I was so happy. "Finally, you admit it!"

"You're still the baby." Beau reminded me.

Earth grunted his agreement.

"You just had to go and ruin it, didn't you?" I complained.

Beau shrugged.

"Lie back." Ethan admonished me gently. "Don't get too excited. Are you cold?"

Blinking my doe eyes at him, I nodded pitifully.

"I'll get a blanket," Ivory said, starting for the door, but

Ethan was already up and tugging the hoodie he was wearing over his head.

"Don't bother," Ethan told her. "This is what he wants."

I lifted my arms happily so he could slide the soft, over-sized fabric down over me. It was warm from his body heat, and the scent of Christmas swirled beneath my nose.

Sighing appreciatively, I burrowed into it, leaning back in the bed.

"He's created a monster," Neo accused, pointing at me but staring at our brothers.

"Like you're any better with Ivory," Earth muttered.

Neo gave him the finger, making Ivory gasp. "How unbecoming!"

I smiled, bouncing my stare between Neo and Earth. "You two are getting along again?"

Earth's eyes slid to Neo, and Neo looked as if he'd swallowed a frog. Clearing his throat, he turned to me. "Well, you needed us."

"But you made up, right?" I pressed, glancing at Earth.

Earth crossed his arms over his chest. "We're working on it."

"Drink some water," Ethan said, nudging a straw against my lips. I listened, sucking down some of the cool drink, letting it soothe my dry throat.

"How are you feeling?" he asked when I released the straw. "Do you want me to get the doctor?"

I grabbed his hand, shaking my head. "No, stay here."

"I'll get the doctor. Someone should examine him," Ivory said, heading toward the door. Pausing, she turned back to the room. "Why don't you all accompany me?"

"Princess can't even find a doctor on her own?" Earth quipped.

A haughty glint came into her eye, and she lifted her chin. "I could find a doctor easier than you could find your brain."

Neo and Beau laughed.

Still exasperated, Ivory put her hands on her hips and glared. "I was trying to offer Ethan and Fletcher some privacy."

Beau smacked Earth on the shoulder as he stood. "C'mon, I need coffee anyway."

Everyone filed out of the room except for Neo who stood at the foot of the bed, glaring.

"Do you have a problem?" Ethan asked, voice mild.

Neo thrust his hand at Ethan. "I had my doubts. Lots of them. But I can see you really care about him."

"Love. I love him." Ethan corrected.

My heart swelled.

Neo made a sound and shook his hand in Ethan's face. Ethan placed his inside, and they shook on it. "Welcome to the family, I guess," Neo muttered.

"If I'd known this was all it took to get you two to get along, I would have gotten hit in the head sooner."

Both men turned, giving me dark looks. "Don't ever do this again!" They both scolded me.

"Aow," I whined, slinking down into the bed.

When Neo was gone, Ethan leaned over me once more, sweeping over my entire face with a thorough cobalt stare. "How are you really?"

"Kiss me."

We'd already established I was spoiled, so of course he kissed me. I really liked it. Being spoiled was pretty good too.

Pulling back, he bumped his nose against mine, his breath tickling my skin. "How much do you remember?"

My heart dipped, and my breathing turned shaky. "I remember everything."

The heat of his palm seeped through my skin when he placed it on the side of my neck. I loved when he did that. The touch was so steadying, as if he were reminding me I wasn't alone. "It's a lot. I know. We don't have to deal with it all at once. I'll be right here for anything you need. Just don't run, okay? Promise you won't run."

I couldn't be upset at the insecurity in his voice. I'd run so many times. The only way to prove to him I wouldn't was through action. To stay. "I only run to you now, remember?"

"After everything, I wasn't sure that would still be true."

I scowled, thinking of Sienna and Preston. "Still not running." I confirmed. "But definitely jealous."

He smiled. "I can work with that."

Nerves bunched inside me. My belly churned with fear. "Ethan?"

"Yes, puppy?"

"Where is she?"

The darkening of his face and even the air surrounding him made me shiver. Concerned, he tugged the blanket a little closer around me and then gently rubbed his hands along my arms to generate heat.

"The police took her away."

Surprise made my eyes go wide. "She's in jail?"

His brow furrowed. "Where else would she be?"

"I was worried Earth killed her!" I burst out, deflating in relief to know he hadn't.

He made a small sound and leaned a little farther over me. "He wouldn't do that, love. He knows it would hurt you."

I burst into tears and immediately pulled the hood up to hide my face. Embarrassed but unable to stop the water from falling, I rolled onto my side, putting my back to him, biting my lip against the pain.

Not only was my head hurting, but my body was too. Just because I held my own against those three guys didn't mean I got away unscathed.

The bed dipped under new weight, and even though Ethan was huge, he somehow scooped me up so gently, shifting so I was in his lap without causing me any discomfort.

Looping my arms around his neck, I buried my hood-covered head in the side of his neck, tears smearing against his skin.

"It's okay." He soothed me, rubbing my back. "It's okay to cry."

I didn't want to cry. Not for her. "She doesn't deserve it."

"No, but you do." He reasoned kindly. "She might be a terrible person, but for a very long time, she was *your* person. The only one you had. For lack of a better term, she raised you. She might not have a heart, but you do, and it's so big and beautiful. So it's okay to cry for her, to not want anyone to cause her harm. Feeling that way doesn't make you bad. It makes you too good for this world."

His words soothed wounds in me I didn't even know were there. I didn't need his permission to feel the way I felt, but honestly, his understanding made it easier. His acceptance that I couldn't just shut off her connection to me somehow made that connection more tolerable to bear.

Sniffling, I lifted my face, peeking at him from behind the now-wrinkled hood. "She's not my person anymore. She hasn't been for a long time. You are."

He dropped a brief kiss to my lips. The tip of my nose. Each wet cheek. I sniffled the entire time, but he kept on landing butterfly kisses everywhere he could reach.

"She's going to be in jail for a long time," I observed solemnly.

"Yes."

"I don't want to see her."

"You don't have to." Reaching into the hood, his fingers clasped my chin. "But if you ever change your mind, that's okay too. I'll take you to see her."

"Are those people really my parents?"

His lips curled in on themselves, and a haunted shadow passed behind his gaze. "It seems that way. But we don't know for certain. They wanted to run a DNA test right away. I wouldn't allow it. I told them they would do nothing of the sort until you were awake and could decide on your own."

The fierceness in his tone calmed me more. Picturing him standing over my sleeping form, refusing to allow anyone to take advantage, was a luxury I never thought I'd have. It also made it easier to say, "You think I'm him."

The sound of his thick swallow echoed in my ears, the answer already reflecting in his stare. "Yes, I do."

I curled back into his body, hiding my face. His arms held me loosely. I needed more. "Tighter," I whispered, pressing closer.

After a brief hesitation, his hold was firm, and I was safe.

"Am I hurting you?"

I shook my head, pressing my lips beneath his jaw.

I thought I might be him too. It seemed impossible, but it *felt* true. How else could I describe the jumpy, uncomfortable way my stomach squirmed when they approached me? How even though they made me want to hide away, my eyes always lingered on where they were.

He played violin just like me.

Her laugh sounded just like mine.

"You look a lot like her," Ethan murmured, his words running parallel with my thoughts. "And the song…" His voice trailed away.

I lifted my head. "The song?"

"That day in Central Park when I heard you playing, it seemed so familiar, but I was so taken with you that I gave it no thought. That was the song you played tonight?"

I nodded. "The music in my heart."

"That's the music in your heart?"

"Been there as long as I can remember."

"Henry composed that song for his son. He played it for him before Samantha even gave birth. They played it for him every day after he was born."

I gasped. "B-but it can't be. I-I must have heard it some-where, some—"

"He refused to play it after you were… taken," Ethan said. "He never once played it in performances or in public. Not ever. Most people didn't even know about that song."

"Then how did you?"

"My family is very close to the Cossgroves. I sort of became a son to them throughout the years." He glanced up, searching my face, hurrying to add, "Not that I could ever replace the boy they lost."

"I know," I whispered, chest aching.

"Anyway, he played a recording of it once. One year on your birthday."

I shot up, nearly tumbling off his lap. Ethan's hands shot out, cupping my body, pulling me back in.

"The fireworks!" I exclaimed.

"Settle down," he insisted, patting my back in an effort to calm me down. "Your voice is strained, and your body is tired."

"Those fireworks we watched, those were for me?"

Tenderness filled his entire face, softening every line and all traces of exhaustion. "Yes, puppy. Do you still think him very lucky?"

I thought it over for a moment, my lip jutting out. "Yes."

"Come here," he crooned, taking my weight, rubbing my back.

I soaked in his comfort, my eyes beginning to droop closed. "I guess that rumor you told me about the woman scorned was true."

His hand paused. "I still think it best to get a DNA test to give yourself some time to process."

"Okay."

"Just like that?"

"Mmm." I agreed, nuzzling into his neck.

Just as I was drifting blissfully to sleep, the doctor interrupted. I kept myself pressed into E, hoping the man would take a hint and get lost.

No such luck.

But he did let me stay in Ethan's lap when he examined me, so I guess it wasn't all bad.

Fifty-Five

A mild concussion. Stitches. Bruises, minor scrapes, and burns.

Fletcher's physical wounds would heal, but it was the ones I couldn't see that worried me most.

How much would he have to endure in his life? The crimes committed against him could irrevocably change a man forever. I was sickened by the woman who'd inflicted this on him. Anger burned within me so bright that jail didn't seem a grave enough punishment.

However, it seemed jail was the harshest punishment Fletcher could withstand. How cruel was life that a woman who really deserved so much worse was granted mercy because delivering everything she truly deserved would only hurt her victim further?

I didn't care about that wicked bitch. I guess it didn't really matter if she got what she deserved. The satisfaction would be lost anyway because someone as vile as her probably wouldn't even suffer the consequences she was handed. Her warped sense of reality likely didn't even comprehend the ramifications of her terrible ways.

And also, even if we had killed her, she'd probably feel at home in hell.

Seeing her in a tiny cell would have to be enough. Caged like the beast she was, locked away for the rest of her existence and unable to cause Fletcher further harm. The cruelest thing to her would probably be the lack of vodka, and I silently wished her dry-out period was wrought with vein-burning pain and horrendous withdrawal.

The door hadn't even closed behind the doctor when Ivory poked her dark head inside. Her blue eyes held apology and were also filled with regret.

"What is it?" I asked, wrapping my arms around the boy still in my lap.

"They're insisting to come in."

"Who?" Fletcher asked, glancing between me and Ivory.

I sighed woefully. "They're still here."

"Yes."

"Now really isn't a good time for this," I said, feeling the guilt I saw in Ivory's eyes, but my concern for Fletcher outweighed it.

"Who's out there?" Fletcher asked.

"I will tell them—" Ivory's voice was cut off by another.

"Please. I just want to see if he's okay. *Please.*"

Ivory's face fell, her eyes darting to mine.

My stomach cramped the moment I heard the sheer misery in Samantha Cossgrove's plea. Her life had not been an easy one. Every moment of every day since her son was stolen, she never felt a moment of true peace.

And now here he was (possibly), found after twenty-two years, and we were keeping her away.

"Samantha," Fletcher murmured, gazing toward the door.

"Yes. She and Henry have been here all night."

"You wouldn't let them in?"

"No." Resolve made my tone hard. Guilt made my heart ache. The Cossgroves really were like second parents to me. In a way, I'd been the son they didn't get to have. So my refusal to them stung us all, but no matter how difficult it was, Fletcher came first.

"Please, Ivory." Samantha's voice floated into the room.

"It's okay. They can come in," Fletcher said.

Ivory looked at me, slightly uncertain.

"Are you sure?" I asked him gently. "You don't have to see them yet. I know it's a lot."

"She's been kept from her son all his life. If I really am him…" His voice paused as he drew in a deep breath. "She just wants to see me. It's okay. Let her in."

Without another word, Ivory stepped farther into the room, holding open the door.

Samantha and Henry hurried in, eyes fixating on the bed immediately. A broken sob ripped from her throat, and she rushed over.

Fletcher went slightly tense, his body wiggling closer, but outwardly, he stayed calm.

"Oh my goodness, look at you," she crooned, tears flowing freely over her cheeks. She started to reach for the bandage on his head, but he ducked his face into my neck. Her hand fell away, and more tears fell. "How badly does it hurt?" she whispered.

"It's okay," Fletcher said, voice muffled.

"Would you like some ice? A heating pad? More blankets? Are you hungry?" She worried. "Henry, make a list," she called out to her husband who was standing at the foot of the bed, face pale, wide eyes fixated solely on the bundle in my lap.

The stark concern in her voice made Fletcher lift his head. "You would do all of that?" he asked, befuddled. I thought back to his early definition of love to me, how he said that person might worry about him.

Having Samantha clearly worrying over him now must have felt surreal.

"Of course," she hurried to say. "I'll make sure you have everything you need."

"But you don't know me," he objected. His voice was not unkind. He was just confused.

"I would like to," she whispered, swiping tears from her cheeks. "What do you like to eat? I'll get it for you."

Fletcher's fingers found mine, giving a gentle tug so I would release his waist and let him hold my hand. "I'm really okay. I don't need anything."

Another sob left her throat. She reached out to cup his cheek. "You are just beautiful. Better than I ever could have imagined."

Fletcher didn't say anything, just watched her curiously. When she reached out with her other hand to fully hold his face, he did not flinch away. "Oh, Alexander. How I longed to find you."

"Is that his name?" he whispered.

Her eyes were so hungry on his face. She had the look of a starving woman who was finally offered a meal. Nodding, she answered, "Alexander Graham Cossgrove."

"That's really fancy. My name is Fletcher."

She smiled. "Okay. Fletcher, then."

"I might not be him." He cautioned her, and I couldn't help but feel as though he were telling himself that and not her. I had a blinding moment of fear that he would grow attached and then find out he wasn't Alexander after all. The hurt that would cause him, having loving parents ripped away…

"You are." Her voice rang with conviction. "I know you are."

"I think it's best if we know for sure." I reasoned, giving Fletcher's hand a reassuring squeeze.

"Will you agree to a blood test?" Henry asked, finally speaking up.

Fletcher glanced at the man. "Okay."

Samantha started crying again, her hands finally back at her sides.

Both of them looked wiped out and rumpled as if twenty years of heartache and misery had finally shown up on their faces. Lack of sleep, Milly's appearance, and now waiting for confirmation for something we all pretty much knew to be true was quite the strain.

"I'm sorry," Fletcher said suddenly, taking us all aback.

Samantha gasped. "Sorry! What in heavens for?"

"That I made you worry for all this time."

Henry made a choked sound, no longer able to control his emotions. "This is not your fault. This is all my fault. If only I'd protected you better. If only I'd never met that woman."

"We're sorry, Al—Fletcher," Samantha whispered, reaching out to take his hand. "We're so sorry we couldn't find you."

When Fletcher said nothing, Samantha spoke again. "How awful was she to you?"

Gently, he tugged his hand from hers. Without waiting, I put my other arm around him, enclosing him in my embrace.

"She wasn't that terrible. I'm fine. So don't feel bad, okay?"

I don't know how he said that lie without it getting caught in his throat. I hadn't even spoken, and I was choking.

Across the room, the family that had quietly filed in shortly after Samantha and Henry all averted their eyes. The muscle in Earth's jaw jumped violently, and Neo's face remained shuttered. I wondered if they knew how bad Milly was to Fletcher. I thought not. I thought if they truly knew the depths of her abuse, Earth would truly have killed her by now.

This boy—no, this man. This person to whom my heart belonged had been wronged and mistreated his entire life. He had every reason to be angry as hell with the people who should have protected him, who should have moved heaven and earth to find him, though he did not rage or lay blame.

He offered reprieve instead, choosing to offer forgiveness and trying to take away some of their pain.

Fletcher was the flower that impossibly grew from a crack in the concrete. He was the tree that did not suffocate in a raging forest fire. He was the rainbow that stretched over the sky in the center of a rainstorm.

I would love him evermore.

The room stayed quiet, emotion swelling to the ceiling, until Henry spoke again. "How did you know that song?"

"It's just always been inside me. I always heard it when I needed it most."

Their emotional reaction seemed to overwhelm Fletcher, his body curling back into mine for shielding.

"I think maybe that's enough for today," I said, kind yet firm.

"But—" Samantha's protest died when Earth stepped forward to escort them out.

"Thank you for coming," Fletcher said, softening his brother's intense presence.

"We will notify your doctor about the blood test. We already gave our samples," Henry told him.

Fletch nodded. "I'll get mine before we leave."

Earth went to the door, pulling it open.

The Cossgroves hesitated.

"Don't worry," Fletcher told them. "I won't disappear again."

Samantha sniffled, and Henry led her out. The second they were gone, Fletcher's entire body went limp against mine.

"That was very generous of you," I murmured, stroking his hair.

"You're too nice," Earth grumped.

"For once, we agree," Neo muttered.

"She hurt them too," Fletcher argued. "All these years, they've missed their son. And now they will find out he's nothing but a misfit."

"What's wrong with being a misfit?" Earth declared.

"Better to be a misfit than some stodgy old richie." Beau agreed. I made a sound, and he winced. "No offense."

"Plenty taken," I deadpanned.

"I'm not at all who they probably expect."

"You're better," I whispered against his ear.

He glanced around from beneath his lashes and smiled.

"You don't need them anyway." Earth decided. "You have us."

Fletcher was silent a moment, thoughtfully so. Feeling his dismay, everyone turned to him, his cheeks bright red. "B-but what if I want to know them? You know, if they are my parents."

Ivory made a stricken sound. "Of course we will support you! The Cossgroves are very nice people. I've known them for many years. They will love you."

"Only Ethan loves me," he whispered. Unable to deny myself, I squished his soft tummy beneath my hands, rubbing him affectionately.

"Always," I whispered in his ear.

"That's absolutely absurd!" Ivory declared, pinning Fletch with a look. "*I* love you."

His belly pushed against my hand with his gasp. "You do?"

"Of course! My goodness, isn't it obvious?"

"Fletcher needs words," I told them all, taking a moment to meet their gazes.

All three of his brothers looked as though they'd swallowed cartons of sour milk. Clearly, declaring their love was not something any of them cared to do.

Pursing my lips, I glanced at Neo. "Even you have trouble saying it?" I admonished.

His eyes went to Ivory, softening just a bit before coming

back to Fletcher. "No. I love you too, Fletcher. Like a brother."

Neo looked at Earth.

Earth looked at Beau.

Even with the beanie perched on his head, I knew his face had turned the color of his hair. Scratching behind his ear, he gazed down at the floor. "Of course I do. Why else would I let you wear my shoes and clothes? I even let you play my Xbox."

That was his idea of a declaration of love? I pitied the poor fool who fell in love with him.

Just then, there was a swift knock on the door, and it swung open, Bree's blond head poking inside. "Special delivery!"

"Ah, Bree, come in," I said, smiling.

She pushed inside with a huge drink carrier filled with cups and paper bags hanging off her wrists.

"Kismet!" Fletcher exclaimed, his voice cracking around the word.

Bustling over, Bree extended the drink holder with both hands and gestured to one of the cups with her eyes. I plucked it out, and Fletch reached for it.

"Hold on, puppy," I admonished. He pouted while I pulled the lid off and took a sip, avoiding the piles of whipped cream. Good heavens! Satisfied it wasn't so hot it would burn him, I surrendered the cup, finally earning a smile.

"Don't drink it too fast. It's rich." I cautioned him, worrying over his stomach.

Half his face disappeared into the cup only to come up covered in whipped cream.

I sighed and wiped it off.

Bree handed over a coffee with cream to me and then glanced over at the group of people watching her.

"Bree." Ivory waved her over and made the introductions

to the three men who I supposed were my brothers now while she handed out the coffee.

When Earth pulled out his cup from the carrier, it left only one behind, which tipped the entire cardboard tray sideways, the final cup nearly toppling to the floor.

Bree gasped and lunged forward, but the bags on her wrists only made her more top-heavy.

Beau's arms shot out, catching the tray in one hand and her in the other.

"Oh my…" Bree gasped, blinking up at him.

"This one for me?" Beau asked, holding up the drink carrier with the cup.

Bree nodded, her blue eyes wider than I'd ever seen before. After helping her straighten, Beau pulled the bags off her arms and handed them to Neo.

"That's food for everyone," she said, pointing at the bags.

The three guys descended upon the sack like a pack of angry vultures, leaving Ivory and Bree to watch in wonder.

"I've tried to teach them manners. I sincerely have." Ivory sighed.

"Ooh! A blueberry muffin!" Beau popped up, holding a white paper sack.

Fletcher looked up from his hot chocolate.

"That's Fletcher's," I announced.

Bree stepped forward and plucked the bag right out of Beau's hands. He gasped, trying to grab it back, but she danced away to hand it to Fletcher, who beamed.

"That was so rude," he told her when she returned.

"He's a patient!" Bree declared. "Get a bagel."

Beau made a face but retreated into the bag for said bagel.

"Earth, I believe you had something to say to Fletcher." I reminded him.

"Me?" Earth mumbled. "No. I'm good."

"Earth, is it really that difficult to say?" Ivory pressed, a look of disdain on her beautiful features.

He coughed around his coffee. "Ah, well…"

"It's okay." Fletcher piped up from my lap. There were muffin crumbs all over us both.

It was entirely adorable.

"He doesn't have to say it. Especially since he doesn't mean it."

A stricken look passed over Earth's usually constipated appearance. "That's not true."

Fletcher shrugged. "It's okay. Love isn't really your thing." Meaning his words, Fletch went back to eating, his lips smacking around a bite as a dark shadow loomed over him.

Pausing he glanced up to where Earth glowered down at him.

Fletch didn't cower into me. He just smiled and took another bite.

With a grunt, Earth bent, resting his hand on the mattress, steadying his eyes on Fletcher's. "It's not my thing, but that doesn't mean some people don't get past my defenses anyway."

The muffin lowered to Fletch's lap.

"You know I love you, kid." Earth's voice was gruff and low.

I took the hot chocolate, and Fletcher flung himself at Earth, wrapping his arms around his neck for a hug. "I love you too, Earth!" He pulled back, beaming from under the white bandage around his head. "All of you!"

I leaned into his ear. "But me most of all?"

His face turned shy as his hands wrapped around his mug. But when his eyes met mine, I saw the answer glowing in their depths. *Yes.*

Everyone dug into their breakfast, the only talk idle chatter.

As we finished up, Fletcher grew quiet. At first, I thought he might be tired, but then I realized something was weighing on his mind.

"What's the matter?" I asked, drawing everyone's stare.

"E," he complained, avoiding the gazes.

"Out with it."

"Well, what if I am their son after all? I won't be a misfit then. Maybe you guys won't like me anymore."

"And he thinks he's not the baby of this family," Beau muttered.

Bree giggled.

"I'm serious!" Fletcher demanded, turning worried eyes on me.

"I'll love you no matter who you are. Always."

Warm lips that smelled of chocolate leaned in and pressed a kiss against my cheek.

"We literally just confessed our feelings to you like we're sitting around some campfire, and that was *after* you got involved with Ethan," Neo muttered. "If we didn't disown you for him, then we won't disown you for anything."

"Straight facts right there." Earth agreed.

Ivory gasped. "Ethan is a fine man!"

Neo smirked. "Then why didn't you pick him?"

Fletcher shot up. "Because he's mine!"

Everyone recoiled at the fierceness in his tone. Neo held up his hands in surrender. "Just kidding. Just kidding."

Fletcher snorted and then crossed his arms over his chest. "Like Ivory and Ethan kissing is a joke."

"What?" I gasped as Neo jumped out of his chair.

It was all fun and games until someone brought up kissing.

Ivory laid a hand against Neo's chest, restraining him with the lightest of touches. "Not recently, Neo. I can explain."

"Maybe someone should," I allowed, staring at Fletcher whose face was beet red but with jealousy swirling in his eyes.

"It was just something that came up earlier with Marco,"

Ivory explained, sliding me a look. "Marco wanted to know if you were a good kisser."

"And you answered," Neo growled.

Ivory sighed. "Of course not. He was asking Fletcher."

Ahh, now it made sense. How Ivory recoiled from my standard cheek kiss greeting at the ball, how she slipped her hand to me instead. She didn't want to upset Fletcher.

Ivory, Sienna, and Preston all in one night… I was shocked he was sitting in my lap.

"I'm tired," Fletcher announced, effectively cutting off the conversation.

"We should be going," Ivory said. "We'll call and check on you later after you get home, okay?"

Fletcher nodded, eyes slipping to Neo. "Thanks for coming."

"Always, little bro," Neo told him, holding out a fist for Fletch to bump.

Once he did, Bree, Ivory, and Neo left the room.

Earth and Beau stood up, bringing their coffees with them. "I've got to check on the bar."

"And I'm having internet withdrawal," Beau added.

"We'll come check on you tomorrow at Ethan's place."

"It's his place now too," I told them. "Not just mine anymore."

Earth's eyes narrowed.

"Ethan asked me to move in with him," Fletcher explained.

"And you want to?"

Fletcher nodded. "Is it okay?"

I made a sound. He didn't need to ask for permission.

"Sure. Whatever makes you happy," Beau replied instantly.

"See you tomorrow!" Fletcher said happily, giving a small wave.

Earth's stare met mine. "You better take care of him."

"I promise."

Earth grunted as though he weren't sure he believed me, but he didn't argue.

And then, finally, we were blissfully alone.

Squirming around in my lap, Fletcher all but lay down on top of my chest. Chuckling, I pulled the blanket up around him, pressing a kiss to the top of his head.

"Do you need some more pain medication?"

"No."

"Do you need to go to the restroom?"

"No."

"Do you want to tell me why you're so jealous?"

"No!"

I smiled at the angry way he shouted his last answer.

I thought he'd settled down when, a few minutes later, his small voice filled the room. "Ethan?"

"Hm?"

"Please don't love anyone else."

As if there were a sinkhole in my heart, it suddenly caved in. Peeling him back like a rag doll, I had to dip my head so I could peer into his averted gaze. "I could never—will never—love anyone the way I love you. I never loved Ivory as more than a sister, and the few brief kisses we had were tepid at best. Surely, she told you that?"

He nodded, still refusing to meet my eyes. "I still don't like it."

"I know, love," I murmured, laying him back onto my chest to stroke his hair and back. "But I didn't really like it either."

"What about Sienna?"

I made a rude noise. "What about her? I wouldn't even kiss her with someone else's lips!"

Fletcher laughed.

"I'm quite serious." I added that on because he thought it was funny when I said things formally.

It earned me another giggle.

A heavy silence permeated the room. Then his voice filled it. "And Preston?"

I caught my breath. I knew this was the one that hurt him the most. I saw the pain in his eyes last night, watched the way he'd disappeared into his violin.

"I never loved Preston. Never. We had friendship… and a physical relationship."

His fingers tightened in my T-shirt.

"I knew you'd been with others… You're too good at it not to have," he said, and I couldn't help but be flattered that he thought I was skilled. "I guess it was easier to not think about when the others didn't have a face."

I made a low sound. "That makes sense. I think I would feel the same way, and I'm sorry you had to see him. To hear that. I had no idea he was coming. I didn't invite him. I would never have. I hadn't seen him in months, long before we got involved. I had no intention of ever seeing him again."

"He's good-looking. Rich. Was he a good kisser?"

Oh, the little insecurities that came out in his voice with everything he said. How my heart ached, and how my fist tingled with the urge to punch Preston right in his nose job.

"I can't remember how he kissed because you erased all memories of anyone before you. And yes, he has a large bank account, but he could never, not even once, fill up my heart. And as far as his looks… I prefer innocent golden eyes, full lips, and a chin that fits in my fingers when I hold it."

"Can I ask you one more thing before I never want to talk about him again?"

"Anything."

"Did you ever do it without one?"

"What?" I asked, confusion muddying my brain.

"You know," he insisted, pushing closer to hide his face.

"I don't know. That's why I'm asking." I confirmed. "Sit up here and look at me."

"A condom!" he burst out, then buried his face again. "Did you ever forget one with him?"

Ahh. A smile blossomed over my face, and I was glad he was hiding because he would probably be irritated that his jealousy gave me the tiniest bit of joy.

"I told you before I hadn't."

"Well, I'm asking again. About *him.*"

This time, I forced him out of hiding. Gripping his shoulders, I waited until he lifted his eyes so he could see the truth in my stare when I spoke.

"I always, always used protection with him. I never once forgot. *You* are the only person I've ever I've been inside bare."

He smiled secretly, lips curling in on each other. "At least I have that."

I made a sound. "No. You have *everything.* Things I never even knew I had to give."

"I feel better now."

I laughed. "I'm glad."

He puckered his lips, and I sealed in every truth I'd told with a kiss.

But not just any kiss.

True love's kiss.

FLETCHER

"DINNER IS GOING TO BE HERE SOON."

The low, rumbly voice above me caused tingles to race over my scalp and chase their way down my spine.

Making a sound of contentment, I curled in tighter, refusing to acknowledge his suggestion that we move. "I'm already full," I murmured.

Low laughter vibrated my cheek when it moved through his chest. "Well, yes, but you can't live on this alone," Ethan replied, thrusting his hips just ever so slightly.

I sighed. Despite the fact that we'd already finished and his cock was softening, my body still held him tight. "I can try."

There was something about how our bodies fit together, something so pleasurable about being physically connected. The intimacy, the reassurance… the warmth. It was a feeling I'd been missing my entire life, a feeling I didn't know how badly I needed.

Now that I knew, I couldn't go back. I wouldn't. If I could, I would warm his cock inside me all night long.

"How are you feeling?" he asked, fingers lightly brushing near the bandaged, stitched-up gash on my head.

"Okay."

"Puppy…" The word held a note of warning as if he wouldn't tolerate any kind of lie.

Propping my chin on his chest, I said, "I'm a little sore, but it's nothing some pain reliever won't fix."

"Did we do too much?"

I snorted. Since coming home from the hospital, all we did was shower and have sex. He'd been gentle and sweet, and it was better than any medicine any doctor could give. "No."

On a nearby pillow, Gwen stirred, making a little mewling sound, stretching, and then walking over to put her face in mine.

I laughed, pushing up to straddle his hips, the movement making him flex inside me. His palms engulfed my thighs, thumbs rubbing slow circles over the skin.

Gwennie's purr grew louder when I scratched behind her ears. "She must be hungry too."

Ethan made a sound. "So you'll get up to feed the cat but not me?"

My smile faded quickly when I focused on his blackened eye. Caressing the traumatized skin, I pressed my lips against it, a silent apology for the hits he took.

"I don't like these," I murmured, moving from the bruised eye to the lump on his forehead.

"Well, I don't like that you have stitches in the back of your head because you got in the middle of me and Milly."

"Like I'd stand there and watch you get clobbered."

A rude sound echoed out of his throat. "No, I had to watch *you* get clobbered instead."

I opened my mouth to let out a very good retort, but he silenced it with a steely look. "Don't do that again, Fletcher."

I admit I liked it when he was commanding. I even kind of liked his bossiness. But I did not like being told what to do, especially when it came to his safety. I had every right to protect him, as he did me. "If you think I'll just cower behind you, you're wrong about me."

"Cowering and not putting yourself in harm's way are two separate things."

"Not always."

His scowl was a clear indication that he absolutely did not agree, and I was about to hear about it.

The sound of the doorbell echoed from downstairs, signaling our time in bed and this conversation was over. At least for now.

I was definitely glad about this conversation, but getting out of bed was more questionable.

"Food's here." Ethan echoed the bell, hands grasping my waist to lift me.

I pouted when he slid out of me, then wrinkled my nose when his earlier release slid down my thigh.

"Wanna watch *Spider-Man* while we eat?"

Forgetting I was pouting, I looked up. "*The Amazing Spider-Man?*"

"As if I'd watch another."

My enthusiastic nod earned me a sharp sting of pain. "Ow," I whined, reaching around the back of my head.

The dark flash in his eyes swirled with regret, regret that I took this hit instead of him. But I didn't regret it, not for a single second. "I'll get some ice for your head," he murmured, leaning over to press his lips at my temple. "Take your time."

He was wearing a designer tracksuit when he stepped out of his closet just moments later, the pants and jacket both having a matching blue and white design.

Ring! The doorbell echoed up the steps again, and Ethan made a face. "The audacity of them to ring that twice! As if I wouldn't come and get the food I ordered."

"Richie," I teased.

The offended look fell from his face, and he laughed. "You're lucky I have to get the door."

I stuck my tongue out at him.

"Put that away." He cautioned me, disappearing into the hall.

My muscles were definitely sore as I slid out of the massive bed and then gently set Gwen on the floor. Cleaning up as quickly as I could in the bathroom, I went into the giant closet to my little section of clothes to select a pair of sweatpants and a T-shirt. Then I grabbed one of Ethan's hoodies, tugging it over my head.

Gwen was meowing at my feet, nearly tripping me with the way she zigzagged between my legs, so I scooped her up to bring her along.

My stomach growled ferociously, the muffin and hot chocolate I'd had this morning long gone. The thought of the burger, fries, and plentiful dipping sauces waiting downstairs made my steps hasten, only to stall when I got to the top of the staircase.

"What are you doing here?" Ethan's voice resonated. He was not at all speaking in the teasing tone he had just minutes before.

"We came to see you—" Adrian Abbott's voice made my stomach drop.

"Now isn't a good time. Leave." Ethan cut him off savagely.

Gwen squirmed in my arms, and I hushed her, hesitating at the stairs, not knowing what I should do. Should I just stay up here?

Stop hiding.

Didn't I tell myself I wanted to be strong enough to stand beside Ethan and not behind him? How could I just leave him to deal with them alone?

"Is Fletcher here?" his dad asked as I stepped onto the top step.

"You don't need to concern yourself with him."

"We want to know if he's okay," Ethan's mother replied,

her voice much softer than her husband's.

Pushing on, I descended the stairs.

"He's fine. Now please go. We can speak later."

"Oh, there he is," Elizabeth said, seeing me.

Ethan turned instantly, eyes sweeping me from head to toe. I stopped a couple steps from the bottom because Ethan was in the way, almost as if he'd positioned himself there to bar anyone from getting upstairs where I was.

"We'd like to speak with you, Fletcher," Adrian said.

My eyes widened. "With me?"

Ethan made a rude noise. "I said no."

"We came to the hospital, but they wouldn't let us in," Adrian said, sliding a glance to Ethan. "Did you hire a bodyguard?"

Ethan made a face. "No. I'm perfectly capable of taking care of myself and Fletcher."

"I can take care of myself," I announced.

"Then who was that scary Asian man?" Elizabeth whispered, eyes worried.

A low laugh bubbled up out of me.

Ethan flashed a small smile.

"That's Earth. My brother," I replied.

"Your brother." Adrian frowned. "That can't be possible."

"Not all family is by birth, Father. Some are chosen," Ethan retorted coolly.

He was in a mood, wasn't he? Geez.

"Anyway, Fletcher, we wanted to—" Adrian began, forgetting the talk of Earth.

"What part of leave did you not understand?" Ethan's voice chilled me. Even Gwennie seemed frightened and let out a loud meow.

"Ethan," I admonished. He glanced around. "You scared Gwen."

"The cat is fine."

Oh, he wanted to be like this, did he? Fine. My lower lip wobbled. "I'm not."

Apology overtook all his coldness, warmth seeping back into his eyes. "I'm sorry I yelled," he apologized softly, grasping me around the waist to gently lift me down the rest of the stairs, depositing me beside him.

Both Adrian and Elizabeth stared at us with open curiosity but also with surprise.

"Ethan…" His mother started, dividing her gaze between us both.

"Fletcher has a head injury. We just got home from a night in the hospital. Can this not wait?" This time, his voice was patient and much kinder. I reached up and patted his back. Maybe he liked praise too.

"We want to apologize," Elizabeth announced quickly before her son really did force them out.

I felt Ethan's surprise. "What?"

"For heaven's sake, you act like we're thugs trying to break in. We just want a civil conversation. I'm your mother."

Gwennie began squirming all around and nearly leaped from my arms. The second I put her on the floor, she went off in the direction of the kitchen.

"She's hungry," I explained when I saw Elizabeth watching her go.

"That is Gwen?"

I nodded.

"She's very small."

"She was abandoned in the subway."

"You brought home an abandoned cat?" She glanced at Ethan, surprise in her eyes.

"We couldn't just leave her there," I answered. Wasn't it obvious?

"Of course not," Elizabeth murmured.

"You can come in, but only for a moment, and if you upset Fletcher in any way, you're out." Placing a hand against my lower back, Ethan nudged me toward the living room. "Come on. You should sit down."

His parents followed silently behind us, my stomach making a loud grumble when I passed the cart with our dinner on it near the sofa. "Oh, it did come," I said as the scent of French fries made my mouth water.

I sat in the center of the couch, the cushions swallowing me, and tugged the blanket Ethan kept there over my lap.

"Please, have a seat," Ethan said graciously to his parents.

I wanted to laugh. I'd never had to invite any of my brothers to have a seat when they came over. They just automatically sat wherever they pleased.

Is that rude? Did their behavior offend Ethan?

"What's the matter?" Ethan asked, suddenly right in front of my face.

I blinked, startled by his sudden nearness but then overwhelmed by his familiar scent. "My brothers just sit wherever they want. Are they supposed to wait for an invitation?"

Ethan laughed beneath his breath. "Like they would wait even if they were supposed to."

That really wasn't an answer, but he was right.

"You two are very close," Elizabeth observed, sitting on a nearby leather chair. His father sat in the chair right next to hers.

Straightening, Ethan faced them again. "Would you like something to drink?"

"No, thank you."

Ethan went off to the kitchen, reaching into the huge stainless fridge and coming back with an ice pack wrapped in a towel. Before sitting down beside me, he tucked it carefully behind my head near my stitches.

Reaching up, I held it in place. "Thank you."

"Last night was quite a scene." Adrian started, voice gruff.

"I apologize that had to happen at our grand opening. I

realize I'll need to do damage control, but it's just going to have to wait. I have other things to prioritize right now."

I almost told him he should go to work if he needed to, but I stopped myself. I didn't want him to go. I wanted him with me. The past twenty-four hours had been a roller coaster, and I was still trying to work out how I felt. Before leaving the hospital, I'd given a sample for a DNA test, and now we would all be staring at the clock, waiting for the truth to come out.

All these years, I'd thought I had no one. Just a mother who despised me and thought I was unlovable. Had all of that been a lie?

Did I really have parents who loved me, who celebrated my birthday more than twenty years after I'd gone missing from their lives? They never gave up hope they would find me.

The woman who hated me didn't hate me because I was unlovable. She hated me because I was born out of love she didn't have. Because she was jealous.

How did I even begin to understand that? To let myself believe it all to be true?

"Don't worry about the business," Adrian was saying to Ethan. "I've already got the PR team on it. Take as much time at home as you need."

"You mean I'm not fired?" Ethan asked.

"Of course not," Adrian replied. "Can't very well fire the heir to the group."

"I meant it when I chose Fletcher."

My stomach clenched at his words, at the reminder of the fight that day in his office. It seemed so long ago even though it had only been a couple days. I didn't want Ethan to lose his family, his job… everything he loved because of me. I couldn't let him sacrifice so much.

"I know that. And you don't have to."

My head came up.

"What are you saying?" Ethan's words were measured.

"We're saying we're very sorry for what happened the other night," Elizabeth said. Turning her eyes on me, she said, "We're very sorry for making you feel unwelcome, Fletcher. It's very clear how much our son loves you, and it's even clearer how happy you make him. I—" Her eyes slipped to Ethan, then back to me. "Could I ask you something?"

Ethan stiffened, but I nodded. "Sure."

"Do you love my son?"

"Yes. I love him," I said, my belly dancing around in my middle. "A whole lot."

Ethan's palm settled over my blanket-covered lap.

"I can see that too."

"You're saying that you accept my relationship with Fletcher? That you support it?" Ethan asked, much more skeptical than I was feeling.

"Well, it would have been nice if you didn't, ah, display your affections so passionately in the middle of our Abbott Group ball last night," Adrian said, face flushing. "But yes, we accept your relationship with Fletcher. We hope that you will forgive—well, I hope that you can forgive the way *I* acted."

"Of course we can!" I said instantly.

Ethan's hand gave my thigh a squeeze. A quick glance in his direction showed that he clearly was not as happy and relieved as I was about this.

"Ethan?"

His eyes remained on his father, jaw hard. "Is this because of Fletcher's true identity?"

"I thought you might say that," Adrian deadpanned.

"You can't blame me for thinking it."

"What do you mean?" I asked, the ice pack slipping a little, its cold edges making my neck chilled.

"Well, if the DNA results come back the way we think, then you won't be some *riffraff* off the street. You'll be Upper East Side royalty. Heir to the Cossgrove fortune and son of the music legend Henry Cossgrove, who also happens to be my father's best friend."

Adrian made a sound.

"You did say you could accept my preference for men if I brought home one with good breeding."

"But I don't want their money!" I burst out, the ice pack falling between me and the sofa. "I don't even want their name."

Reaching between me and the cushions, Ethan fished out the ice pack, placing it on the coffee table close by. I didn't realize I was shaking until he tucked an arm around me, anchoring me into his side. "Calm down," he whispered.

The back of my head bumped on his shoulder when I flung it back to look up. "Ow!" I hissed, slumping forward to avoid any further contact on the stitches.

Elizabeth jumped up to rush forward, but Ethan held his hand out, stopping her.

"Let me see." His voice was gentle, meant only for me. The pads of his fingers were warm against the iced skin of my scalp as he tilted my head down to lift the bandage slightly to look beneath it. "Looks okay," he announced, smoothing everything back into place and then tugging me partially into his lap. "Stop jumping around so much," he scolded, but it was more of a plea.

"But I really don't want their money, E. Really!"

"I know that," he replied, sincerity in his eyes.

"Besides," I said, turning back to his parents, "even if I do turn out to be their son, I'm still me. I was still raised by a criminal. I'm still from the Grimms. I don't even have a violin anymore."

Images of my busted violin with broken strings and splintered wood lying on the ground last night flashed behind my eyes. I would never feel her under my fingertips again. I'd never feel the subtle, unique way she vibrated when I played. The bow that bore the indents from my fingers, the wood that was worn in all the places I'd gripped it tightest... All of those things were gone.

A deep, hollow sadness blew through me like a bitter wind in an empty city alleyway, leaving behind something terribly lonely.

That violin had been my most prized possession, the one thing I felt was truly mine.

It had taken me years to steal enough for a new one after Milly busted the one I'd brought home from school. The school had made me pay for it because I broke it.

You break it, you buy it. That's what the teacher had said, and that's why it took so long for me to get another of my own. I was too busy trying to pay for the one I'd lost.

The joy that coursed through my body the day I finally bought my used "new" violin was something I would never forget. It was probably the best day of my life until I met my brothers and then Ethan. I cherished her and protected her, took great care to make sure Milly never caught sight of her. I'd spent endless hours busking in crowded subway stations and on sidewalks with her perched on my shoulder. That violin was my friend when I had no one else. My savior when I was lost.

And now she was gone.

Destroyed beyond repair.

I would never again hear the sweet harmony we made together.

A sob caught in my throat, clinging to the rock of hard emotion already trying to choke me. To me, it wasn't just a violin. It was a piece of my soul.

I turned toward Ethan, and he welcomed me in. Burying my face in his broad chest, I hid my tears and distress from the people I thought could never possibly understand. These stupid tears and emotions probably made me look weak, but I couldn't push them down.

I mourned for that piece of me that had been taken away.

Hell, I would have a physical scar on my head from its final demise forever.

"Your name doesn't matter." Ethan soothed me, trying to calm me down.

Another sob escaped, and I pulled back to stare up at him. "She destroyed my violin."

Understanding melted his gaze, and a rough sound echoed in the back of his throat. "I know," he crooned, hugging me again. "I know she did."

"She took everything," I said, breath hitching. I wrenched back, feeling my eyes flash. "She even tried to take you!"

"She didn't." He assured me. "I'm right here."

Breathing unsteady, I pressed on, words spilling out that I didn't even know I needed to say. "I know you're angry I got in the way," I whimpered as our unfinished conversation bubbled up inside me. "But I couldn't let her hurt you too. I can live without my sweet violin if I have to, but I could never survive without you."

Ethan made some comforting sounds, scooping me even closer. I couldn't even be embarrassed his parents witnessed my outburst because I was still too upset to even comprehend what they were seeing. I had a feeling I might be like this for a little while, fine one moment and unable to process the next.

"I'm not mad, puppy. I promise. I understand why you did that, okay? I'm sorry I was hard on you before. I'm sorry."

I clutched his shirt tighter, trying to quell my uneven breathing.

"You did so well," Ethan murmured beside my ear. "You stood up to her for all the awful things she's done."

"I couldn't let her hurt you," I whispered as his praise soothed my most exposed nerves.

"I know," he murmured, dragging his hand up and down my spine. "You should go," Ethan said, reminding me that his parents were still here, that they were seeing me have a breakdown. "I told you this was too much."

Great. Now they'll think I'm unstable along with everything else.

"I'm sorry," I said, voice raspy from emotion.

"Don't apologize," Elizabeth implored. "Please. I am so sorry. We just felt it important to come by and tell you this before the DNA results."

Ethan made a noise.

"We wanted to tell you we accept you no matter what the outcome will be. We felt it might seem more insincere after the results," Adrian said. "I do hope you are Alexander. God knows my friends deserve to have their son back, but that's the only reason. We will still accept you as our son's partner even if you aren't."

"Why now?" Ethan asked.

"Honestly, because of last night. Because of the way you leaped in front of our son, Fletcher. We saw everything. How she was threatening you and then turned to Ethan. You didn't even hesitate. You put yourself in front of him. You took a hit meant for him," Elizabeth explained.

Adrian picked up right where his wife left off. "It's very clear that you are a good man, Fletcher. And I… regret the way I spoke to you. I'm an old man set in his ways, but I promise to do better. I am grateful that my son found someone who would go to such great lengths to keep him safe."

Cupping a hand over my ear, Ethan hissed, "Don't encourage him."

"I still heard you," I retorted.

Ethan lifted his arms so I could sit back, blinking the wetness from my eyes.

"I understand why you did it. I'm not mad, but that doesn't mean I want you doing it again," he explained.

My lower lip jutted out.

"Don't give my son such a hard time, Ethan." Elizabeth scolded him. "Just look at him."

Ethan's eyes flashed up to his mother. "You're taking his side?"

"Of course!"

I smiled.

"Well, we'll be going. It's been quite a day. You two need your rest. If you need anything at all, please call. And let's have dinner when things settle down."

Ethan started to get up, but Adrian waved him back. "Just stay there. We can see ourselves out."

"Mom, Dad?" Ethan said after a few beats of silence. I glanced over the back of the sofa to see the couple turn around.

"Yes?" Adrian asked.

"Thank you."

"You don't owe us thanks for doing what parents should do. I apologize it took so much for us to get here."

Ethan didn't say anything, but I felt his hand curl into a loose fist at my back.

"Don't worry about work." Adrian spoke again. "Take as much time as you need. Work will be there when you're ready."

Their exit was punctuated by the quiet latching of the large front door.

We stayed quiet, relaxing into each other for long, blissfully quiet moments.

"I'm sorry I got upset before," I finally said.

He made a soft sound. "Don't ever apologize for showing emotion and for not keeping it all bottled up inside. I admire that."

"But your father probably thinks I'm weak."

"Maybe if my father was better at showing that he cared, things wouldn't have come to this point."

"Do you think he meant what he said?"

"I think so." Ethan agreed. "But I guess time will tell."

"Time will tell us a lot of things," I whispered.

"Mmm." He agreed. "But the most important thing I already know."

Pushing up, I stared into his summery blue eyes. "What's that?"

"How much I will always love you."

Giddiness rushed me, pooling in my belly and making my heart speed up in rhythm. "Does that mean our love is timeless?"

"A love greater than time and measurable only by fate."

Ethan made me feel as though I'd been asleep in a nightmare but awoke to a fairy tale.

"My prince. My one true love."

We met halfway, lips melting together in a kiss that belonged in storybooks, but incredibly, this wasn't a book, and my prince was real.

Epilogue

Ethan

"FLETCHER!" I CALLED, MY VOICE ECHOING THROUGH OUR home. "You have a delivery!"

The sound of an elephant parading through the house made the delivery man's eyes go wide under his hat.

The pounding was preceded by a man of less-than-elephant size rushing into the foyer, golden hair flying wildly around his head.

"What is it?" he exclaimed, eyes going wide at the large box sitting at the man's feet. "That's for me?"

I pointed to the label on the box. "Says so right here."

He shook his head. "I didn't order that."

"I need someone to sign for it."

I took the pen to scrawl my signature across the tablet. "Ethan, that's not mine. You shouldn't sign."

"Thank you," I told the man, ushering him out.

When I turned back, Fletcher was scowling. "I didn't order that. You should have made him take it back."

"Maybe it's a gift."

His beautiful eyes lit up but then turned suspicious. "It's probably something weird from our fans." His suspicion turned to horror. "Or something from our antis!"

Antis was what Fletcher called our haters.

I think he read too many comic books.

But honestly, it was kind of fun to see what would come out of his mouth next.

Since the ball a few weeks ago, our relationship basically went viral. Photos of me kissing him in the middle of the ball spread like wildfire online and then again when someone released photos from the same night when I'd been shielding him on the ground with my body as Milly attacked.

So it wasn't just the Upper East Side that was buzzing but, in fact, the entire country.

"A modern fairy tale couple," the press had dubbed us.

Fletcher thought it was romantic, and I thought it was ridiculous. I had to admit, though, it was good for business.

I thought the news of Abbott Group's heir being gay would hurt the stocks and all our accounts. Sure, we'd lost a few, but we gained more. Abbott Group was applauded for its modern, nondiscriminatory values, and our public image actually rose.

Of course, you couldn't have a fairy tale without a few villains (aka antis). With Milly in jail for the rest of her life, our villains now consisted of people who disagreed with our type of relationship.

Our type of relationship?

You'd have to ask those tallywackers because, to me, our type of relationship was one of great love, and I frankly saw nothing wrong with that.

"What if it's a bomb?" Fletcher announced. Pulling out his cell phone, he said, "I'm calling Earth."

Lunging forward, I snatched the phone out of his hands before he could hit send. "First of all, why would you call Earth if someone sent us a bomb?"

"So he could kill it."

See what I mean? He's ridiculous. It was incredibly charming.

It took effort to hide my amused smile, but I succeeded.

"If someone mailed us a bomb, I would protect you, not Earth."

"But I don't want you to get blown up!"

This was an entirely absurd conversation. "Fletcher, that is not a bomb."

"How do you know?"

"Because I'm the one who sent it to you."

His mouth fell open. "Really?"

"A man tries to send his boyfriend a gift, and he thinks it's a bomb," I muttered, rubbing my forehead.

"Gwennie, Daddy sent us a present!" Fletcher called, bouncing over to the box.

The alpha I could not deny that lived inside me flared to life. With it, something hot and nearly uncontrollable took over.

He squealed when my arm snaked around his middle, pulling him away from the box and into my body. Glancing over his shoulder, he looked up, the confusion in his face morphing into sweet vulnerability as he recognized my mood.

"What did you just call me?" I growled.

He opened his mouth, but no sound came out. He tried again. All that came out was a rush of breath.

Whirling, I pinned him to the door, clasping his wrists in one hand and anchoring them above his head. His eyes were surprised, but the desire was there too.

Despite how totally I leaned into him, he arched closer, offering up his body, rubbing along me like a giant cat.

"Be a good boy and say it again," I demanded.

His body vibrated against mine. Desperation started to creep into his hazy expression. *"Daddy."*

I crushed my mouth onto his, the urge to claim so urgent inside me that if I'd been coherent, I might have been scared. Sucking his lower lip into my mouth, I worked it until he whimpered and his knees gave out.

Lifting him, I only went a few steps, carrying him to the table nearby, sitting him down, and tugging off our shirts.

His nipples were already erect when I drew one into my mouth, sucking and nipping at it with my teeth. Arched up into my mouth, his upper body draped over my hand while sinful little moans floated up the stairs to fill our home.

I moved to the other nipple, working it just as thoroughly as my free hand pushed at the waistband of his pants until they fell around his ankles.

Taking advantage of the way his body was offered up, I nibbled and sucked down his torso, swirling my tongue around his belly button before licking across his engorged head.

His body going completely slack, I lowered him onto the cold surface of the table, watching as he barely registered it against his inflamed skin. His chest rose and fell rapidly as he watched me with eyes that were narrowed into slits.

As I backtracked across the foyer toward the table I'd tossed my keys on, Fletcher whined, so I pulled off my pants to let him see what was coming back. I was already so hot I practically hurt, so even as I reached into a drawer for the lube I'd stashed, my other hand stroked over my cock, making me shudder.

Fletcher reached for himself, and I made a noise, stopping him.

"No you don't, puppy," I declared, going back to fit between his legs. Slapping both hands on the table on either side of him, I claimed every ounce of his attention. "You will come on my cock and my cock alone."

"Please," he whispered, arching up.

Oh, how I wished I could just sink right in, but I would never be that kind of lover. I would never put my urges before his comfort, so I took my time, stretching him open with my fingers and the lube.

When he was dripping and stretched, I grabbed his

ankles, sliding him across the table until his body bumped mine.

I thought about flipping him over, taking him from behind, but in that moment, I wanted to see him. I wanted every noise he made, every expression that flickered over his face. I was greedy and possessive, and I wanted every last detail of him I could get.

Both of us groaned when I pushed in with a single thrust. His legs that had been hanging off the table locked around my hips, and his hands reached for mine.

Instead of giving in, I captured his wrists again, pinning them over his head, laying him out on display beneath me like he was an all-you-can-eat buffet.

My hips snapped forward, and he cried out, moaning in delight at the way I hit his perfect spot.

"More," he panted, heels digging into my back.

I set a punishing pace, pushing us both hard and fast to the edge, then backing off just a little to keep us teetering in place.

"Please," he begged, wiggling his wrists to try and get free.

"Please what?" I growled, bending over to nip at his lips.

Turning his head to the side, Fletcher rose to brush against my ear. "Please, *daddy*. Please let me come."

I let go of his wrists at once to grab his hips and thrust into him with ferocity. "Come for me, puppy," I demanded as his eyes rolled back in his head. The beginning of his bliss was all it took to push me over, and we both hit climax together.

When I finally came back from wherever I had spiraled, I smiled at the ribbons of pearly white decorating his belly and chest and a boy who looked completely blissed out.

"You," he panted, "have a total daddy kink."

I growled. "Keep saying that word and you won't walk for a week."

"Tempting, but I already can't feel my legs."

Chuckling, I peeled him off the table to take him into the bathroom so we could clean up.

He was still wobbly when we were done but insisted on opening his present. So he sat on the stairs, and I put the box in front of him.

"What is it?" he asked, eyes sparkling, cheeks still flushed from our romp.

I cut the tape off the top and then gestured for him to look inside. Honestly, I couldn't wait until Christmas because Fletcher was pure joy in everything he did. I could hand him a pair of socks, and he would rip at the paper and coo enthusiastically as though he'd never seen anything better.

Paper and bubble wrap went flying, decorating the floor and the stairs.

"*Ahh!*" he exclaimed, looking up from inside.

I smiled.

Diving back in, he tugged out the contents, which were fairly large. "You got me a Spider-Man!" he yelled, holding out the statue to stare at the red and blue hero.

"Well, you said you thought Julius Cesar was creepy."

Gasping, he looked over at the table we'd just had sex on, realizing the statue was no longer there. "Hey, where'd that old guy go?"

"I told him to find somewhere else to live. We need room for Spidey."

On wobbly legs, he navigated around the packaging, carrying the statue over to the table. Fletcher perched it in the center, then stepped back to admire the view.

It fit there relatively well, even if it didn't match anything at all in this house. If my designer saw this, he'd likely have a coronary.

I thought it was perfect.

Spider-Man was crouched in his signature pose, holding out one arm wrist up, ready to shoot a web.

"Do you like it?" I asked.

Fletcher flung himself into my body, arms and legs looping around me. "I love it so much! Thank you, Ethan! Thank you!"

I laughed as he peppered kisses on the underside of my jaw.

Fletcher pulled back, arms looped around my neck, and looked up with Bambi eyes. "Do you think he's offended we had sex on there?"

I threw back my head and laughed.

"I'm serious," Fletch muttered.

There was a knock on the front door, making both of us turn to stare. "You expecting someone?" I asked him.

"No. Are you?"

"No."

I went to the door, pulling it open.

Henry and Samantha stood nervously on the other side. I pulled the door a little wider so Fletcher could see them.

"We're so sorry to drop by unannounced." Samantha began, eyes going straight to her son.

"It's okay," Fletch said. "We said you could come by whenever you want."

The DNA test confirmed everything we'd suspected. Fletcher officially became Alexander Graham Cossgrove, the missing prince of the Upper East Side, and Henry and Samantha finally found their son.

Fletcher, who still went by the name he preferred, had taken the news well but was still cautious with his usually easy affection. Who could blame him, though, after everything he'd gone through?

The Cossgroves were slightly nervous, but I knew he'd come around, and once he did, my second parents would be bombarded with so much innocent love they wouldn't know how to act.

"Is now a good time?" Henry asked, eyes raking over the box and all the mess Fletcher had thrown on the floor.

"Ethan just gave me a present," Fletcher announced. "Come in and see it!"

The couple stepped inside, and Fletcher held his hands out, presenting the large statue of Spider-Man.

"Oh my goodness!" Samantha exclaimed. "That's a very interesting piece."

"Spider-Man," Henry said approvingly. "The best super-hero there is."

"That's what I think too!" Fletcher exclaimed. "It's a lot better than the guy who died."

Henry and Samantha turned alarmed eyes to me, and I chuckled. "Julius Caesar."

Realization dawned. "Yes, well, he was a dreadful man." Samantha agreed.

"Ethan, we should get them a statue for their house!"

Samantha's eyes welled with tears. "I would love that. It would match nothing, but I would love it."

Ahh, she and I understood each other well. I made a mental note to order another statue.

"I actually brought something for you as well," Henry said, holding up a familiar-looking case.

We moved into the living room where everyone could sit down. Fletcher had turned quiet and was staring at the case.

He'd refused to let me replace his violin, saying he wasn't ready yet. Sometimes I would find him staring out over the city in an eerily quiet room. I would ask him what he was doing, and he would say he was remembering his violin.

I told him when he was ready, I would buy him a new one, any one he chose.

"It's not the same," he'd say and then change the subject.

I knew it couldn't go on like this forever. Music and violin was as much a part of him as his soul, and without it, he would be incomplete. I was afraid to push too much too fast, though. Having his entire world turned upside down and meeting new parents was enough.

"Since we are both violinists, I wanted to share something with you. I thought you might appreciate it." Henry began, turning the old, worn case to its side to undo the clasps.

Fletcher's head bobbed, his Adam's apple doing the same in his throat.

"I know she destroyed your violin that night," Henry told him, looking up. "And I also know that it likely felt like a death to you."

"It's been really hard," Fletcher whispered. "I miss her a lot."

"I know, son." Henry empathized.

Samantha and I shared a look, noticing that neither of them realized what Henry had called him. It just was natural in the moment.

Samantha's eyes filled with tears, and she blinked them back while pressing her fingers against her lips.

"Remember when I told you I had an old violin that was my favorite?"

"Is that it?" Fletcher asked, eyes widening.

"Sure is," Henry replied, opening the case to reveal the worn instrument.

Fletcher made a sound, his face mirroring awe. He went around the table to stand close to Henry, dropping to his knees to peer into the case.

Honestly, I thought it just looked like an old violin, but the way Fletcher's eyes shined made me realize the closest I would ever get to experiencing what he saw as he stared lovingly and longingly at that instrument would be second-hand through his expression.

And even that was overwhelming.

"It's so beautiful," Fletcher whispered, lightly running a finger over the wood. "She's an old soul, isn't she? Wise and strong."

"Yes." Henry agreed, emotion ringing in the word. "We've been through a lot, this old girl and I." Henry went on, throat bobbing. "And now I thought perhaps you'd like to have her."

Fletcher's breath caught, and his hand pulled away from the instrument as though it were suddenly on fire. "Me?"

"Well, yes. You need a violin, and this one is very special. I think you two would bond quite well."

"B-but why?"

"That song you know? The one I wrote and played for you as a baby? I wrote it on this girl. She knows the music in your heart quite well."

A new glimmer came into Fletcher's eyes, one that hit me right in the feels. He stared down once more at the violin, pure longing in his face. "Thank you, but I can't."

"Perhaps you might reconsider?" Henry said without heat. "I never imagined that my son would be a prodigy, my intense love for the violin passed down to him. It would make me so proud to have you play with this. So proud."

"You want me to play her?"

"Oh yes."

"Perhaps you could try her out now," Samantha suggested. "Play something for us."

"You want to hear me play?"

"Oh, honey, we would love nothing more."

Fletcher turned to me. "Is it okay?"

What was it about this man who turned everyone around him into an emotional mess? One simple question, one request for reassurance, and I was near putty at his feet.

"Yes, puppy," I said, trying to hide the emotion welling up my throat and thickening my tongue. "It's okay."

He picked up the instrument slowly, holding it reverently. I honestly felt a little jealous watching how he handled her, the way his eyes scanned every inch and his fingers caressed every curve.

As he explored her, a small smile bloomed on his lips, and a brightness I hadn't seen in a while lit up his face.

And then he started to play.

To say that he played beautifully was a massive understatement. He basically stood there before us and laid bare his soul.

Every single note was perfect as if he were in fact somehow bonded with that instrument, as if it really did understand the music in his heart.

I didn't know how long he played, but even after he finished, my cells vibrated with the echoes of the music and tears wet my eyes.

Samantha and Henry were both openly crying, and when Fletcher finally looked up, he radiated with pure peace.

"You, my son, are far more talented than I will ever be. And that is no longer my violin. It could only be yours."

He nodded once as if he, too, realized that she chose him and they were already tethered together.

I glanced across the room, catching Henry's eye.

Thank you.

The pleasure is entirely mine.

After that day, the Cossgroves were bonded, and the curse brought on by a woman scorned was broken, for the king and queen's castle was no longer empty but filled to the brim with love.

And of course, we all lived…

Happily Ever After

Once upon a time… There was a writer who loosely planned some of her book and sat down to write. Then from the very first chapter, her characters, whom she loved so much, laughed in her face and said, "We do what we want here."

That writer is me.

Those characters are Ethan and Fletcher.

I'm actually not much of a plotter, but going into any book, you need to have sort of a grasp of the plot and the characters and where you want to go. I usually also have random scenes floating in my head that the characters have already shown me that I need to work in somehow. I had all of that, and basically, these boys were like, "Hold my Kismet hot chocolate," and did whatever they pleased.

When I wrote *Ivory White,* I fell in love with Fletcher. He was my most favorite character in the book. I loved his innocence and his acceptance of everyone. I loved how "soft" he was in such a hard world. I couldn't wait to write his story, and when he pretty much swooned seeing Ethan on TV that first time, I was hooked on these two.

Going into *Prince,* I was nervous. I was unsure because Ethan wasn't all that loud in my head. I wasn't really sure who he was other than a "prince" of the Upper East Side, very fashionable, and very rich. But I wanted him to be more than that. I wanted him to have his own personality... so I started writing and was so worried he would come out stiff and proper and wooden. And frankly... boring. But in that very first chapter, he was like, "I get migraines," which took me by surprise. And so did his derision of his father's elitist attitude. AND THEN he went to the forest, aka Central Park, and he basically fell in love with Fletcher at first note. I did not expect him to fall so hard so fast. I did not expect him to be putty in Fletcher's hands. He practically melted in that park, and it gave me butterflies and surprised me so much. I was like, *Holy crap, this guy is besotted with him.* And then his inner alpha came out. I love how he is SO protective of Fletcher. He accepts Fletcher the way he always wanted to be but never felt like he was. Ethan suddenly loved Fletcher the way he wanted someone to love him. I love how strong he is but also vulnerable at times, and I especially love how he basically spoils Fletcher rotten.

And Fletcher, he was everything I expected him to be, but he was also more. He surprised me with some of his crazy comments, like all of his thoughts about Julius Caesar and how he thinks waffles are very considerate pancakes. I love how he never lost the light in him, the innocence he was born with despite his horrible mistreatment. I think many think Fletcher as weak, but really, he is one of the strongest. He kept himself alive; he kept himself from turning bitter and villainous. In a world where he had every reason to hate and rage, he remained loving and sweet. I love how he was just himself. How he would cry when he was sad, hurt when he was hurt, and be angry when he was angry. I think in today's society, men often feel like they can't show all their emotions like that, and it's nice to see someone who does. I won't lie. I worried a bit that people would dislike Fletch because of that innocence, how he tends to run and basically "submits" to Ethan in a lot of ways. But then I decided I wouldn't change him to fit a mold of how people think a man should act. Fletcher—just like all of these misfits (even Ivory and Ethan)—is a products of his environment. And that's okay.

I hope there is a clear message in this book that you can be whoever you want. It doesn't matter if you are rich or poor. Accepted or not accepted. It doesn't matter if you're gay or bi or straight. Everyone has value, and everyone deserves a happily ever after.

I do believe this is the longest book I've written to date, and to be honest, I probably could have written more. I truly love these two. I feel like I wrote this book for me, and I haven't written a book that way in a long time. Saying that, it still was not an easy book to write. As I said, these boys did what they wanted all the time. I'd be like, *Okay, today we will do this, this, and this.* And they were like, "Nope, nope, and nope." Instead, they were kissing on the couch, sharing shoes, and eating pancakes. I'm like, *Excuse me. Can we get on plot here?* They kissed way sooner than I planned, they had sex way sooner than I planned, and Ethan just blurted out the L-word when I wasn't expecting it. I learned fast that fighting their plot was detrimental to my mental well-being. I do realize I'm speaking about being mentally sound and, at the same time, telling you all that the people in my head were making me write things. Ironic.

I ended up rewriting a big section of the book and altering it a bit because it felt off. And then I felt as though I'd written myself into corners for the rest. I just followed what they said and then lay in bed at night and worried I would never be able to resolve the plot or that it was too much to work out. And then Ethan would do something that would make me sit back and be like, *Oh, so that's how it is.* LOL. I would think, *How you gonna get out of this, Ethan?* Then he'd respond, "Watch me," and then kiss Fletcher in the middle of the ball. He called a private detective and found out about Milly. He sent Sienna packing after insulting her boob job. Great gods! LOL. That's another thing… What's up with the great gods saying? Ha-ha. He's just a richie.

Anyway, all in all, I am happy with how this one tied up and still a little surprised I managed to tie it up. I do also think that some of the things in this book need to be inferred. As in the reader must realize things, know things by what they are seeing and hearing. You know? I feel like I didn't spell out everything Fletcher survived as a child, but he painted a pretty clear picture of the abuse he endured. I also kinda liked how he never quite told Ethan everything he went through, because, for Fletcher, living through it once was enough and he didn't want to relive it by talking about it all. I used to sit and worry that I needed to explain things down to a T. But then I thought to myself, *My readers are smart. They'll know.*

I hope it feels "fairy tale-ish" to you in a modern world. Unlike *Ivory White,* this is not a retelling. I was inspired by *Sleeping Beauty* for this one, but instead of the baby being sent away with fairy godmothers to be kept safe, he was kidnapped by the villain. I owe that gem of inspiration to my friend, Amber, who honestly helped me so much with this book. We would bounce ideas around and talk about the characters. She actually had some good ideas I didn't get to use because Ethan wouldn't let me, lol. So a moment of thanks to Amber for all her pep talks, readings, and listening to me go on about the boys in my head.

I hope you enjoyed this one, my first male/male romance that is not set in the GearShark world. I didn't realize this until after I was done writing, and I'm glad because that thought is very intimidating. I think *Prince* is different, but I hope their chemistry speaks for itself and that these boys have burrowed a place in your heart like they have mine.

Thank you so much for reading this one. I hope you will

enjoy the rest of the House of Misfits books I will be releasing. As always, thank you so much for your support and encouragement. See you next book!

~XOXO~
Cambria

Cambria Hebert is a bestselling novelist of more than fifty titles. She went to college for a bachelor's degree, couldn't pick a major, and ended up with a degree in cosmetology. So rest assured her characters will always have good hair.

Besides writing, Cambria loves a pumpkin spice latte, staying up late, sleeping in, and watching K drama until her eyes won't stay open. She considers math human torture and has an irrational fear of chickens (yes, chickens). You can often find her running on the treadmill (she'd rather be eating a donut), painting her toenails (because she bites her fingernails), or walking her chihuahuas (the real bosses of the house).

Cambria has written in many genres, including new adult, sports romance, male/male romance, sci-fi, thriller, suspense, contemporary romance, and young adult. Many of her titles have been translated into foreign languages and have been the recipients of multiple awards.

Awards Cambria has received include:

Author of the Year 2016 (UtopiaCon2016)

The Hashtag Series: Best Contemporary Series of 2015
(UtopiaCon 2015)
#Nerd: Best Contemporary Book Cover of 2015 (UtopiaCon
2015)
Romeo from the Hashtag Series: Best Contemporary Lead
(UtopiaCon 2015)
#Nerd: Top 50 Summer Reads (Buzzfeed.com 2015)
The Hashtag Series: Best Contemporary Series of 2016
(UtopiaCon 2016)
#NERD Book Trailer: Best Book Trailer of 2016 (UtopiaCon
2016)
#Nerd Book Trailer: Top 50 Most Cinematic Book Trailers
of All Time (film-14.com)
#Nerd: Book Most Wanted to be Adapted to Screen: (2018)
Amnesia: Mystery Book of the Year (2018)

Cambria Hebert owns and operates Cambria Hebert
Books, LLC.
You can find out more about Cambria and her titles by
visiting her website:
http://www.cambriahebert.com

The Heven & Hell series
The Death Escorts series
The Take It Off Series
The Hashtag Series
The GearShark Series
The Amnesia Duet
The Public Enemy Series
The BearPaw Resort Series
The House of Misfits Series

Standalone Titles:
Moth To A Flame
Mr. Fantasy
Distant Desires
Maneater
Blank
Whiteout

www.ingramcontent.com/pod-product-compliance
Lightning Source LLC
Chambersburg PA
CBHW021239200726
48288CB00014B/48